TORN APART

Mom yanks her arm out of Copper Head's grip and stumbles toward her youngest child. But before she can come within a meter of Anka, the corporals grasp her elbows. While Mom squirms, the taller soldier rams the butt of his gun into her belly. The other presses the tip of her weapon to Mom's forehead, yanking on her earlobe with her other hand. The agony distorting Mom's sharp face indicates that if she could do more than whimper, she would scream.

Copper Head turns to me for the first time. His irises have the gray sheen of cold steel; they send shudders down my spine. He mouths, *I'm so, so sorry.*

Stop apologizing, I want to snap. But I refrain—I don't like talking to strangers, because my high-pitched voice makes me sound fragile. It might give the Beaters more ways to amuse themselves.

Mom opens her rough, dry lips for the first time. "Just wait," she rasps to me.

The officers drag Mom out of our home. Struggling against them with the remainder of her strength, she kicks Tinbie by accident. He topples over, clicks twice, and powers off. The yellow radiance vanishes from his eyes.

Copper Head follows the Beaters, hands behind his back, eyes on the ground. Before the group passes through the doors, Mom gives me a hard stare, her dreamer's eyes bloodshot. "You've always been ready for this," she says. Then she's gone.

OTHER BOOKS YOU MAY ENJOY

Burn	Walter Jury and Sarah Fine
Catalyst	Lydia Kang
Champion	Marie Lu
Control	Lydia Kang
Guardian	Alex London
Legend	Marie Lu
Prodigy	Marie Lu
Proxy	Alex London
Scan	Walter Jury and Sarah Fine
The Young Elites	Marie Lu

To Sadie —

You're a ★!

DOVE ARISING

KAREN BAO

speak

SPEAK
An imprint of Penguin Random House LLC
375 Hudson Street
New York, New York 10014

First published in the United States of America by Viking,
an imprint of Penguin Group (USA) LLC, 2015
Published by Speak, an imprint of Penguin Random House LLC, 2016

THE LIBRARY OF CONGRESS HAS CATALOGED THE VIKING EDITION AS FOLLOWS:
Bao, Karen.
Dove arising / Karen Bao.
pages cm – (Dove chronicles ; 1)
Summary: "On a lunar colony, fifteen-year-old Phaet Theta does the unthinkable and joins the Militia when her mother is imprisoned by the Moon's oppressive government"—Provided by publisher.
ISBN 978-0-451-46901-4 (hardcover)
[1. Science fiction. 2. Space colonies—Fiction. 3. Militia movements—Fiction.
4. Government, Resistance to—Fiction. 5. Moon—Fiction.]
I. Title.
PZ7.B229478Dov 2014
[Fic]–dc23
2013041198

ISBN 978-0-14-751243-7

Printed in the United States of America

1 3 5 7 9 10 8 6 4 2

TO MY PARENTS

DOVE ARISING

1

UMBRIEL SAYS I'M SO GOOD WITH PLANTS because I'm as quiet as they are.

He might be wrong. According to the oldest people here, green growths weren't always silent: leaves once cartwheeled in the wind, and storms snatched branches from trunks with deafening cracks. But these plants surrounding me are mute apple trees, strawberry bushes, and cotton shrubs with fibers and filaments of cellulose that would, if they could, complain about never anchoring in the earthen soil and never seeing the light of day, except through the carbon-reinforced glass of the Greenhouse 22 roof.

I used to imagine their limbs lengthening toward the tantalizing sliver of a sphere along the horizon, trying to stretch away from this barren, cratered satellite and reach the Earth we all came from. I stopped sympathizing with them at thirteen, when I converted the energy of my childish fancies into relentless concentration in Primary Education. Now we come to the greenhouses after class to make extra money. I don't try to understand the plants anymore. I just take care of them.

"Phaet!" Umbriel says. Because my name's pronounced "fate," it sounds like destiny's calling every time someone addresses me. "This one's growing quickly. Can you bring me the stake?"

He stands a few meters down the row of flowering apple trees, scrutinizing a branch that has gotten too long and upset the balance of the sapling. It looks like one of those old Earth buildings called "skyscrapers," shrunken down and ready to tip over. Ironic, that name. We are closer to the sky than *they* ever were.

To reach him, I leap across the plants between us. There are no grav-magnets above our heads, so acrobatics unimaginable in the rest of Base IV are possible here. I relish the sight of my billowing, white clothes until gravity pulls me back down.

We strap a pole to the sapling's trunk so that the lengthening branch doesn't cause it to tilt farther. Umbriel's awkwardly tall body resembles the skinny tree we're disciplining, a likeness intensified by the matching green of his clothes. Smiling, I scoop smelly compost from a box with a small shovel and spread it in a ring around the base of the trunk.

Moisture hits my scalp while I work: the spray nozzles in the ceiling have released water onto the left side of my head. Umbriel bunches his sleeve around his hand and uses it to soak up the droplets in my tightly coiled hair. "Let's hope this dries before Dorado sees. Heh—aren't you a waste of water."

H_2O is dear to us; it costs three Sputniks for a one-liter canteen of the stuff to drink. If we're lucky, Dorado, the head Agriculture specialist, who never enters the greenhouses himself, isn't watching the cameras closely. He's old, at least seventy, and dozes off on the job unless he's shaking his cane at us clumsy young folk. In spite of the inconvenience we've caused him, I think he likes us.

When we were eleven, Umbriel tripped over a pumpkin vine and landed face-first in a clump of *Vaccinium-8*, a bioengineered variety of fist-sized blueberries with savagely poisonous leaves. Dorado heard shouts of agony through the security screens, saw splotches of scarlet erupt on Umbriel's skin, and summoned a team of Medics on the spot. It was a special case, he'd told us, because we were young; normally he wouldn't call Medics for workers' nonlethal accidents. That's when I began hoping to become a Bioengineer—so I'd get to work on projects like reducing the plants' toxin levels while increasing their nutritional content.

I don't usually slip up—and neither does Umbriel, not anymore. We trained under heavy supervision for three years before they gave us duties, and for good reason. Greenhouse plants supply the bulk of the base's nutrition, as well as the cotton in our robes and the oxygen we breathe. Above my head, solar-powered filters dump carbon dioxide into the greenhouse and pump oxygen to the rest of the base.

I'll admit that I'm distracted today. This morning, my mother left for her job in the Journalism Department with circular blue imprints under her eyes. She hasn't looked alert for a few days but has refused to say why. Apprehension has been thrashing around in my heart, unspoken and squashed down by my will. Regardless, I can't hide my worry from Umbriel.

"What's bugging you? Not the flat-ended bees, I hope. The hive people had to harvest honey today. Neither species was very happy about it."

Umbriel knows that being surrounded by organisms—sprouting and growing and *living*—usually puts a serene, if not content, expression on my face. When the slightest crease appears on my forehead, he feels he must erase it with a joke or two.

"I know—it's that chemistry test. You probably *bombed* it. Your name's going to flop off the top of the science-area listing."

Now he's appealing to my pride by bringing up my Primary ranking, the reward for long nights of studying, of pinching my forearms to stay awake and mumbling formulae to drown out the complaints of my empty stomach. It'll someday get me a job in the Bioengineering Department—and along with that position, state-of-the-art equipment to tinker with and design team members who'll give me both respect and space to think. The entire *base* gave respect and distance to the Bioengineer who modified honeybee homeotic genes to strip the species of stingers. I, too, want to create something new with the tools nature has provided. I'd also earn an engineer's high salary, though that's secondary.

As Umbriel straps another tree to a post, he studies me with eyes so dark I can't tell where the pupils and irises meet. Stumped, he slaps his gloved hands together three times, as if dusting them off. It's an old signal of ours. We'll talk later, when there's greater likelihood of privacy.

"Guess you're just tired, then," he says.

He taps the back of his left hand and turns it toward me. His handscreen—the circular layer of flexible polymer fused with his skin—reads 16:58. Two minutes remain until we can go home to the Residential Department, him to the Phi complex and me to Theta.

When we've finished off the compost, we walk past other temperate fruit-bearing species to the perimeter of the dome. Our two-person transport, made of fiberglass embedded with carbon nanotubes, has a nose shaped like an old-fashioned bullet. It's a retired Militia ship that has been stripped of its tinted shell and fitted with a storage bin on the rear, into which we pile our shovels, hoes, empty compost sacks, extra stakes, and soiled gloves. The thing miraculously didn't explode in space combat or get piloted into an asteroid by some novice soldier during its fighting years. Today, it sports only a few scars where the self-sensing material grew back after being punctured by small particles.

I take the driver's seat and enter the password—6, 8, 8, 6—into a keypad, another relic from the past. Nowadays, secure access doors and vehicles all have fingertip scanners.

Umbriel parks himself next to me, patting my shoulder the way he does when he's not sure what to say. Last year, we took our first pilot's tests, excited at the prospect of flying the endless distances between the Agriculture terminal and our assigned greenhouses instead of hitching rides with older workers. Because I had scrutinized the steering mechanisms—and studied the transport manual—I passed the written and practical portions in half the time allotted. Umbriel didn't; he forgot the scientific names of the delicate plants over which we're not allowed to fly and failed the written. I'm secretly glad that he can't travel far by himself. For convenience's sake, Dorado still assigns us to work the same plants at the same times.

I crank the bottom-thruster lever all the way up. With a sputter, the old transport lifts us two, four, six meters in the air. I set the transport to lateral mode, push the joystick—I try three times before it stops jamming—and we're flying over the garden below.

Umbriel sucks in a breath, uncomfortable with me doing

something as "dangerous" as piloting a transport. "I'll never get used to this. . . . Next year I'll pass that, er, *exam*."

I glance at him and laugh as he polishes his incisors with his tongue—our code for "blast, how dumb." Not far from sticking our tongues out like annoyed little kids, which is precisely the point.

There's the familiar whoosh of cool air and the change of scent from plant fragrances to plastic and glass as we exit Greenhouse 22 into the main terminal of Agriculture. My eyes painfully adjust to the shift from soothing green to blinding white. The entire interior of Base IV is white, which best insulates us from the volatile temperature fluctuations of the Moon's crust. My body slumps as the grav-magnets in the ceiling repel the diamagnetic water molecules in my system to make me as heavy as I'd be on Earth. If not for the magnetic force supplementing lunar gravity, everyone would shrivel from muscle atrophy or osteopenia.

We zip past the greenhouses, each half a kilometer in diameter and climate controlled to suit its plant species. Greenhouse 17, tropical fruits; 14, cotton and indigo; 13, coniferous forest. Last year, when Dorado assigned us to 12, paddy crops, we wore bizarre rubber overalls and sowed rice, poking each other with muddy fingers whenever we finished a row.

Finally, I park the transport in the lobby. Leaving the transport in its designated spot, we step out and enter the expansive Atrium, where Base IV's complex network of hallways meets. Each of the six bases has its own departments needed for subsistence, from Agriculture, where food is grown, to Culinary, where it's prepared, to Market, where it's finally sold. Law, Defense, Sanitation, Recreation—they all serve concrete purposes in our lives. We always know where to go when we need something, but many departments are off-limits to nonemployees—like Journalism, where my mother works.

Umbriel slings an arm around my shoulder. People push and shove, all wearing the robe colors of their respective apartment complexes. Scattered throughout are black-suited clusters of Militia soldiers, or as we call them, "Beetles." Their shiny-visored black helmets obscure their faces, mimicking the reflectivity of insect shells.

Wrongdoers must hide their activities from both the Beetles and the two-meter-high convex security mirrors that stretch toward the ceiling. Civilians are supposed to check the security mirrors and report suspicious activity to the nearest Beetle, but I've never seen any criminals in action. Maybe that's because I don't pay enough attention—I don't *want* to approach the intimidating Militia.

Headlines from the *Luna Daily* roll across the domed ceiling in block-shaped print:

MISSION TO OBERON SUCCESSFUL—SAMPLES TO BE TRANSPORTED TO GEOLOGY LAB

BASE III MILITIA HALTS EARTHBOUND ATTACK

The capital letters on the high-resolution screens worsen the visual clutter, and the pulsing crowd makes my discomfort around large numbers of people impossible to ignore. Umbriel clutches me tighter, using his height and sure footwork to drive us through.

STANDING COMMITTEE COMMENDS BASE I AGRICULTURAL PRODUCTION

Sometimes, the Committee—the six people, one from each base, who govern the Moon—directly addresses the public. I'm glad they're not appearing on the news tonight, because they'd make my head spin even faster from fear. Whenever they give a public address, they use lighting that reveals only their silhouettes, turning them into towering black shadows. Hiding their features allows them to lead quiet lives outside of the government buildings; they also use pseudonyms. If I met the Base IV representative in Market, I wouldn't recognize her.

Fortunately, the chances of an unknowing encounter with a Committee member are tiny, because the Committee resides on Base I to facilitate meetings. The oldest Base is located all the way near the North Pole, on the rim of the Peary Crater. In contrast, Base IV is a few kilometers from the equator, on Oceanus Procellarum—one of the dark basalt seas formed by ancient magma deposits—and slouches against the wall of the Copernicus crater, which protects its western portion from meteorite bombardment.

After exiting the huge dome and bumping along arched white hallways barely wide enough for me and Umbriel, we reach Theta, one of twenty identical apartment complexes. A four-meter-high letter "Θ" greets us out front. The can-shaped elevator takes us up to the eighth floor. At my apartment, 808, I press my fingertip to the scanner, and the doors slide open.

We stop in the white cylinder of a bedroom I share with my sister to stow Agriculture's shovel, trimming knife, and gloves under the shelf that holds my little moss garden. The stuff grows under the angiosperms in the greenhouses; Dorado considers it parasitic, so we pluck it away. But I once snuck some home, filled a tray with pilfered soil, and laid stripes of light green sphagnum and brownish cap moss across its surface. I'd get locked up if anyone found out I'm cultivating unregulated life-forms, but it's worth the risk. The moss brings me peace in a life of constant studying, working, and looking over my shoulder. It's the most low-maintenance companionship one could ask for, and it reminds me that things are more than what they seem. Its uneven clumps look like shrunken versions of Earth's rolling hills, and the sporophyte stalks resemble trees. Not that I've ever seen the hills, except in old pictures. But I've tried looking, even though I know the Moon is too far away, by squinting at Earth through the greenhouse windows while the sun shone.

My room is so small that when Umbriel and I sit on my cot, we see both the moss garden and our reflections in the desk mirror. I uncoil my hair and pick apart the braid, shaking loose the feeling that someone's been yanking on it all day. Agriculture, like many of the scientific departments, expects females to bind our hair so we don't shed or tangle it in expensive equipment. The style is a headache to create every morning and literally a headache to wear during the day.

I lower my cheek onto Umbriel's solid shoulder, but because our faces are pointy from daily bouts of hunger, the pressure soon hurts my bones and I have to sit back up. We both have tan skin from working in the greenhouses and eyes the same shade of onyx: mine long and sloped, his wide and penetrating. Our hair was the same color too, in our childhood, but now mine is shot through with silver veins, the tails of miniature comets hurtling across my head. The rest is dark as the spaces between the stars.

Looking at my hair, Umbriel clicks his tongue. "Take it easy, will you? There's a whole new section here that's gray. I'm starting to worry about your worrying." The fingers of his right hand untangle the knots at the ends of my hair—fingers that have vexed me time and again by snatching fruit off shrubs and depositing them in his pockets. For free produce, he's willing to risk spending a few days locked up—though he's gotten so good at evading security that I think he no longer worries about the danger.

Before he continues the conversation, we sit on our left hands to cover the microscopic audio receptors on our handscreens. It's a common practice, but I still grin for a moment. It's always funny to me that people having the most serious talks look the silliest, hands firmly tucked under gluteals.

Powered by our blood circulation, handscreens perform the functions of old Earthbound computers and link us to the Base IV network. Every five-year-old must report to the Medical Department, fall unconscious under morphine, and remain so while specialists fuse flesh with technology. We use handscreens to compute figures, read uploaded books, watch news broadcasts, and view other peoples' statistics on demand; Medical also uses them to monitor our vital signs, like heart rate and body temperature. However, we can't send messages or receive communications unless they're transmitted directly from a department. And everyone knows—though the Committee doesn't tell us—that in some undisclosed location, their agents listen to the multitude of handscreen feeds to root out threats to national security. Maybe the Committee's okay with our knowing because it discourages bad behavior. I've never felt unsafe—but I wish they'd leave us alone.

"What was bothering you earlier?" Umbriel says. "My guesses have all been wrong so far . . . Oh?"

A third person appears in the mirror, fragmenting our short-lived privacy. We turn away from our reflections. Umbriel huffs in annoyance, but I don't, not after I see who it is.

My ten-year-old sister, Anka, stands at the door, staring at us with eyes identical to mine, except that hers glisten with innocence—and at this moment, fear. She could have been me five years ago, with her full cheeks and black hair, but she allots herself more words per hour than I ever did. I tug Umbriel to his feet.

"Um, can you guys come out?" Anka's voice is a nervous whisper, turned down to about five percent of its usual intensity. Her hands are clasped together, right palm concealing her handscreen. "There's this weird boy. . . . The door light blinked, and I forgot to check the camera, and I opened up, and now he won't leave."

No. We haven't had an unexpected visitor since last year, when my brother, Cygnus, was quarantined for a vicious stomach virus. Three weeks later, Medical dumped him on our doormat, having hoisted away 20 percent of our savings for his treatment.

I remember learning that Earthbound creatures like mice and birds have such high heart rates that their pulses sound like humming. I'd never thought that my own heart could take off at a pace that might rival theirs.

But as the three of us tumble into the main room, it misses beat after beat. Saving them up for what will come.

2

THE ONLY NOISE IS THE FAINT WHIRRING OF our half-meter-tall maintenance robot, Tinbie, as he zips around on rickety wheels and sucks up debris. His eyes light up yellow in victory whenever he rids the floor of a particularly large chunk. But machines, even rotund benevolent ones, are insensitive in difficult situations.

Cygnus crosses his arms over his chest, trying to make his lanky thirteen-year-old body appear imposing. Like Umbriel, he looks as if someone grabbed both ends of his prepubescent self and pulled. He holds his right shoulder higher than his left, a result of spending so many hours fooling around on his handscreen.

Tinbie darts between my brother's feet and circles the boy—almost a man—who faces him. Our visitor wears the ultramarine robes of the Kappa complex and the white cross badge of a Medical assistant. His hair shines like a roll of copper wire. And his right hand is fastened onto the left arm of my indignant little mother.

I've always thought of her as little, regardless of my own size. Not only is she small compared to other adults, but she has a petite nose and the hands of a child. After years of pressing her lips together, sucking them in as if worried she'll say something she shouldn't, her mouth has become tiny too, a pink contour framed by deep creases in her skin.

"Mom's *not* sick." Cygnus's voice cracks in his agitation. "Don't take her away."

"It's a passing bug," Mom insists, annoyed. "On its way out. Don't squander a Medical room on me."

The Medical worker glances at the floor. "I'm sorry, Ms. Mira, but my supervisor told me that another assistant marked you as an infectious threat. Your handscreen sensor indicated that you had a fever of 310.7 Kelvin this morning. We've got to quarantine you." His diminutive voice has a slight rhythmic lilt and a slow, muffled quality; he sounds like he's talking through cotton balls.

"No." Anka grabs Mom's limp hand. "You're making that up."

As if taken aback by Anka's impertinence, Tinbie tucks himself under the kitchen table, his vacuuming duties finished. Cygnus scrambles to put Anka's meaning in gentler terms for the benefit of the Committee's handscreen eavesdroppers.

"Mr. Medical worker, there has to be a glitch in the system. She's *fine.*"

Frowning, Copper Head applies an adhesive thermometer to Mom's forehead. His vertebrae are stacked one on top of the other, ironing out the natural arch of his back. But I notice he pulls back from Cygnus. Maybe he's as nervous as we are.

"She's at 311 Kelvin now . . . no glitch, sorry to say."

This morning, I thought Mom was simply fatigued. But upon closer examination, I see that her breath is too fast and her complexion too pink, as if all the blood is trying to escape the surface of her skin. Why doesn't Copper Head let her sit down? I compress my eyes and lips into a glare in his direction.

Whoosh. The doors to our apartment slide open. I gasp, even though extra visitors shouldn't come as a surprise after Anka's outburst. My sister yelps; Cygnus shrinks away from Copper Head. Umbriel edges in front of me, chest squared to the new arrivals.

"Is there a problem here?" In stride two Militia corporals, their special rank denoted by the yellow patches on their jackets. Their boots clack in unison as they finish walking. The shorter holds a glossy handgun by her side, her finger on the trigger.

Copper Head looks bewildered by the Militia's intrusion, but like the rest of us, he should have expected it. "I—I didn't require backup. . . ."

The taller soldier draws his finger across his throat, silencing Copper Head.

I've never been this close to Beetles before, let alone officers. In the midst of my panic, what strikes me most is their cold efficiency, developed over years of patrolling, prodding, and pummeling. Not only have they survived Militia training, during which many initiates die of exhaustion, decompression, or sabotage, but they've either outplaced dozens of their former peers or fought their way to a higher rank. Maybe they've even traveled off the Moon in the name of serving the Committee.

The taller corporal's featureless head swivels as he takes in his surroundings: our bare walls, plastic furniture, spotless floor.

"Ah!" When he spots Tinbie, he hurries to the table, squats beside the robot, and rubs the top of his cubic head. Tinbie emits a series of clicks. "Cute. I haven't seen one of these since I was a trainee."

So much for efficiency. I will the corporal to continue indulging his penchant for antique robotics, thankful that we never saved enough money to replace Tinbie with a newer model.

Across the room, Mom kisses the top of Anka's head. My sister begins to whimper, and the corporal, forgetting Tinbie, swings around to point the handgun at her throat.

I let out a hiss. How could anyone show more compassion to a robot than a human girl?

Mom takes Anka in her arms, turning her back to the soldiers. She looks over her shoulder at them, teeth bared.

"Usually we aim at the forehead." The corporal's pronunciation is distorted, his vowels too narrow. Although a helmet masks his face, I know he's smiling. "I want to take out the brat's voice box instead."

Cygnus jams a hand over Anka's mouth, his face sallow and still.

The corporal sends a violet laser beam into the wall by their heads. When my siblings hold each other closer, eyes shut tight, he cackles.

"Beaters," Umbriel whispers in my ear. The revulsion in his voice sets that word aflame. My throat convulses with disgust.

Beaters—Militia members, usually higher-ranked officers, who adjust too well to positions of power—are a Lunar legend. No one starts out cruel, I've heard, but after years of answering to hardly anyone, these soldiers grow sicker than anyone they're assigned to quarantine or imprison.

"Every minute this quarantine is delayed," drawls the shorter corporal, "heightens the danger surrounding Mira Theta as an infectious threat. Medical needs two or three months to treat her."

Umbriel squeezes my shoulders tighter, keeping me upright.

The Committee quarantines sick people for treatment because in the cramped bases, infection spreads quickly. As Medical can fix anything else in a matter of hours, extended stays are reserved for life-threatening cases.

The shorter Beater continues, "Her children may not see her or speak to her during treatment. Mira, come quietly."

"Ow!" Cygnus cries.

Fighting to reach Mom, Anka has bitten Cygnus's finger, but he grabs her again. Mom yanks her arm out of Copper Head's grip and stumbles toward her youngest child. But before she can come within a meter of Anka, the corporals grasp her elbows. While Mom squirms, the taller soldier rams the butt of his gun into her belly. The other presses the tip of her weapon to Mom's forehead, yanking on her earlobe with her other hand. The agony distorting Mom's sharp face indicates that if she could do more than whimper, she would scream.

How many times have the corporals performed this maneuver, amused by the helplessness of their prey? If these are the lower-ranking officers, the malice of their superiors—who take orders from the Committee and no one else—must be even more repulsive.

Copper Head turns to me for the first time. His irises have the gray sheen of cold steel; they send shudders down my spine. He mouths, *I'm so, so sorry.*

Stop apologizing, I want to snap. But I refrain—I don't like talking to strangers, because my high-pitched voice makes me sound fragile. It might give the Beaters more ways to amuse themselves.

Mom opens her rough, dry lips for the first time. "Just wait," she rasps to me.

Of course I'll wait for her to come back. My siblings and I have never gone a day without seeing her. Now she'll be away for at least two months.

The officers drag Mom out of our home. Struggling against them with the remainder of her strength, she kicks Tinbie by accident. He topples over, clicks twice, and powers off. The yellow radiance vanishes from his eyes.

Copper Head follows the Beaters, hands behind his back, eyes on the ground. Before the group passes through the doors, Mom gives me a hard stare, her dreamer's eyes bloodshot. "You've always been ready for this," she says. Then she's gone.

I begin my life without Mom by looking backward. For nine years, this feeling has been first on my list of things to forget: impermeable stillness, a gnawing hollow between my lungs.

Dad's hands were rough when he showed me how to swing a chisel-tip hammer—against Mom's wishes—but his arms were soft when he hugged me after I got it right. He brought home surface samples from his Geology Department lab and pointed out all the glittering crystals you could see if you held a rock up to one eye and closed the other. He spoke of the little things in our world people too easily overlook: the ever-changing clouds that blanket distant Earth, the spread of colors that appeared on a wall when he held a test tube of water to the sun. Rainbows without rain, and he made them just for me.

He died. When he went to the Far Side to excavate the misnamed Love Crater, a ten-minute long, 5.1-magnitude moonquake tipped his supposedly first-rate topographical utility vehicle, shook and shook the thing until its pressurized interior burst. I was six.

When we got the news via handscreen message, it felt like this. Only Mom and I remember that time—but I try not to, and she pretends not to.

Anka interrupts my thoughts with a wordless wail.

"We're all sad, Anka." Cygnus's voice wavers. "Don't make it worse."

"Yeah, and don't *you* either." Umbriel catches Anka's hands mid-flail and kneels before her. "We'll be okay. Your mom will be okay."

I approach them, unsure how to comfort my sister.

"No, we won't!" Anka sobs.

"Shh," Umbriel coos. "Phaet's thinking hard. . . . She's the smartest girl I know. She'll come up with something. We'll forget this whole Medical deal in a few months. Right, Anka? Right?"

When Umbriel sees me hanging my head, his hand wraps around mine. My index finger traces circles around the new blister between his thumb and palm. He's so accustomed to my presence, and to getting blisters, that he doesn't notice.

"Sorry," Cygnus sighs through pursed lips. "I was being mean. . . ."

"You're *always* mean." Anka's voice has stabilized, to my relief.

"Stop bickering and come over for dinner," Umbriel says. "With Ariel and my parents. We can fix everything. Well, we can fix *some* things."

After our quiet trek to the Phi building, the circular, white elevator opens onto their floor. In their apartment, Caeli Phi, Umbriel's mother, cries loudly and wetly. Tears spill over her creased tan skin, giving it the sheen of polished wood. Her long arms set bowls and silverware on the table, repeatedly hug Cygnus, Anka, and me, and whirl with her body as she multitasks. She's the closest thing to a hurricane we'll ever see.

Ariel, Umbriel's twin brother, and Atlas, Umbriel's father, stand dry-eyed in the living room, just out of the storm's reach.

"Oh dear, look at your hair." Caeli's a tall woman; she riffles through my mane with stubby fingers. "Even more gray. Ay, poor Mira—your poor mother . . . and no one to write the news, or cook, or watch over little Anka!"

Atlas circles the kitchen table, pulling out stools for everyone. "Sit, sit, and we can talk this through." A mid-level counselor in the Law Department, he's accustomed to calming people in a civilized fashion, the first step of which is to have them take a seat. Atlas is tall, like his sons, but more solid; he serves as a human buffer when Caeli tells the boys off. Although the hair on the top of his head has seen denser days, he has the same thick eyebrows as Umbriel. I've never seen him use them to intimidate people, but I suppose he might in court.

Everyone sits on a stool, covering their handscreens, except for Caeli. She bustles about, spooning onto each plate a mash of celery, carrots, and apricot-colored potato fortified with beta-carotene. *After the storm comes the harvest*, Dorado would say. Cygnus's foot bounces with no predictable pattern; Anka squirms and sniffles in her seat. My siblings' fight-or-flight reactions still haven't run their course.

Through a mouthful of potato salad, Atlas asks, "Have you three gotten an official notification from a department yet?"

I shake my head. When a family's situation changes—a death, an arrest, unemployment—its members receive instructions on how to proceed. Our message, when it arrives, won't be pleasant. Without Mom's work in the Journalism Department, we have no income but my pitiful earnings from Agriculture, two hundred Sputniks per month. Mom writes—she *wrote*—for the Opinions section of the Committee-funded *Luna Daily*. The Committee dictates which opinions suit the newspaper's needs, so Mom never had to think on her own. No wonder they paid her only 1,200 Sputniks per month.

I might not like all the Committee's choices, but they've ensured the Lunar Bases' survival on the ecologically hostile Moon. Tomfoolery resulting in leaks and broken filters—or an epidemic of illness—could kill off a whole base. They watch us to prevent catastrophes. We keep them in power, and they keep us alive—a good enough bargain for me.

"Dad!" Umbriel's fingers grip the edge of the table. "Couldn't you wait to ask? They just took Ms. Mira half an hour ago—"

"Who's 'they'?" Atlas asks.

"Corporal Beaters," Cygnus says. "I don't know why they didn't send privates."

Ariel and Atlas shudder.

"That's awful," Ariel says. "And strange. You'd think corporals had more important things to do. Maybe the notification will explain—it should come within the next thirty minutes." He frowns too, highlighting his resemblance to his twin. Unlike Umbriel, though, Ariel has pretty features and a slight frame, traits that make him seem younger. His skin is paler from staying out of the sun; even his lips are redder, like the peel of a Gala apple, and his nose rises to a graceful point. While Umbriel stares at people intensely, sometimes accusingly, Ariel gazes at them, his huge eyes closed halfway.

Anka draws her knees to her chest. "I don't want to know."

"Ay! Enough sadness. Eat, you kids." Caeli takes her place on the last empty stool. "I spent all morning mashing potato."

As I squish a bite of salad with my tongue, a vibration rattles through my left hand; it travels down my spine, giving me the sensation that someone has dropped ice down the back of my robes. Anka's and Cygnus's shoulders jump to their ears. They've also received the notification.

"Someone else read it," says Anka.

"Grits, my eyes must be coding wrong to my brain." Cygnus holds his handscreen a decimeter from his eyes, blinking. "It's from . . . from Shelter."

Atlas groans.

I open the message on my handscreen, reading silently as Cygnus reads aloud.

"CONDOLENCES FOR MIRA THETA'S MEDICAL CONDITION. REPORT TO THE SHELTER DEPARTMENT WITHIN TWELVE HOURS. GIVEN THE DEFICIT IN THE FAMILY'S JOINT ACCOUNT AND PROJECTED MEDICAL EXPENSES, THIS IS THE OPTIMAL AND ONLY COURSE OF ACTION."

Translation: unless my family finds another way to support ourselves, we must give up our home and live in sordid Shelter, dwelling among vermin and disease and crime, and subsisting off the Committee's meager handouts. To stay in Theta 808, we'd have to scrape together all the money to cover our dues to the Committee, rent, and Mom's Medical bills in twenty days. It's impossible. Part-time Agricultural assistant is probably the most lucrative job someone my age could hope for, and still the pay is not enough. Working in a high-paying Department, like Chemistry or Aerospace Engineering, is out of the question. It requires Specialization training, which I won't complete until I'm twenty-three and have spent my required years in the Militia.

We must obey Shelter's directive. Cygnus knows it—and judging from her continued weeping, Anka knows it too.

"They should live with us!" Umbriel blurts. "Please, Mom?"

Caeli clears her throat. "My darling, we don't have space for three more. As it is, there's barely room for our family. . . . They can still come over for dinner, though."

"They can't if they're in that pit of a department," says Umbriel. "Shelter residents need permits to leave."

"Umbriel, if we had the resources, you know we'd keep everyone out of there," says Atlas.

"Anything would be better than *Shelter*." Umbriel grimaces before turning back to me. "Can't you work more hours in Agriculture?"

Anka shakes her head, examining a wad of cucumber on her fork, and pulls a sour face.

"Not enough for Medical bills and rent and stuff. That's with low estimates." Cygnus pokes his handscreen, his elbows on the table. One foot is tucked under his behind; the other dangles from the stool. He's not bobbing back and forth, which means he's concentrating hard. "We've got 1,293 Sputniks. Food costs us four hundred per month; rent and Committee dues add up to a thousand. The projected cost of Mom's treatment, medication and all, is a little over fifteen hundred. They're going to send us an official message tomorrow, but I got hold of the numbers a few minutes ago."

He's still working on his hacking skills, but in a few years I doubt any of the bases' servers will be safe. Sometimes I wonder who is the greater liability between Umbriel and Cygnus. Umbriel steals food, while Cygnus steals information.

"I could work in Sanitation full-time," Cygnus offers. "Another four hundred Sputniks per month."

"You're funny," Umbriel says. "You'd have to be older and more . . . coordinated."

My brother will have to wait until he's fifteen to meet the age requirement for Sanitation employment, and I'm glad. I grimace at the thought of him scurrying through dank tunnels under the base, surfacing only to disinfect public facilities and collect waste and turn it into compost. It's tiring, thankless labor that would detrimentally affect his health.

"Ha-ha. I'm overqualified in breaking and entering. They'll never know it's me." Cygnus strokes a beard that isn't there. Despite all the joking, he really thinks he can fake his way in. I love him so much when he's being unreasonable.

Atlas scoffs, drumming the table with the knuckles of both hands. He deals with many cases of underage workers; they go to Penitentiary for three or four days and then return to Primary with documentation of the crime defacing their handscreen profiles. "Well." Cygnus stands, not bothering to smooth his crinkled robes. "I give up."

"Already?" says Anka.

"I can't think of anything, except illegal stuff."

Funny he should say that—because I can't either.

"You don't think about much else," Atlas says.

Yesterday my siblings and I were normal, hardworking students; today we're destitute, on the verge of becoming outlaws or Committee dependents. If Cygnus and Anka weren't at my side, I'd allow myself a few tears and swear words. If we don't check into Shelter within the next eleven hours and fifty-one minutes, the Militia will haul us there. There's a chance Beaters will appear at our door again, one I'm not willing to take.

Cygnus sighs, turning to Anka. "So let's check out Shelter."

"Okay," says my sister. "Ms. Caeli, thanks for dinner."

As Anka and I prepare to leave, Umbriel jumps from his seat. "Hold up! I'll come with you."

"No!" Caeli rises, knocking over her stool. "Haven't I told you never to go near that place? Please. Let Phaet take care of her own family."

"I don't think he makes a distinction between hers and ours," Ariel says.

Caeli looks from one son to the other, bewildered. Although Umbriel often disobeys her, it's rarely with Ariel's support.

"We'll be fine," Umbriel tells her. "Maybe Shelter's not as bad as people say."

He's wrong. It's worse.

3

SMOKE RESIDUE AND OTHER GRIME HAVE stained Shelter's ceiling a mottled brown, but the filth is nothing compared to the stench rising from open excretory pots and bodies that haven't entered a shower chamber in eons. The floor is lower in some places than others, and yellowish liquid sits in the depressions—not flowing, not even rippling. It's sitting, just like the people—if one can call them that—around the cavernous space.

They cover their flesh with scraps of robes that have lost their color and display brown stains like those on the walls. Nearby, two people scuffle for a dilapidated cot, even though it looks hard as petrified wood and about as comfortable as the floor; one surrenders, his nose pouring blood. Other residents huddle together and shiver, cocooned in raggedy blankets. Shelter's as chilly as a Culinary Department refrigerator; the Committee sends this place just enough heat to keep its inhabitants alive.

When the dinner buzzer goes off, able-bodied residents—60 percent or so—scramble to line up at an enormous black tub in the center of the dome to be served brown vegetables. A girl about my age shrinks from the groping hands of the man behind her, coiling around the malnourished baby in her arms. Poor thing has an oversized head and matchsticks for a body.

Shelter workers ladle stringy food into people's hands.

Without utensils, the Shelter residents must eat like Earthbound beasts. Beetles stand by, using glass truncheons to strike those who reach into the tub for more. Often, ignoring the pain, the victims claw food out of their neighbors' hands.

Most people slouch onward. Younger ones cluster in circles to share pipes and inhale wispy black smoke. Dumb pleasure suffuses their faces. The Committee declared a ban on depressant drugs decades ago, but in Shelter they haven't enforced it. Artificial satisfaction keeps these addicts from causing more dangerous kinds of trouble.

On the far right side of the dome, Militia soldiers surround a transparent quarantine tent for the ill, shoving new additions in with the butts of their laser blasters. The people inside lie in restless sleep, punctuated by frequent shudders and the occasional moan.

Anka and I shelter our faces with our sleeves.

"I want to go home," mutters my sister. Umbriel, Cygnus, and I refrain from pointing out that within the next few hours, this place will *be* home.

In spite of what I've heard about Shelter before, I'm shocked the Committee allows people to live in total degradation. The Shelter Department should care for people without the means to care for themselves, but these residents are just in a holding area, waiting for death. *Do people know how horrible things are here?* If they did, would they be upset or keep ignoring what's going on?

Ripples of light roll through the crowd as the residents' handscreens simultaneously receive an official message. Most people don't bother to lift their arms. I peek at the handscreen of the man before me, whose blood vessels, visible through translucent flesh, loom dark against the artificial pigments comprising the message.

REMAIN SEATED AS MEDICS QUARANTINE DISEASED INDIVIDUALS.

"Phaet—we always knew that living here meant getting dirty," Umbriel whispers. "Didn't know it'd mean seeing Meds and Beetles all the time."

As if on cue, a herd of Medics strides through the Shelter dome's back entrance. "If you have the streptococcus infection, please come forward," says an older Medic with a lazy eye, his voice amplified through the speakers on the residents' handscreens. "We know who has a fever and who doesn't. Don't make us come find you."

Groaning and spluttering, several lumps on the floor find their feet and stagger to the tent. Soldiers point them to empty spaces on the ground. Some avoid physical contact, while others use the butts of their guns to knock the Shelter residents into place. The Medics roll up their new patients' dirty sleeves and inject antibiotics. Drug production and administration aren't cheap, but I know why the Committee sends workers to treat Shelter residents and soldiers to keep them caged. It's more efficient than taking each individual to Medical—he or she would be unable to pay the bill, anyway—and it prevents the outrage that would result if everyone in the dome got sick.

"Hey." Umbriel tugs my arm. "Beetle's coming over."

I stand straighter as a young soldier approaches us. Her jacket sports the white circular private insignia, and her visor is pushed up so that her deep-set eyes, dreary gray like the lunar landscape, are visible. They're not cruel eyes, just tired ones.

A hollow surrounds each, likely resulting from strain and lack of sleep. She must be assigned to regular duty in Shelter, a job that's mentally rather than physically taxing.

Her chest heaves with an exasperated sigh. "You checking in?"

"Still deciding," Cygnus lies. There's no decision to make—if we don't move in now, we'll be forced to return within a few hours.

Something tugs the ends of my hair, gentle but insistent.

"Shoo!" barks the private at whatever's behind me. "Blast, Belinda, I'll have your daddy tie you to his wrist if you keep on . . ."

I turn around. A little girl steps back, tucking her hands under her chin. Moments later, she sneezes into them. She could be anybody's child, fresh from playing in dirt—muck masks the original color of her skin and the precise proportions of her features.

"Her handscreen profile says that her grandmother died last year," the private explains. "Says she'll touch anyone that looks like her."

Umbriel makes a grab for my arm, but I evade it and squat to get a better look at Belinda. Her smile, her movements—they're quick, bright, and *normal*, like Anka's when she was that age. I wonder how long they'll remain that way, how much time Belinda has before numbness becomes routine and joy a hazy memory.

Belinda draws her index finger from my right nostril to my chin, where I'll have a frown line like Mom's in thirty years or so. "Nothing there!" Her voice is a hoarse whisper.

This isn't the first time a child has puzzled over my gray hair and smooth face. I smile, and creases appear.

"Found one!" Belinda rasps.

"Good for you!" says Anka. She's probably glad that there's someone around who can look up to her.

"Thanks," says Belinda. "Are you big kids going to stay?"

Anka laughs, flattered that she's been called a "big kid." "I don't know."

"What's it like on the outside?" Belinda asks.

I feel a surge of pity for this child, who knows nothing but Shelter misery.

My sister opens and closes her mouth several times, struggling to decide where to begin. "Outside of here, it's—"

The private interrupts her. "Belinda, why ask about the rest of the base when you're never going to see it?"

Shelter children must pass a rigorous exam to gain access to Primary. Odds say Belinda won't try, let alone succeed.

The private grabs Belinda's wrist, saying, "Something sounds *off* about you."

Belinda cries out in pain.

Fuming, I step between them, using my arm to break the private's grip. Belinda hunches over her arm, whimpering; the private's dull eyes light up with anger.

Too late, I realize my effort was futile and idiotic.

The private pushes me. "Back off. I could truncheon you for this." Her hand seizes Belinda's chin. "Open up, blast it."

Glancing from me to the private, Belinda drops her jaw.

"Knew it. Those white dots . . ." The private—Gertrude Zeta according to the voice-recognition software on my handscreen—taps twice on the back of her left hand. "Quarantine!" she hollers into the receiver.

An indigo blur—probably a Medic—bursts from the sick tent and sails across the floor, dodging clusters of people whose heads follow its trajectory. Sudden movements must be rare in Shelter, a place where life itself slows down until it eventually halts.

"You people are going to put a *kid* in that tent?" Umbriel demands.

Gertrude shoots him a look filled with equal parts annoyance and alarm.

"Someone could roll over and squash her," Umbriel continues, "and that's the best-case scenario!"

Near the sick tent, three Militia helmets swivel in our direction.

Out of selfishness and fear, I turn to Umbriel and pretend to dust off my hands: *Stop talking!* People have gotten arrested faster for protesting less.

Umbriel swallows the rest of his tirade. To my relief, the three Beetles across the room turn away, scanning Shelter for more obvious troublemakers.

The Medical assistant skids to a stop at our side.

"All right, Belinda." Copper Head glances at my family and takes a step backward. He's either too embarrassed or scared to face us. "I'll bring you to the big tent over there. We have medicine just for you. Okay?"

Anka points a quivering finger at Copper Head. "I thought we were done with you!"

Dozens of Shelter eyes fix upon us.

"Calm down, people." Cygnus shows everyone his open palms. "Nothing's happening."

Seemingly ignorant of the fact that her temper has already caused the Militia to appear at our apartment, Anka continues ranting. "Stop taking people where they don't want to go."

Gertrude's hand drifts toward her truncheon. I swallow hard, willing Anka to hear my thoughts; her disobedience could result in punishments ranging from a twenty-four-hour detention for her to additional surveillance for Cygnus and me.

"And leave us *alone*!" Anka tells Copper Head, who holds his hands up as if surrendering.

Although I sometimes wish Anka could flatten her emotions like I do, it would destroy me if she lost her vigor, that radioactivity in her belly. I want to grab her and Cygnus, spirit them out of Shelter, and ensure they never enter again. Here, Meds and especially Beetles could steal them at any moment, hide them in a tent or find some other excuse for separating us. And if they don't, I'll have to watch my siblings' wills dissipate until all three of us are motionless lumps on the floor.

"I promise you won't see me anymore." Copper Head applies an adhesive thermometer to Belinda's forehead, just as he did to Mom several hours ago. His mouth curves into the faintest of smiles. "I'm to join Militia next week."

Anka's face slackens as if he's slapped her—despite her fury, she's not above sympathy. Neither am I. For Copper Head, the next two years of mandatory soldiering will bring relentless competition, frequent boredom, and sudden danger on the Moon, the Earth, and in the empty space surrounding both. There's a chance he won't make it, as serious injury and death are not uncommon for new recruits. The Committee officially acknowledged the death of nine Base IV trainees last year—*trainees,* not active soldiers. Who knows how many more have died off the charts?

"Open wide," Copper Head instructs Belinda, ignoring Anka's sudden tranquility. "Aaaaaah."

Belinda drops her jaw without moving any other part of her face. Light from Copper Head's handscreen illuminates white spots on the scarlet throat tissue.

"You've contracted the infection, but it doesn't look too bad. Off we go!" Copper Head and Belinda shuffle toward the tent, her dirty little fingers in his big, gloved hand.

Gertrude huffs, uncrossing and recrossing her arms. "You Thetas ready to finish this check-in? Need an answer from the head of the family."

Do I want to check into a life that's no longer life? I'd give anything not to participate, to avoid even observing it.

Maybe that's why Copper Head smiled when he mentioned Militia. Soldiering means spending months away from this place—although there's a small probability that if he survives the eight-week training course, he'll have to monitor Shelter, like Gertrude. If he becomes a private, he'll serve two years and move on to Specialization, remaining the same tongue-tied civilian he is today. But if he ranks high enough during training, he'll make more in prize money than he would earn in a year as a Medical assistant. As an officer, he'd command other Beetles and likely stay in the Militia for life.

"Phaet?" Umbriel squeezes my shoulder. "She's asking you."

My eyes scan the crowd, falling on the indigo figure that has nearly reached the quarantine tent and the stoic soldiers whose ranks he will join. Countless grimy faces point our way—seeing, perhaps even understanding, what is happening.

One hunched-over man summons the strength to shake his head at me. *Get out while you can.* I frown at him, knowing it's all but impossible. Unless . . .

Gertrude taps her foot. "I'm *waiting.* If you don't check in soon, your presence here will be considered trespassing."

I glance from side to side, almost expecting Mom to handle this situation for me. Letting us stay here would be out of the question—she'd spin a tapestry of words to get us out to clean air.

Looking over at Copper Head in the tent, I utter the first thing I've said today: "I'm going with him."

"Wha . . . ?" Umbriel whispers. "To Mili—You can't. You're too young. Phaet—"

I take Anka's elbow and Cygnus's wrists. Ignoring their confusion and Umbriel's demands for clarification, I lead my family toward the Shelter exit. As we shove past the clumps of humanity on the ground, several people stretch up and touch the ends of my hair. Even layers of grime can't mask the awe—and in a few cases, the jealousy—on their faces. Maybe they wish they'd walked out of here while they still could. *You did the right thing*, their eyes say.

"Why are they staring at you?" Anka whispers.

Because I found a way out.

After we escape the vile dome, the air becomes breathable again. Never have the scents of plastic and steel been so sweet.

I inhale and exhale almost violently to clean out my lungs, but I can still feel dust and smoke residue clinging to the walls of the air sacs within.

Umbriel grabs my upper arm, forcing me to a halt. "What in the name of the Committee was *that*?"

"Say you were kidding about Militia," says Cygnus. "I think that Medical assistant could clobber you in a fight, and he's probably below the fiftieth weight percentile for eighteen-year-old boys."

Because trainees earn their rank by competing with one another, strength matters whether they're on duty or not. We've all heard stories about the top few sabotaging one another—often with deadly outcomes.

"Militia . . ." Anka trails off.

Cygnus throws up his hands, asking me, "You sure you want to do this?"

You don't have to be eighteen to enlist in Militia. Occasionally, seventeen-year-olds who want to Specialize early join; I've also heard about the rare sixteen-year-olds who desperately need money. But out of the nine trainees who died last year, seven were younger than eighteen. Seven dead, out of twelve who were under the official draft age.

What are the odds for a fifteen-year-old? Enlisting at my age has never happened on any base in all eighty-one years of Lunar history.

Costs: potential injury and death, for me. Benefits: a hundred Sputniks per week as a stipend throughout training and a small chance of ranking high and earning enough to pay Mom's Medical bill. In objective terms, one person's risk could bring four people's reward.

I'm determined to carry out my plan for the people I love past reason. I resign myself to the next two years, which will be very different from how I originally envisioned them: filled with textbooks and flora and family.

That's if I even last two years. And if I do, will all of me come away intact?

"This isn't the place to argue." Every few seconds, Umbriel glances over his shoulder to see if people are watching—fortunately, they simply part around us, too concerned with their own problems to care about ours.

As I walk with my family and best friend to the Phi complex, perhaps for the last time, I envy the monotony of their existence. At least they know what tomorrow will bring.

"But it's three years too early!" Ariel sits cross-legged on his bed, left hand under his rear. Although his body beneath his green Phi robes is relaxed, his eyes are restless. "Giving up on Primary is a total waste of your brain. You could check into Shelter, take that blasted exam, and be back in class by next month."

"Don't worry about it." I yawn. It's close to my bedtime, and well past Anka's, but my siblings and I didn't want to reenter our apartment, where this trauma started. For now, we're in Caeli's home, although she has politely hinted that she'd like us to leave. It's getting late. In the living room, Anka has fallen asleep, her head on Cygnus's lap. The twins and I have relocated to their cramped bedroom so they can keep trying to change my mind. They're continuing from where their parents left off. Atlas doesn't like that I'm leaving my siblings alone in

Theta 808 with only a maintenance robot for company, even if it's better than Shelter. Caeli has agreed to feed and supervise Anka and Cygnus, as long as I compensate the Phis with a small percentage of my trainee stipend.

"Ariel's going to miss competing with you if you leave," Umbriel says.

In Primary, Ariel and I usually earn scores within a fraction of a point of each other, setting the curve. Our rivalry has become a running joke. Because of our families' friendship, we study together and collaborate on group projects rather than sabotage each other. And despite our lifelong academic game of one-upmanship, Ariel's always been honest with me.

"In all seriousness, Phaet, you could lose yourself there." Ariel's voice is mellow, unlike the rumble Umbriel emits when emotion strikes but petrifying all the same. "Like this girl who graduated Primary last year—I saw her slugging a little boy in the Atrium a little while ago."

"But wasn't she always sort of . . . emotionally unstable? Phaet's different. Not the Beater type." Umbriel turns to me. "But when you're on your own, people might beat on *you*."

"See, Phaet?" Ariel says. "Your plan's going to hurt you, and everyone else too. Especially *my brother*, and you both know why."

Umbriel flushes crimson beneath his tan, opening and closing his mouth like a koi as he struggles to think of a biting retort.

Ariel has ventured into taboo territory. Umbriel and I have never discussed . . . *that*, keeping it tacit like our other understandings. I've known since we were ten, just as I know the night will be cold when my kneecaps hurt during the day: after we complete Militia and Specialization, we'll carry on as we always have—guarding each other and communicating without words—except with adult responsibilities and, someday, a family. Our plans may sound premature, but we're lucky. Having someone to trust, even without the "chemistry" Primary girls giggle about rather than study, is more than many citizens dare hope for.

Ariel shrugs off our discomfort. "I only hope this one"—he pokes Umbriel in the ribs—"won't up and join Militia just because you did, Phaet. He'd steal something dumb in his first week."

Disobedience in the Militia means immediate dishonorable discharge and permanent pariah status. Consigned to society's waste bin, Umbriel would have nowhere to go but Shelter.

Cringing, Umbriel dusts off his hands; not even Ariel knows about our secret signal. Umbriel needs to talk to me later, and I'm not looking forward to it.

"What are you two plotting now?" Ariel asks. "Listen, Phaet. If you enlist, you won't have anyone to talk to—I mean, no one else understands this sign language you guys use. Won't you wish Umbriel was there? And over here, he's going to miss you like he'd miss sunshine."

"We'll *both* miss you," Umbriel says.

"Sorry," I tell him. "But my mind's made up."

"You can't do this to us!" Umbriel exclaims.

"Or to yourself," adds Ariel.

"I can, though." As long as I have a chance at success in Militia, a chance at seeing the twins again after it's over, I won't surrender my family to dirt and disease. "I will."

4

THE EXAMINATION ROOM SMELLS LIKE bleach and ethyl alcohol.

"Phaet Theta," the tall twentysomething man, Medic Canopus Epsilon, reads off his handscreen. He scrolls through my stats, making assumptions about me based on my birth date, apartment number, IQ, bank balance, parental occupations, et cetera. When he presumably gets to my disciplinary history—my only misdemeanor is stargazing with Umbriel at the greenhouses after hours, long ago—he lets out a choppy laugh. "I hope you're not that lazy anymore!"

When I don't laugh or smile, he returns to official business, looking put off by my silence. "Fifteen years of age. Why are you joining Militia so young?"

Shrug.

Canopus raises a perfectly groomed yellow eyebrow, the color of one of Saturn's rings; his Epsilon robes are the same shade. The white light and white walls of his office match his skin. "Well, let's see if you're fit to serve. Looks good so far, except for the hair."

"Genetic," I explain.

Mom's grandmother, long gone now, was completely gray before she turned thirty, though Mom still has hair as black as the outer reaches of space. My great-grandma was born on Earth, in a place called China, which she left to study in the United States. During the petroleum embargo, she fled into the sky with the rest of the Lunar Bases' founders. If she hadn't left, she would have suffered through cataclysmic flooding, economic turmoil, and even civil war. She helped design the irrigation system for Agriculture. Mom says I would have liked her, that if she hadn't been so old, and me so young, we would have gotten along. "Maybe she came back through you," Mom said.

Canopus pats the examination chair. "Well, have a seat and make yourself comfortable."

I do. I feel the cold glass backing through my robes and shiver as Canopus fastens buckles around my wrists and ankles. The chair springs into action, measuring my weight and then stretching out into a cot of sorts to take my height. When it suspends me upside down to test my inner ear fluid balance, I fight to keep nausea at bay.

A painful time later, Canopus recites my results. "Average height for a fifteen-year-old female, weight below regulation. Blood composition, heart rate, blood pressure, internal organ function, eyesight, hearing, sensitivity, all normal. Muscle mass percentage relatively high."

Pride tugs at the corners of my mouth, and Canopus smiles back. Lifting sacks of compost, hacking at wayward tree limbs with a knife, and crawling between dense crops, all while avoiding the spray nozzles in Agriculture's ceiling, require more exertion and coordination than people imagine. My strength will serve me well in training, as much of my competition hasn't done physical labor outside of standard conditioning classes in Primary.

"Bones of slightly porous consistency. Take vitamin D tablets during training, okay?" Canopus leans in and whispers: "Listen here—according to your body size and composition, and taking the workouts into account, you need to eat a little over two thousand, two hundred kilocalories a day to maintain your weight. But I'm going to program in four hundred extra. It'll help."

"Thanks," I whisper, genuinely grateful. Maybe I can put on a few kilograms during training.

Raising his voice back to normal, Canopus finishes, "You're all clear."

I offer him the back of my left hand. He presses his thumb to my handscreen, waiting for it to register his fingerprint, until CLEARED FOR MILITIA appears in green letters.

"Next!" he calls.

As I exit Canopus's office, an enormous boy with a bulbous forehead saunters in, looks my small frame up and down, and shoots me a quick smile. I return it, happy that I've gotten a pleasant, if not sympathetic, reaction from another member of my trainee class. As Canopus bustles about, gathering equipment, the boy uses the sweat from his palms to slick back curls the color of pecan shells. I laugh quietly—is he *preening* for a medical examination?

Umbriel is waiting in the lobby of the Defense Department's Medical quarters. It's a testament to the magnitude of the Militia that they get their own on-site hospital. "All good?"

Nod.

Although his face distorts with disappointment, he recovers quickly. "That's great. You show them what you've got on Wednesday."

Every two months, eighteen-year-olds fresh out of Primary start training in a group. The training lasts eight weeks, until the trainees are sorted into their respective units. Each base has its own Militia, but together we are known as the Lunar Forces (I wonder if the physics pun was intended). The need to unite hardly ever arises; Militias individually ward off stray attacks from Earthbound cities, collect intelligence, and police the citizenry.

The last time the Forces acted together was thirty years ago, when the Earthbound superpowers attacked Base I, resulting in the Battle of Peary.

That was when the then-Committee instituted a temporary "emergency rule" that has lasted to this day. They say they're too busy to schedule elections.

Both my parents fought in the Battle of Peary, driving off the Earthbound for good. Mom rarely speaks of the experience, except to whisper, "What a pity," when she thinks her children aren't listening.

Umbriel and I wander out of Defense and into one of the wider pedestrian hallways. Everyone keeps to their right, so traffic is smooth.

"Don't do this," Umbriel repeats for the forty-third time this week. He's agitated, so he strides quickly. I have to jog to keep up. "It's not too late to drop out. Cygnus checked the reward money for each Militia rank: you'd have to get seventh or higher to make over fifteen hundred Sputniks in prize money. And that would only cover your mom's treatment. While we're waiting for that, four hundred a month in stipends won't even cover your rent."

We reach the entrance to the Education Department, and I

drag Umbriel inside. Sensing our body heat, the automatic portal opens upward for us. As soon as it closes, I grab his wrists. They're so big in my hands.

"Umbriel, stop."

"Stop what?" He tickles my palm, but I'm in no mood to laugh.

"Stop talking. I'll make the top seven."

"But you're younger, and smaller, and, er, weaker—"

I tap my right temple with a forefinger.

Most people in our three-hundred-member Primary Level Nine class only know my name because Ariel or I finish first in nearly every subject. Electromagnetism, Human Biology, Calculus, Language Composition . . . Lunar History is one of my two weak areas. It consists of tedious retellings of scientific developments, and Earth Studies is no better—dull scrutiny of the unfortunate beings we left in chaos a century ago.

Because the Earthbound are so disorganized compared to us, that last subject is a particular pain. Earth has too many micro-civilizations to count, each with different languages, governments, and parts-per-million toxicity readings. Although the wild ecology of the planet fascinates me—how does life relate to other life without human interference?—I couldn't care less about the people. They can't keep track of themselves; logically, I can't either. Small wonder Ariel, whose frontal lobe processes the feelings and motivations of countless individuals with ease, always beats me at Earth Studies.

The entryway of Education is dark—it's late, 22:00. To maintain our bodies' circadian rhythms during the 352-hour lunar diurnal cycle, all public Departments and main hallways have their lights turned off for ten hours a day to mimic nighttime.

"Look up." Umbriel's arm presses me to his side.

Through the small circular window above, I glimpse hints of constellations. Gemini, the twins, glows especially bright. Unwelcome emotion bubbles from my chest up into my throat. I try to withdraw to a thoughtless space inside my head, as Mom once tried to teach me, and ignore this bodily contact and my unwelcome future in Militia.

"I won't see you tomorrow, because I have late hours at the greenhouse. And your day off isn't for another month." He steps away, shoves his left hand into his roomy pants pocket, and lowers his voice to a whisper. "So . . . here goes."

Umbriel pulls a short stalk of something green and red from his pocket. It's a rose, one of the most expensive plants in the greenhouses because it serves no other purpose than decoration. He must have used all his tricks to smuggle it out.

I don't understand why he brought me a flower instead of the usual pear or handful of strawberries. It'll wilt soon, and I can't eat it.

Then the anxiety hits. Did someone see him filch the flower? Is anyone listening through our handscreens, or observing us through security pods, objects the size of a big toe that hover soundlessly in the air?

"Phaet . . . I've—I've wanted to know something for eons. We've been friends since—since we were born, right? I've needed you for school stuff, and you've needed *me* for people stuff. . . ."

It's true. After Dad died, I despaired of fielding sympathy, retreated inside myself, and let Umbriel deal with everyone on my behalf. I'd once been talkative, but I soon realized that words wasted my breath. Our arrangement worked so well that when girls in seventh-year Primary mocked my hair and boys yanked it on dares, Umbriel teased them back—and in severe cases, made their belongings spontaneously disappear. Soon they didn't dare come within a meter of me.

". . . and now things are going to be harder for both of us. So will you—will you accept this?"

I offer a cautious nod, understanding that his gift has sentimental rather than practical value. What that value is, I'm not sure.

He places the flower into my hand. One of the tiny thorns catches my thumb—Bioengineering hasn't gotten rid of them yet. A miniature red orb rises on my fingertip, and I figure it's payback for Umbriel stealing and killing the rose in the first place.

He sighs my name in relief. A chin digs into my forehead; the smell of unripe fruit enters my nostrils. One of Umbriel's hands cradles my neck, while the other tugs at the small of my back. Something in the air has warped, and I don't like it. I'll deal with Umbriel when—if—I get out of Militia alive.

"Sorry," I splutter, sounding like the apologetic boy from Medical who abducted Mom. I extract myself from Umbriel's arms and turn back to the entrance, not caring whether I've vexed him. Since Mom left last week, I hardly care about anything.

Umbriel walks me home, all the way to my white cylinder room. When he's out of sight, my fingers uncoil from the short rose stem. As the flower falls to my desk, another thorn scratches my palm.

5

I HOLD MY SIBLINGS TIGHT, ONE IN EACH arm. Anka can't seem to grab enough of me, while Cygnus squirms, his wiry arm hanging over my shoulder. Since he turned ten, Mom has had to ask him to hug me. He's squeamish when he thinks things are "corny" or "girly."

In contrast, Anka cries freely, pounding her fists against my back in sadness or anger—maybe both.

Cygnus holds the tears in like me. "I'll make sure Anka gets to class all right, and I won't play too many sim-games, and if anything gets weird, I'll run over to Umbriel or Caeli like you told me. . . ."

I squeeze him tighter, and the display of affection finally becomes excessive. He wriggles free.

"It's 6:45." Anka wipes tears away as if she's mad at them for being there. "You should go."

These two will be fine on their own. At least, I hope so. I hug them again, so that in the absence of loving words, they know how much I care.

For Mom, I remind myself.

My biceps give a spasm of resistance before I let go of my brother and sister.

ↀↀↀ

Our training begins with a review of Lunar history, intended to excite us but accomplishing the opposite.

"A hundred years ago, Earth was in chaos," an instructor drones, reading from her handscreen. She's young, unlike the two men standing behind her, but by her carriage I know she abandoned girlhood long ago. Her eyes are long and angled like mine; her face, nose, and lips narrow, as if someone shaped them with a razor. According to my handscreen, she's Captain Yinha Rho; she holds the minimum rank needed to instruct trainees, and in a full-scale combat situation, she could command up to two hundred soldiers. I'll always have to remember that she's more powerful than she looks.

"The last oil and natural gas reserves were depleted. Temperatures were rising and so were the seas."

Three meters from me, a lanky dark-haired girl in maroon Beta robes yawns without bothering to cover her mouth. She can't be any more bored than Yinha, who's probably given this exact speech to each batch of soldiers every two months for years.

My eyelids grow heavier as the history lesson progresses. Ice caps collapsed and lowlands flooded; oil-producing countries started a global economy-crushing embargo. Inundated cities constructed massive rafts and floated off to sea, the financial burden leading to civil wars and international breakdown.

"Two superpowers grew out of the chaos," Yinha says, "the destitute but aggressive Pacifian alliance, and the Battery Bay bloc, riven with liberal debauchery, which it still tries to spread. Both spew poison into the environment and propel themselves across the oceans, seizing the few pitiful resources that are left."

Yinha tells how Earthbound governments poured money into researching bizarre geoengineering schemes and how our scientist ancestors, from many different countries, knew the schemes would fail. They collected the funds, started constructing Base I, and brought their families with them to the Moon.

I feel bad for not paying more attention, because I'm thankful to live on the Bases. The founders thought of the Moon as a last refuge for the human species, and my family was lucky to have a place here.

To finish, Yinha holds one hand toward us, palm facing up. We join her in shouting the motto of the Lunar Bases: "A beacon of humanity for the glory of science."

Our first assignment in protecting the beacon is to shed our loose robes and change into trainee suits. The instructors laugh at our confusion as to where to do it.

"Right here," Yinha says.

"Change in front of twenty-five hormonal teenage guys?" The tall girl next to me wears the familiar green robes of Phi; the color is striking against her dark olive skin. Around her eyes, she has the beginnings of crinkles, radial like the veins on a gingko leaf, from constantly grinning. "See? Stripy-hair is *freaked*."

She's referring to me, perhaps even mocking me for being the blatant outlier in this group—or I'm being defensive because of nerves. My heart is propelling so much blood through my head that I'm getting dizzy.

But she's also challenging a captain, one who seems to relish authority. None of us knows whether Yinha also enjoys abusing it.

Captain Yinha scrutinizes the girl's frizzy black curls, which refuse to stay in the knot required for women, and glances at her handscreen. "Nashira Phi, I'll tolerate your cheek for now, but other officers might not."

A few trainees exhale, relieved. We hadn't expected such leniency, instead bracing ourselves for Nashira's verbal or physical punishment, for Captain Yinha to enjoy making an example out of her.

"That said," Yinha continues, "don't expect privacy in the Militia. Here, men and women are equals in every way. Do I make myself clear? Cool."

Mom always told me not to judge people by their handscreen profiles, and I rarely look at anything but the name. But self-preservation gets the better of me; glancing down, I see why Yinha was terse with this girl. Nashira—who "prefers to be addressed as Nash"—gets decent marks in Primary but has a reputation for asking "unnecessarily specific" questions in Lunar History class.

The trainees spread out, trying to find contraptions to duck behind. This is the famous Militia training dome, where a flick of a switch can alter gravity, where a linoleum floor can sprout a forest overnight, where sound takes half a second to cross the room and bounce back. Rumors fly that the laws of physics don't apply here, but that's nonsense. They're just manipulated.

Nash disappears behind a wall with various handholds meant to simulate rock climbing on Earth. Noting the stares I'm receiving from other trainees—sizing me up, because I wasn't in their Primary class, because I look so young—I hide behind the same wall. But I choose a spot far enough from Nash so it doesn't look like I followed her.

Hands shaking and fumbling, I discard my white robes, sliding into a snug black shirt and loose pants full of pockets. A tough canvas jacket goes on over the shirt.

"Done yet?" Yinha's voice booms across the white dome,

magnified because it's coming from everyone's handscreen as well. "Cool. We're running a kilometer to warm up. That's two laps along the perimeter. Get behind the green line."

Neon green flashes to my left, indicating our starting point. The trainees saunter in its general direction; several shove one another in order to get there first.

"Hurry up," Yinha says. "You've got loads of exercises before we're done today."

Nash sprints toward the line, showing off her long, powerful legs. Though all I want is to keep hiding behind the wall, I tail her, holding myself tall. We're among the last to reach our destination, and we end up behind a swarm of eager trainees. *Why are they so desperate, when we're not being scored?*

"Go!" barks Yinha.

Nash pulls ahead. I hang back to gauge my body's aptitude for running and to observe the competition. I'm of average height among the girls, but small overall; with my proportionally short legs and long torso, I need to make up for my smaller strides with a higher frequency.

While I strategize, unaware, someone's foot stomps on mine.

"Watch it, granny!" shouts a girl with a runny nose. Strange she should call me that, since I'm closer in age to any younger siblings she might have.

By the second lap, I overtake a panting Nash, but my lungs burn and sweat trickles into my eyes. I was never good at this during conditioning. Looking ahead, I see two boys race neck and neck toward the finish line. One's tall and stocky, pain obvious on his face. It's the friendly landmass who fixed his hair in Canopus's office. The other boy, who has a smaller build, takes leisurely strides that barely ruffle his reddish hair.

Oh no. Bitterness simmers within me as I remember his curt repetitions of "sorry" on that awful day, the meek apologies that couldn't make up for leaving three children without a mother, and his artificial civility when we saw him in Shelter. Despite the dangers in Militia, he grinned when he told Anka he was about to join. Now I understand why. He's looked forward to outdoing the other trainees and to an ego boost.

As the Giant begins to tire, Copper Head prances past him. Then the Giant rams into his rival, forcing Copper Head to stumble onto an outside lane. The Giant's open hostility tempers my satisfaction at seeing Copper Head put in his place.

They cross the finish line together.

Thirty seconds later, I follow in the midst of a swarm of trainees. If I'm to pay for Mom's treatment, I have to improve, and quickly.

"The last twenty of you, move it!" Yinha commands the stragglers. She nods with approval at the Giant, who rests his hands on his knees, and Copper Head, who stands off to the side to stretch his quadriceps. "Nice job to the two who finished first. Seems we have some well-conditioned trainees."

Immediate recognition—that's why they pushed themselves so hard. Although training has just begun, the instructors are already paying attention to them as potential officers.

"Today's workout will be cardiovascular conditioning," says Yinha, "so take a moment to catch your breath and stretch. Next, we're jumping, crawling, and doing other stuff that gets your heart rate up. We'll finish with another half-kilometer run. Got it? Cool."

A grid of torn muscle fibers, swollen and blotchy at the microscopic level, comes to mind. If I'm lucky, a single-digit percentage of the cells in my arms, legs, and torso will end up like that by tomorrow. Sometimes I wish anatomy class had been less graphic.

We divide into groups of five, each of which gets a hundred-meter-long straightaway to work with. The original circular track disappears, and neon lights indicate the new paths.

We sprint. We hop on one foot, back on the other. We crawl on hands and knees, and crawl on one hand. We tackle cartwheels, roundoffs, and forward rolls with varying degrees of success.

"This is how you get in shape!" Yinha hollers as motivation.

By the time the cooldown run arrives, my kneecaps pound and the room around me jolts with every step.

Copper Head finishes a full five seconds before everyone else and jogs around Yinha, avoiding her eyes.

Who is he? The day he came for Mom, I was too upset to identify him using the voice-recognition software on my handscreen. I'll learn his name soon enough—but more important, how do I reach his level?

6

THE MESS HALL'S THICK TABLES ARE EMPTY when the ravenous trainees troop inside for dinner. I sit near the end of the room with Nash and two other girls, my back against the wall.

"You following me again?" Nash says.

I shake my head and drop my gaze to the tabletop, wishing Umbriel could back up my denial. No, I wish I were home with my family, or in the Phi complex. Anywhere but here, surrounded by hot glares that could incinerate me at any moment.

On my right is a sensor for my thumb. I scan myself in; the little bar on the top reads, THETA, PHAET. 2,650 KILOCALORIE DIET.

"Leave the kid alone, Nash," the lovely girl across from me says. Her skin is bronze and freckled, her hair is wavy and black, and her eyes are shot through with gold. "She's probably my little sister's age. Chitra's terrified of boys, and we're about to see boys with *guns*."

Biting back a laugh, I decide I like her wit.

Nash scowls. "Itty snob. Look, Vinasa, she's ignoring us, like we're not worth her breath."

No, that's not it. I shake my head, panicked, but Nash has turned her attention elsewhere.

The tables rumble as decades-old conveyor belts carry our personalized meals from the walls to our seats—it's nothing like having Mom ladle vegetables onto our plates and watching Anka wrinkle her nose if she smells horseradish or okra. *Are they missing me like I miss them?*

The square section of plastic before me tucks itself away, revealing hot food in a circular compartmentalized tray that rises and screeches into place. Dinner is knobs of whole grain bread and a vegetable soup with bits of lab-grown beef drifting in the hearty broth; dessert is a personal cantaloupe, a new fruit the size of an orange with skin that peels away just as easily. Cygnus and Anka would be jealous, not because of the food's quality—Mom could make even an underripe eggplant taste delectable—but its quantity. I'm going to finish every last crumb of bread, every last drop of soup, and my cantaloupe too.

"I don't care where I place, or how much Defense pays me," the short girl sitting across from me is saying to Vinasa, who compared me to her little sister. She has white skin and hair as orange as a marigold blossom, cropped short like Cygnus's. "Actually, I'd rather rank low so they don't put me on Earth recon."

Earth recon missions are unpopular but necessary assignments for high-ranking soldiers. From what I've read in the *Luna Daily*, Battery Bay and Pacifia have more problems between them now that we leave them alone—but we make a point of keeping an eye on them. My Earth Studies teacher once joked that the two cities are like teenage lovers: fickle, silly, bickering. They float atop the ocean, sometimes chasing each other and sometimes speeding in opposite directions. They've each tried to get as many other countries on their side as possible; now, most of the planet's population belongs to one of the alliances.

Vinasa swallows some bread and looks as if she's trying

not to hiccup. "Don't know if you can bet on that, Eri. Beetles have seen more Earth ships nearby these past few years, so the Militia's sending more people to dispatch those ships and on actual recon missions."

"Ugh, and the food on the ships is probably even worse than *this*. . . ." Eri hasn't touched her meal; she glares at it, as if doing so will turn it into fresh sushi and fluffy coconut cake. "Think we can get our parents to send some real bread?"

Groans of assent arise from around the table. These girls surely grew up in middle-income families, eating the kind of food mine only bought for special occasions. White bread, still warm from the Culinary steam ovens, filled with fruit paste or lab-grown meat. Water infused with carbon dioxide and sweet stevia leaves that bubbles delightfully on the tongue.

I whisk my soup with the spoon, aiming to create a smooth, sloping vortex until I admit to myself that the chunky liquid will never cooperate.

Nash's low voice wafts from beside me. "It's not that bad, Eri. At least they care about our health."

Defense is feeding us now so that we can do their bidding before either completing our service or dropping dead. *Great investment*, I think with a sardonic smirk. We might as well take advantage of their generosity.

"You know who's going to place at top two and end up on recon?" Vinasa winks at Eri, whose face turns the color of a radish. "Wes Kappa."

I wonder if she's talking about Copper Head.

"Yeah, Eri, your *stalk-ee* ran like a comet today—I mean, if comets could run," Nash adds. "I saw you staring at him like . . . well, the way you've stared at him since Level Ten Primary. . . .

Top twenty in every subject! Pretty hair like the surface of Mars!"

Eri hunches over her food and shovels a spoonful of the soup into her mouth. Now's a good time for her to eat it, when she's so embarrassed she won't notice the taste.

She swallows. "Fuzz off, Nash."

About ten years ago, some colorful individuals derived the swearwords *fizz, fuzz,* and *fuse* from nuclear fission and fusion, violent processes from which the best lunar weapons draw their power. I'm unused to profanity, but given Militia's coarse environment, hearing such phrases shouldn't be a surprise.

"But it's so much fun to tease you!" Vinasa erupts into laughter, clutching her middle. "Also, you do *nothing* about him, even though he'll *never* make the first move."

Nash snorts. "Vin, Wes is right there, with Orion. Quit with the giggles unless you want them to hear."

Indeed, Copper Head sits at the end of a nearby table full of babbling trainees, facing the wall and watching the evening news on his handscreen. The fellow responsible for most of the mirth—Orion, I suppose—has peachy skin and wears his wheaten hair in a stubby ponytail at the nape of his neck. His face and shoulders are so strong, even the hairstyle doesn't make him look effeminate. While he makes conversation with the unfortunate girl beside him, her spoon misses her mouth and stew spills down her front. I let out a snort of amusement.

Oblivious, Copper Head spears his bread with his fork and chomps it with his premolars, on the side of his mouth. Something on the news holds his attention, or he's pretending it does. Because I'm in a similar social situation, I feel a sudden closeness with him, but I repress it. He deserves no empathy from me.

After dinner, Colonel Arcturus Theta, an older officer with a round, ruddy face and gray hair shaved close to his scalp, delivers a lecture on rules that focuses on our 23:00 curfew—"23:00, and not a second later!" We mustn't wander about after curfew; boys and girls must be in their respective halves of the barracks after curfew; handscreens must be silenced after curfew. . . .

"People call him Arcturus the Assiduous." In the row above me, Orion whispers loudly to Copper Head. "Because he flips grits every time people don't follow his exact directions. And he's super picky about squat technique. *Ass*iduous. Get the double meaning?"

On a better day, I might have laughed. It would feel wrong now, with my family scattered all over the base.

Arcturus's eyes dart to our section of chairs. When he turns to a different part of the crowd, his droopy cheeks wobble.

Twenty minutes later, he finishes. We drag ourselves to the barracks, where cots for all trainees are stacked in columns—girls in one half of the room, boys in the other. I gulp, wondering how I'll fall asleep with so many people around.

I dart to a quiet corner and claim a top bunk. I've always liked to see everything. Even though the lights are still on, and the cot is too bumpy for restorative rest, my eyelids begin to close as soon as I orient myself horizontally. With a stranger's soft breathing in the cot next to me instead of my sister's, I drown in the loneliness that's been seeping into my blood all day. In a futile attempt to fight it off, I imagine Mom's dark eyes watching me as I wander into the void.

7

THE NEXT DAY INVOLVES STRENGTH TRAINING, which works muscles I didn't know I had to the point of misery. I had hoped that my time in the greenhouses would prepare me for this kind of exertion, but I was sadly mistaken. The Giant does the most push-ups, crunches, and squats, with Wes Kappa a close second.

Periodically, I glance at my handscreen clock and wonder about my family—at 16:00, in the middle of a pull-up, I think, *Did Anka get home?* At dinnertime, while in my usual seat against the wall: *Did Caeli remember to make food for two more people? And Mom . . . oh, I hope her fever's subsiding. . . .*

Later in the week, we spend hours reviewing form and martial arts techniques. My sore muscles bewail every punch and parry. The double roundhouse kicks are the worst, requiring a quick pivot in midair to hit the left and right flanks of an opponent. Most satisfying is the axe kick, which aims to crush a bone or two beneath the heel. I earn myself dirty stares when my foot flies up past my collarbone. Years of crawling and twisting in the cramped greenhouses have kept me flexible.

When Yinha orders us to pair off so she can critique us two by two, I lurk near Nash, Eri, and Vinasa, who argue over which two will form a pair and who will face someone new. Eri shuffles off into a crowd of trainees, and I follow—she seems like a safe opponent.

Before I summon the courage to approach her, the Giant swaggers over to Wes Kappa and grabs his arm. Trainees scoot backward as they face off.

"Would you like to partner up?" Wes asks his rival in a civil tone.

"Stop being sassy, Kappa." The Giant pulls Wes into his body and traps him in a headlock. "I've waited so long for this . . . now I'm giving you a preview."

The Giant uses the strength in his back and arms to throw Wes down. As Wes hits the floor, he rolls on his back to absorb the impact. I remember how the Giant rammed him on the track last week—Wes seems like his perennial victim.

Without Umbriel by my side to fend off bullies all through Primary, I might've endured the same treatment I'm witnessing now. My best friend wouldn't stand by if he were present.

While the other trainees watch in fear—Eri looks as if she's about to cry—I run forward, my hand extended to help Wes up. He might've taken Mom, but he doesn't deserve to be tormented as the Beaters tormented her.

He takes my hand, his grip gentle, and his legs—stronger than they look—do ninety percent of the work in getting him to his feet. He appears uninjured. We each avoid the other's eyes, but I read utter surprise on his face. Maybe he wasn't expecting the Giant to hurt him outright. Maybe he wasn't expecting anyone to step in afterward. Especially me.

The Giant's hooded eyes focus on *me*. "You Kappa's little minion or something? I'll spar with *you*—I'm a little sore. We'll take it easy."

Oh no. How could I have been so stupid? I've earned the enmity of the brawniest trainee, who's clearly not the harmless landmass he seemed in Canopus's office.

My knees quiver, but I fight to keep the fear off my face.

"Jupiter, let her be." Wes hovers around me and the Giant, trying unsuccessfully to edge between us.

The Giant—Jupiter—ignores Wes and extends his mammoth hand to introduce himself. When I offer mine, he squeezes my fingers until my knuckles grate against each other. This trainee doesn't broadcast his stats to everyone's handscreen by speaking his name aloud. He has no reservations, however, about examining my information. As he reads, he arranges his lips into a square shape around his teeth.

"Damn, you're only fifteen?" But he sees something else, and his caricature of a smile falls away. "But this IQ . . ."

Looking warily from me to Wes Kappa, Jupiter cracks the knuckles of his right hand against his hip. I lean away from him, filled with dread. Does he consider me even more of a threat now that he knows my IQ?

I check my handscreen: Jupiter Alpha is the Giant's full name.

As I wiggle my fingers to check for damage, a warm hand finds my shoulder. The feeling is so familiar that I expect to see Umbriel in the flesh when I turn around. To my disappointment, I behold only the coppery hair and tranquil features of Wes, who I assume wants a go at Jupiter himself.

Wes focuses metallic eyes on me for a heartbeat before looking away and removing his hand. "Stay low, all right?"

I archive his advice in my mind. Keeping close to the ground against a larger opponent makes perfect sense.

"All set?" roars Yinha. "Cool. Everyone hit the viewing platform."

A stampede ensues as the trainees move off in pairs.

"Good. That was a lot quicker than yesterday. Today we're sparring until one person falls and stays down for more than three seconds. Who's first?"

"Us!" hollers Jupiter.

"Hmm . . ." Yinha's face hardens with concern. So she's not completely callous; pitting the youngest trainee against the biggest one seems to bother her. "Fine—I won't stop you. I like to see volunteers."

The seats that Jupiter and I occupy rise up from the rest of the viewing platform, carry us through the air, and lower us into the middle of the empty training-dome floor. When we stand up, the chairs retreat to their original positions.

"Go!" Yinha yells.

Jupiter stampedes toward me, leading with his prism-shaped head. With his bigger mass and higher top speed, he can achieve a greater momentum than me any time of day—and knock me over like a bowling pin in that useless Earthbound game.

Stay low, I repeat to myself, crouching and pivoting on the balls of my feet to face right. Before Jupiter barrels into me, I execute a forward roll and regain my footing immediately.

Jupiter zooms past, slowing with great effort.

"Can't run forever!" He comes after me again, with heavier feet this time, and stops in front of me, aiming a massive fist at my face. I raise my crossed forearms to block it. The impact jars my bones. He throws more punches at different sections of my upper body and scores a hit on my sternum. Ouch.

Instead of continuing to block his fists, which would only

reward me with extra bruises on my forearms, I step back, slowly at first. Jupiter leans farther and farther forward—if I sufficiently shift his center of gravity, he'll fall.

"Get on the offensive, Stripes!" a boy yells from the stands.

I aim a fist at Jupiter's stomach. He turns my forearm aside; the collision jars my wrist and elbow. I deliver a vicious kick to his left shinbone, eliciting a yelp of pain, and backpedal away. A collective squeal arises from the female half of the trainees.

Jupiter stalks backward, putting a distance of ten meters between us, and charges again with the speed and certainty of a missile, arms outstretched to prevent a rolling escape on my part.

I should tire him. If I were fighting Wes, with his steely endurance, I'd try something else, but Jupiter looked exhausted by the end of yesterday's workout and probably won't last more than ten minutes running.

I shuffle toward him this time, but veer to the right seconds before we collide. He swears on several human anatomical features and pursues me, losing momentum all the while. I run in a circle, leaning my torso inward to gain speed and maintain balance.

But because he'll eventually attack, I zigzag across the floor at full throttle. Jupiter grunts in frustration, dumbly rotating his head to find me. I sprint behind him and knee him in the groin, which elicits another roar, this time of pain.

The crowd hoots in approval at my dirty trick.

I'll do what I must.

While Jupiter's incapacitated, I back up and shoot toward him, planning to push him over. But he swivels around, grabs my arms, and throws me down. Before my head hits the floor,

I realize that I must have missed his essential organs, and that he's a better actor than I had supposed.

I land hard. It feels like several of my ribs have swapped places. I also may have bruised my brain.

"Sorry, little birdy." Jupiter thwacks me on the nose, and I taste iron in the blood trickling into my mouth. Fighting to stay conscious, I watch his black boot press into my chest.

"And that's three seconds," announces Yinha. "The victor is Jupiter Alpha!"

I hear a few lonely shouts of approbation before blacking out.

8

I OPEN MY EYES TO BEHOLD WHITE EVERYwhere. Spots of color float above me; I blink, and the dots unify into one blob, which materializes into Eri's face. Vinasa loiters by the door; she approaches when she notices that I've woken up.

"Hey," Eri mumbles through a yawn. "Thanks so much for helping Wes earlier. . . . That was real brave."

It wasn't brave as much as stupid, but it's earned me respect—if not fondness—from Eri. I'd underestimated the depth of her puzzling infatuation with Copper Head.

"Yeah, and it landed her here in the Medical quarters." Vinasa turns to me, extending a hand.

I extend my hand too, touching her handscreen with the pad of my thumb so that it can register my identity.

"Phaet. That means 'dove,' right? Associated with peace throughout Western Earthbound culture. Don't know how much that name's going to help you here." Vinasa looks at my stats once more, and her mouth forms a little *O* of surprise. "You're . . . you're only fifteen? I knew you were young, because you weren't in our Primary class, but . . . wow. I'm not saying you can't get through training, though. Some of the nonaligned floating cities—Dakota and Benthos, specifically—have used child pirates for centuries, and they're really fierce."

Vinasa's breadth of knowledge takes me by surprise—like Ariel, she has a mind structured more like a database than a calculator.

"Vin's big on History; she'll work there first chance she gets." Eri smiles sadly at her friend. "If there are any spots left."

"You heard the Committee cut another fifth of the department last month?" Vinasa pouts. The Committee only pays big money for what's essential to the Bases' survival: administrative essentials, as well as scientific discovery and innovation. "Journalism and Visual Design are having the same problem. My dad thinks a nonscience Specialization is a ticket to Shelter, only the ride's longer."

"There's still time to change your mind, Vin." Eri looks at her handscreen, frowning. "Canopus says we have to leave by 18:00."

How long have I been unconscious? It's 17:56. Seeing the worried look on my face, Eri says, "You weren't out for too long. Everyone else is having dinner. I brought you some!" She shoves two slices of stale brown bread at me. I peel them apart to check for anything suspicious. Between them are four slices of lab-grown chicken egg with crumbling grayish yolks. There's also an apple, some water, and a few dietary supplement pills.

"Thanks." I gratefully bite into the bread. "Have you eaten?"

"Yeah, we did," Vinasa says. "*Very* quickly. Set new records, I think, but the Militia doesn't track stuff like that." A smile darts across her face. "The rest of the matches weren't as entertaining as yours. Nash scratched me on the cheek."

"But the Medics fixed Vin in a minute!" Eri says. "And Wes beat Ganymede Zeta with your knee-in-the-manly-areas idea."

Ganymede is one of Jupiter's meatier cronies, with a shaved head and a skinny snake tongue.

Eri sighs. "Callisto gave Jupiter crap for beating up a girl—don't know why she puts up with him."

"Callisto?"

"Jupiter's girlfriend, the one with the pimples. They fight a ton."

I've seen the girl hanging off his arm—her face, though finely formed, is cratered with acne scars like the moon of her namesake. Her hair has stripes like mine, brown and yellow rather than black and silver.

"Oh—Wes came in here about an ankle sprain that turned out to be nothing," Vinasa says, eliciting a frown from Eri. "He hung around and asked us if you were okay."

I stop chewing and gawk at her.

"Probably wanted to congratulate you on nearly sterilizing Jupiter," Eri says defensively. "Those two never liked each other. Wes transferred from Base I when we were all fifteen, 'cause our Medical Department had a better job opening. He had to apply for a transfer permit and everything. Well, Jupiter ignored Wes until he saw him run in conditioning class, then tried to pick on him, but Wes almost kicked Jupiter's teeth out. Since then, Jupiter's steered clear of him . . . until today."

People rarely relocate from one base to another—I suspect that the Committee tries to thwart interaction among the bases so that trouble on one doesn't slither into the other five. If the other bases didn't appear in our news reports and history texts, we'd risk forgetting they exist. As the first transfer I've ever met, Wes might as well be an alien.

"You sure Wes transferred for a job?"

"It's all he ever told anyone."

I'm down to the calcium pills, which I swallow without the aid of water.

"How you feeling?" Eri gives my hand a squeeze.

"Better." My vision blurs again, and my eyelids threaten to fall of their own accord. The food had a sedative in it, maybe melatonin.

"It's nice that they give us the nights off," Vinasa says. "Why don't you take a nap? It's still early, but we should get some sleep ourselves."

Before I can respond, everything dissolves again.

I wake to a dark world, energized. If every object weren't in such sharp focus, and if my bladder weren't so uncomfortably stretched, I'd believe this was a dream.

After using the toilet, I tiptoe through the empty hallways and find a domain of wonders—no security pods in sight. Curiosity about the Medical facilities takes over, and because curfew doesn't go into effect for another twenty minutes, I decide to explore.

The hall is devoid of Medics and patients alike. Because we haven't fought real battles in so long, fewer active Militia members are getting hurt. Most Medics are in the civilian Medical Department, contending with a recent bout of influenza that has afflicted a good part of Sanitation. Those moles get sick a lot.

Before I get to the end of the hall, footfalls approach. They're too frequent to be the echoes of my own. Sudden dread seizes me—what if it's someone who will tattle to one of the instructors and guarantee me negative points before the first evaluation? If that happens, I won't be able to pay Mom's Medical bill; the prize money of a low-ranking trainee can't even buy her a maintenance robot to keep her company. I press myself against the wall, heart pounding, as a shadow sprints around the bend.

"Hello?" calls a male voice.

He approaches. The emergency lights on the floor illuminate copper-wire hair.

He shouldn't be here. He's not in recovery; he's nothing but an overly ambitious trainee—*oh, Medical assistant*. That's how he broke in.

"Stripes? What are you doing out of bed?"

My right toes cross over my left foot, and I pivot to face the way I came. My bare feet carry me away from him.

"I don't feel that I thanked you enough today—won't you come back?"

Considering his speed and strength, it may be useful to put my distaste aside to observe and analyze his training methods. I pivot again and walk until I'm close to him—but not too close. The fingers of my right hand itch to wrap around my handscreen; his forearms twitch as well, because this upcoming conversation may hint at sensitive matters. Blocking one's handscreen is a gesture of trust; it communicates to the other person: *let's keep this between us, and no one else.*

There are few people I distrust more.

As we size each other up, I try to appear as alert as he does. When I stand my straightest, I'm exactly his height. He holds out a hand for me to shake, which is polite but unnecessary, because he's been to my home and probably knows my name. Though his palm is calloused like the bark of a sapling, the contact is gentle. Mom says that soft handshakes indicate soft personalities, which I'm good at dealing with, but I still don't like him.

Moments later, my handscreen reads "Wezn Kappa," followed by his stats, which I examine for my own safety. He has an above-average IQ and zero policy infractions; his mother and father reside on Base I, apart from him. Fittingly for a Medical assistant, he has blood type O negative, the universal donor—but it would mean more if the practice of donating blood still existed. We manufacture the stuff by the liter now.

Looking down at my information, he says, "Nice to meet you again, Phaet." Again, his slow, deliberate speech pattern catches my attention. Maybe they speak differently on Base I. "You took some blows for me today—even though there was no need. Much appreciated." He rocks awkwardly back and forth on his heels. "I thought, er, it was only polite to learn more about you."

I want to know what he's doing here. I question him with a raised eyebrow and a jerk of my head down the hallway.

"Oh, just running. It's not curfew yet . . . I should be fine."

Perhaps he doesn't see me as a threat to his supremacy, even after viewing my academic stats. Wes wears a neutral, if not pleasant, expression—although he seems averse to looking me in the face.

He's your competition, my prudent side reminds me. *And he took your mother.*

But why not learn something from the most capable of the fifty of us, despite my unhappy associations with him? With Wes's old job in Medical, and the wide-ranging contacts he must have in other departments, he could find out how Mom is doing—if I ever become comfortable asking him for favors.

"*I* should've fought Jupiter. . . . He has no mercy—bludgeoning someone *half his mass*." Even though his eyebrows are knit in consternation, Wes doesn't raise his voice above a murmur. Maybe he *does* want to keep this chat from prying ears. "Stay away from him—please?"

Nod.

"You're a talkative girl." While examining something on the spotless floor, he dimly smiles, a passive expression that doesn't involve parting his lips. I don't see the point, because it's like switching on a neon lamp and throwing a cotton sheet over it.

"Well. I'm going to keep running—please don't tell anyone. Thanks again for earlier and, er, see you tomorrow!" He sets off at a pace that would induce cramps in anyone else.

As that dim smile fades from my mind, I decide to keep him close. He could help me get what I need.

9

DAYS PASS, EACH FILLED WITH UNFORGIVING exercises with torture devices ranging from jump ropes to the climbing wall. While many trainees don't finish the assigned workouts, I try too hard and sometimes end up on the floor because of my clumsiness. Eri continually complains about blisters on her feet. My own muscles smart every time I move, but I know the tears in the tissue will soon heal and increase my strength. On days when we run less than two kilometers, I jog around the training center after Yinha dismisses us, hoping that Cygnus and Anka are sleeping soundly and growing tougher along with me.

Although I miss home, I'm no longer lonely. After a few days and nights sleeping near my new acquaintances, I feel I'm better integrated into the group, though Nash still tries to ignore the fact. Slowly, I learn how to socialize with three people at once—and female ones to boot.

One day at lunch, I catch Vinasa staring in my direction. Not into my eyes, but at the top of my head. "I wish I had your hair, Phaet. Mine's such a wild mess! It's so thick, I can't hold it all in one hand."

"Cut it off, then!" Eri laughs.

The two girls look at me, heads tilted to the side, and wait for my reply—something I'm not used to from my friends. From Umbriel, that is.

"Straight hair goes in one direction," I say. "Downward. Unless you're in zero-grav. It's not much fun."

As my companions laugh, I almost feel the table rattling.

"Vin's hair is more downward-oriented than mine," Nash says, glancing at me with a smile. "I'm half Saudi, a quarter Nigerian, and a quarter Jamaican. Makes for an explosion on my head when I get up in the morning."

"Indian and Irish," Vinasa shoots back. "Kapow all the same."

Nash admits defeat. "Cheers," she says, and the two girls clink their water bottles together. Amused, I spear three kidney beans with my fork and eat them one at a time. Nobody's ever complimented me on my strange hair before.

Sometimes younger people jabber about the Earthbound countries their ancestors came from. Although most of those places don't exist anymore, discussing them makes people feel special. They're proud of their forebears' accomplishments, and I'm not immune to that immodesty. After a long-ago conversation with the Phi twins, I peppered Mom with questions and learned that China's coast once boasted magnificent cities with willowy steel structures and frolicking lights, but the buildings toppled and the lights fizzled when the sea spilled onto the land. Whenever our teachers in Primary hear these discussions, they ask us to focus instead on our Lunar national identity. A few kids consider their particular genetic inheritance a source of superiority; if they do anything to show that belief, the incident shows up on their criminal records.

For that reason, talk of ancestry also is supposed to be taboo in Militia.

"You worried, Stripes?" Nash teases me, lowering her voice. "It's too loud for the Committee's toadies to hear us. I mean, they shouldn't be listening, anyway."

"Shh!" Eri says. "Don't get us in trouble."

"Trouble dee, trouble doo." Nash dares herself to speak out against the Committee, as if testing to see how loudly she can talk before she's caught. Her behavior frightens me, but I like her for it. If only more people were brave enough to state the obvious.

As Eri smiles and Vinasa giggles, a sudden pleasant thought fills my mind and makes my blood run warm through my veins: I have more of a social life in Militia than I ever did in Primary.

When the first evaluation arrives, the soreness is mostly gone and I'm ready to show the instructors what I can do.

Today, it's not Yinha's grating voice sounding in my ear but Colonel Arcturus the Assiduous's. "There's a point system, trainees. No need to know the details. We will simply watch you run, perform feats of strength, and spar with one another."

When the trainees run laps, I place myself just behind the fastest few. I manage forty push-ups before collapsing, a fifty percent improvement from a week and a half ago. After the jog, Arcturus announces point deductions: two off for three girls who skipped instead of ran, even though they insist that it kept them motivated. He docks points from five people, including Vinasa, for inadequate push-ups—they failed to bend their elbows a full ninety degrees. Taking into account my improvement and Arcturus's critical eye, I estimate that I'm at the seventieth percentile. Wes sits at the ninety-ninth.

The instructors assign us our sparring partners this time, usually of the same sex.

"Vinasa Epsilon and Halley Nu," Arcturus reads off. "Io Beta and Phaet Theta."

Io is the dark-haired girl who yawned conspicuously on the first day of training; she's proved to have a tendency to daydream and has hazel eyes that can't decide whether to stay open or closed. This round should be no problem.

"One point off Io's score for untied shoelaces," Arcturus says.

Io squats in the middle of the floor like a child and manipulates the string into clumpy knots. A strangely parental feeling warms my heart. I hope that I won't give her any serious injuries during our match.

This time, I'm conscious during the other fights, so I'm able to observe. Fights between girls are skittish, those between boys, ferocious. Nash loses to Callisto and, swearing hoarsely, exits the ordeal with a bruised collarbone and a sprained ankle. Callisto breaks down weeping. "I didn't mean it! Oh, Nash! Didn't mean it!"

Behind me, Jupiter's de facto sidekick Ganymede snarls: "Tell Callisto to watch out, Jupe. Nashira's people started that sneaky oil embargo; who knows what *she'll* do? It's in her blood. . . ."

Nash is one of those citizens, like me, whose Earthbound origins are plain in her features. And Ganymede's one of those rare idiots who derives superiority from genetic inheritance. I wonder if he's ever gotten in trouble for it. His confident brutishness makes me suspect not.

"She tries anything, and I'll break her damn nose," Jupiter says.

Furious, I consider telling off the two bigots. But I don't, because I shouldn't make enemies.

Vinasa swivels her head and does it instead. "Say that to Nash's face next time, vacuum-heads."

I add, "Yes, you won't be saying much afterward."

Eri and Vinasa gawk at me for a long time before giggling with satisfaction. Jupiter and Ganymede look away, their jaws set like stones.

Soon it's my turn to fight. I breathe deeply, forget Ganymede's comments, and focus on my opponent.

The lights blink green. Io canters in a winding path toward me. Before we collide, I swerve to one side and hook a foot behind hers. She trips and sits dazed on the ground. Three seconds later, we're done. It's the shortest fight of the day, which should help my ranking, though I'm offended that the instructors gave me such an easy opponent. Perhaps they thought Io was all a fifteen-year-old could handle.

The last fight pits Jupiter against Wes. If Wes wins, his score will be dangerously high, but I'm rooting for him.

The crowd takes a colossal inhale as the two boys face each other. Jupiter's forward-leaning posture and flexed muscles inflate his stature even more. Wes, who has just over half Jupiter's bulk, stays loose by shifting his weight from left to right. He can't win by normal means, but recent observations considered, I don't think he's normal.

"Ready for a week in the Medical quarters?" Jupiter hollers, wanting us all to hear.

Wes chews on his lips in concentration.

"Go!" shouts Arcturus.

As Jupiter makes his customary stampede forward, Wes turns on his heel and bolts in the opposite direction.

Callisto stands, hands clasped to her heart, her striped hair disheveled. Ganymede pulls her back down by the wrist. On the floor, Jupiter puts on an extra spurt of speed. I hold in a snort—he leans so far forward that a push from behind would land him on the ground, bulbous forehead first.

Wes has been running straight this whole time, and he's getting precariously close to a wall. Jupiter gains from behind.

A moment before they collide, Wes launches into a handspring and pushes off the wall with his feet into a complex flip. While Jupiter grabs at empty air, Wes extends his legs and knocks his adversary's head into the wall.

Jupiter rocks in agony on the ground, but only for a moment. His arms stir. Wes darts in the other direction and stops in the middle of the floor to catch his breath. He beckons with his hand to Jupiter, who doesn't have the breath to curse at him. When Jupiter nears him, Wes takes off in a perpendicular direction, and Jupiter overshoots once again.

"Go, Wes!" shouts Eri, adding her voice to the cacophony. In my excitement, I grab her hand, and she squeezes back, hard.

Jupiter slows to a jog, with little malevolence left to sustain him. Sensing weakness, Wes shoots forward and launches an aerial side kick at Jupiter's jaw.

Jupiter stumbles. With his other leg, Wes delivers a kick to the rib cage, which finally fells the massive boy.

Wes doesn't give him a final satisfactory stomp or even put his foot on Jupiter's chest, as Jupiter did to me. He simply waits, his fist drawn back in case the bigger boy tries to get up again.

One, two, three.

We drown Wes in claps and cheers. Even Arcturus's announcement, "The victor is . . . Wezn Kappa!" dissipates in the din.

As Wes shyly waves at his new devotees, I feel the same amazement as when I first watched a ship take off in a miasma of dust.

10

TWO DAYS ELAPSE BEFORE RANKINGS ARE posted on the scoreboard in the training dome.

This evaluation is important, but there are three more left, each with progressively more weight, for a total of four. The Committee has always liked the number four. It's a perfect square, the number of directions on a compass, the number of limbs on a human. Mom hates it. When she was young, her grandmother told her that the word for "four" in her native tongue sounds almost the same as the word for "dead." I believed four was unlucky until first-year Primary math showed me that numbers are just quantities.

Wes's name crowns the top of the list. Next is Jupiter. Orion Nu follows, then Callisto Chi. I'm fifteenth—surprisingly high, but not good enough. Cygnus, Anka, and Mom need me to do better than this.

Beside me, Callisto turns around and gives a thumbs-up, a weak sign of approval supported by a weak smile. She runs off before I can respond. *Why is she so civil to me?*

"Congratulations, Stripes," says a knowing female voice behind me. It's Yinha, riding on one of the hover-chairs. I've never heard her speak without crackly amplification. "You've made a lot of progress recently. Cool."

She pats me on the shoulder before gliding off.

To my right, a cluster of people congratulate Wes on his placement. He stares down, not meeting their eyes. When he sees me seeing him, he gives me a low-wattage smile before looking elsewhere.

I get a feeling in my stomach reminiscent of free fall.

"Hey, Stripes." Nash's voice jolts me from my inexplicable nausea.

I snap to attention.

She's standing to my right. "I placed twenty-second. Not great, but not bad either. You, lady, seem to have a shot at the top."

I think of Wes, with his flying kicks around the floor, and shrug.

"Also . . . thanks for sticking up for me to Jupiter's posse. Yeah, I heard about that."

"You're welcome," I say.

Nash suddenly looks bashful. She checks her handscreen. "Well. It's only 16:00 and we're off for the rest of the day. I'm gonna go to the Exchange and buy some stuff with Vin. Want to come?"

I don't have money to spend, but I'm grateful that she's trying to make up for her former coldness with an offer of—could it be?—friendship. I shake my head.

"I'll see you later then." Nash pats my forearm affectionately and takes off.

With all the noise, I feel an acute desire for solitude. Sliding out of the training center, I venture into the huge complex of the Medical quarters. I'm not sure if it's allowed, but if Wes does it, so can I, seeing as the instructors haven't stopped him.

My muscles feel pretty good. We only did some light strength training and basic weapons instruction before the rankings list was posted. So when I reach a long, empty hallway, I set the timer and distance counter on my handscreen and run.

The rhythm feels natural; my strides have become longer. It feels as if springs on the bottom of my boots propel me higher and farther. Although the rubber was engineered to give lift, I like to think my burgeoning muscles contribute as well.

After jogging in a huge circle for exactly twenty-nine minutes, I manage to log five kilometers. My clothes are damp, my knee joints smart, and my throat is grainy with thirst.

Fizz, I forgot my canteen in the barracks.

This place is quiet without my footfalls, allowing my ears to pick up another set of steps somewhere behind me. I dare to look.

Wes Kappa flits to me, jogging in place. He looks ridiculous, trying to be courteous while maintaining an elevated heart rate. "Hey."

I open my mouth to say something, but only a rough *whoosh* comes out.

"Want to get some water? I've been running on the floor upstairs for a while now, so I need some too. You can come with me, if you'd like." He takes off.

Somehow, I have it in me to match his pace. The exertion gives me a rush that energizes me like a caffeine tablet. Maybe it's the thrill of unofficial competition with the best of us.

"One suggestion," he says through even breaths, watching my feet. "Actually, I have two."

Nod.

"Don't land on your heel so much; aim for the middle of your foot. Better already. Also, don't turn your toes inward. I used to run that way, before I got knee problems. Whenever I took a step, it felt like my ligaments and bones were getting into fights."

I angle my feet outward until they're pointed straight. The pounding in my joints lessens significantly. I didn't even know I was pigeon-toed, or that it could affect my stride so much.

Wes gives me a thumbs-up.

Many painless seconds later, we reach a set of double doors, sealed so tightly that not even air can enter the space they guard. To my bewilderment, Wes marches up to the fingerprint scanner on the wall and presses his thumb to it.

When he sees my look of amazement, he says, "Remember? I worked as an assistant in Medical, so I'm solid in the health care system."

The first set of sliding doors part lengthwise, the second up and down, revealing a dark room that lights up in our presence.

We're in a high-caliber lab. My fingers ache to tinker with the scales, which are rumored to be accurate to the microgram, and to slide cell samples under the electron microscope. Hundreds of years ago, these microscopes took up a whole room, but now they're fifty centimeters high and can achieve magnification in the tens of millions. If I ever join the Bioengineering labs, I'll be able to do so much more than stare.

Stop that, I tell myself. Survive Militia first. Save your family.

Wes taps me on the shoulder and shoves a standard cylindrical plastic canteen at me. I hadn't even heard him fill it. I nod my thanks and force myself to drink slowly. But I take one desperate gulp too soon, before my epiglottis closes, and I cough until the precious water threatens to squirt through my nose.

Wes raises a hand, as if he's going to pat me on the back like Umbriel does. But he seems to think better of it. "You're funny. You choke louder than you speak."

I laugh through a series of coughs, using a hand to hide my smile. After I've stopped making hacking noises, he says, "Want to stretch? Otherwise our muscles will make a racket when we wake up tomorrow."

With legs straight, he rolls down to place his palms flat on the ground and drums a rhythm of sorts on the white floor. We stretch every muscle, every tendon in our bodies. Wes's joints are silent as he arranges them in extreme angles, while mine crack from the unfamiliar twists. Each time it happens, he chuckles, feeding my envy.

We return to a sitting position and simply breathe. Wes inhales and exhales as steadily as if he were sleeping, while my befuddled mind keeps interrupting my rhythm.

Why's he being so *nice*? Does he feel guilty for dragging my mother off to a hospital bed? He's not naturally extroverted; on the contrary, he prefers solitude, like me. But he's giving it away in favor of my company.

On the other hand, I'm so quiet that I might as well not exist. Mom says that people who talk less have more stories to tell. I used to think she was trying to console me about my silence, but her aphorism is applicable to the boy beside me.

The object of my befuddlement opens his eyes, and I detect a spark in them. But he quickly looks down at his hands, folded in his lap. "Will you practice sparring with me tomorrow? I need a partner so my skills don't deteriorate."

Fascinating—I may have formed an alliance with the number one trainee. It was much easier than I'd expected.

"Okay," I mutter.

Wes gives me a huge smile, pleased that his new accomplice isn't mute, and one side of his mouth pulls up farther than the other to expose slightly crooked teeth. It shocks me more than anything he could have said.

11

THERE'S A CERTAIN ITCHINESS IN MY BLOOD that results from being alone in a dark hallway with someone who could incapacitate me in a matter of milliseconds.

We may have been sparring on and off for fifteen minutes or fifteen hours. It's hard to tell time when Wes is aiming fast but light jabs and kicks at every part of my body, and it's all I can do to deflect them with my forearms and shins. Anyone listening to our handscreen feeds would hear only whacks and grunts. What bothers me more is that Umbriel would lecture me ad infinitum if he saw me putting myself at the mercy of this combat machine.

"Try not to step back so often. Find a way through my defenses."

It's difficult. His feet change positions about three times a second, and he has already hit me twice: once on the cheek, once in the gut. In frustration, I lash out with my right foot and whack his knee.

"Good!" His voice is throaty, betraying the pain behind the compliment. Using his vocal cords distracts him, and I manage to elbow him in the chest.

But my victory distracts *me*, and Wes gains the upper hand again, pushing me back until I hit the wall. As I slump against it, he backs away. Unless he's pummeling me, it seems, he can't stand being within two meters of my person.

"That was much better than last time. Although you should try harder to shield your face with one hand or the other. Good work. I think we've had enough for one night."

I retrieve my canteen from the side of the hallway and zip up my jacket. According to my handscreen, we've been here for an hour.

Wes gazes off into some unknown place, possibly daydreaming, and makes no move to leave. I question him with my eyebrows: *Are you coming?*

"I think I'll stay here, if you don't mind." He kneels on the floor and stretches his left hip flexor. "I like the quiet."

After waving good-bye, I amble out of the Medical quarters, wondering what in the universe he's doing there—poking around, maybe, or practicing his Medical skills. Most likely, he's exercising even more, outworking people like Jupiter in order to outplace them in the end.

I wish he wouldn't, because he's crossing into the realm of the inhuman. It would be a relief if he revealed his physical limits—providing he has any.

This week, the trainees exercise for no more than two hours a day. We spend the rest of the time sitting on our behinds learning about the Militia's arsenal of weapons. The most devastating, hydrogen bombs and intricate bioweapons, require large groups to coordinate and deploy; only top-ranking officers go near them, and only Base I has them. The Bases have never had occasion to use one, so we're not even sure how much damage they can do. Another weapon, the Gamma gun, generates rays that cause radiation sickness and death within a day. We've never used that one either.

More standard arms include the popular laser blasters: sleek, transparent weapons small enough for a soldier to carry on a utility belt. They're not difficult to aim and almost never need recharging, so like generations of trainees before us, we affectionately call them "Lazies." The manual warns us in red letters of their one weakness: SHOOTING AT A REFLECTIVE SURFACE MIGHT CAUSE BACKFIRE. Wasn't that obvious, by the nature of the laser mechanism? I suppose some unfortunate trainees who didn't read the manual or forgot basic laws of optics fired at glass or steel and blinded themselves—perhaps projectile weapons make better arms for people like them.

To guard against metal Earthbound bullets and the electromagnetic waves from the lasers, we carry heavy ballistic shields to supplement a special type of body armor. But despite the wealth of technologically advanced arms at our disposal, the training dome is devoid of them on the first day of weapons instruction.

"We're going to start with this." Yinha draws a small, straight knife from her boot, and the trainees groan. "Unlike our other weapons, the dagger has been around since Earthbound prehistory. It's an excellent tool for building reflexes. And in actual fighting, it's useful as a backup in case a Lazy runs out of power. Good for close combat. You can also throw it. And if you look at your boots, they have cool little pockets for storage."

The instructors pass out standard daggers to all of us—silver, symmetrical, made of the lightest, strongest polymers available. The weapon in my hand is the size and shape of my old trimming knife—but I won't be pruning plants with *this*.

"Partner up with someone you trust. We're going to study basic form. To further your training, I'm also going to deactivate some of the grav-mags, so get ready for moon-grav. Am I understood? Cool."

Nash grabs my hand. The gravity settings in the training center shift until I feel as light as I used to in the greenhouses. My eyes close; I can almost smell the soil and the unripe-fruit scent of my best friend. Mom would be waiting for us at home with a small but intricate dinner, listening to Anka's chatter while prompting Cygnus to look up from his trigonometry homework and talk about his day at Primary. . . .

No. Until she leaves Medical, she can't be more than a muddle of wonderful memories.

We arrange ourselves two by two in a line. Wes picks the fourth-place trainee, Orion, and twirls his dagger around his forefinger while he waits for instructions. Instinct makes me want to tell him to stop lest he slice his hand open, but—he's *Wes*. He knows what he's doing.

We ease into thrusts, strokes, and parries. With a certain degree of focus, I find a rhythm in using the dagger and a grace I never felt in the greenhouses, where every cut, precise to the millimeter, met with arboreal resistance. Now, with no plant fibers in the way, I feel as if this weapon were designed specifically for my use—it's small, silver, and silent, exactly like me.

Not everyone experiences the same affinity.

"This thing is useless," Nash grumbles as she parries at an angle twenty degrees too far clockwise. "And the moon-grav doesn't make it any better."

I disagree. The ease of the blade, along with decreased gravity and Wes's nightly help with hand-to-hand sparring, makes this feel like dancing. I jump over Nash's head multiple times and even manage to do a forward roll in midair.

"Hey, don't kill me." Nash retreats with a distressed expression.

I freeze.

"Where'd you learn to be so good at this?"

Shrug.

"Okay. How about I attack, you parry. That way I won't end up in the Medical quarters again."

We chuckle as she makes a haphazard slash in my direction.

"I'm not actually going to use this undersized knife in the field. Right now, it's for the giggles—hey, Stripes, *check that out*!" Nash points over my shoulder.

Orion is attacking Wes with perfect form, his right arm elegantly parting the air. Both boys laugh as Wes evades every stroke, spinning on his toes or swinging his dagger with a series of flourishes to block Orion's. Every now and then, he jumps and twists in midair, folding and unfolding his limbs like the petals of a black morning glory. When Orion catches a break, which is rare, he fans himself with his thin shirt, exposing a well-defined chest that I'm sure distracts Nash a good deal.

She whistles crudely at them.

While Orion busies himself winking at her, Wes taps his flat abdomen with the equally flat side of the dagger. "Gotcha."

Orion snarls playfully, and the acrobatics resume.

When I find the lower half of my face abnormally stretched, I realize I've been grinning at the spectacle of grace. I don't notice the shadow sprinting closer to them—not until a sliver of silver meets a plane of black, and Wes staggers, clutching his right arm to his chest. Rivulets of red flow between his fingers.

That same red coats the dagger in the hand of Jupiter, who's slowing from his mad dash.

"Everybody stop!" Yinha's amplified voice shouts.

My breakfast churns in my stomach, threatening to rise into my esophagus. Wes's blood, like burgundy poison, pools on the floor.

"Jupiter, do not spar with anyone other than your partner."

"It was totally an accident!" insists Callisto, threading her arm through his. But no one believes her. Jupiter has hit a bloody new low.

"Orion, please escort Wezn to the Medical quarters." Yinha's voice crackles menacingly. "Jupiter, you have earned a ten-point deduction from your total score. Everyone can resume sparring now."

No one does.

Jupiter grunts; the brutish sound echoes through the silent dome. He should show more appreciation, considering that Yinha should have suspended him from Militia for attacking another trainee without permission; if she did, he'd go to Penitentiary, fail to secure a Specialization, and head straight to Shelter. There must be a reason why she didn't—perhaps he's demonstrated too much potential for Defense to give him up, or he's bribed her in some way. "A Sputnik can always set you straight," Mom often muttered while typing news reports.

Orion slings his arm around Wes even though Wes looks stable, albeit pale. I shudder out of revulsion and confusion as the boys limp between Nash and me, Wes staring directly into my face.

His irises have never looked more like mercury.

12

EVERYONE GIVES JUPITER A WIDE BERTH after the incident, but we cluster around Wes as if he's a magnet pulling at the trace metals in our blood. When I visit him in the Medical quarters that night, a mostly female crowd surrounds his cot. I only manage to slip him a smile before curfew.

Otherwise, training continues as usual. We practice aiming Lazies and wielding ballistic shields. The shields are deadweight heavy and give me aching muscles by the end of each session, but I stubbornly run my laps around the Medical quarters every night until curfew. The beating of my feet clears my mind.

I observe myself in mirrors when I practice knife throwing, aiming at various points in my surroundings and always checking my form. After a few disastrous attempts, it gets better. Late at night, I run calculations in my head, trying to determine a dagger's spinning motion, to picture the graph of the blade's angle to the ground oscillating in a sine wave. The launch angle needs to counteract the parabolic path caused by gravity, so during evaluations and such, I'll have to account for different grav-mag settings. With practice, instinct rather than computation guides the daggers where I want them.

After a few days, Wes resumes training and shows up in the Medical quarters to exercise. I touch his left bicep with a questioning expression.

"I feel a lot better," he answers, and I drop my suddenly graceless hand. "They erased what Jupiter did to my arm. I can prove it to you right this second." He slips into fighting stance, saying, "Have at you, Theta!"

Okay.

I trade blows with Wes for ten whole minutes, according to the timer on my handscreen, and land a few punches and kicks before he fells me. Although I'm still pathetic compared to him, we're more evenly matched than before.

"I might actually be afraid of you," he admits. "Want to take a break? Let's go for a run. I found something I think you'd like to see."

He leads me off, covering the circular perimeter of every floor before sprinting up a flight of stairs. We repeat this pattern seven times before we reach the top of the tower. Finally, he stands still. I try not to breathe too loudly. It would disturb the quiet, which is punctuated only by the whirring of disused medical equipment.

Side by side, we tiptoe into a small room, presumably a single-patient facility.

"Now look up."

Through the small glass window in the ceiling, I see Cancer twinkling far, far away. I never knew the Medical quarters had real windows on the top floor, but I'm glad Wes did. This is my first glimpse of the sky in weeks. I never thought I'd miss it, but now I long to grab every cubic centimeter of space's murky blackness and clutch it to my chest. I mustn't shift my eyes from the stars to anything else, because if I do, maybe some will shoot away so fast that I won't find them again. It's a silly thought—the universe isn't expanding quite that quickly—but there are thousands of light-years from their location to ours, so the way I see them, as they were ages ago, could be different from what they have become. Just as Cygnus and Anka—and Mom—may have changed from the way I see them in my mind.

Wes sits down on the cot and pats a spot nearby. I take it, making sure to stay at least half a meter away. Umbriel would chastise me if he were here—especially if he saw Wes sitting on his handscreen, finally not fidgeting. I've never had a blocked-handscreen conversation with anyone outside my family or Umbriel's. Nevertheless, I slide my hand underneath the seat of my pants out of reciprocal courtesy.

"In my old home, we could see the entire sky from an observatory."

How beautiful the sight must be. Base I, I've heard, has more windows than any of the other five. It isn't any wealthier, but it's less efficiently constructed because when our ancestors built it, they hadn't yet found their moon legs, and they sacrificed insulation and shielding for aesthetics.

The greenhouses are the only buildings in Base IV with full glass ceilings. How lucky I was to see stars at all.

Willing my voice not to crack, I speak slowly. "I used to lie on the greenhouse floors with my best friend and pretend I was falling into the stars."

Upon hearing a complete sentence leave my lips, Wes gawks at me. The Earth's reflection creates an arc of sapphire across his eyeballs. I smile—he can be funny too.

"When you do speak, Phaet, you do it so . . . imaginatively. Like you can see the words take shape, and you pick only the most interesting combinations to say out loud. Is that what you spend your quiet time doing, writing pretty things in your head?"

I'm liberal with smiles today. I give Wes another.

Wes leans back on his hands and contemplates the circle of sky in the ceiling, a serene expression passing over his face. Tapping noises, tiny meteorites striking the carbon-reinforced glass, reach our ears. On the Moon, our only precipitation is "grit-rain," a phenomenon that leaves small dents on the exterior of all our buildings. Calling someone a "piece of grit" is a routine insult.

"Your best friend—would she be angry with me for putting that bruise on your cheek?"

"*He* probably would." Umbriel might nick surgical scissors and mow down Wes's shiny hair during the night.

"A bit protective, no?" Wes chuckles, expelling every ache in his body instead of mere carbon dioxide. "How long have you two been friends?"

"Fifteen years."

"Since you were born?"

Nod. Our fathers, both named Atlas, were close companions in Militia. They had their first children at nearly the same time and raised Umbriel, Ariel, and me together. Mom likes to remind us that Atlas Phi taught me the alphabet in an hour, and that Umbriel took his first steps with his hand in Atlas Theta's.

Then Dad was sent on that botched topographic assignment. Our families kept going after that, and sometimes I wonder if going on is all we know. Shutting my eyes, I summon Umbriel from my memories, imagine him sitting here, fussing over my hair and asking how my day was. It's sweet and painful all at once.

"Was he the tall boy in your apartment, the one with you in Shelter?"

Nod.

"That explains a lot. Is he the reason you don't talk? Because he has spoken for you all your life?"

I jab my right forefinger at my handscreen, and then promptly resume sitting on my left hand.

"It can't be only handscreens that keep you quiet. Look at you now—we're sitting on ours, but I'm the only one talking. Maybe you've got something to hide, or maybe words scare you because they're so permanent. Don't you hate that you can't ever erase what you say?"

"Not really." I've never felt dislike so strong it became hate—but yes, the longevity of the spoken word in the files of the Committee's eavesdroppers, and more so in the memory of other people, irritates me.

His fingernails dig into his palm. "Did I upset you?"

"Don't worry about it."

"Sorry."

The more he says, the heavier the air grows. With my eyes, I trace the seams between the tiles on the floor, searching for the shortest pathway from my left foot to the doorway.

Wes doesn't stop pushing, but in spite of his efforts, I am as inanimate and immovable as one of the tiles. "Fine, fine, forget everything I've said, but answer this one question: What are you so afraid of?"

He talks as if he can peel back skin and muscle and bone to see straight into my soul. I'm so uncomfortable that I could faint—*I'm* usually the perceptive one.

Wes bunches the fabric of his pants in his fist. "If your best friend were asking, you'd probably tell him, no? I wish I were close to someone, like you are to him. . . . What did he say about your joining up so early?"

"Umbriel said enough." His prolonged opposition is nothing I care to repeat.

"Forgive me for what I'm about to admit. . . ."

I blink at Wes expectantly.

"I wish he'd tried harder to stop you. For physical and mental health reasons, no one should face this Militia ordeal until they're ready, or until they absolutely must."

I close my eyes so that he can't see my exasperated eye roll. What useless words! I *know* I'm an underage trainee and constantly in danger, but there's no way to reverse the decision that brought me here and no need to critique it.

"And there's another line of reasoning, saying even in the worst of times, live on for life's sake—don't gamble it away—"

I seize his wrist, pinching two of his tendons between my thumb and middle finger.

With his left hand—now unprotected—he gestures frantically for me to cover my handscreen.

Glaring, I cross my arms and block the audio receptors.

Wes again places his hand under his rear. He lets out the breath he's been holding. "Sorry, I should've kept that to myself."

"Hmph."

He struggles to pick up our discussion from the point at which we dropped it. "Er, now you've seen why I didn't make many friends in Primary, or in Medical. Things inevitably turn awkward when I try."

I won't indulge his self-deprecation. "You're fine here. People have reasons for associating with the top trainee."

"You too, I presume."

"Of course."

Wes sighs and musses his hair. It falls perfectly when he's done. "At least you're pleasant to spend time around."

"The same."

We listen to the grit-rain on the ceiling. I hug my knees to my chest and rock back and forth on my tailbone. This is like sitting with Umbriel, but quieter. Despite his physical prowess, Wes has a less commanding presence than my best friend.

"You know, even though a lot of people here pretend to ignore you, they can't stand to see you do badly. Maybe it's because you're just fifteen." He yanks the laces on his boot, finally getting nervous at talking for so long.

"Is that why you're helping me?"

Though Wes inhales like he's going to respond verbally, he decides against it and settles for a shrug.

After we descend the stairs and say good-bye, Wes lets me start walking to the barracks first. Unlike Nash or Umbriel, he doesn't want to publicize his companionship with me, fragile as it is. It's better this way.

When I arrive, Eri squeezes me hard. Her cropped hair tickles my cheek. "Where were you?"

I respond with an ambiguous facial expression and shuffle with great concentration toward my cot.

"Stripes, I also wonder where you hop off to. Every night now." Nash matches me stride for stride. "I have a few theories. One: to Jupiter's cot to sock him senseless. Two: off on hot dates with one of the boys. More than one of the boys? Three—"

"Don't worry about it," I cut in.

The lights in the barracks go out, and we're sunk in darkness. Good-nights and sleep-tights are exchanged, but I stay silent.

In my top bunk, I'm unable to decide if I should sleep on my right or left side tonight. For the first time since I joined Militia, I can't find slumber.

13

"OW . . . I SWEAR, THIS THING HURTS WORSE than a kidney stone." Eri reclines on her cot, rubbing her hand over the sole of her foot.

"Ever *had* a kidney stone?" Vinasa asks.

"No, I'm too young; but *you* try walking around with a blister the size of your eyeball. . . ."

The blister on her left big toe is not, in fact, the size of her eyeball. It isn't even as big as a typical kidney stone, which would have a diameter of two centimeters or fewer. Eri should stop complaining. After a hard day's work, we'd all stab noisy people to get some quiet, and the girl two cots away from Eri is looking particularly murderous.

Eri weeps into her hands, mumbling about *real* shoes, *real* food, a *real* cot. . . .

"Want me to take you to Medical?" Nash offers.

"Oh no. They'll laugh at me. It's only a *blister*."

What a stubborn, spoiled girl. I'm fond of her, though, and know how to fix the problem in the most cost-effective manner possible. I swing over the edge of my cot and plummet a meter and a half to the ground, landing squarely on my feet. "I'll get Wes."

As Eri beams, her pale face glows against her halo of orange hair. Her head bears an uncanny resemblance to the sun; the blushes on her cheeks could be solar flares on a much smaller scale.

On the boys' side of the room, Orion and Wes sit on a cot, playing handscreen chess. The names of the pieces used to be aristocratic and religious, outmoded words like *queen* and *bishop*, but the Committee changed them about twenty-five years ago to things like *general* for the most important and *privates* for the expendables. The players move them by touching and dragging, and they need to be meticulous. A move outside the rules causes that person's handscreen to vibrate jarringly for five seconds or so.

I'm not surprised when Orion snarls and slaps the back of his hand on his knee. "Ooh, damn it! Didn't see your colonel there! I was *so close*."

Wes grins dimly, and that's his entire reaction to winning.

He's not grinning anymore when we arrive at Eri's cot, although she is.

"I have a teensy bit of a blister," she explains. "We tried draining it with a knife, but we couldn't get through."

Wes prods Eri's toe, producing a whimper of pain from her. "Give yourself more credit—this thing's got to be punctured with a needle. Most of it is hidden under that monstrosity of a callus. . . . Hold on; I've brought some Medical knickknacks with me—it's under my cot."

When he's out of earshot, Eri says to me, "Thank you *so much* for inviting him over! You're such a good wing-woman."

I gather she doesn't mean I'm good with spaceship wingtip weapons.

Nash cackles. "Chill, Eri. She brought Wes because Wes can fix your foot."

When Wes returns with his Medical kit, Eri studies him as attentively as she should have been studying her weapons manual. If he were any other boy, I might find it comical.

Wes scatters first-aid miscellanea all over the floor: a needle, ethyl alcohol, bandages, scissors, and a miniature drill—which I hope he won't use, for the sake of Eri's mental health. He rubs the needle with the alcohol.

If Eri's feet stink, his face doesn't show it. He prods her toe with the blunt end of the needle. Now that I'm closer to the infamous blister, I have to admit that it's quite infected—it changes color depending on where pressure is applied.

"You're gonna be okay, baby." Nash squeezes Eri's hand so hard that both girls' knuckles whiten.

Eri begins to cry.

Wes stacks his hand atop theirs. "It's all going to be over soon. Are you ready?"

Eri gapes at the pile of hands as if she can't believe Wes's is really a part of it. "Okay."

"This is one of many unglamorous parts of Militia." Wes flips the needle around and shoves it into Eri's toe.

I shut my eyes before he pulls it out, and then wait five seconds before daring to look.

Wes is mopping up the pus and blood with a piece of gauze. Though Eri weeps and wallows in the crisp memory of pain, the fully drained patch of dead skin won't bother her anymore.

After Wes cleans the needle, he bandages her foot. Pointing to a lone boot on the floor, he asks, "This yours? Would you mind if I have a look?"

"Nope," Eri pants.

As Wes examines the shoe, he makes a *tsk* noise with his

tongue. "Height-enhancing boots—really? These slope downward from heel to toe, which is causing rubbing at the front of the foot, especially with all that sliding around in weapons training. Get yourself normal boots the next time you go to the Exchange. As for the blister, take off the bandages in two days, and don't pull off the dead skin, or it'll get infected."

"Thank you so much." Eri tips forward as if she's trying to count his eyelashes. "You're *amazing*."

Terror crosses Wes's face before he bends down to clean up his Medical tidbits.

As Wes hurries away, he shoves the last of the supplies into his kit. He narrowly misses ramming his forehead into a bedpost.

Although I'm laughing along with Vinasa and Nash, I don't like seeing Wes so uncomfortable. The next time Eri gets hurt, I'll take her to Canopus instead.

Just like Eri, I need better boots. Mine are worn out from the running, jumping, sliding, and all-around roughness of my time here, so I go to the Exchange with Eri and my other friends the next day. Orion, Wes, and a burly trainee I've seen them with before join our burgeoning group. Nash can barely contain her excitement at the thought of seven people doing something together besides train, and she buys each of us a small pouch of tangy dried cranberries in celebration. I pocket mine to eat later as a post-workout snack.

Purchases at the Exchange, or anywhere else, are simple. As soon as someone walks out the door with merchandise, its price is deducted from their account balance. Vinasa decides upon some faintly glittery elastics for her hair, because "why not feel pretty without getting busted?" She uses one to tie off the end of her braid and coils it in a bun, tucking in the end to hide the sparkle. Defense has the strictest dress code of any department, so she'll have to wait two years before she can properly show off her bauble. Neither men nor women are allowed ornaments because they make us easy targets. In contrast, the History Department, where Vinasa hopes to work, allows women to wear their hair unbound, and they can even adorn it with accessories, as long as the decorations aren't unpatriotic.

In the footwear section, rows upon rows of seemingly identical black boots line the walls. They all have special features: steel-weave, good insulation, superior traction. Eri picks up lightweight, flat-soled boots, and with Wes's approval, decides to buy them without blinking at the exorbitant price of two hundred Sputniks. *Two hundred.* I was right about her family's wealth.

New boots are more than I can afford, but I manage to find a mildly used pair with "extra-durable" soles and built-in sheaths for five standard-issue daggers. I almost leave them behind because they're a full twenty-six Sputniks. But Orion says, "If they get you a higher rank, it'll make up for the price pretty quick." So, with a twinge of guilt in my intestinal region, I stroll out of the Exchange, the synthetic leather already molding to my feet.

14

OUR STRESS HORMONES REACH NEAR-critical saturation as the second evaluation approaches. The instructors don't reveal anything about its content, but I suspect it will include knowledge and skill assessments concerning the myriad of arms in the lectures and workouts.

Even after an introduction to an array of other instruments, my weapon of choice is still the dagger. I perform decently with a crossbow, another weapon of old, but I find guns with copper bullets too clunky. The reloading is also a pain. I like Electrostuns, electrocution guns of an old Earthbound design, but they're inefficient weapons, taking too much time to incapacitate an opponent. Militia members on patrol prefer using them to stun rule-breakers. My aim with the standard Lazy was at first shaky, literally, because I trembled whenever I pointed one at a moving target. The thought of putting a destructive violet beam through a living thing still disturbs me far more than the act of stabbing. It's less organic.

When evaluation day arrives, the instructors surprise us with a written test, which makes me cheer internally. "You'll get more than enough practice with the weapons later on," Yinha says. "But if you didn't want to study them, we don't want *you*. Today we'll pick out who paid attention and who was just toying with them. Cool?"

On all sides of me, trainees groan.

Parts of the training floor invert to become rows of desks equipped with large touch screens. There are one hundred open-ended questions, such as "What is the percent efficiency of the standard laser blaster, and what is the wavelength of light emitted?" and "What are the dimensions of the 'Little Sagittarius' warhead?"

It's just another test in Primary. As I submit one answer after another, I feel grateful that I absorbed the weapons lectures, when quite a few of the other trainees stared off into the distance, talked with friends, or even slept.

Forty-five questions in, I allow myself a break. I wiggle my fingers and roll my head in a circle, cracking the stiff joints in my neck. In the desk to my right, Nash crosses her legs, jiggling the top foot. Two desks behind her, Wes hunches over his desk, his head tilted in confusion as if the text were displayed sideways.

I calculate projectile trajectories and draw collision vectors. I type out redox reactions illustrating the effects of chemical agents on humans and, thinking back to Primary class, describe the source organism or process involved in producing the agents. Although most of the questions don't worry me, three make me wrinkle my nose and guess. I'm not the best at remembering which Earthbound civilization created which ancient weapon.

This time, the results come out quickly. My heart plummets when I read the name at the top: Callisto Chi.

Wes is second. A month ago, I wouldn't have cared; I would have even cheered Callisto on because she's a female in a position usually occupied by a male. But the fact that Jupiter's girlfriend beat Wes annoys me. And with Jupiter placed sixteenth, I'm impressed that he hasn't stabbed *her* in the arm yet.

My name appears next to the number eight; I'm satisfied, but frustrated all the same. If I had just remembered who invented the musket, I might have made top seven and would have been en route to paying off Mom's treatment.

That night, at the Medical quarters, Wes and I go for a long run. I always run faster when he's around, as if something's chasing me, but I can't figure out what it is.

"What happened?" I can't help but ask.

"You mean on the written examination?" he clarifies, his breathing regular. "Unfortunately, I forgot some obscure facts. Like what exact model of Lazy the Lunar Forces used when they fought off Pacifia and Battery Bay." The sarcasm in his voice practically drips onto the shiny floors. "Honestly, I didn't pay attention during the weapons lectures. I thought I was done memorizing things after Primary."

"It's hard not to learn when Yinha's shouting facts at you."

"I'd disagree. . . . Tell me, do you have an easy time memorizing random bits of babble?"

"As long as they're interesting." Ancient history surely isn't.

"I'm no good at it. Too much memorizing in biology; small wonder I had issues there." He exhales deeply and lowers his voice. I can barely hear his whisper over our footfalls—and hopefully, neither can anyone listening to our handscreen feeds. "Well, I'm glad someone else is ranked first now. I needn't fret about Jupiter's miniature death squad as much."

My palms grow sticky with sweat, not from exertion but from genuine alarm. "Has he tried to harm you again?"

"His sneaky associate did. Ganymede. If Orion hadn't gone to the toilet two nights ago and found him hiding near my cot, I'd have a slit Achilles tendon . . . or so I'm told."

I stagger at the horrifying image.

"Orion and my other friends agreed to rotate cots every night, so Jupiter's minions have a harder time finding me in the dark." Wes continues down the hallway, easily outpacing me.

How resourceful and kind of them. "Whose idea?"

"Mine." The pride in Wes's voice rings through that one word.

We jog onward, giving the handscreen eavesdroppers nothing but footsteps to hear. When we've had enough, we return separately to the barracks, Wes unreasonably cheerful and me reasonably worried for him.

After lights-out, I coil into a ball under the cotton coverlet and peruse Jupiter's stats—all of them—which I've been putting off. He's been accused of disorderly conduct and physical harm dozens of times, but the charges were always dropped, so they don't show up on his quick-view profile. His mother works in Culinary—interesting—but his father's employment is "Not Applicable." If his family is broke like mine, Jupiter has a financial motive to thirst for a top trainee position. But he looks too well fed for that to be the case, and he couldn't have bribed his way out of criminal charges, a common practice in Law trials, if he were poor.

My handscreen lights up brighter with a new message, sending a vibration up my arm and making my teeth chatter. In the cot across from me, Vinasa flips onto her stomach and pulls a pillow over her head—she takes a while to fall asleep, I've noticed, and is grouchy when she's trying.

What bothers me more than the light is that no other trainee received a notification. With many a nervous swallow, I open the brief message, which turns out to be a joint communication from Medical and . . . Law?

MIRA THETA HAS RECOVERED ENOUGH FOR TRANSFER TO THE PENITENTIARY. BAIL: 3,500 SPUTNIKS.

To stifle the scream clawing at my insides, I bite down on my right fist.

The system *must* have had a glitch. Mom *was* sick that day, with a disease that painted her skin pink and wrung air from her lungs. Even Wes, a supposed physiological expert, seemed to believe she needed treatment—unless he was pretending.

And Penitentiary? Jail is for lawbreakers, not quiet Journalists like my mother, who has the same chance of causing trouble as, say, a daisy. She wouldn't grumble in public, much less commit a crime worth 3,500 Sputniks of bail when that for petty theft is generally below 200. The only deeds involving that kind of money are murder and public offenses against the Committee—something like ranting against them before a crowd of thousands, which hasn't happened for decades.

But corporals, not privates, appeared at her "quarantine," indicating its significance. And all the reasoning in the universe can't counter the fact that official communications never—*never*—say what they don't mean.

Or do they? The Militia first took Mom to Medical. If she were destined for Penitentiary in the first place, why didn't anyone say so? Did her "fever" merely serve as a reason to carry her off? I think of the Committee, six shadows on a screen; now

I'm seeing just how shadowy the reasons behind their behavior are too. But the realization feels like stepping into the light.

I pound a fist onto the lumpy Militia cot, causing Nash in the spot below me to toss and grumble. So I tuck my knees and my revulsion into my chest, shuddering into the night.

15

ON OUR FIRST AND ONLY DAY OFF, MY family fills my field of vision; everyone else on the training floor vanishes into the periphery. Cygnus is getting ever closer in height to the two curly haired twins who stand head and shoulders above the crowd. The three boys wear solemn expressions, their eyes cast forward and their mouths tight at the sides. One look at the group, and I know that they've gotten the same notification I received last night.

Anka clings to Umbriel's hand. When she sees me, she races over and attaches herself to me as if she has suction cups on her arms. Her eyes are shiny and swollen, her cheeks caked over with a film of salt. My sister has no tears left, and it chips away at my composure.

"We missed you." She's more careful than before not to say what she's thinking.

"You look tired," my brother says in a monotone.

I rise on tiptoe, squeeze him tight with the arm not holding Anka, and plant an audible kiss on his cheek. His robes are now filled with as much air as flesh.

When Cygnus pouts, embarrassed, Anka says, "Phaet, you're acting like . . . like Mom. It freaks me out. Just a little."

Someone conspicuously clears his throat.

"*Umbriel!*"

Cygnus and Anka step aside so I can dash to Umbriel and throw my arms around him. Though my full body weight accompanies the embrace, he doesn't stagger. "How are you?" Umbriel asks a normal question to pass us off as a normal group.

Nod. *Good.*

"Your arms got buff." He sweeps his palm over my deltoid and triceps.

I affirm his observation by squeezing his waist even harder.

"Is training as nasty as people say?"

"It got better. I had help."

He and Ariel look relieved to hear that.

Nash is busy talking to her family; to their left, a tiny woman fusses over a rather annoyed Jupiter. Wes and Orion stand together, chuckling at something the latter just said.

"Phaet, who are those people?" Ariel asks. "You seem preoccupied with them."

"Hey!" hollers Orion. The two boys jog over.

In preparation for their arrival, Umbriel squeezes my wrist once. He doesn't know Orion is of the more benevolent Militia sort, and even if I said so, Umbriel would still be uncertain. As for Wes—my distrust of him has reached a new height. Did he know Mom's final destination when he helped take her away? If so, why has he trained me; why hasn't he done me harm?

Orion introduces himself *and* shakes everyone's hand, prompting Ariel to ask if everyone in Militia is so "approachable." A meter away, Wes studies his own feet. Maybe he knew what Mom's quarantine really was—but this, his signature awkwardness, is ordinary. It proves nothing.

"Why don't you join and find out?" Orion garnishes his words with a wink. Laughter bubbles from Ariel's belly as he tries to hide the bloom on his cheeks—how could anyone laugh so much at such a time? His anxiety must be causing him to overcompensate with geniality.

Ariel and Orion chat about mutual friends, funny things they've seen recently, each trying to make the other laugh harder than he did before, until two young women with Orion's wheat-colored hair—his sisters, I guess—pull him away.

With his companion gone, Wes scans my face, looking for either permission to stick around or an order to leave. Hoping not to appear rude, I shrug. *Do whatever you like.*

But my brother turns his back on Wes. "Hmph."

"Wes, the guy from Medical," Anka says matter-of-factly, offsetting Cygnus's insolence. I can't imagine my siblings having warm sentiments toward Wes, so Anka's good manners are a surprise.

"Are you two part of Str—Phaet's family as well?" Wes asks the twins.

"For all practical purposes." Umbriel reaches a hand backward and latches his fingers onto mine.

Wes's eyebrows shoot up. "Ah."

"Wes helps me with endurance, strength, martial arts . . ." I offer. "For rankings."

"Thank you," Umbriel mumbles to Wes. "I'm glad she's safe."

"I'm sure she would have been fine on her own. Stripes takes pretty good care of herself." Wes peers at my hand, enveloped in Umbriel's, and says, "Anyhow, I should be off. Nice seeing everyone again. Wish you the best."

He's his usual self. He must not have known he was taking Mom, ultimately, to a jail cell and not a hospital room. Medical or Law wouldn't inform him—a low-level assistant—about a heinous crime, especially one against the state.

"Bye, Wes," says Anka, before whispering something to Cygnus.

Wes jogs away through the crowd.

"He seems nice but . . . uncomfortable," Umbriel comments. "Like he's hiding something. Where's his family?"

"Base I, he said. Does it matter? He's trying to help, and he's the number two trainee." I dust off my hands, telling Umbriel to hold back on the subject of my mother until we find privacy.

"Then I'm glad you're on his good side." Umbriel squeezes my hand harder, pulling me toward the exit of the Defense Department. "Let's get you home."

Anka's handscreen projects a three-dimensional view of the night sky into our dark bedroom, throwing pinpricks of light on her face. She has drawn imaginary animals and figurines around the stars of nine constellations; smooth and graceful, each seems to be stretching toward something unseen. I'm glad she has made something lovely over the past month instead of wallowing in sorrow and rage.

She zooms in on Cetus, the Whale, holding her handscreen far from our faces so that it picks up less of our conversation. "See that red star in the middle? Right there—it's Mira, our mom."

How sweet of her.

"My teacher said that Mom's name means 'wonderful' or

something nice like that. *My* name means 'phoenix.' How come you never told me that?"

"You never asked." I poke her nose. "It's Arabic."

"What's Arbick?"

"An old Earthbound language."

Anka zooms out from Cetus and shows me a different constellation. "I missed you a lot too, so I drew Columba. The Dove."

I can't help but hug her.

"Here's Phaet, the dove star." Anka points at the biggest white dot, right where the bird's eye would be. "And this is Wezn—'weights.'"

It's a smaller dot, down in the cardiac region.

"Are you good friends with Wes? You should be. You're in the same constellation."

"Not every Pollux likes every Castor, and those stars are both in Gemini."

My little sister throws her hands above her head in mock exasperation. "You know what I mean! A lot of people's names come from Gemini. No one pays attention to Columba." She studies the constellation, purses her lips, and shifts them rapidly from side to side. "Do you *like* Wes?"

I shake my head, amazed that Anka has the time and energy for such trivial accusations. And when did she start emphasizing random syllables with assertive inflections in her voice?

Even sitting, I can tell that she's gotten taller. Anka has hit puberty with no mother to guide her through its mysteries—and thanks to the Militia, no sister either.

Anka shuts off her handscreen and sits on it. "Do you like *Umbriel*?"

"Don't worry about it."

"Are you *sure*?"

I dodge the question with a question. "Do *you* like someone?"

She sticks out her tongue, a persistent gesture from her younger years. "Yuck."

Her extravagant reaction makes me wonder. "I won't tell if you do."

"Okay. You don't talk to anyone *really*, so, um, someone in my class. Rigel." Anka giggles into my shoulder. "He called my star map pretty, and he helps me with algebra. Which is so embarrassing." Her smile turns upside down. "Why can't I be good at math like you?"

The sudden despondency in her voice rubs my heart the wrong way. Those who fall behind in Primary mathematics can't Specialize in scientific fields. Not that Anka would want to—she'd rather draw. But she won't earn a decent living from that, even if she nabs a spot in the oft-ignored Visual Design Department. Still, I allow myself the hope that Anka can find her place.

I hug her again. "People will always need something pretty or interesting to look at." Even if it's just a tray of stolen moss or a colorful Committee poster. "You'll make it for them."

She grins, even laughs. "You and Mom are the only ones who get it." Then she says, "I love you, Phaet."

"Love you too," I slip in, before she starts her Rigel chatter again. Rigel is so *smart*, so *nice*. I wish I knew how to get her mind off him, because she should concentrate on other things. When I was her age, I didn't get excited about Umbriel, maybe because I knew him too well. So much for being a good big sister.

"Lunch!" the twins holler from the kitchenette.

As we step over a pile of discarded robes, I try to disregard the mess in the apartment. The chairs aren't pushed in, the table isn't clean, the plastic furniture isn't dusted, and old Tinbie hasn't been fixed. He's still under the table, toppled over, the yellow light gone from his eyes. I should've predicted that if I left the apartment to topsy-turvy Cygnus, everything inside would end up topsy-turvy too. I roll Tinbie under the plastic sofa, but one of his wheels falls off. I kick it out of sight.

We take our usual seats at the table, except for Umbriel, who sits at Mom's old place. He and Ariel have assembled sandwiches with soy patties in the middle; I hope Umbriel didn't snag them from Culinary. It's the best meal we've had since Cygnus's last birthday, months before this whole Militia mess. Their efforts make me want to cry with homesickness.

"Thanks," I manage. "You didn't need to make all this. The food is more than enough in Militia—"

"Who cares? Just eat it," Cygnus snaps. So I do, and the mild food is more savory than an enormous Militia meal, its flavor enhanced by the labor of the people I love.

We clean every bite of food off the table. It takes prodding from Anka for Cygnus to finish his sandwich, but eventually he nibbles away the last of it and grabs a banana for dessert.

Finally, everyone's hands are free. Cygnus, unwilling to wait any longer for our critical discussion, tucks his left hand under his right upper arm.

We follow suit, covering our handscreens in various ways. Anka squeezes her hand between her knees.

As my brother speaks, the weight of heavy things sucks the life out of his voice. "You know me. I can't sit still when something bad happens. Last night I poked through Law Department files—those zipperheads have *no* idea how encryption works—and found out what they busted her for."

"Cygnus . . ." Umbriel glowers at him, looking parental.

"It's not a joke, Umbriel; I saw it on the screen. Disruptive print . . . is never a joke."

Silence falls, interrupted only by Anka's whimpering.

"Disruptive print" means that the authorities believe the defendant has threatened the unity of the Bases by writing blasphemous statements. I'm more shocked than devastated. Mom couldn't have committed such a horrible crime; she's too smart. Besides, if she's ever angry about a new law, or if a Militia member disrespects her in the corridors, she rants to Atlas, who pats her shoulder and mumbles placating words. Although these incidents always made me uncomfortable, they provided an outlet for Mom so that she wouldn't need to hash her feelings out in print. Spoken tirades against the Committee or the Militia are smaller crimes: they're called "disruptive speech," which is harder for law enforcement to detect and less threatening to authority because it can't be spread as easily.

Punishment for disruptive print is subjective, depending on how unpatriotic the accused's writing is deemed by Law. Some convicts leave jail within a decade. Others are imprisoned for life, the same sentence suffered by murderers. The death penalty, as the Committee claims, has never been implemented. But they've lied to me once.

Ariel takes over. He works as an unpaid secretary in Law, where his brain stows every interaction it encounters. "Judging from the bail amount, I bet the prosecution has written proof against her."

Cygnus nods. "All they have to do is prove that she wrote it—whatever 'it' is—with software that analyzes how much she uses certain words, sentence length, et cetera."

"Basically," says Ariel, "over time—and if things go their way, they'll have a *lot* of time—their evidence will remain unchanged, while the witnesses my dad plans to call on to help your mom will gradually lose interest."

"*Your dad* is her defense?" I'm impressed that the Phi family has already made plans to help us, even though I never asked them to. We'd be alone and afraid without them.

Ariel's face falls—he thinks I'm insulting their efforts.

"Unless you want to waste seventy-five hundred Sputniks a month on someone else from Law," says my brother. Apparently, the planning also involved Cygnus. He tosses the banana peel into the compost bin and hunches over his handscreen.

"As I was saying," Ariel continues, "we need to have the trial soon. Before the witnesses get bored—and they will, if we wait a year. We need that bail money, to get your mom out of jail soon *and* to speed up the trial."

It'll have to come from me—all thirty-five hundred Sputniks of it, along with Mom's fifteen hundred Sputnik joke of a Medical bill. I've got to push harder in Militia training. Ranking top seven won't be good enough; I'll have to shoot for fourth or better.

"And . . . the nature of Mira's 'crime' means we'll have a harder time winning." Ariel's expression is bleak. "Disruptive print is pretty rare—the only instance when someone was found innocent was thirteen years ago. I overheard Phobos Xi—he's a colleague of Dad's—telling that story when I was outside his office pretending to fill my canteen. He laughed at how he doesn't think their strategy will work for your mom. I had Cygnus look into it last night."

Cygnus shakes his head. "The family's joint account shrank by 6,392 Sputniks after the trial."

"Bribe," I mutter.

The money needed is so far beyond our reach, we might as well go to Saturn to fetch it. But why not try? The practice is more widespread than the Committee would ever admit.

They'd also never admit to letting official communications tell children their only parent is in Medical while she's really bound for the Pen. I'd hate to throw my hard-earned money at Law, but between indulging my sense of righteousness and saving Mom, I choose Mom.

"If we want to bribe them, Phaet has to become a sergeant—it's the highest rank attainable out of training and without a commission from the Committee. There's a new one in every batch of trainees. She has to place first out of fifty. All our other expenses considered, it'd take two months of sergeant salary—five thousand Sputniks, give or take—to get the bribe money together, while we still pay for rent, food, dues, all that. It'll be tough, but do it for Mom. In case they say she's guilty."

I thought training was going well, but now I need to adjust my goals. First-place trainee. Sergeant. My family knows it's nearly impossible, so there's no use complaining. I feel a surge of resentment against Cygnus, who punches numbers on his handscreen all day and has no idea what he's demanding of me: to top Jupiter, Callisto, *Wes*—or deplete myself trying.

Then I feel a flicker of ambition as I imagine myself as the victor. I always did enjoy beating Ariel and placing first in Primary.

But if I do win? I could assume command of less important missions, and in combat, I could direct a forty-person platoon. Officers' contracts last longer than other soldiers' because the Militia prizes continuity in the upper echelons. And if I do well enough for five or six years, the Committee might give me a commission to become a captain like Yinha. I might have to shelve my dream of becoming a Bioengineer and watch it gather dust.

"That's all I had to say." Ariel checks his handscreen and wipes his mouth with the back of his hand. "I should get back to Law. . . . There's a case I need to set up."

"Don't go," Anka pleads.

Ariel makes a sad face. "My apologies. Later, Anka." He pinches her cheek and elicits a snarl. Laughing, he whisks out the door.

"Nerd." Umbriel chuckles. "Well. Let's keep talking about our options—"

"Blah, blah, blah," says Cygnus, stirring his water with his spoon.

Umbriel shoots him a dirty look.

"All you guys do is talk." Anka stands without warning, knocking over her stool. "I just want Mom back." She storms down the hallway to our room, sealing the white circular door with a *snap*.

"I'll do something about her." Cygnus scuttles down the hallway in pursuit. I want to follow them but wouldn't know what to say.

Mom is good at this sort of thing, comforting people and

picking tender words out of midair. Once, when some bully told Anka that she was stupid, Mom said, "A dog will bite others because it can't bite its own tail." It was almost certainly another old Earthbound saying from our great-grandmother, yet Anka understood that Gemma Lambda was the one with real insecurities—she got the same algebra marks as Anka but could hardly draw a stick figure. The bullying continued, but for the most part Anka didn't let it bother her.

Now Umbriel and I are alone, and I can tell he's been waiting for this moment. He scoots his chair closer and takes my right hand in his clammy one.

"We miss you around here."

I know. They have time to immerse themselves in emotion, while I've been focusing every iota of my energy and attention on learning how to destroy people. I can't look at Umbriel's scrunched-up eyes, so I concentrate on his forehead. A loose curl, shaped exactly like a question mark, meanders between his brows. He should get a shorter haircut as per Agriculture regulations before the patrols shave his head bald.

"I worry about you. I can't sleep. I want to join Militia myself, like Ariel said."

My silvery hair is reflected in the liquid pooling along his bottom eyelids. I hope he doesn't cry—I don't want to deal with that—but luckily Umbriel keeps his tears inside, like me.

"Look at how much you've changed already." He gestures at my clothes, at the new muscles visible through my shirt. "Will we still know each other when you're done with this whole mess? Will you still—"

"Of course." Apart from my biological family, I love Umbriel best out of everybody in the universe, and I've missed him enough to know we shouldn't be apart.

Elated, Umbriel stands up; his left hand slides into his pocket, while his right pulls me to my feet. He shows his perfectly straight teeth in an awkward grin.

I've gone too long without seeing it. I return his smile.

"Come home and you'll be this happy all the time," he whispers, even though we know it's not possible or true. "You know how I feel about Militia?"

Because there's no one to see us, he unabashedly sticks out his tongue instead of licking his incisors. I laugh out loud.

We hear small footfalls, and our heads swivel toward the sound. Cygnus and Anka solemnly stride into the kitchen, Cygnus with his arm around her, Anka rubbing tears off her cheeks with the back of her hand. I used to do that, before I stopped crying altogether.

Anka hooks an arm around Umbriel's free one, and Cygnus does the same to me, so that the four of us make a tight circle. Half white, a quarter green, a quarter black.

"Can you promise something?" Anka looks at the three of us in turn, her expression hopeful and challenging. "That we'll all be together after this? Mom too?"

I think hard before replying, "No guarantees."

Anka rolls her eyes, sighing. "Okay. Wrong question. Can you guys *try* to make it happen? I'm only eleven. I can't do anything but wait."

I resist the urge to tear up, swallowing hard. It was Anka's birthday a week ago, and I forgot. Eleven is the fifth prime number—and the number that Anka would wish upon whenever it showed up twice on her handscreen's digital clock.

"We're trying everything," Umbriel says. "We'll bring Ms. Mira back; I know it."

It's sufficient for my sister, who gazes at him with adoration.

They both disappoint me. Umbriel shouldn't make promises he's unlikely to keep, and Anka shouldn't believe him when he does.

16

HAVING A TASTE OF HOME MAKES IT SO difficult to come back to the training floor, which has been converted into a huge launchpad. All of yesterday's talk about Mom's trial haunts me, and I try to imagine her in Penitentiary. Are the guards Beaters and the cells sickeningly filthy, as I've heard? Is she thinking of us too, wondering like me if Anka and Cygnus are holding themselves together at school?

I must keep myself from falling apart so I can give my best in training.

I blink away grogginess, a product of last night's perusal of the handscreen-accessible Militia flight manual. Because the instructors only uploaded it yesterday, most trainees didn't bother to read it. However, I felt compelled by old Primary habits—and the faint promise of *winning*—much to Vinasa's annoyance. My handscreen emitted light until an indecent hour, knocking hours off her beauty sleep.

Ten identical destroyer ships are spread across the floor, each large enough to carry a team of five. Each looks somewhat like an Earthbound shark, with a sharp nose, sleek body, and fins for steering. Interlocking ribs in the midsections allow the crafts to bend.

Some of the trainees, like Nash, squeal in excitement; others clutch their bellies, anticipating motion sickness. I do neither.

For each ship, there's a pilot, a copilot, two wingmen to control the computer-aided blasters on each side, and a flight leader to check the route, communicate with the team leader and base, and carry out other administrative tasks.

The main steering, just as in my greenhouse transport, is simple: a joystick for direction and levers for speed and nose angle. However, the array of other buttons inside the cockpit is not to be trifled with. Thus, for many missions, the ships follow a previously calculated autopilot route until they near their destinations, rendering flight straightforward and safe except in emergency situations. We've heard stories of pilots so accustomed to preset routes and zero confrontation that they panic and crash in actual combat.

"These spacecraft don't fly," says Yinha, to a chorus of grunts and moans. "You'll participate in a simulation with the controls, for practice. It's pretty cool."

Jupiter perks up as if he's been Electrostunned. Turning to Callisto, he remarks, "If this is anything like my sim-games, my rank's going to go through the roof."

Hopefully, his rank number will shoot upward, maybe even into the double digits—tenth, twentieth, fiftieth—as he idiotically said. And maybe mine will drop into the smaller numbers, where I want it. If my greenhouse piloting skills haven't left me, I could do well here.

My team consists of Orion, Eri, a courteous brunette named Cassiopeia, and a not-so-courteous platinum blonde named Sunova.

Orion pouts with disguised amusement at being the one boy on our team. Cassie pats his arm and brushes chestnut bangs out of her eyes. "You can be the leader if you want."

He counters by patting *her* arm. "Only if you ladies agree."

One by one, we enter through a small hatch on the belly of the ship. Orion, the biggest of us, barely manages to slither through. Inside, we find walls that are black where they aren't covered by grids upon grids of backlit buttons, all different colors and sizes, as well as switches and meters to measure pressure, missile inventory, and engine heat. There are three radar screens, each on a different scale, a blinking blue ship schematic, and five seats with sleek black helmets hanging above them.

The other girls, who admit they haven't glanced at the flight manual, persuade me to be pilot among a glittering shower of compliments. Only Sunova dislikes the idea.

"Why leave the hardest job to a *kid*?" she sneers.

However Orion approves, and commands Cassie and Sunova to take over the wing weaponry. Eri sits next to me as copilot, moaning, "I don't want to shoot stuff!"

"Don't worry," Cassie reassures her. "Keep telling yourself it's just a sim."

Once we buckle in, our world goes dark. All around us is a projection of the open sky, with the blue orb of the Earth in the middle. In rearview, the simulation Moon shrinks as we push off. The training dome's magnets decrease the gravity in our ship until we'd float if we weren't wearing seat belts. For this sim, the instructors do the difficult work of launching us, so I don't have to set off the controlled nuclear fusion reaction that will combine hydrogen atoms with helium ones and lift us off the Moon.

"Asteroid approaching," declares Orion.

Indeed, a chunk of dirty metal hurtles toward us head-on. According to the flight manual, the ship's hull can repair itself if it's punctured by objects less than three centimeters in diameter. This asteroid doesn't fall into that category. I jerk the joystick to the left, causing the craft to lurch. Amidst grumbling from my team, I remind myself that these controls are more delicate than those of my clunky transport.

"Can I blow it up?" begs Sunova.

"Nah. We should save ammo." Orion doesn't use a condescending tone but states the facts. "Enemy spotted."

A gaggle of battleships approaches in the side window, each looking like a collection of gray building blocks glued together. These are likely from Battery Bay; they have altogether too many right angles, like everything else there. Despite the Batterers' ugly designs and the inefficiency caused by unchecked arguments among their alliance's diverse peoples, they are not to be trifled with. Only the most powerful Earthbound cities can access the resources for space flight.

"Can we blow up *these*?" Sunova's voice rattles with anticipation.

"I think that's why they're here," Cassie says.

"Go ahead," Orion says through a laugh.

I don't have the pleasure of incinerating the ships but must dodge their fire instead. Making sure to be delicate with the controls, I pilot us away from their slow missiles with minimal disruption to our digestive systems.

To my right, Sunova rotates various knobs and fires three beams in quick succession, two of which hit enemy targets. "Yes!"

I think she's played these kinds of games before too.

"Oops," murmurs Cassie. "I think I shot a missile instead of a laser."

Indeed, she has. It finds a large enemy ship, drawn

magnetically to the metal in its exterior, and cooks it in an orange conflagration that also fries a nearby craft.

"Real fighting can't be this easy," Orion says. "This is a low-level sim."

All the talk has broken my glassy-eyed concentration, and an enemy shot finds its way into our right-wing weapon stash. *Wham.* The ship rattles. I imagine the shark choking on something, bending in upon itself.

Fizz—I'm that careless crew member, the one who let her focus slip in the crucial moment. *What if this simulation hadn't been a simulation?*

"For grits' sake, Stripes!" swears Sunova. "Why didn't you wait a few more years before trying this whole pilot thing?"

"We should stress more about the ship," scolds Orion. "Eri, can you fix the damage?"

Eri gulps, examining the rows upon rows of buttons before her. I remember reading that among them is a set of controls for two repair arms that can access the stash of spare parts in the back of the craft.

"I didn't study the repair section of the manual! I don't know how to do this!"

The ship rocks again, knocking my tailbone into the hard pilot's seat. We've been hit once more, on the belly of the craft. I hadn't noticed a Batterer ship in that direction.

As the entire ship goes dark, Sunova swears on the sun and the moons of all the planets. This sim is over.

"Very cool, team," Yinha's crackly voice addresses us out of our handscreens. "You made it farther than we thought you would."

The instructors didn't have great expectations.

The ship's windows let in the acute light of the training floor. Blinking wildly, Orion says, "Thanks, ladies. It's been real." He opens the hatch and pulls himself out. He usually knows the most comforting thing to say.

But I agree more with Sunova's snarky last comment: "That could have gone a fizz ton better."

17

LEARNING ABOUT FLIGHT MAKES TRAINING surprisingly enjoyable—more like Primary. The instructors lecture us on the features of different ships, and I clear out space in my brain to absorb them. The largest are the Colossus models, which can each hold twelve nuclear warheads and a few hundred civilian passengers. Why anyone would transport the two in the same vehicle boggles me. The smallest are the Pygmettes, two meters long. These are used by on-base patrols and off-base scouts who need to fit into small spaces. But we still do simulations with the destroyer ships, because they are the most frequently used for both defense and recon missions.

If the crafts' fusion generators fail, ion thrusters keep the craft running. Should the entire ship break down, there's a spherical escape pod nestled into the ship's tail.

Nash thinks the pods make the destroyers' rear ends look like "pregnant chicken butts." I decide not to point out how physiologically mistaken she is.

Lectures and simulations beat strength workouts, even though they remind me of the classes and labs I'm missing in Primary—my classmates are probably synthesizing orange and purple transition metal complexes now. I try not to let my mind wander too far along that path, but in moments of weakness, I find myself cataloguing the course work I need to make up.

My body has a chance to recover from the grueling month of physical conditioning and combat training. If not for Wes, whom I suspect might be addicted to exercise—and to running in particular—I'd let my muscles atrophy. But he won't have it, coaxing me every night into the Medical quarters to run, lift heavy objects, or spar. The extra exertion stresses my body but mitigates the fear that I won't be strong enough or fast enough to place in the top few.

Though it's dangerous, we sometimes draw the daggers out of our boots and slash at each other until we can't lift our arms. While I try to attack, Wes calls out, "Stay farther away," or "Smaller steps. Lighter grip."

When I'm careless, he cuts me, but it's happening less frequently. Each time, Wes pulls out a tube of scar-erasure cream and dabs the green goo on my face or limbs, his hands heavy and surprisingly clumsy for a Medical worker who has performed this simple task hundreds of times. I struggle to keep quiet, unsure whether I'm reacting to the stinging pain or the smoothness of his fingertips on my skin.

Once, I manage to nick Wes on the cheek, and though I apologize profusely, he declines even a bandage. He pats the crimson slash, which suits him. "It'll remind me in the future that a girl had a quicker wrist than I did."

But he still fixes me up every time he cuts me, no matter how much I protest. "You're too young to be carrying around scars, kid. And what'll your, er, best friend say if he sees?"

Kid. Even though no other trainees heard him, I'm stupefied by how much I wish he hadn't called me that.

I'd forgotten that my friends wondered about my location when I was away at night. One evening, I walk to the barracks, worrying and checking my siblings' handscreen profiles to make sure they haven't made trouble.

Nash and Eri corner me in an empty hallway. Although Eri looks upset, Nash wears a grin.

"You'd better watch yourself—it's almost curfew! We don't know where you disappear to every night." Nash giggles through her words. "But we know who you're with."

My stomach lurches and my feet grow roots into the floor, tangling in the linoleum.

"Orion told us that Wes disappears but comes back around now too," Eri mumbles.

"I was right about what you do when you disappear." Nash wags a finger at me. "Hot dates with one of the boys. But why *Wes*, out of all of them?"

Fortunately, my dinner has been well digested. I wouldn't want to offer it as a sacrifice to the shining floor. "He's—he's been helping me. Running, strength, sparring."

Nash's forehead scrunches with skepticism. "For the past *month*?"

"It's why I've gotten better. In the rankings, I mean."

"*Really.*" Eri's face colors with hope.

Nod.

"Makes sense," Nash says. "You used to be an average runner, but now you're one of the best. And I wouldn't want to be anywhere near an angry Stripes with a knife. But . . . why would he help you? Mr. Lethal, Ginger, and Handsome doesn't seem to like company."

"Remember when Jupiter beat me up? Wes felt bad," I say.

Nash paces, heel to toe, deep in thought. "M'kay. I believe

you. We won't tell anyone. . . . And I'm sorry we worried you were a dude-hustler."

I nod in genuine appreciation and start walking away, but I realize I forgot to clarify something. "Nash, what you were implying—I wouldn't do that to Umbriel."

Eri leans forward. "Who?"

"Aww, Phaet has a little boyfriend!" Nash affectionately flicks my shoulder. "Bet we could search his stats on our handscreens, if we knew his full name. What complex is he from?"

Shrug.

"She's not going to tell us," says Eri. "So, what's he like? Is he cute? This means Wes is available, right?"

I consider answering, *Protective. He's all right. Do what you like.* Instead, my mouth opens in a yawn that I hope is convincing. "Tired."

To their disappointment, I trudge away to the clamor of the barracks.

18

"WELCOME TO YOUR THIRD EVALUATION," says Yinha from the front of the hovering viewing platform. "I hope you like to race. First team to the finish line gets the most points, with slight variations for individual accomplishments. You're going fifteen kilometers through mountains, valleys, some lunar lava tubes, before looping back to base. For many of you, this will be your first time outside, so keep in mind everything we've studied, all the safety stuff. If you're not ready for it now, after these weeks of prep, you're not going to be ready as full recruits. If something happens out there, it's *your* fault. Understood? Cool."

She taps her handscreen, and a crack opens down the middle of the familiar floor of the training dome. The two halves slide apart until we see ten *real* destroyers lined up on the floor below, fiberglass plates glinting like scales.

As the platform descends, I clutch my hands in fear. We'll finally see the wild landscape of the Moon, a vista we've studied since Primary but have never seen firsthand. With the adventure comes probable dust storms, meteorite bombardment, and—worst of all—moonquakes. I'll also have to deal with my randomly assigned team, which includes my scatterbrained first-evaluation opponent Io Beta, a low-ranking guy named Triton, Jupiter, and Wes. I grumble internally until I recall

Jupiter's penchant for simulation games and Wes's levelheadedness. If the former doesn't try to assassinate anyone, we might do well.

We file off the viewing platform and assemble with our teams. Wes opens the hatch of our destroyer, and we climb inside. The pulsing buttons, the hum of the engine, and the numerous clicking monitors almost fool me into thinking this spacecraft is alive.

Jupiter makes himself flight leader, and no one argues. Wes gives me a long look accompanied by a miniature smile, indicating that we shouldn't listen to the bulk of the orders he'll give.

Before Jupiter can assign other positions, Wes asks, "Io, would you like to be copilot?"

Io doesn't respond until I tap her shoulder. Wes repeats his proposal. She nods vigorously—her new job requires the least concentration.

"I want Stripes on pilot," Jupiter interjects. "She's better at steering than the rest of you. Triton, get on left wing. Kappa, you're on right."

I wouldn't have allocated jobs any differently. Maybe Jupiter isn't as stupid as he seems.

Fully realizing that my actions mean life or death to the team, I sit in the familiar cockpit, flex my fingers over the controls, and flip through the operating manual on my handscreen, hoping I remember every line of print.

"Stripes." Wes's eyes lock with mine and he inhales, about to speak—but decides against it. Instead, he raises his right hand to his forehead and salutes me with two of his fingers.

"Shut up, you two," snaps Jupiter.

"They weren't saying anything," Triton points out.

"Now *you* shut up." Jupiter hunches over the numerous communication devices and screens at the flight leader's seat, his forehead bulging more than usual. He probably wishes he'd made himself pilot instead.

A massive door opens before us, and all ten ships move into the air lock.

"All trainees prepare for start. Ten seconds," says Arcturus's voice from one of the speakers in our ship.

Triton frowns, rolls his eyes, and sticks his tongue out. I bite the inside of my cheek to keep from laughing out loud. Remembering the helmet, I pull it over my head. Everyone except Io follows.

"Io!" Jupiter hollers.

I fasten her helmet over her quivering head.

The buzzer sounds, and the last hatch opens. I crank the engine to full power, holding back the speed lever with one hand, waiting until there's sufficient power to go. I press a few buttons, reshaping the wings to make the ship as sleek as possible, which includes stowing the wingtip blasters.

On the radar screen, I see the nine other trainee teams. Some have tried to move and failed, so their ships trip and teeter at the gate. I imagine Arcturus sighing as he watches the footage and deducts points from the pilots' individual scores.

When the power is sufficient, press the speed lever to full throttle and expel the engine exhaust. I follow the instructions, letter by letter. Because we won't be escaping the Moon's gravity, "sufficient power" is a fraction of that needed during the sim. Without a hitch, we shoot across the dark gray Oceanus Procellarum.

"Whoo!" Triton's voice congratulates me through our helmet headsets.

My eyes seek out the path ahead of us, marked by yellow lights on each side.

"Everyone shut up. Stripes, dodge those damn hills."

"The instructors can hear you, mate," Wes says through his teeth.

Jupiter shuts up.

According to my radar screen, the track will take us through a row of rugged mountains up ahead—the Montes Carpatus. We can't fly over them or we'll lose the path, so I'll have to steer us through the narrow valleys between. If only Io would help instead of daydreaming.

"Stripes! Move! There's a damn ship!" hollers Jupiter, jarring my ears.

He's correct, much as I don't like to admit it. Team Two is approaching us from behind, and they're going 150 kilometers per hour—their pilot is willing to risk hitting something for a higher top speed. That something happens to be us.

I fire the starboard-side thruster. We jerk to the left, and Two pulls ahead, leaving us in a cloud of exhaust.

"Damn it, now we're gonna hit a mountain!"

We're about to collide with a peak. I clack my jaws together in irritation. *Focus.* My hand twists the steering rod right, but another precipice bars our way.

Wes clacks at his keypad; an instant later, the wingtip fires some of our more powerful ammunition—not the lasers but the missiles—straight at the peak.

"What in the . . ." Jupiter trails off as the missiles strike. Clouds of dust rise from the impact; our ship trembles. Debris pings against its exterior. I grip the controls tight, relying on instinct and luck until the windshield clears.

"Whoo, Kappa!" Triton cheers. "You sure we're allowed to do that?"

"It's better than breaking our skulls open," Wes deadpans. "Anyhow—Phaet, good job, but concentrate."

He's treating this like another nighttime training session. Feeling some semblance of calm from hearing his voice, I steer us away from the area and back onto the track. Two more ships have passed us, but at least we didn't crash.

If we had, though? We'd suffer severe burns before dying and languishing in nothingness forever, with no pressure to hold our cells together—like Dad.

The path takes us into the mouth of a cave—a lunar lava tube, formed by hardened lava and traversed by magma, but now open like an empty blood vessel. I fold the wings, hiding our artillery but decreasing our surface area.

Inside the lava tube, it's dark except for the track markers and the taillights of Team Six's ship ahead of us. The walls inch closer and closer, until the vein opens into a space taller than five Atriums stacked atop one another. Here, a mammoth bubble in the magma formed and cooled. Team Six and Team One are engaged in combat with a fleet of ugly prism ships.

Jupiter launches into a nuke-oriented series of curses. Everyone but me joins him.

19

"TEAM EIGHT, BECAUSE YOU ARE ENTERING the interior of the shield volcano, we are transmitting an important announcement," Yinha's canned voice says. "Battery Bay's ships have been detected, but the evaluation will progress regardless. Points will be awarded to teams that destroy enemy spacecraft."

A click and she's gone.

How could the Batterers *possibly* get in here? Is this some sick practical joke from the instructors?

A gray block about our size swerves into our headlights before I can unfurl our ship's wings. While we wait for the artillery to reemerge, I point the ship straight up and perform a corkscrew maneuver, dodging the Batterers' fire. When the weaponry is ready, Triton incinerates an enemy ship, but the explosion also rocks our own vessel.

Jupiter sees more ships behind the remnants of the first and grunts in frustration. "The enemy is closing in on left, right, and front! Move the ship forward-right! And do it now!"

That wasn't my idea. I check the radar. Nothing above us. Wearing my own version of Wes's dim smile, I tilt the nose of the ship upward and put on an extra spurt of speed that jars everyone's spines. Batterer fire streaks toward us from below.

I jerk the controls again, but a small missile grazes the belly of the ship.

Pinpricks of light sparkle above us, clustered together in a small circle. *Stars? Here?* We've found the vent of the dead volcano. Even if flying through wouldn't help us get away from the enemy, I'd still do it out of curiosity.

I fire more exhaust, and we speed toward the night sky.

"What are you *doing*?" hollers Jupiter. "Where's the damn track?"

"She'll find it again, don't you worry," Wes tells him.

Our ship is once again flying over the lunar surface. Far below, yellow dots line the path back to the distant crater that contains our home.

But there's something in our way: a gargantuan Batterer ship languishes in the middle of the track. Three destroyers weave around it, all using full firepower. The cruiser is an old model made to house dozens of passengers, dating back to Battery Bay's diplomatic fiasco.

Triton fires a series of shots. He manages to strike it once, yelling, "Whoo! Got it!"

Though I like Triton, I'm disgusted. He hit a passenger ship, the spaceflight equivalent of attacking a horde of civilians. I retract the wing weapons, to Jupiter's irritation, and push the speed lever all the way forward. Our ship zooms over the civilian cruiser and finds the track again.

"You piece of grit!" Jupiter's face is probably swelling like a tomato. "We get more points for blowing up enemy ships!"

"That was a civilian vessel," Wes sputters, sounding lost.

"Are you sure?" asks Triton. "What if it's a military ship that just looks like one?"

Io whimpers into her hands.

"Well, we get points for any enemy ship." Jupiter fumes. "Turn us around!"

I ignore the order, although I'll lose points for doing so. I'd condone incinerating military ships out of necessity, but never civilian ones. Within the privacy of my helmet, I mourn everyone who might've been on board that cruiser. My fingers on the levers urge our destroyer onward. Soon, we overtake Team One.

But as we approach Team Five, a missile zooms toward our ship. I tilt the nose downward just before the missile would hit us head-on; it scrapes us, and we lurch forward as our velocity is abruptly reduced. Glowing metal scraps bounce off the windshield.

"Team Five did that!" Triton shouts. "That's *definitely* not allowed!"

"Callisto!" Jupiter's bellow is hoarse with indignation—somehow, he's sure that his girlfriend is the one who attacked us. "Extract the wing weapons, damn it!"

I keep the wings folded, preferring to lose points for insubordination rather than friendly fire. Since we're on a plain, with no mountains to protect us, I brace myself and tap the joystick from left to right, egging our ship on to the finish line. Let them try to hit us now.

"You're gonna make me barf," Triton grumbles, his voice oscillating with the shark's lopsided swimming.

As the green finish line draws ever closer, I push us past 160 kilometers per hour. Soon enough, we're right behind Team Five, bathing in their exhaust. Every time I try to pass them, the ship swerves to block us. And when we reach the finish line, we're still behind them.

Jupiter swears violently to show his fury at his girlfriend's antics. But within a few seconds, his face returns to normal—he looks pleased—and I wonder if they made some intra-couple agreement beforehand.

The last part of the evaluation involves docking the ship. To take us out of full speed, I shut off propulsion and fire the reverse exhaust.

We trail the victors into the Defense training hangar. I release the wheels, used only for takeoff and landing, and we follow them back through the first gate and the air lock.

"Well," crackles Yinha's voice. "Nice job, Team Eight. You realize that you win, right?"

Triton's cheering and Jupiter's dumb yelling force her to stop talking for a few seconds.

"Team Five was disqualified for friendly fire. Congratulations. You're guaranteed high scores, even with those nonregulation tricks."

Wes chuckles. She probably means his stunt with the missiles, and my flight away from the cruiser to protect innocent lives.

"You showed ingenuity in unpredictable situations. Like how you dealt with the unmanned old Batterer ships we stuck in that volcano for you."

I puff out my cheeks and exhale, slowly releasing the air and the tension. The visor of my helmet clouds. The Batterer ships were fakes: no one got hurt.

"And Stripes, cool piloting. Haven't seen a trainee do a roll like that for a long t— No! Watch out!"

A great impact from behind throws our ship nose first into the second gate. My seat belt catches me before my head knocks into the controls. I gasp for air, thankful all my bones are intact, and glance backward.

The first gate now sports a massive dent. As it creaks open, the third-place ship hobbles in, left wing hanging onto the belly by a hinge. The polymer exterior around the disconnected limb has melted and then solidified into a lumpy mess.

I gawk at the mangled destroyer, horrified that all the flat training statistics I've read have become reality. *Who's in that ship?*

"Do not move!" Yinha's voice booms from the sound systems within both our ship and the hangar. "I repeat—trainees, do not move! Do not enter or leave the air lock! This is an emergency. Instructors, registered Militia, and Medics will get the situation under control."

Outside the half-open gate, three more ships prepare to land—how will the trainees within them react? Within the next few minutes, all fifty of us will have seen the collision or heard about it. Our superiors may be able to clear away the debris from the crash, but they'll never contain the echo.

20

OVER THE NEXT HOUR, I PIECE TOGETHER what happened from stray slivers of sentences. Team One and Team Four were racing nose and nose toward the hangar, pursued by "Batterer" ships, when Team One's pilot tried some complicated maneuver he'd "read about" and lost control of his craft. The ship slammed into the air lock gate. Four team members will spend the week in the Medical quarters.

The fifth, Vinasa Epsilon, was assigned to left wingtip. The impact threw her onto her weapons controls, breaking her ribs and stopping her heart.

Nash crushes me in a cinnamon-scented hug. I'm aching from my grief, but hers must be crippling. I've only known Vinasa for six weeks. I never explored the landscape of her mind, as I have Umbriel's, and I didn't learn everything that existed behind her biting pleasant humor, the golden backlit glow in her eyes, her appreciation for things long gone by. Compared to Vinasa's lifelong companions, Nash and Eri, whose faces are distorted in misery, do I deserve to feel this devastation? Compared with them, I lost only the promise of a friend.

We read our new rankings, unable to keep from thinking, *It could have been me.* One mistake during that evaluation, and any of us could have been in Vinasa's place.

I'm ranked second, one place behind Wes and one in front

of Orion, and Nash has moved up to sixteenth; I feel no joy. Jupiter has risen to fourth, while Callisto dropped into the twenties; I feel no satisfaction.

The instructors should have expelled Callisto for her friendly fire stunt, just like they should have expelled Jupiter for stabbing Wes. I need to find out what's going on—why both Callisto and Jupiter are still around.

I disappear behind the climbing wall, where, on the first day, I swapped my civilian clothes for Beetle black. How much has changed since then?

CALLISTO CHI, I type into my handscreen.

Unlike Jupiter, she doesn't have any policy infractions listed. Her father, now deceased, worked in Financial. Her mother's occupation, like that of Jupiter's father, is "Not Applicable." Neither the amount of money in her bank account nor her apartment number in the Chi complex is accessible. Frustrated, I close her profile.

She's as sinister in the intra-base network as she is in the flesh.

At night, I run endless laps around the Medical quarters until my mind is numb and my system is full of endorphins. Running is cheap, a temporary barrier to unwanted feelings.

Afterward, I creep through the silent halls, knowing I have stayed out past curfew.

A tiny squeak reaches my ears; my heart thumps in my rib cage, deep and hollow. I crouch, listening hard. Human hissing ensues. In these echoing halls, I can't tell where it's coming from.

I fight down trepidation, which persists even after the hissing stops. Maybe there's nothing.

"Hey, little Stripes." A smiling Callisto steps out of a doorway. "Let's talk."

Dim light from the hall catches her curls, which puff out around her head like polyester pillow stuffing.

Jupiter swaggers over to her. He tosses an arm around her shoulders, and she leans inward, her face a mask of romantic satisfaction.

"I'm so, so sorry about Vinasa. You were friends with her, yeah?"

I look at Callisto without even a nod; I don't want to discuss this topic, and judging by Callisto's saccharine tone, she doesn't care.

"Well, it's really sad, what happened. But it's a sign that we trainees need to work together better—you and Jupe have sure had a few misunderstandings, hmm?"

Jupiter nods. I don't. I rest my left hand on my right shoulder, adopting a posture that ensures my handscreen will pick up everything she says.

Callisto simpers, licking her lips. "What I really mean is, let's forget all that and talk about Kappa. Jupe heard him muttering in his sleep—something about keeping you in line—oh? You think he's playing fair? He wouldn't let you get what he's wanted forever, now, would he?"

Alarmed, I listen harder.

"Sweetie, you're fifteen. Too young to tell a backstabber when you see one. We went to Primary with Kappa. There's a reason he never had any friends. How's this: we protect you from anything he tries to pull."

It sounds too abrupt to be true, especially after a 180-degree turnaround on Jupiter's part. I cross my arms and make my most affected, superior face at them, though objectively it's neither affected nor superior.

"As payment, you help us place first and second. You can be third—it's higher than anyone expects of a little kid, anyway."

For grits' sake, they think I'm a child who can't recognize blatant ambition when she sees it. "No thanks."

Callisto disentangles herself from Jupiter, removing his limbs from her body while gazing intently into my eyes. "Oh?"

I shake my head to restate my point.

"Aw, she's rank-hungry too. What a pity."

She's right. I want to prove that Jupiter's initial wariness of me was warranted. "Pity," I agree.

"Well . . ." Callisto looks to Jupiter for a nod of approval. She gets it. "Why don't we tell Yinha and Arcturus what's going on with your mom? We'll throw in the rest of the trainees for good measure, hmm? Actually, we could say it right now, with everyone's handscreen uncovered—"

"No!"

How in the universe do they know about Mom? I dare not ask.

Jupiter and Callisto want to place high at any cost. If I teamed up with them, I'd be easier to sabotage; they could ensure that I placed much, much lower than third.

"I still say no," I tell them.

"What a pity," Callisto repeats. She nods to Jupiter. In the darkness, I see a flash of silver.

An instant later, something chilly runs down my thigh, and Jupiter holds a bloodied knife half as long as his arm.

I thought bleeding was supposed to feel warm, at least as

warm as the stinky arm around my neck and the anger festering in my stomach. I consider screaming for someone, anyone, but I can't even inhale. In less than two minutes asphyxiation will knock me out, and the stars only know what these two will do to me before someone picks up my handscreen readings and comes to help.

"So quiet," Callisto muses, pacing. "Not fit to be a leader in the Militia. Don't you have friends to run to? Ah, of course not. You think you're too good to even talk to people here."

Jupiter puts a hand over my mouth, just in case. I try to kick and squirm. He needn't worry. He's twice my mass and, unlike me, has access to oxygen.

"Oh, right." Callisto pats my cheek, sneering. "You can't run."

The chill invades my other leg; I sway back and forth. Their shapes grow blurry, lose their definite edges. I could give up. I could slip under, let the pain stop, and never know what they'll do to me next.

Stop it! Wes's voice in my head says, the way he sounds when I've made a dumb sparring maneuver. Thinking of him reminds me that I'm cleverer than this. I clamp my canines onto Jupiter's hand, which snaps back. His curses echo around us as I elbow myself free. Blurriness recedes from my eyes and brain as I gulp for air, trying to find a way to defend myself against their long knives.

I have short knives; they will have to do.

I crumple to a sitting position on the floor and make stupid sobbing noises into my knees, screaming intermittently with all the breath in my lungs. To assess the damage, I brush my hands along my legs and find a sticky gash, deep into the muscle, trailing up each thigh. I'd better end this quickly. My fingers find their way into my boot and pull out one of my daggers, fiddling with it until I hold the hilt in my fist and slip the blade into my sleeve.

"Get up." Callisto yanks me up by my hair, and Jupiter reestablishes his death grip around my neck.

If I survive this, I'd like to slap her, something I've never done to anyone in my whole life.

But first I need to escape this choke hold—again.

Jupiter is about thirty centimeters taller than me, but he's slouching, so I should aim approximately twelve centimeters above my head. My right hand reaches up behind me and smacks the hilt of the dagger into the joint where his jaw connects with his cheek. His mandible slides leftward with a *crack*. He collapses without even a whimper.

If Wes were here, he'd be pleased with my use of his sneaky trick for knocking people out. Moving the mandible triggers the cranial nerve and causes immediate unconsciousness.

But one major concern remains, and she's furious.

"You *fusing* piece of *grit*!" Callisto pulls out another long knife.

With the dagger, I block her first blow, an obvious one at my chest. But if I can't move my legs without losing even more blood, I can't keep fighting. Leaning against a wall to stay upright isn't proper sparring technique.

Callisto rains blows onto my body, managing to slash my upper left arm. It goes cold as the blood flows free.

This is the end of my time as a trainee. If she manages to take off a limb, I'll be unable to pay for a reattachment operation or a prosthetic. I'll become a cripple, leaching off society, and my siblings will have nothing, not even a mother.

Callisto slashes my left shoulder, cutting even deeper.

Soft white light approaches us in the hallway. Is the sun coming up already, or are my senses disintegrating?

"What is this mess?"

I never thought I'd be so glad to hear Yinha's voice.

Everyone stops moving. Yinha's narrowed eyes take in Jupiter's limp form, the puddles of blood at my feet, and the long knives of my assailants. Jupiter begins to stir.

"Two against one—and against the youngest trainee I've ever seen? I thought we taught you to fight fair—or at least not to steal scimitars from weapons storage."

With her here, I let myself dissolve into a bloody pile on the floor.

"Hang in there." Yinha kneels, takes off her jacket, and ties the sleeve so tightly around my arm that it no longer feels hot or cold—just *numb.* She types something onto her handscreen. "Someone from Medical is coming to help."

Callisto pleads in a nasal, high voice, "Captain, we can explain everything."

"Good. Now if you'll answer a few questions for me . . ." Yinha rises up and pokes her handscreen until it shows Callisto's and Jupiter's heart rates, hormone levels, and vocal quality. She hands them each a pair of glasses that will track pupil size and eye movement. I sit straighter so I can see Yinha's handscreen from behind.

"Put the glasses on, Jupiter. No, not that low—on the bridge of your nose! How did Phaet sustain her injuries?"

"She attacked us," says Callisto. "We were so scared . . . after curfew and all. . . ."

"She pulled a knife," Jupiter adds.

I'd object to every word, but there's no need. Yinha's handscreen shows that their pupils are dilating and their eyes shifty.

"Okay," says Yinha, unconvinced. "Why'd I hear Phaet's voice instead of either of yours?"

"She was trying to get sympathy." Callisto stands motionless, though her heart rate is on the rise. "You don't understand how tricky this little girl is."

Jupiter's cortisol level approaches a peak. "She's going to come after the other trainees next. I know it."

"Enough." Yinha snatches the eye-monitoring glasses from their faces. "I'm reporting you both based on conclusive evidence that you attacked another trainee." She gestures at the blood on the floor. "I do in fact have eyes."

Callisto sneers, dropping the innocent façade at last. "Yeah, and we can never tell when they're open."

Yinha and I stiffen at the attack on our shared Chinese ancestry.

"You can't hurt us, *Captain*. Jupiter's dad, the Base IV Militia *general*"—Callisto pauses for emphasis—"will get rid of you before you've opened your mouth to report me. And so could my mom, you know, on the Standing Committee."

Yinha flexes her narrow jaw, speechless. Jupiter's father runs the Base IV Militia; Callisto is the daughter of Base IV representative Andromeda Chi. These must be unspoken "secrets" among the instructors. That's why Yinha didn't expel Jupiter and his cronies after the knife slashing, the friendly fire, the failed ambushes—why she deducted points from their evaluations in tiny amounts and why Arcturus ignored their transgressions. It's why they had so many points to begin with. Callisto and Jupiter control Yinha as much as she does them.

Now I understand why no one from Defense or Medical showed up to investigate my abnormal handscreen feed—and why Callisto and Jupiter knew about Mom's predicament.

"Sorry, Phaet," says Yinha. "I should have hauled myself here faster, before they hurt you . . . hey, who am I to tell you trainees to move it?"

Soft footfalls approach, rubber against tiles, as familiar to me from hours of trying to match them as my own. No one else seems to notice—especially Yinha, who continues mumbling apologies.

At once, the dark hallway is less of a menace.

Everyone ogles Wes as he rounds the bend and skids to a stop. His eyes reflect the light from Yinha's handscreen. When he spots me, he drops to his knees, props up my back with sturdy hands, and pushes the mussed hair back from my forehead.

"Oh God. Which of these fiends gets retribution from me first?"

"Shh," I mouth. He doesn't need to punish anyone. Being here is enough.

I release my grip on consciousness. Everything dissolves like spiral galaxies through an unfocused telescope, everything except an alabaster oval and two specks of silver.

21

SINGING. A BOY, SINGING. FAT GREEN FRUITS hang above my head; long, pointed leaves cast shadows on my white robes, which spread across the ground beneath my back. I'm in the greenhouses, watching sunlight fade into shadow, clasping Umbriel's hand. I never knew he could sing my cares away, open up space in my heart for sunshine and music and the clean green smell of chlorophyll.

But Umbriel's real voice is a rumble like the deep whir of the solar-powered generators. Even when he was younger, it was never silky like the inside of an avocado, never capable of low timbres and high hums.

I open my eyes, expecting to see him. And there he is, tan skin and all, with the mole beneath his left eye and the question mark lock of hair dangling between his brows. But Umbriel's face has the haze of a dream, as if there's a scratched-up plastic film covering it—one that I can't peel off, because I can't find where it ends.

"Stripes?" Would Umbriel ever call me that?

The music has stopped.

I blink in my dream, open my eyes, and open them again to take in reality. I'm in the Medical quarters, with Wes bent over my cot, looking intently into my face. He has eight little freckles across the bridge of his nose. There's a definite zigzag pattern. If they were connected with little line segments, they would make a path, jagged like the constellation Draco, from below the center of one eye to the area beneath the other.

"Did I wake you up?" Wes retreats to a standing position, hands clasped to conceal his handscreen. "Er, sorry if that was the case."

"Where's Yinha?" I croak. Last night, if I wasn't hallucinating, she acted so strangely, speaking comforting words to me . . . using a finger, not a handscreen, to check my pulse.

"Officer duties," Wes says. "She asked me to stay when she needed to leave, but following orders isn't the only reason I'm here. I'm glad to see you conscious."

So Yinha's kindness wasn't my imagination. Neither is Wes's. Checking that my left hand is completely covered by the blankets, I say, "You were singing?"

Wes's cheeks flush the pink of cherry blossoms, though his narrow scar doesn't. I'd never known his skin could be anything other than eggshell pale.

"I liked it."

He turns pinker. "I think they might've hit your head too hard. I'd do no such thing. Public singing is punishable by adhesive over the mouth for twenty-four hours."

He's teasing, but he's also right—on the Bases, only patriotic songs are allowed. A while ago, Psychology ran a study that proved that people remember things more easily if they're set to music, and the Committee decreed non-nationalistic singing a public disturbance. Mom thinks the lyrics of "Luna," our national anthem, are juvenile. Looking back, I realize she only said so in our apartment, while sitting on her handscreen. Her offhand criticisms made me squirm for reasons I only understand now, but back then I wasn't brave enough to critique them. Maybe she wrote something far worse than insults directed at a song to get charged for disruptive print.

I grind my teeth together, wishing I'd confronted her then.

"Your song didn't hurt anyone." I pat the covers by my left leg, gesturing for Wes to sit.

He does. When I bend my knees to accommodate him on the cot, the chilly pain I feel brings back everything: Jupiter, Callisto, scimitars, blackmail.

"You all right? Please tell me—does anything hurt?"

"No," I lie.

"Do—do you know what you looked like last night?" Wes has difficulty speaking, as if the words are too big for his mouth. "Blood all over your clothes, cuts everywhere? God, it was—"

"Don't worry about it," I rattle off.

"All the evidence on you is gone. The Medics got rid of every mark. Thank God."

Why does he keep saying "God"? If the security pods are on, he could get in trouble for indecent spirituality, which runs counter to unbiased scientific advancement—a core tenet of Lunar life. Religion incited conflict on Earth before and after the embargo; that's why the Committee banned it.

"What if Yinha hadn't come? You'd—argh, please, will you watch out a little more? Maybe switch cots with your friends, don't travel alone, tactics like that."

Digging around in his pants pockets, Wes pulls out a pair of glasses. "Here. These provide infrared vision. Nothing and no one will be able to ambush you in the dark again."

"Thank you," I murmur. With all the concern for my safety,

he's reminding me of Umbriel. "I haven't seen these before. Are they from Base I?"

He nods.

"Cool," I remark, even though the glasses are primitive compared to the latest sonar-vision eyewear.

Oh. Gadgets. We're due to learn about field equipment, for earthen and lunar missions, in the final two weeks. I've missed at least a day.

"What happened in training?"

"Not much. Yinha reviewed team basics, equipment maintenance, and space-suit operation."

They've started wearing pressure suits already? If I don't learn how to use one by the time I venture into the lunar plains, I could die from temperature fluctuation or decompression. I'll have to read the lengthy manual myself. "But—"

"Let yourself rest. Both of us have worked too hard lately."

"I'll sleep if you sing." Music will take me somewhere that isn't cold, hard, and painful. Better than any medication.

He shakes his head but says, "If that's what you want."

After a long moment, he starts quietly. His eyes close, and he sways as if he can feel wind around him. I briefly wonder what wind must be like, all that air moving at once.

"Have an olive,
No, have two.
Wear a dress of leaves
As the sun warms you . . ."

This time, his smooth voice reminds me of water, drizzling out of the greenhouse ceiling to nourish the plants beneath. The words stick in my mind, growing into my synapses like roots in fertile soil. Something prickles behind my ribs and spreads to my belly. I can't explain what it is, only that it's multicolored and alive and makes me hold my breath, wrap my arms around my chest, and rock myself back and forth, trying to cage it in.

> "Little girl, little friend,
> This day will never end.
> Our day will never end. . . ."

Too soon, he stops, eyes still closed, and the silence is part of the song.

When the silence reaches an acceptable length, I say, "Is there more?"

Wes opens his eyes and has to think before replying. "I don't quite remember it."

"But you do. Why don't you want to sing the rest?"

He frowns. "Well. It's my sister's absolute favorite."

He has a sister? And she listens to music? I don't remember anything about her in his stats, and I don't recall any evidence that such singing is permissible anywhere on the Moon.

"Where is she?"

"With my parents."

"Do you miss her?"

"Slightly."

"What's her name?" I can't help myself.

"Murray," he mutters cryptically, as if memories of her pain him.

Interesting name. "Is that a star?"

"It's a comet that orbits a binary star a few hundred light-years away."

"I've never heard of it."

Wes scratches his cheek with a forefinger, right along his scar. "Not many people have."

"How old is she? Is she strong, fast, and *daring*, like you?"

Eyes downcast, he chuckles at my sarcasm. "Murray is a few years older than I am. She prefers more domestic activities."

"Cooking and cleaning like Earthbound women?"

"Not necessarily," Wes retorts, but he doesn't elaborate. "What about your family? I'd like to know more about Cygnus and Anka, since you obviously adore them."

The thought of my siblings floods my brain with dopamine, that happy chemical. "Cygnus is thirteen and already wants to run everything. Before I joined Militia, he was plotting to fake his age and work in Sanitation. But InfoTech would be a better fit."

"Ambitious."

"Anka relies on him completely, and they're as close to each other as I am to Umbriel. She's eleven and entering a feisty phase that I never experienced."

"Right. I can't imagine you ever causing trouble—intentionally."

"Mm."

Pause. "What are your parents like?"

Wrong question. I fight to keep a grimace off my face.

"I'm sorry," he says. "I was never good with delicate things. Will you forget I said that?"

"It's all right." I cough away the lump in my throat. "Well, you already know that Mom's not home."

"Would you like me to fetch water?" Wes starts to stand, but I grab his forearm. I need to finish.

"Dad died on a Geology expedition when I was six."

"That's so sad to hear." A straight crease appears between his eyebrows. "Not to be callous, but I think I know why you joined Militia so early."

When I remain silent, he guesses, "Money?"

Exactly.

Sympathy and sorrow cross his features. Does he see why I've worked so hard? Will he listen to that small, merciful part of himself and let me, his de facto protégée, have the ultimate honor?

"I would help you place first, now that I know this. . . ." he trails off, and my heart swells with hope. "But I can't."

Why?

He shakes his head.

The hope crumbles to nothing. I want to hit him for letting me amass it in the first place, for withholding the reason he needs to be first. Wes is stockpiling information away from me, just when I thought we were starting to rely on each other.

"Second is fine," I spit out, though first would mean three hundred extra Sputniks, the title of sergeant, and a salary large enough to free Mom even if the Committee finds her guilty.

Second is not fine for either of us.

I'd rather he not let me win—Ariel never did. I'll get more satisfaction through my own efforts.

"I'm going to sleep," I stammer, cuing him to leave.

"That's good." Standing abruptly, he reaches a hovering hand down, as if he'll brush a runaway strand of hair from my face. He decides against it at the last instant.

The fluttering thing in my chest slows and plummets. As Wes's footsteps fade, I hum his lovely song to myself. But it doesn't remedy the fact that I might have lost him: the boy who salvaged me from mediocrity, gliding out the door.

22

"STRIPES!" THE NEXT DAY, WHEN I TROOP into the training dome on steady legs, Nash ambushes me with open arms. Since Vinasa's accident, Nash has grown bubblier, overcompensating for grief. As per our instructors' expectations, we act as if Vin never existed—actively denying the past. Our behavior disturbs me, especially because Vin, an aspiring History worker, would hate it.

"You're back! I stayed up these past two nights worrying about you and sneaking banana peels under Callisto's bedsheets."

"Was that necessary?" I ask.

"Having insomnia or making her smell funny? Yes to both."

Eri sits down with us on the viewing platform and embraces me in turn. Unlike Nash, she has grown more serious since the third evaluation.

"We visited you," Nash says. "Actually, half the trainees tried to visit you. But Canopus kicked us out. He said you had major recovering to do."

"Speaking of that," Eri says, "you should sleep in my cot tonight, so Jupiter and Callisto don't get you. Orion says Wes switches off with him and some other people. We should at least *try*—I don't mind."

"But Callisto might . . ." I'm grateful for their hospitality but worried for their welfare.

Eri grimaces. "I think we should protect each other."

Protect me—by putting herself at risk. However, it would be idiotic to keep sleeping in my usual cot, and I remind myself of my purpose in Militia now: to come out on top, because my family deserves to be together again. "If you insist."

Yinha's voice fills the room. "We'll continue our field training now. Trust the instructions from your headset. Get it? Cool."

Recorded commands play from our helmet speakers. Today, training involves excessive physical activity and little thinking. We follow every word in every sentence—at least, we're supposed to.

The training area has been altered to resemble Earth, complete with plastic-smelling trees and a squashy floor imitating mud. Even the dome's ceiling has changed from white to a sickly green-gray, mimicking the polluted sky. Each of us is weighed down by ten kilograms of equipment and supplies on our backs: jackets, heavy all-purpose helmets, weapons in our belts, and ballistic shields. I feel like one of the pack animals used by the ancient Earthbound.

A crackly voice commands me to take cover behind this tree or set up a grenade under that rock. Sometimes the orders are more complex: set up a lethal trip wire between two points in a group of three or guard the southwest corner of a hexagonal building while other unit members infiltrate the interior.

Though I'm fatigued, I pass the night sleeplessly in Eri's cot. It smells like her, spicy and sugary, but *off*—a constant reminder that up on my cot, her snoring form is exposed to danger. Thankfully, nothing stirs in the darkness.

The training area is still disguised as an Earth forest when we return for more soreness the following morning.

Yinha strides in. "Yesterday, many of you were dragging your feet. Were you *tired*? We're going to take care of that today. Have fun jogging with all your equipment. Five kilometers. Let's go."

Although all the other trainees groan, I don't let myself join them. This reminds me of the first week, when we ran in circles around the perimeter of the dome, but this time, rocks and roots bar our way, gusts of air blow from the walls to slow us, and kilograms of equipment weigh us down. I watch my feet constantly to avoid tripping. Soon, a pattern in the obstacles emerges: two low roots, a high root, a rock, a mid-sized root, an overhanging vine, and two low roots again. I break away from the horde of trainees and set a steady pace behind Wes, who, as usual, overachieves in front.

"Hello, Stripes," he says without turning.

How civil he acts, considering we haven't talked in two days! There's something different about him now that he considers me a real threat to his standing.

"Good morning." I tail him, letting his bigger body block the directed airflow so that my own running is easier.

"Are you upset by what I said?" He gets right to the point. "I was being inconsiderate—please forgive me."

There he goes with the apologies. Remembering Mom's pink skin the day everything began, I pound my simmering frustration into the ground, causing my strides to lengthen. Good, I've made practical use of my emotions.

"My family needs the prize money too. I wish I could change the situation so that this . . . pettiness . . . wouldn't come between us—"

"You can't."

He must come from poor stock as well. He had to take a small job as a department assistant, like I did. But how did he find time to practice running, fighting, and shooting? Who taught him those skills? The best explanation is that his parents are low-ranking Militia officials, but in that case they would still get decent pay, rendering the financial motive implausible. Also, if Murray is his only sibling and has a job of her own, no one is dependent on him. I wish I could find out more about his family, but my handscreen won't provide information on citizens who don't reside on Base IV.

Nothing makes sense. I dislike thinking in circles even more than jogging in circles.

"Phaet, will you please run next to me? I want to see you."

Sighing, I comply.

"I promise I will explain it all when I can." So there is something else. "We should meet back at the Medical quarters tonight. At the least, we can stay in the top two."

"Fine."

Matching our strides, Wes and I pass the slowest trainees, who have shamelessly resorted to walking. Eri whoops as we race past her, but I barely notice.

My instincts are funny. The first time I set eyes on Wes, I didn't like him. Something within me knew to beware those cold, shiny eyes.

That night, I fight with Wes as never before, testing my limits and his. We're sore from the day's labor, but our movements build to a frenzy, an ephemeral kaleidoscope of limbs. He doesn't call out suggestions anymore, needing to concentrate wholly on our duel. My fists fire like tiny sparks at his face and torso; my feet whip out in attempts to trip him.

He hooks a foot behind mine and pulls my heel from under me, the same tactic I used against Io Beta in the first evaluation. Before I fall onto my back, I throw all my weight into a punch aimed at his chest, which he deflects with his shoulder. His fingers capture my wrist; he pulls me in and hooks his elbow behind my neck.

"Gotcha." His breath tickles my ear; his sticky cheek presses against my forehead.

Inexplicably, his arm around me slackens—as does his focus. Wes *never* loses focus.

Out of concern rather than malice, I punch him in the gut. I feel a sour surge of satisfaction before his torso collapses inward, curling around itself like a withered stem. He anticlimactically plants his rear on the floor.

I retract my guilty hands and join him. "Sorry."

"I'll recover soon enough." His voice catches on a few syllables as if he's hurt. But he's emitting some kind of mirthless laughter. "You absolutely amaze me."

I inch away. Part of me had prepared for a surprise resumption of our match. "What?"

"You heard me." Wes draws himself up and raises a flat hand perpendicular to the ground. Is he going to hit me? I've never encountered this peculiar gesture.

"This is what you do—we call it a high five. Raise your hand like this. Exactly."

He slaps my hand, stinging it a bit, but it makes me feel accomplished. Victorious.

"Not so hard, is it?" he says between laughs. When he's this agreeable, it's hard to stay upset with him.

I glower at my hand in puzzlement. "So that gesture of goodwill was for socking you in the stomach."

"In essence, yes." Wes's face turns serious again. "Please don't be upset with me anymore, Phaet. We've helped each other so much."

It's true, at least in part. Wes has raised my ranking by more than a dozen places and turned me into a carbon-based fighting machine. "Besides the Jupiter debacle, how have I ever helped *you*?"

"You let me beat you nearly to a pulp on multiple occasions."

I almost laugh.

Wes tousles his hair, searching the air around us for adequate words. "All joking aside, remember how I said I'd never really found a friend in the world?"

I do.

"You might not consider me one. Not like Umbriel. But you're like the little sister I never had. You showed me what real companionship could be. . . . No matter how unlikely it seemed that we'd get along."

He called me his first friend, a little sister. An Anka of his own, as if he and I share a multitude of lovely things from childhood memories to specific sequences in our DNA. I'm not sure why, then, I feel incomplete, or what else I expected to hear.

"Come on, ready for another go?" he says.

Though my muscles burn and my back is dotted with spots of soreness, I get up. Our conversation has exhausted me as much as the workout; I put my hands on my lower back, rolling my head from side to side. My neck makes loud cracking noises.

"You all right?"

I return his previous frankness. "Sore."

We trade blows for a minute or so, but when I reach around for a right jab, pain shoots from my shoulder down my arm and through my fist. *Weak*, I think as he grabs my hand and forces it down.

He drops the fighting stance. "I don't think you're actually all right. Want me to take a look?"

I vigorously shake my head.

"It'll take a minute at most. You see, carrying heavy packs tends to strain the lumbar vertebrae and the shoulders, especially in women."

I narrow my eyes but note that he indirectly called me a *woman*—not a girl, not some imaginary little sister.

"Well—the sexes are equally valuable, yes, but their bodies are built quite differently. Not that differences shouldn't be embraced."

"Whatever." Now I sound like Anka.

"Er—you'll need to be still." Delicate fingers probe the grooves between my back muscles through my shirt. Several times I jerk, either because a nerve fires with pain or because chilly goose bumps rise on my arms.

"Knots everywhere, or as Medical calls them, myofascial trigger points. After overuse, the muscle stays permanently flexed and causes lactic acid buildup. It's not too hard to remove them with massage. Er—perhaps lie down on your stomach?"

After I do as he says, Wes sits down beside me. His cool hands roam my upper back; I suddenly feel too warm and wonder if my shirt is damp from sweat.

"Ow," I carp when he pinches the flesh over my left

shoulder blade. It feels like he's picking up the muscle and dropping it somewhere else. But after he lets go, I feel relief.

"Oops." Wes pats the area. "I should have mentioned that targeted massage can be quite painful."

He pinches again and again. Soon I'm squirming when it hurts and giggling when it tickles. "This isn't massage; this is you rearranging my back."

"I could rearrange your neurons too, if you'd like." He taps the back of my skull with his knuckles.

"You probably just killed fifty of them."

"Kid like you has a few to spare." There he goes with the compliments, but . . . "kid," yet again.

I stay silent and still for the remainder of my "treatment." Wes takes a while to finish both sides; my back feels looser but I'm still too warm.

"Thanks for being a good patient—minus the initial squirming. Would you like to walk back to the barracks now?"

Unlike the other nights, Wes wants to come with me. I could argue against his offer in a number of ways—he could get in trouble for going near the girls' cots, people would say nasty things about us, it would take longer for him to get to the boys' half of the room—but my tongue sticks to the floor of my mouth.

Wes's company provides protection, but the twinge of guilt in my gut won't leave. Had Umbriel stolen into the Medical quarters and lurked in the darkness, he would have accused me of fraternizing with my competition.

And when I lie in Eri's cot, again losing a battle with insomnia, I see Umbriel kneading his brows in disapproval as clearly as if he were imprinted on the back of my eyelids.

23

THE TENSION AMONG THE TRAINEES stretches to a breaking point as the last evaluation approaches. Jupiter lands Orion in the Medical quarters after "accidentally" positioning a trip wire near his feet. Paranoia sets in. I never wander around after lights-out without wearing Wes's infrared glasses. Nash and Eri chatter about their concern that life as a soldier will be even tougher than life as a trainee. I disagree—by then, I'll know my placement and will be freer to visit what's left of my family.

After the night he redistributed my back muscles, Wes and I get along admirably, preferring to compete as a team rather than as enemies. If we can beat the other forty-seven, the top two spots are ours. But I need the money of the first-place trainee, and I want to surpass everyone's expectations of me—even my own.

Only the number one rank will satisfy me, but to preserve our alliance, I don't say so.

In the training dome, Arcturus takes over and gives us strategy lessons for the field. The eyes of most trainees glaze over with indifference; they won't become officers anytime soon, but the highest-ranking among us sit attentively, typing with our index fingers on our handscreens. We might give orders of our own in a matter of weeks.

"Never send troops into completely unknown territory. Send a small recon team first to gather intelligence about the geography and the people. Secure the highest ground. Play to the capabilities of each soldier in your unit. Do not pause in your directives for long, lest your soldiers panic. Follow the orders from your own superiors at all times. And always secure a meeting location if anything goes wrong."

The morning of the evaluation, no one knows what to expect.

"Hope you all slept well," Yinha announces. "Today's will be the most difficult of the evaluations. We're going outside again. There will be one team of twenty-four and one team of twenty-five, each guarding a cache of supplies, represented by a green box. The object is to find the other team's box and bring it to your side of the arena. Everyone will be individually evaluated based on what we see in our cameras, set up around the area. Simple. Straightforward."

Each trainee is issued a gray pressure suit, the better to blend in with the regolith—the dusty mess that is the lunar surface's poor imitation of soil. The suits aren't as bulky as old Earthbound astronaut garb but leave a good half-centimeter of air between our bodies and the plastic-like material. I seal my limbs inside my suit without complaining, like some of the girls, that it makes me look "fat."

We've dealt with the outdoors before. I can't fathom why this will be the hardest evaluation of all—harder than that race through the Montes Carpatus.

"Outside, it's nighttime, but you may not use any illumination. The yellow team will wear helmets with dim yellow lights on the forehead and rear; the blue team will wear helmets with blue lights. This will be the only means of team identification. Shooting at the lights with your simulation Lazies and hitting them will result in the victim being physically removed from the contest."

We'll be virtually blind for this evaluation, which will make it both difficult and dangerous. I glance at Nash, whose arm envelops a hyperventilating Eri.

Vinasa—no one speaks of her, but everyone thinks of her.

"We are trying to mimic ground combat," says Yinha. "So our two top trainees will lead the teams. Follow their orders as you would any officer's."

The thought zaps me into shock. I'll be in charge of over twenty other trainees, pitted against Wes and his bloc. If we lose, my score could take a nosedive.

Yinha reads off the teams. Nash, Orion, and Io are with me on the Blue Team. Wes has Eri and the notorious trio of Jupiter, Ganymede, and Callisto on Yellow. Our teams are evenly matched in terms of skill, but Wes must deal with the three most dastardly suckers ever to pass through training. They'll probably refuse to listen to him, and the judges will find him an ineffective leader. Worse, Jupiter and Callisto won't hesitate to use their parents' power to place ahead. It's not fair, and it makes me wonder if someone in the high command is setting Wes up to lose.

The instructors issue the usual burden of equipment to carry on our backs. Then they shoo us into a Titan ship—one of the medium-sized models—and even with a suited-up Nash by my side, I panic as soon as the ship exits the air lock chamber.

My fingers and toes shake; every sound seems to arrive at my ears after a long, echoing journey. No one talks to me, though, because we're all asking ourselves the same two questions.

Will someone die today, like Vin? Will it be me?

We have fifteen minutes to explore the marked-off area and strategize before the evaluation begins. Every step I take pushes me higher and farther than I'd anticipated, but soon I remember how to move efficiently. I triple-check the gauges on the inside of my helmet to be sure that my pressure suit won't spontaneously explode in the near-vacuum that surrounds us. If Dad were here, I wonder if he'd be relieved, or proud, or concerned. . . . I don't remember him well enough to know. Would he lose his nerve, as Mom would if she knew I was in space? After his accident, she wrung her hands and screamed whenever Anka got too close to a window.

Trainees from years past have been here, traversing the sloping terrain. Patchy footsteps pepper the regolith. Boulders litter the ground, many taller than I am—perfect for cover. There's the dark outline of a low hill close to the back of the Blue half. Yellow's side is nearly the mirror image of ours, so that from the start, no one has an advantage. First things first; I'll need to change that.

I turn on my microphone. "Hi."

A few people greet me in return.

"Ideas?" I want us to think together, rather than have me make decisions in spite of having zero qualifications. Wes will likely follow standard procedure and decide everything himself, but I figure that my fifteen-year-old mind, in conjunction with twenty-three older ones, might match his genius.

A gaggle of responses overwhelms my eardrums.

"One at a time," I chide.

"The rocks are tippy," a dreamy voice replies. According to my visor screen, it's Io.

"Yeah, I tried to move one," says a boy named Pan. "They're really light; three people could pick one up."

Huh. Each rock looks as if its mass were a metric ton. Of course—the instructors designed this field to be manipulated and probably inserted fake boulders—hard shells stuffed with foam. Moon-grav also contributes by making everything lighter, about one-sixth its usual weight.

"What if we make some kind of defensive formation with the smaller rocks?" Pan says.

The rest of the team jabbers their approval before tossing out other ideas.

"A wall."

"A fortress."

Some proposals are downright ridiculous, like "chuck the boulders at the other team."

But a female teammate suggests, "Make a fort, just don't put the box in it."

I stop in my tracks. "Yep, make a circle with the boulders at the top of the hill. Good one."

"Thanks!" she gushes. "But where will we put the box?"

My team starts chattering again, sounding like twenty-three Ankas. "Put it in someone's backpack."

"Yeah, have someone carry it so that it keeps on moving."

But the simplest idea is the best. "Dig a hole," suggests Orion. "Dig a hole and stick a boulder on top. Have some people guard it."

Instead of talking, I have resorted to what I do best: listening. While arranging our defenses, we decide on a passive strategy of hiding behind boulders and ambushing attackers. Orion will lead the stealthiest of us on a miniature recon mission to discern the location of the other team's box. I'm going to hide within the boulder structure on the hill, because as Orion points out, there will be pandemonium if I'm shot down. But just in case, I give secondary command to Nash, whom people seem to like.

It's all the planning we have time for. Too soon, the match begins.

24

"GO!" YINHA YELLS.

From my vantage point, I see my team hunker down behind boulders while sinister shapes stalk toward our territory. Now that my eyes have adjusted to the dark, I can make out the fuzzy outlines of human forms. Their helmets bob up and down with each step; they're not used to moon-grav.

Orion, Pan, and a girl named Libra, on recon, cross the dividing line of lights and send me real-time updates on the other side. Yellow shoots down Libra. Once the programming in her helmet jerks her to the ground, a pair of painful-looking pincers removes her from the regolith and carries her toward the Titan.

"I can't see Wes, little piece of grit," Orion fumes. "And we have no idea where their green box is. He hid it good."

I hear frantic whispers from my teammates on defense. Wes's team is making headway.

"It's the yellow team," Nash says from below. "They're running to our side and jumping up on the boulders. Then they shoot. I think *Wezn* read your mind and knew you'd tell us to hide. We're getting killed here."

He knows me too well; I should have anticipated this. I issue new orders: "Team, get to higher ground before they reach the hill." I gesture frantically with both arms, hoping to draw the Yellow Team's attention away from a crucial boulder far to the left, the one hiding our box. "You'll have more of a vantage point if you come up here."

Several blue lights dance toward the hill. Yellow ones follow, too close. I get out my simulation Lazy, peep out from behind the boulder shielding me, and shoot at the enemy lights. It's tough, as they're continuously bouncing in different directions. Wes probably told his troops never to move in straight lines. I cheer inside when one of my shots turns a yellow light red.

"Callisto's down!" cheers a group of Blue girls.

I let myself laugh. Better that the regolith slaps her than I do.

Though Nash motions me to duck, I stay standing and continue trying to pick off the Yellow Team. I don't score any more hits, but two other lights turn red thanks to the shooting of my teammates.

I remember Arcturus's advice to keep talking. "Good work, defense. Orion, how's the other side?"

Orion turns on his microphone, panting. "You won't believe it. We made it to the top of their hill, where they had the box, and as soon as they saw us, they started chucking it to each other. Someone throws it; someone else catches it—Pan, duck!—and they take cover. We can't keep this up forever. I've lost two people already."

"Nukes on a stick," Nash swears. "Hang in there, O."

I try not to overreact. "Any ideas?"

"Half of us stay here," says Orion. "The rest go stomp on them."

"Yeah," Pan agrees. "A surge would be nice."

My legs tense, itching for action. "Orion and Pan, keep an eye on that box. I'm coming with reinforcements. Nash—*stay here.*" She protests, but I shush her with a finger. I name ten other people, and tell them to wait near the dividing line while I make my way over through enemy fire and fake boulders.

"When I say go, we run straight down the sides of the area. There are too many Yellow soldiers in the middle. Ready? Now!"

The eleven of us rise from behind boulders and sprint. We're fresh, whereas Wes's people move languidly. He's exhausted them, forgetting that not everyone can lope for kilometers on end like he can.

Orion's voice crackles in my headset again. "Hey, Stripes, I shot Ganymede pretty good. His face landed right on the ground, where it belongs."

A number of us snicker into our collective sound system.

By now, the entire Yellow Team has noticed the intruders. Their jerky movements indicate that they're waiting for a certain smooth voice in their headsets to order them around.

In my peripheral vision, I see one such confused trainee and shoot at her head. A red light appears, and I let myself whoop—alien as it feels to my vocal cords—along with the nearby members of my team. My first one-shot knockout. An invisible force, probably magnetic, knocks her to the sand.

According to my headset, it's Eri. I immediately regret my outburst.

I take cover behind a nearby boulder and catch my breath. My teammates have tracked down the throwers and are shooting at them. All is well.

Suddenly, arms embrace me from behind—one around my shoulders, one around my belly. Why didn't I check the area before I moved in? As Arcturus watches the footage, he's probably shaking his round bald head.

Is it Jupiter? He's the only one who could get such a steely hold on me, even in a pressure suit. Or is it *him*?

My assailant presses the tip of a Lazy to my helmet, over one of the blue lights. His helmet touches mine. Through the air and polycarbonate between us, I hear his voice.

"Hello." It's Wes. His voice is woolly and quiet, though I know he's yelling so I can hear.

Callisto was right—he's the sort to fix my back one day and put a simulation-blaster to my helmet the next. I want to hit myself for thinking any better of him.

With this victory, he'll be the top trainee. My ranking might drop all the way to tenth, or worse. Why betray me? And if he can't help it, why now? I'm so close to freeing Mom.

"How did you find me?" I can't help but ask.

"You always like to be able to see everything."

My heart pounds so hard I feel it in my temples, and not entirely because of rankings and points. The fear of what Wes will do next makes me want to shriek.

He continues, "I heartily apologize in advance for— *Oof*!"

The lights on his helmet turn from yellow to red, and he belly flops onto the regolith.

Sprinting away from us is a figure topped by a yellow-lit helmet, so mammoth in its pressure suit that it could only be Jupiter. If he's in luck, the instructors will pretend they never saw the friendly fire in order to keep the General happy.

Wes squirms for what seems an eternity before the pincers seize him and lift him out of sight.

THOUGH I'M PETRIFIED WITH SHOCK, I OPEN up the link and relay, "Wes is down. Hit by Jupiter."

Confused burbling streams into my ears. Orion sums it up best: "This may be the biggest favor that sucker's ever done you, but I still want to sock him for it. I think he mutinied to take command of Yellow."

"Hey, team, don't shoot Stripes," Nash warns. "She's nicer than Wes."

A few people laugh uneasily.

"Focus," I cut in. "Jupiter might know where our box is—that's why he's moving so quickly." As I speak, a micrometeorite, the first in an oncoming grit-storm, bounces off my pressure suit.

Half a dozen Yellow Team members race toward our side. Taking advantage of his immunity to rules, Jupiter likely used the zoom function on his visor before the match began, saw Blue digging a hole, and remembered which boulder we pushed on top of it. He waited until now to reveal his knowledge. With Wes gone, he can claim glory—and points—for himself.

"Everyone on the enemy side," I call. "We need to get their box. Now."

Three Yellow Team joggers still play catch with the box.

They're okay, moderately fast. But they're distracted by the laser fire of Pan and other good shots. And I'm faster.

One of them falls, and I hear Nash's low chortle.

"Nash! I told you to stay back."

"I'm more useful over here! Say you're okay with it so I don't lose points for insubordination."

"Fine . . ."

I turn my attention back to the two remaining Yellow guards. They're far from each other, tossing the box to and fro over boulders. If the one on my left continues in a straight line, I'll be in a perfect position to catch it right before it gets to him.

"Go," I tell myself, pushing up off the regolith and scurrying alongside the Yellow boy, too close for him to shoot.

His eyes grow shiny with surprise as the box hurtles toward us. It's set to go right over my head and into his hands. I elbow him in the ribs and stretch both arms to my left.

The wooden crate lands in my hands. The thing is heavier than I expected, even with moon-grav; no wonder the Yellow Team seemed weary. But I can't be like them. Putting on an extra burst of speed, I scamper in a zigzag pattern, hoping to avoid the shots I imagine are aimed at my head.

The dividing line glows a hundred meters away. The boulders are sparser here—and that's when I see the enemy. Several silhouettes, one of them noticeably bigger than the others, are positioned every few meters along the line, barring my way.

"I've got it, team. I'm coming!" I raise my voice to an unprecedented loudness. "Obstruction at the dividing line."

The shots behind me grow closer and more frequent. I dig

my boots hard into the regolith, trying to lengthen my strides, but I only bounce higher, making me an easy target.

Jupiter and comrades have noticed my flight and are firing at me too. Meanwhile, my teammates assault my ears with bad news.

"They've taken down more of us!"

"They're digging! With their hands!"

This is a comprehensive disaster: if I get shot down, Blue probably won't be able to retake the box.

What would Wes do? He wouldn't have gotten into this situation in the first place, surrounded in the open on enemy terrain, but if he somehow did, he would observe, think, and get out. I scan my destination again. Two of my teammates canter toward the dividing line. Someone shoots down Jupiter, and whoops when he falls face-first. Behind him, surveying the chaos around her, is Io. She's so close.

"Io! Hold your arms out!" I give simple directions in the hope that she might actually follow them.

So much for all the physics I've learned. I don't have the time to run calculations in my mind before applying a diagonal push to the back of the box, which sails in a parabola over the line. One of Jupiter's troops leaps up to catch it, but he overestimates the force needed to match its height and hovers in space as the box passes under the bottoms of his boots.

That's all I see before the suit locks up around me, and I fall into the regolith's embrace.

26

WHITE. BLAST, IT STINGS. AS MY PUPILS shrink to accommodate the lighting inside the Titan, I become aware of cheers erupting on the right side of the cabin.

Sitting on the shoulders of the rest of my team, Io cradles the green box in her arms as if it were a newborn.

Blue won.

"Amazing job, Stripes," says a smooth voice, distorted because of the helmet I'm still wearing. I behold the person I want to both hug and strangle, kneeling beside my prone body and offering a hand to help me up.

I bare my teeth.

"Shh." Wes grabs one of my limp, gloved hands, and with a minimum of contributions from me, arranges my body into a sitting position. He gently removes my helmet.

Without receiving any instructions from my conscious mind, my arms pull him to me in a hug. He doesn't respond—have I done something wrong? But soon I feel the warmth of his hands on my back and relax into them.

"There you are. Number one." His breath moves the hair on the right side of my head.

Number one, unbelievable as it is. I jerk my arms, letting out a little yelp. How could mere flesh contain so much happiness?

Even with my dumb luck, I probably accumulated an astronomical number of points from my stunts—and I'm proud of every one of those antics.

Mom can leave her prison cell. When I become a sergeant, I'll have enough bribe money from my first month's salary to preserve her freedom, no matter what happens at her trial. My heart swells with the love that has sustained me these past weeks—and with liberation, however fleeting, from duty. Now I can rest, having played my role in bringing normality back to Theta 808 and survived.

But Wes needed to place first too. "Sorry for taking your spot," I say.

His shoulders move under my embrace. "Watching you out there was almost as good as winning."

I squeeze him one last time before pulling my arms back where they belong. Already, members of my team have shifted their attention from Io to us. I scramble to my feet like a sprout growing off kilter and steel myself for the hugs and handshakes to come.

Three hours later, in the dome, trainees pile on top of each other to get a glimpse of the final rankings. When I see them, I bounce on the balls of my feet and wring my hands, unable to contain my joy.

1. PHAET THETA precedes 2. WEZN KAPPA. I'm relieved, because he could have slipped further down. Third is Callisto—what else was I expecting? If she placed any lower, her mother would fire Yinha and the other instructors. Fourth is Orion, who deserves every point he got. Fifth is Nash, who must have scored high based on her performance as my second-in-command.

Jupiter comes in at sixth. His bulbous forehead appears even bigger now that he won't stop seething.

Ganymede, who doesn't have powerful parents, places somewhere in the thirties with the likes of Eri. With a laugh, I realize that Io's lucky catch moved her up to twenty-eighth. My heart warms at the sight of her dreamy smile. I never thought I could grow to like such a funny-minded person.

Yinha's amplified voice ends both the celebration and the fuming. "Everyone sit on the viewing platform in order of ranking. Cool?" She's standing on a smaller floating platform with several other officers, including Arcturus Theta and a giant man with a protruding forehead who wears the general insignia, a clockwise swirl representing a mighty spiral galaxy. He could only be Jupiter's father.

I take the seat on the lower left with the number 1; the chair feels too wide, as if my little frame and little personality don't fit my new role.

When Wes sits to my right, it registers: I beat him. It's not as satisfying as I imagined, because his efforts got me here. But he's wearing a joyful expression, not the dimmed smile I've come to expect, so I erase the doubt and color my perception with gratitude.

A projected image of the lunar flag appears on the far wall. It's a square, with a black top half and a white bottom half. Three white stars form an arc in the black section, just as three black stars form an arc in the white; together, they make a hexagon that represents the six bases. Since three bases are usually in sunlight and three in darkness, it's a fitting symbolic image. Mom always said the flag reminded her of an old Earthbound design; I forget the name, remembering only that it's two syllables that start with a *y* sound.

As the lights dim, Yinha invites us to stand and sing the national anthem.

> "Luna, Luna,
> Once a sphere on high,
> Now our home in the sky.
> Survive and prosper
> Take the bounty nature offers.
> Oh, the Earthbound below
> The truth they'll never know.
> Silver mountains, blackest seas—
> Only here is mankind free."

Lights illuminate the dome once more, and the trainees—rather, soldiers—cheer. Chills climb up my spine, as if someone's icy fingers were tickling the vertebrae one at a time. It's the first time I've sung the words and thought about their meaning, into what I will now fight to defend. We're "free," but from what? Not material want, heaps of which I witnessed in Shelter, or direct commands, which govern my life here.

Jupiter's father rises and speaks in a magnified voice, his tone deep like Umbriel's but crystalline with cunning. The General's son may be rash, but the father is as composed as a sheet of graphite.

"Congratulations on completing training and joining the Base IV Militia. Many of you may celebrate these next two years as an opportunity to serve the Moon. A number of you dread them. But I tell you this: we live in the greatest civilization ever created by man. It is a privilege to defend it!"

Forty-seven trainees—all of us except me and Wes—hoot their approval.

"Every one of you," he says, "should swell with honor as you ride your hover-seat to the platform and allow me to attach the private insignia to your jacket. I did the same when I was young. I never left. I continue to serve the honorable Standing Committee. My fervor led me to become general of the Base IV Militia."

"Here we behold an excessively humble man," Wes observes out of the side of his mouth.

Yinha calls names, starting with trainee number forty-nine, Europa Nu. Upon arriving at the platform, she tumbles out of her chair in her eagerness to shake the General's hand and receive her adhesive insignia, a white circle of cloth with a simplified representation of an atom, complete with a nucleus and electron cloud, stitched upon it.

Somewhere in the teens, the insignia changes to the special private symbol, a bigger white circle with a benzene ring. As one ascends the Militia hierarchy, the symbols grow larger in scale, from the atom of a private to the spiral galaxy of a general. Objects, such as the sergeant's microchip, represent things the Militia considers indispensable. Jupiter, number six, receives a violent pat on the back from his father and a yellow square labeled CORPORAL. Upon the patch is an animal cell—a compartmentalized blob with short cilia on its surface. As Jupiter trudges away, the General glares at his back, his eyes blaming his son for not being good enough. Beside me, Wes chuckles.

Nash, Orion, and Callisto solemnly receive their patches.

The first two, to my surprise, don't grin or laugh; I thought they would find something funny in seeing a huge, middle-aged man frowning at the people who bested his son.

"Wezn Kappa." As Wes rides to the platform, the General continues, "Typically, second-place trainees don't rank higher than corporal. But this cohort is unusually talented. Upon careful consideration, we have decided to award Wezn the title of sergeant."

He produces a red diamond with a gold computer chip stitched upon it and presses it to Wes's jacket. As Wes rides back, I notice his name stitched in small letters below the word, SERGEANT.

If he's a sergeant . . .

"Our last trainee has displayed unusual physical and mental discipline, as well as leadership and bravery, in spite of being only fifteen years old. What you will hear next is unprecedented," the General says in a monotone. Despite the obvious praise, he doesn't seem to like me.

"After much *deliberation*"—he emphasizes the last word with a brief incline of his head—"and with a formal commission from the Standing Committee . . . We award Phaet Theta the rank of captain."

27

DISBELIEF CLOUDS MY VISION EVEN AS MY chair lurches forward. Ecstatic, I nearly topple off; the lower half of my face smarts from smiling.

The applause deafens me. I disembark and walk toward the General on the platform. Like Jupiter, he squeezes my hand so hard that the bones chafe against cartilage.

The insignia is a squat silver dagger that reads CAPTAIN, with PHAET THETA embroidered below. Yinha beams at me as the General attaches the badge to my chest, indicating her own with a reedy finger. Like her, I now have teaching privileges and, in wartime, command of a company of soldiers. It's the first time I've seen her smile.

When I return to the viewing platform, the General makes more tiresome comments about pride and patriotism. Finally, he lets the restless trainees leave. We must pack our things away; tomorrow we'll move into new quarters in the main part of the Defense compound, and neophyte trainees will take our place in the barracks.

I don't have much to bring, only a few sets of shirts and pants and my old white robes. I thought my load would contain more, but I realize that the things I was preparing to take aren't material. They're people. Nash, Eri, Orion . . . With my new title, I won't see them often.

Nash voices my thoughts. "Training was . . . tough. And I'm sorry for being mean to you the first week. But I was glad to have you around—I'll think about you a lot, Stripes."

When she embraces me, she plants a sloppy kiss on my cheek that makes me feel happy and sad at the same time.

Other people come up to my cot and hug me. The finality of this farewell hits like a side jab from Wes, hammering in the reality again and again. If I ever see my friends, it will be to lead them on missions or patrol. I'll give them direct orders and evaluate their performances. Two years from now, when they go on to Specialization or return home, I must stay in Defense.

What about the greenhouses? Finishing Primary? Finding a job in Bioengineering, as I've studied to do for ten years? And Umbriel—will he want to spend his life with a soldier? I'll never have the life of quiet innovation that I'd imagined.

Ninety-nine percent of base doors are now open to me via my captain's fingerprint, but hundreds of intangible ones are shutting tight. I *did* join Militia without thinking about the long-term repercussions. If I hadn't left home for this place—to rescue Mom, to keep my family safe—I could still be looking at my future with a hint of happiness.

Instead, my life is on autopilot.

But there on my handscreen are 3,500 Sputniks, waiting to leap out of the family account and free Mom.

Mind fuzzy, I make my way through the twisting corridors to the Defense exit. Yinha is waiting for me. She grabs my arm.

"I need to talk to you for a few minutes. It's important—about your new job."

"Gotta go." I accelerate, but Yinha's fingers dig into my flesh. Her inconsistency hurts my head. I don't know when she'll act friendly or push me around like a superior, a position—stupefying, no?—she no longer holds.

"Where to? It must be important, because I've got urgent advice for you. Your captain duties technically started the minute you got that insignia. Thought you'd want some pointers from me before you mess up."

I freeze. Leaving Mom in Penitentiary for a second longer than necessary pains me, but she must wait a few minutes for me to dampen Yinha's obvious suspicion by complying.

We walk into the busy dinnertime hallways of Base IV, where the security pods spread their attention among hundreds of commuters. The clamor will muffle whatever Yinha wants to say. People stand straighter as we pass, moving out of our way when they see the patches on our jackets. We reach the Atrium in record time. Adding to the strangeness is the realization, when I peek into a civilian security mirror, that Yinha is shorter than I remembered—shorter than me, in fact.

"First of all, congratulations. Saw something in you from day one." Yinha's tone isn't condescending or flat; she doesn't even utter the word *cool*. She pulls me into the entrance of the Market Department. People are buying groceries or sitting at small circular tables, shoveling cooked food into their mouths.

"Dinner's on me. That's nonnegotiable." She reaches into a refrigeration unit and snatches two packages of sushi; each piece has been molded into a star shape, with either white or black rice. Her handscreen flashes as Sputniks are deducted. I'm too shocked to object. I've never had sushi before; seaweed cultivation and laboratory meat formulation are notoriously costly. Will my new life be like this—having the money to casually buy luxury dinners for other people?

As we move toward the rear of Market, a dark-eyed private, at least four years older than me, emerges from a group of friends and presents me with the back of his hand.

"Captain? Can I have your autograph?"

Beside me, Yinha smirks but remains silent. One of the other boys whispers something, causing the rest to snigger into their palms.

With my forefinger, I open a blank document on the private's handscreen and shakily scrawl my initials. Only thirty minutes have passed since my promotion, but it has been enough time for my notoriety to spread through Defense. This soldier wants to get a piece of me, before it reaches the remainder of the base. People will discuss me when I'm not around, which is bad enough, and not because I discovered or invented something useful. Base residents admire our best researchers and engineers but fear top military personnel. I don't want to be feared.

"Thank you! I'll keep this close to my heart." The private inclines his head and takes off with the rest of the group, leaving my cheeks too fiery for my liking.

"Typical fan boy. He was supposed to *salute* you first. Not cool." Still wearing a superior smile, Yinha chooses a tiny table at which we're enveloped by noise. She opens her sushi but otherwise ignores the food. Her dark eyes rotate, scanning the vicinity for security pods and finding none. Those things wouldn't stalk two officials with clean criminal records.

"Do you know why you're a captain?"

"My training score?"

"You scored well, but you had only three points more than Wezn. And we employ enough captains in Militia already."

Does Yinha consider me a threat to her position? It's plausible, but no ill-meaning officer would buy her colleague a dinner of sushi—maybe cucumber salad.

"Who had the idea to rank me so high?"

She pulls a sour face. "The General. Jupiter's father."

My mouth drops open. To cover my surprise and vulnerability, I drop a piece of sushi on my tongue with the sterilized glass chopsticks. The wasabi sticking to the roll hits my eyes, which involuntarily leak tears.

Yinha continues. "Some people in the scoring panel didn't like your little stunt during the third evaluation—steering the ship away from the enemy target against Jupiter's direct orders. You're lucky you got the points that you did."

"But it was a civilian ship—"

"It would've been a threat to the Bases if it were really Batterer. If there had been soldiers aboard, if they were posing as civilians and later carried out an attack— Well, chaos."

Yinha chomps on a piece of wasabi-laden sushi. Her eyes don't water at all. "Some of them didn't like your leadership style in the last evaluation either. Not enough valor, they said, though I argued that you displayed an unusual amount."

"Thanks."

"They know about your workouts with Wes, but they liked the effort, so they let those continue. There are *so* many security pods zooming around Defense, several of which filmed you. They're even in the troops' residences."

Surveillance—I guess I expected that. "Are they watching me now?"

"There are at least three pods in your new apartment. I know because I counted three in mine."

The rice from the sushi sticks in my throat.

"I don't like being watched but, obviously, it's for my safety and the security of the Bases."

I make a big show of checking the time on my handscreen.

"My family's waiting for me," I say, telling a quarter of the truth.

"Pity." Yinha crosses her arms and drums her fingers on her triceps. She doesn't believe me. "Hold on a few more seconds and let me finish—cool? Listen, I don't interact much with the higher-up commanders. But I know them. They have some larger motive for promoting you to captain—larger than putting you in an apartment with three pods to watch you—but I don't know what it is. Be careful, Stripes."

I don't want to listen anymore, because she could very well be right. Disregarding my manners, shuddering at what the Militia's "larger motive" might be and whether it has anything to do with the accusations against Mom, I stuff my mostly uneaten sushi into my empty canteen and rise from the table. "Thanks for the food. My sister would love to try sushi."

"Be back before curfew," Yinha says. "I need to escort you to your new home."

Not quite. Home has never been anywhere other than apartment number 808, Theta complex. This new apartment will simply be where I sleep.

28

I SPREAD MY FEET AS WIDELY ON THE FLOOR of the Law lobby as I can without looking absurd and point in a haughty manner to the insignia on my chest. Several of my Militia subordinates line the walls, giving me an extra incentive to look authoritative.

"I'm here to pay Mira Theta's bail."

The middle-aged receptionist flips through the touch screens around her desk. She has smooth, dark skin and a wide nose that looks proportional when her lips stretch into an even wider smile.

"You're her genius older daughter, no? She told me stories about you."

I drop my stiff Yinha face, taken aback.

"I'm usually with the prisoners, keeping them in line—well, Mira never needed to be kept in line. Today is my desk day."

We shake hands; she pulls back as soon as my profile appears on her handscreen, intimidated by my Militia rank. Glancing down at my handscreen, I learn that she's Deima Upsilon, Penitentiary warden.

"Now put your left hand up on the counter. . . ."

I pull up my family's loaded bank account and present her with my handscreen.

"This is a great day for Mira. She's getting out of custody *and* finding out her daughter's a captain."

Is she worried? She sounds overly optimistic.

Deima taps my handscreen and presses her thumb to it. The touch screens on her desk flash the words, BAIL AUTHORIZED. Without the bail money, my family still has more than two hundred Sputniks to spare. Good.

"All righty," says Deima. "Your mom's trial just got moved up about fifteen months, to this August the twenty-fourth, 17:00, in Law Chamber 144. Sound good?"

I'm so relieved I could skip across the lobby. My family now has a year and a half less to wait. Maybe the change means Law will treat Mom with mercy. I breathe slowly, fighting the sudden hope. It'll probably lead to disappointment.

"*Mira*culous." Deima laughs at her own pun. I can see why Mom got along with her. "Enough dallying. Come with me."

Deima takes me through the lobby and two sets of doors into the dimly lit Penitentiary tower. We board an elevator with graying walls.

"I'm not supposed to let people into the prison area, but you shouldn't have to wait any longer to see your mom. Besides, *Captain*, you're part of the 0.2 percent of Base IV's population that's allowed up here."

Deima's clever. I'm glad that Mom had her.

We get off at the fourteenth floor. My pupils dilate as soon as the elevator doors close behind us. Floor 14 is completely dark and completely silent. Using my handscreen for illumination, I discern long spans of identical doors curving into the distance on my left and right. Militia guards are positioned every fifty meters or so along the wall. The halls branch off quickly. The architects of this place did a good job ensuring that it would be difficult for anyone to get in or out.

Deima stops at Cell 1494. What an unlucky number.

"Don't be scared when you see your mom. I . . . I didn't do this to her," Deima says. "It was the other wardens. Really, don't be scared."

Her words don't have the effect she intends. They terrify me.

Deima presses her thumb to the scanner, sticks her tongue out for another contraption to verify, and says slowly into some sort of microphone, "Deima Epsilon."

All three detectors blink green. One by one, three sets of double doors slide open to reveal a tiny white cylindrical cell so small that my arms can span its radius. There's a stool in the center of the room, with a sad little pail pushed underneath to hold human waste. Other than that, there's something I can barely identify as a person, curled on a ragged mat, robes torn and browned with grime. She seems to be sleeping, if it's possible to sleep while in such a state.

My mother's waist-length hair is gone. Black fuzz covers her skull; her head is small and bumpy, unrecognizable. But the intelligent eyes that fly open when the doors slide apart are indisputably my mother's, as are the flared nostrils and the overall expression of disbelief.

"Phaet—you came for me." My mother stretches out her hand, but I'm too paralyzed with joy to do anything but stare. "Welcome to my luxury apartment."

"I'm here to evict you," I fire back, pulling her into a hug and doing my best not to crush her. I'll never let go of her again.

"You two are free to go," Deima says. "Good luck with the trial, Mira."

"Thank you." Mom takes Deima's proffered hand and stands. She puts her hand on my cheek, as if checking to see whether this strange soldier is really her offspring. She squeezes the skin over the bone, as she used to do when I was younger, but it hurts far more than when my face was fleshy and her fingers weren't feeble twigs coated with greenish skin.

Deima claps her on the shoulder. "You're my favorite inmate. I'm going to miss you."

"You were my favorite warden. I'll miss you as well, but I hope I never see you again."

All three of us laugh.

I take her arm, and we shuffle back the way I came. My mother slips every few meters, her legs clumsy with disuse. Seemingly smaller than ever, she positions herself behind me whenever we pass a helmeted guard, like a novice private caught in enemy fire. The Beetles ignore us, except to salute in response to my insignia.

When we reach the bustling Atrium, Mom staggers again from the sudden increase in sensory input, shuts her eyes, and jams an index finger in each ear.

I pull her to a bench on the side of the dome, as she used to do for me when I was younger and all the people in the Atrium frightened me. If everything were as nature meant it to be, Mom wouldn't lean on me for another twenty years.

In the security mirrors, I see people staring at us with morbid inquisitiveness, drawn by the irony of what probably looks like a streaky-haired crone guiding a starved, black-haired boy to refuge.

Mom points at the insignia on my chest. "Congratulations, my girl." She sounds anything but happy. "Militia—of all the things in the universe . . ." Mom sits on her handscreen, lowers her voice to a whisper, and puts her lips by my ear. "Do you have friends there? Do you feel safe?"

I nod, even though both my friends and true safety are now far away.

It's enough for Mom. She straightens again. "Would you come home, maybe once a week?"

"Don't worry about it."

She looks away. "This might not be justified—but I worry that you'll change, Phaet. You're so strong and brave, and I like to think I've taught you well . . . but what if you forget where you come from?" She pulls back the sleeve of her stained robe to expose open cuts and half-formed scabs. "My guards seem to have forgotten."

I lean back, repulsed by her festering wounds, even as grief constricts my trachea.

"Full-powered Electrostuns, Phaet. They sliced my hair with a dagger, and my scalp along with it." Mom's voice rises. "They drugged my water, giving me dreams of you three—distorted and hazy dreams. And they laughed—they thought everything was funny—seemed to enjoy tormenting me—"

"Mom, stop!"

"—and I could hear them playing handscreen checkers when they were done with me. Checkers."

Mom spent fifteen years sheltering me from the darker departments. She's always hidden the important things—like when I had a sister on the way; I didn't know until I asked Dad what was wrong with Mom's belly.

Mom's head droops so that her chin nearly touches her visible sternum. "I'm sorry I told you these horrible things, Phaet. But you're growing older, and you deserve to know all about the organization you've joined. Oh, I wish you hadn't! In training, you could have been paralyzed, or dead, or made mentally ill for the rest of your life."

"All for you." She's doing something that I'll never understand, something that mothers inexplicably do: agonize about their children in the most hypocritical of instances. She shouldn't concern herself with my health; she can hardly stand, while I'm stronger than ever.

"I can't find words in this Journalist head of mine to sufficiently thank you for it." Mom squeezes my hand hard; the gesture seems to use up all the strength in her body. She rises, takes a few staggering steps, and then looks back. "Let's go to Cygnus and Anka."

I tail her and latch onto her arm. Although she smiles back at me, her eyes glaze over and avoid contact with mine. Now that I've become a captain, she can't look at me the way she used to. She can hardly look at me at all.

I watch Mom sleep for two hours and sixteen minutes while Cygnus and Anka drift in and out of her bedroom. Mom clenches her fists and kicks the covers so frequently that I'm relieved when she finally sits up, sweating but shivering. Despite her exhaustion, wakefulness seems more peaceful than reliving the horrors of Penitentiary in her dreams.

"Tell me this is real, dear," she rasps.

Indeed, she's safe, with not a Beater in sight. I mop her brow with a scrap of cloth torn from one of Anka's old robes. Now that Mom's woken up inside her own home, maybe she'll realize how much better things are.

She begins to laugh and finishes with a cough. "You didn't answer. That's how I know it's really you."

As her knobby hand tucks a strand of gray hair behind my ear, her eyes flick to the mole beneath my bottom lip. Then she catches sight of my jacket's black collar, and her left hand darts under the covers.

"I apologize—my guards wore the same black jacket. For a while, I'll be confused as to where I am." Her voice is a whisper that hardly makes it past her throat. "Is your brother home from Primary?"

I point toward the kitchenette, where my brother is toying with his handscreen and our Hemispherical Registered Processor, or HeRP. He's probably blowing off homework to mine a department or two for information that'll help in the trial; tunneling is more urgent than ever now that the date has been moved up.

Mom's eyes are cast downward. "Can you fetch him?"

She must want me to leave; she wants to enjoy being home without a reminder of how she got here.

Miffed, I walk into the living room. As I pass the kitchenette, my boots clack and echo. Four and a half pieces of leftover sushi wither on the table. After months of eating bland root vegetables, my siblings couldn't stomach the riot of flavors that Yinha so easily swallowed down.

Anka looks up from her handscreen, upon which she's doodling a floral pattern, with the same scared expression she wore when Wes first visited Theta 808. For her sake, I relax the muscles in my face before proceeding.

As I suspected, Cygnus hunches over our outmoded HeRP, waving his hands over the dome-shaped structure like some Earthbound fortune-teller. The HeRP is about as big as the top of his head; its entire surface is a screen that sheathes the other working parts. A spotted banana peel lies limp on his lap.

Coming closer, I see the screen is pistachio-colored rather than the white I remember. What's he *doing*? I squat beside the HeRP, tuck my left hand between my knees, and gesture until Cygnus notices me.

"Hi," he says, sitting on his handscreen and continuing to work with one hand. "I've been trying to jailbreak this thing for a week. 'Cause the processor's a lot faster than the one on our handscreens. That's why the color's all weird."

"Hmm."

"I'm going to remove the limits of the civilian operating system. We'll be able to change the wallpaper to whatever we like, upload stuff, run searches, contact anyone. Maybe I can even find out what they *say* Mom wrote. Just in case it'll help prove she didn't write a thing, yeah? I jailbroke my handscreen a few years ago, remember?"

"Altering HeRPs is riskier," I observe. The punishment for his trick must be hefty, and I hope he found a way to hide it.

"Not a problem." With his index finger, Cygnus drags a red box labeled ENCRYPTED KEYSTROKES to the top of the hemispherical screen. As he types, incomprehensible letters, numbers, and symbols roll across the box. "This is a Keyscrambler. After I started the jailbreak and removed the downloading restriction,

I could finally get it. Generates gibberish so no one can see what I'm typing."

"Won't someone find you?"

"Psh, no one will notice activity from this address. I'm going to put in private networks, proxies, tunnels. They won't have any idea what we're—I mean, I'm—doing, 'cause it's impossible to crack or track."

When my brother speaks in tech-talk instead of English, I wonder if he has neurons or microchips between his ears.

Wheezing coughs reach our ears from Mom's room; she must be getting impatient. Cygnus freezes. "She all right?"

Forgetting both me and the HeRP, he rushes into Mom's room, coming to kneel by her side with his handscreen under his rear. Although a wave of sickly smells hits me, I follow him until I reach the doorway, still hoping to be included in the conversation.

Mom picks a stray eyelash off Cygnus's cheek with her cracked yellow fingernails. "Give your eyes a break from that thing once in a while."

"I'm *fine*. If stuff gets blurry, then Phaet can buy me bionic eyes from Medical."

Mom ignores the reference to my—our—improved financial situation. "What are you working on now?"

"Jailbreaking. Changing the HeRP settings so that we can access other systems on the base, like I do on my handscreen—but faster. Thought it would help you."

"Fascinating. And timely." Mom turns toward the door, registering my presence. The parentheses around her mouth deepen. "Phaet, you don't need to stay. If your superiors need you back in Defense . . ."

But I want to stay. And I will, because something's off, and it's not just the color of the HeRP screen. Not only is Mom saying I can leave; she *wants* me to leave.

"Do you want to take anything with you? Blankets? Something to eat? The kitchen's empty, but I'll start cooking when I feel better. I remember the utter mediocrity of Militia fare. . . . Should I bring you something later this week? Pepper lasagna? Papaya juice?"

I shake my head, though Mom's offer makes my mouth water and my heart fill with gratitude. Not only would a Theta-to-Defense delivery service embarrass me in front of my older colleagues, but it would also heighten my homesickness. "I have everything I need now—my apartment's supposed to be really nice, and I can buy things from Market."

"You sure?" Mom pinches her lips, dejection in her tired eyes. "I wouldn't go in. You could meet me at the Defense entrance."

I clench and unclench the muscles in my legs. Does she still see me as a child, after everything I've accomplished? "I'll take care of myself."

Mom's glumness turns into irritation, and I realize my mistake. "For fifteen years, I've given you the best I could . . . with my Journalist's pay. I tried, but now Militia tends to you better than your own mother."

"I didn't mean that—"

"I'm sorry, my girl." She swallows hard, moving the sagging skin hanging from her hollowed-out neck. "It's just that . . . it's hard to look at you, with those weapons clipped to your belt, and still see the child I raised. They used those same weapons on me."

"But Shelter." Let her imagine what my siblings and I would have endured if I hadn't become a trainee.

"Better than Defense. Safer, and with fewer threats to the goodness of your soul." She turns to Cygnus, irritating me more. "If you were a stranger and saw this captain in the hallway, what would you think? Wouldn't she frighten you? You'd wonder what she did to become a captain, and if she'd hurt you to remain one."

"I . . . I don't know. . . ." Cygnus looks desperately at the door, his escape.

"Phaet," Mom says, "I apologize for my honesty, but . . . I wish you hadn't joined."

"Stop it!" I shriek, straining my vocal cords. In Mom's eyes—maybe in Cygnus's too—I'm bordering on Beater behavior. I'll show her that I haven't changed, treat my family the same as before I left, if not better.

We hear the patter of small feet rushing to the doorway. Anka tumbles into Mom's bedroom and dashes behind Cygnus, using him as a shield against me. "What's Phaet yelling about?"

Me, yelling?

"Oh, Anka," says Mom, "you don't need to witness this. Phaet, can you take your sister outside and help her with her homework?"

I stare at Mom, not moving, not even blinking.

She lowers her head; her chest heaves. When she looks back up, she's crying. "You've entered another world now."

I stamp my black boot on the floor. Anka shrinks farther back, and Mom clenches her eyes shut, squeezing more tears out.

"See?" Mom glares at where I've put my foot down as if she's expecting to see a pothole there. "You've changed. I'm not sure how to deal with you anymore."

"Phaet, calm down. . . ." says Cygnus. I know he doesn't mean to alienate me, but it's happening nonetheless. I extracted Mom from Penitentiary and my siblings from Shelter, and now they treat me like an outsider.

"I'm sorry, dear Phaet," Mom says. "Maybe . . . maybe we need some time apart. I can love you from a distance, but I haven't an inkling how to do it up close. It's impossible to know what to think of you anymore."

She's cracked something inside me wide open. I stride to the door, but I can't leave just yet.

"*Fine*," I say, infusing the word with venom. "Then don't think about me at all. You're on your own now."

I return to Defense two minutes before curfew.

"Not cool," Yinha scolds me, powering up her Pygmette speeder. The little ship, suitable for both on-base and outdoors, is shaped more like a clown fish than a shark. As its three-pronged stand retracts, it lifts Yinha into the air. "A traffic jam in the Atrium and you would've been late."

"Family's important." I avoid Yinha's gaze; so much pain courses through me that one look in my eyes would give it away.

"You sound like my mom, kiddo. Are you okay?" Yinha leans forward. "Your face looks like a parachute that's about to spring a leak."

"Don't worry about it."

I vault into the seat next to Yinha. We zoom through the

lobby, through twisting hallways that lead to the housing wing, up a spiral staircase, and through doors, spaced throughout our journey, that progressively require more identification. At the fourth, I watch over Yinha's shoulder as she jams her thumb on the sensor, tugs her eyelids apart for a retinal scan, extends her tongue to an unseen camera, and types MILKI8WEI8 into a keypad lock.

At first, I'm confused as to why there isn't an elevator, but I realize that the endless stairs provide either a cardiovascular workout or steering practice for anyone who can afford a Pygmette.

The door opens and we zoom into the next leg of the staircase.

"All the privates live on the first six floors," Yinha says. "The seventh is for corporals and sergeants. The eighth is for us and the majors—there aren't many of us, but our apartments are bigger. Don't bother visiting the top two levels. The four colonels and the General live there. I'm pretty sure that if you're not a Sanitation maid and you try to intrude, some kind of Electrostun will zap you into a pile of human compost."

Yinha parks the Pygmette in front of two doors with silver daggers, which are taller than I am, painted on the front. She opens the one on the right, orders me to sleep tight, and disappears into the apartment on the left.

My new living space reminds me with every generously furnished square meter that I live in a different world from my family. If I were happier, I'd run laps around the living room, cartwheel across the dining table, drown in the shower chamber, and bounce across the bed. While I reside here, I won't shiver at night under the heat-retaining gel comforter or wish for a glimpse of the outside landscape. With shaky steps, I approach the floor-to-ceiling window made of tinted photovoltaic glass.

The graphite-colored swells and dips of Oceanus Procellarum spread out below me, and a small peak rises in the distance like a curled knuckle raised to the sky. But enjoying the magnificent view dredges up guilt. I adjust the window glass so that it blocks all sunlight and turn to face my clinically clean apartment, devoid of people and even small personal comforts, like my moss garden. Has Anka remembered to water it?

I drag the comforter to the memory-foam sofa and lie down, taking a massive burden off my feet. I wish for dull dreams, to take up space in my mind and relegate the hurt from Theta 808 to the margins.

After what feels like only seconds of sleep, my apartment flashes like a blue strobe light. I roll off the couch and stumble to the door barefoot to find Yinha suited up. "Look sharp, sleepy. Skat wants to see you at headquarters. Pay attention on the way there—next time, you've got to find the place yourself."

Good. Militia has an assignment for me, something to distract me from the situation at home. "Skat?"

Yinha rises on tiptoe and positions her mouth next to my ear. "Our boss, a major. I'm pretty sure some officer paid for him to get promoted—he's so lazy, I don't know how else it could have happened. Whatever he asks you to do, no matter how scary or stupid, just say yes and walk out, okay?"

I throw on my boots and tuck stray hairs into the bun I wore yesterday. Yawning, I tail Yinha to the top floor of the residence tower and march with her into the conference room, where ordinarily only colonels and the general are allowed. We salute as we enter, two fingers to our foreheads.

The room has a commonplace domed ceiling, but screens cover every inch of space with a plethora of figures and charts. A map of Earth, with its scantily populated continents, looms above us. Our satellites track each of the major mobile island cities.

Blinking orange dots represent cities in the Batterer cohort, while blue dots represent Pacifian allies. Green icons indicate nonaligned cities. We also track all of Earth's manmade satellites, which provide excellent hideouts for our enemies when they pass close to the Moon—especially the Apollo crafts, which, according to the screen, orbit 350,000 kilometers from Earth's surface.

Yinha, her face filled with wonder rather than worry, watches the icon of the largest satellite, which has been tagged with a red marker. Pacifia appropriated the International Space Station, or ISS, shortly before the Battle of Peary, to intimidate us. By attaching thrusters and accelerating the ISS, they moved it closer to the Moon, a strategy cheaper than launching their own space station.

The now-abandoned satellite's orbital path has grown eccentric because the thrusters are still attached, and it nears us at odd intervals. Now, it's aligning with the Moon, and therefore is a great place for our Earthbound enemies to launch an invasion.

Seated around the circular table are the General, who absentmindedly examines his Lazy, and a short, slouchy man in his thirties whose insignia reads MAJOR SKAT YOTTA. His head has been shaved on the sides, leaving a strip of black hair that runs from his forehead to the nape of his sunburnt neck.

Skat greets us with little more than a yawn. "So, this the new kid?"

Tearing her eyes away from the miniature ISS on the ceiling, Yinha says, "This is the new kid."

Skat turns his head toward the General; the rest of his body doesn't move. "Just the patrol duty for now?"

"We've been over this," snaps the General.

"'Kay, new kid." Skat inspects his fingernails, picking off bits of skin at the cuticles. "We have an important assignment for you . . . but it's not ready for discussion. For now, you're on Atrium patrol from 12:00 to 17:00 daily, starting the day after tomorrow. Means you oversee the privates. Can't have you sitting pretty around the Defense compound."

"Yes, sir!" I holler, sounding more excited than I feel. I grow restless thinking about the monotony of endless laps around the Atrium. I'd rather oversee privates' workouts or check on the bioweapons and nukes we've deployed in space. I'd even lead a debris cleanup team, using a special magnet and laser-equipped Titan ship to remove stray pieces of space junk, the pieces of metal and other materials left by sporadic Earthbound launches that interfere with our Earth remote-sensing and spaceflight capabilities.

But because I'm new, it's silly to wish for a better assignment.

"Yinha, show her around so she doesn't get lost," Skat adds.

"Yes, sir!"

The General takes over. "Remember, Yinha, you also have a meeting with Colonel Arcturus to prepare for the new trainees' arrival. Don't be late."

"Yes, sir!"

Crossing his feet on the table, Skat chews off part of his middle fingernail and examines the result. "What you waiting for? Leave."

That's all? They called me and Yinha up here to assign me to patrol the patrols? I imagine pulling Skat's chair out from under him so that he falls, squirming, onto the floor.

For one day, I have Yinha's tour around Defense to keep me busy.

The privates exercise in a cylinder-shaped room shabbier and larger than the training dome. They salute us halfheartedly. Only Eri smiles at me as they jog by in formation; the others stare with either mild interest, like Io, or disgust, like Ganymede. Even people who weren't in my trainee class give me looks that guarantee they'll talk about me as soon as I turn my back.

The officers' gym, one floor above the privates', looks and smells better. Expensive equipment and rows of adjustable free weights line the walls. After watching me strain to work the bench press, Yinha lies down and hoists the bar above her chest with perfect form—until a man around her age begins flirting with her, addressing her as "Yee-haw." She curses at him and leads me away to the Medical quarters lobby, where scores of soldiers wait for voluntary injections such as painkillers, caffeine shots, and muscle-enhancement drugs. At night, she scans in my thumbprint, retina, tongue, and chosen personal password of 08TO03M97 so that I can access my apartment, the Defense intranet, and the mid-level Militia files on my own.

She bets me ten Sputniks that I'll forget the "too-numerical" password within a week.

Every day after that, while Yinha's indoctrinating the new trainees, I walk endless loops around the Atrium, chastising unfocused privates and checking the civilian security mirrors for infractions that never occur. In the evenings, I grow uneasy with the absence of a sibling to help or a friend to be with. I explore to ward off loneliness and the longing to run home for a long hug—from anybody. But I can't. Neither can I approach Umbriel, who has likely heard about my actions. I'm sick of rejection.

My thumb gives me access to every department, from Shelter to Law. On my handscreen, I peruse the operating manuals for all military equipment and view the blueprints for almost every structure on the six bases scattered across the surface of the Moon. They're similar in setup, though Base I has the most complex floor plan.

I don't look up statutes on disruptive print or check the status of Mira Theta's trial.

Despite the new information crowding my head, I also don't forget my password. A week later, Yinha unhappily transfers ten Sputniks to my family account.

I'm more comfortable alone with her than in public. In Defense, lower-ranking soldiers, including my former fellow trainees, salute me wherever I go—but that's not the worst of the unwanted attention. People goggle at me when I'm on patrol; a week after I became captain, Journalism aired a news report filled with video clips from training, and the reporter commented on my "selective muteness." I had the misfortune of seeing the report in the Atrium but the fortune of wearing my helmet, whose visor I slid down before anyone could identify me.

Young girls braid silver string into their hair to mimic my gray stripes, and despite my uninviting glower, mothers approach me to ask for advice, hoping to give their daughters an edge in Primary and Militia. If I'm walking with Yinha, she apologizes about our next meeting or training session—appointments that she fabricates on the spot—and punts me in the shin, indicating that we can escape.

Worse, my training friends are slipping away. I manage to wave to Nash only once, in a corridor. As for Wes—Eri has been assigned to his platoon, so she can talk to him all she likes. Her fiery head bobs alongside his coppery one as they traverse Defense. To avoid encountering them—together—I bury myself in my handscreen and hurry away. Every instance leaves me with a frigid soreness buried so deep inside that no amount of heat therapy could wring it out.

The monotony of Atrium patrol breaks down after a week and a half.

From my perch on the third-floor terrace, I notice a knot of people dressed in green and white exiting Market. They've stopped moving, forming a "roadblock" with respect to the surrounding crowd. Shiny black helmets zigzag toward them—privates trying to prevent a traffic jam. I descend one floor to get a closer look.

It's my family.

Mom has fallen. Although she can hardly stand, she probably insisted on walking without help. Atlas hoists her to her feet, his hands under her arms. Umbriel and Cygnus look like they want to help, but they're holding piles of vegetables—bought with my income, I imagine.

I turn away, gloom already gathering atop my shoulders to weigh me down. In another life, I might have walked with them, carrying those groceries or looking out for Beetles. Now I'm the enemy, hiding from my family while they bolt away.

They pushed me up here. I can't flip up this visor and reveal myself as long as they turn their backs on my existence.

29

THE NIGHT THAT GEOLOGY'S SEISMOLOgists say a big moonquake is coming, I huddle under the table in my empty apartment, trembling. Quakes shouldn't worry us, because the metal that composes the bases' exteriors is mixed with a flexible polymer that bends without breaking. Besides, most quakes are so tiny we can't feel them. But they remind me of Dad, and they scare me more than everything except death.

Before Dad set out on his last Geology expedition, Mom saw the forecast about the Far Side's upcoming moonquake and pressed her face against his shoulder, begging him to stay. I'd never seen her so scared—but I had seen them arguing over the previous few weeks. Although they tried to hide it from Cygnus, Anka, and me, I heard feverish whispers late at night. About something that happened long ago, and whether they should *ever* tell us about it. I still don't know how any of it fits together. Maybe it doesn't.

That last night, Mom left the bok choy and tofu in the pressure cooker, and the dish turned to mush. We didn't have dinner, but I don't remember feeling hungry.

"What'll they think of me if I don't go?" Dad said over and over. Maybe he meant his coworkers and his lab's principal investigator, or the Committee itself.

"Where are you going?" I asked. I babbled quite a lot as a child. "Can we come?"

Dad picked me up in his strong arms, even though I was a big girl, already six. "You, my dove, help Mommy while I'm gone." He kissed my forehead twice. "Okay?"

"I promise, Daddy."

He never came back, but I kept my word.

The door light flashes blue, pulling me into the present. I slide out from under the table, which is trembling even more than I am, and let Yinha in. Her unbound hair hugs her face, emphasizing the sharpness of every feature.

"Stripes, you okay? I, uh, saw your stats, and figured you might want company. This quake's going to be magnitude 4.3—definitely a doozy."

The first tremor rocks the residence tower back and forth like an upside-down pendulum. Through my window, I see clouds of dust obscure the mountain in the distance.

I clasp Yinha's hand and drag her farther into my apartment. We huddle under the oversized table, and she snakes a scrawny—but strong—arm around my ribs. I can't fully inflate my lungs, but it's a cozy feeling. "Thanks for coming."

"Thanks for letting me in," she says. "I *hate* quakes. The only thing worse than sitting through a quake is sitting through a quake alone."

I cuddle closer to her as the tower rocks again. "Aren't you a recon officer? You could go to Earth to get away from them—be gone months at a time."

"I could, yeah. But that wouldn't be cool for my big brother."

"Hmm?"

The tower bounces up and down as if we're resting on a

giant's jiggling kneecap. Yinha cringes. "Yeah. Bai was a special private, lost his leg on a recon mission. A year ago. Right around the time I got promoted. I stick around to make sure he's doing okay. Why didn't you know about him? Didn't you check my stats?"

"I don't like to make premature judgments."

Even in the dark, Yinha's face looks green. "You don't check stats? So you don't know about my cruddy Primary scores either. I used to pretend stats don't exist, just like you. But when you're a captain, you see suspicious stuff everywhere. And sometimes, knowing someone's stats is enough to save your behind and whip theirs. Since I *was* your instructor and *am* your neighbor, I thought you'd at least run a background check. Or, you know, sneak extra surveillance pods into my apartment."

She doesn't laugh—Yinha never laughs at her own punch lines—but I do. When my body is shaking with mirth, the tower's quivering doesn't feel so bad anymore.

"Recon is full of combat situations. And I'm an *awful* soldier." Yinha waves her hand in front of her nose as if she smells something foul. "Disgustingly bad."

I pull an incredulous face. She can shoot three arrows into three dummies at once and pilot a Pygmette through the smallest crannies in the Defense compound.

"Really. When I was a special private, the corporal in charge always told me not to look into people's eyes if I had to shoot them. I kept looking, anyway. Looking and missing. It's easier teaching the mechanics of killing people than actually *doing* it."

I know for sure that she approved of my refusal to attack the fake Batterer cruiser. I feel even safer, and so glad that she has taken me under her wing.

The tremors stop. Lights on my ceiling blink green, signaling the all clear. We emerge from under the table. My robe rack has been knocked over and the fruits from my countertop have toppled onto the floor, but nothing is irreparably damaged.

"Cool?" Yinha asks, dusting off her black uniform.

"Mm-hmm."

My handscreen lights up with a message delivered during the quake—it's from Defense headquarters.

CLASSIFIED MEETING, TOMORROW 07:00. CAPTAIN PHAET THETA, PRESENCE DEMANDED.

"Huh," says Yinha. "About time they gave you something to do."

"How've you liked Atrium duty?" Skat drawls, his feet perched on the table in the top-floor command center. "Well, that'll be over soon. Things are about to get more . . . more . . ."

"Labor intensive," finishes the General. He jabs a button on his handscreen, and the satellite-tracking icons disappear from the ceiling. Now, the Committee's silhouettes loom around us in a ring as if we are ten-centimeter-tall midgets trapped in the center of the conference table. The six members stare down with eyes that nobody can see.

They're making one of their rare appearances—for me.

When Umbriel and I were in first-year Primary, we made up nicknames for the Committee members, whose real names we had to memorize and match with silhouettes for class. The featureless black masses petrified us, hardened our tongues into stone until we imbued them with absurdity. The Base IV representative Andromeda Chi, the only female, became Lady A. The others—Hydrus Iota, Cassini Omicron, Janus Lambda, Nebulus Nu, and Wolf Omega—became Stouty, Spider Hands, Frowning Mustache, Handsome Profile, and Eyebrow Man.

The Committee members rise when they see me. Like a string of robots, the others in the room follow. Skat yawns.

Though flustered, I salute. Is this the proper way to greet the most powerful people on the Moon?

"No need for formalities." Cassini's voice rustles like desiccated leaves. As he speaks, his creeping fingers tug at individual strands of his beard.

"We took time out of our busy schedules to meet *you*." Hydrus's voice oozes like maple sap, as saccharine as the unhealthy food he must have eaten to make his neck disappear.

"The youngest captain in our military history," drawls handsome Nebulus, whose silhouette is like that of an Earthbound marble statue. The youngest Committee member, he was only in his twenties when he ascended to the post. He begins scrolling through his handscreen—maybe he's checking my stats.

"And a girl, no less," Andromeda adds. Her hair, as curly as Callisto's, is almost as short as a man's, but her body is rounded enough to peg her as a woman. She gives Nebulus a look of disapproval—he shouldn't be on his handscreen during a meeting—and he puts both hands down by his sides. Even Committee members have to watch their manners, I think. But only with each other.

"What we're asking of you, *Captain* Phaet, is *indispensably* important," says Hydrus. "A recent Earth recon mission has informed us that Pacifia may be planning another strike on lunar territory."

Searching for emotion in eyes I cannot see is unnerving, to say the least.

"We need someone *competent*, not necessarily needed here on the Moon, and above all, *inconspicuous*."

Wolf Omega turns left, then right for approval before he speaks; his bristly brows protrude from his face in silhouette. He raises his trembling hands.

"It was serendipity when we heard about a new captain from Base IV. You are among the *greatest* specimens of our great nation's youth. Be honored to do our *great* work, to be ambassador of our *great* philosophy, to rid the Earth of uneducated filth—"

"That's enough," whispers Andromeda, patting Wolf's shoulder.

Shivering, I process what I'm hearing. I'm going to Earth within weeks of finishing training. Although I've internalized operating manuals and my new authority, I doubt I can apply them outside of an evaluation or sim. I certainly won't be ready to touch down upon that shifting blue marble on the horizon, which will surely be much more intimidating in person.

Yinha's earlier warning comes to mind. As a captain, I must take charge of and assume liability for entire recon missions. *Is the Committee trying to hurt me? Or are they giving me a chance to prove myself?*

"I can take over from here," the General says. "I know you are all busy today."

"Thank you, General. Yes. We must resolve the energy

dispute on Base II," says Hydrus. I scrunch my eyes shut and shake my head, hoping to clear the fog of agitation. Base II was built near Base I eighty-five years ago as an emergency shelter in case of attack or infrastructure problems. No evacuation ever occurred on Base I, but Base II still has a purpose. On rare occasions, Base I uses more solar power, water, or food than it produces on its own; Base II often makes up the difference.

"Pay attention, Captain," the General orders.

My eyes snap open. The Committee has disappeared from the walls, replaced by the rows and columns of figures, the images of Earth and its satellites. "Yes, sir."

"Don't let me catch you daydreaming again. Am I understood?"

Do all officers ask their underlings some variant of that question, as if we don't comprehend English? Will I do so myself in a few years, or worse, a few days?

"Yes, sir!"

"You will lead this recon mission. You will not reveal your assignment to anyone. Your team includes capable subordinates who have already demonstrated loyalty to you."

My handscreen flashes. Nash, Io, Orion, and Wes will accompany me to Earth. Within me, the stubborn loneliness begins to thaw, and the corners of my mouth jerk upward. I don't care if the Committee sees.

Then I see our departure date: August 24—the same day as Mom's trial. I teeter on unsteady legs before my hand reaches back and finds the plane of the door.

I mumble like the fearful daughter I am, "Thank you, General."

The General swivels his chair, giving me the back of his broad head.

Skat flicks his hand at me. "That means you're dismissed. Shoo."

I salute the two officers and inch backward out of the room.

Yinha paces in circles around my apartment, forehead wrinkled.

"That's an intense assignment. They could have asked me or someone with more experience—especially when they know I'd like to take a break from teaching incompetent teenagers."

But you're a horrible soldier. You said so.

She lowers her voice, surveying our surroundings for one of the security pods. "And Pacifia? It might be the second-biggest city on Earth, but its technology is *gritty* compared to ours. They couldn't hurt us decades ago, and they definitely can't now."

Yinha widens her eyes at me before slowly blinking twice. *Oh.* I wonder if she knows that Mom will be on trial while I'm spying on Earth.

"Strange, the timing. Usually, they give teams a month to prepare for an Earth mission. This is your first assignment, and they're giving you *two weeks*."

Oh, yes. She knows everything.

Maybe they gave me the position of captain so that they could send me to Earth on Mom's big day—and have me assume responsibility for anything that goes wrong. Did they think it would help them win?

My absence will make no difference to the Committee, but without me, August 24 will be a hard day for Cygnus and Anka.

I can't abandon them on trial day, leaving them huddled at home. But I also can't abandon my team's Earth recon assignment and disobey direct orders.

"I've got to go to training now; it's almost 08:00." Yinha passes me on her way out of my apartment. For an instant, she's close enough to whisper in my ear. "Be careful, Stripes."

30

I POUND ON THE DOOR TO MY BROTHER'S room.

"Cygnus! Hurry!"

"Go away! Didn't Mom want you to stay in Defense with your new friends?"

I hesitate, remembering that awful falling-out, and decide to convince him using the facts. "The Committee assigned me to Earth recon on the same day as Mom's trial."

My brother lurches toward the door, footsteps uneven. When it opens, I behold a boy whose eyes are so glazed I can almost see the reflection of a handscreen in them. We hurry to his cot and plant our rears over our left hands.

"So you're back. Why? You were going to throw us your money and make us deal with the trial alone."

"I got mad last time. Came here to say sorry." I also have something to ask, but I'm not sure how.

"So what can I do for you?" Cygnus demands. "I'm busy already, data mining Law."

"Help me."

Cygnus tilts his big head to the side. "You'll be gone."

Nod.

"Going to Earth is dangerous. Those pieces of grit majors! Why don't they go instead?"

I grimace. "It's the Committee that's sending me. . . ."

He waves me off with a flip of his hand. Like his head on his scrawny neck, it's oversized compared to his skinny forearm. "Anka's going to go ballistic. Well, not literally, but you know what I mean."

He's already doing too much—babysitting Anka, administering Mom's medication and food, and reconfiguring parts of the digital world. It's like we're characters in a malfunctioning sim-game, assigned task after grueling task before we've accomplished the preceding one. Guilt can't describe how I feel about asking him for more, but I have to be here on August 24. What if Cygnus or Anka needs me?

My voice cracks. "Is there a way to skip it?"

His jaw drops, and he meets my eyes for the first time. "Skip . . . skip your *mission*?"

"Break into Defense intranet? Enter a fake ship launch?"

"Hack Defense? That's . . . hard! Hardest on the base!"

If anyone could do it, Cygnus could. "I could launch the ship," I say, "then ride the escape pod back to the base. Record my voice now and play the files to my superiors later."

"What about your team? I can't get their voice samples. And trust me, there'll be people listening in on your ship. Even if I could get clips, there's no way the conversation would sound natural! You're just asking for more problems. Mom's already in trouble, and if you get caught, you'll be kicked out of Militia. Or . . . worse. Then you'll both be in jail—and—and if the Committee goes gritty and decides *not* to show mercy . . ."

. . . we will all *go to jail.*

"I'm sorry, but . . ."

As I watch his reddened eyes and swollen fingers, I can't suppress the shame. I swallow it down, but it merely sits undigested in my stomach.

I never had a choice about going to Earth.

"I'll take care of Anka. And . . . and Mom. Just don't die, I guess. I'd be sad if you did."

"I won't," I say, even though it's probable.

He throws his right arm around me. "You should talk to Mom. Every time someone mentions you, she gets this sad look. Sad, not mad, so don't be scared. She just wants the old you back."

I nearly scoff at his optimism. Healing my bond with Mom will be more complicated than showing her I'm still the same person. Cygnus didn't hear her tell me I'd destroyed myself, implying that the old Phaet, whoever she was, had vanished and wasn't worth trying to salvage.

"Why wait? Mom's sleeping in the next room—" Cygnus raps his wall. "Right there."

"Don't worry about it." I squeeze his middle, hanging on until I feel his skinny arm squeeze me back. "Thanks for trying to help."

"Then will you talk to her soon? I don't want to be in the middle of this anymore." He returns to prodding his handscreen.

Somewhere inside, Mom and I are the same. She must be suffering from our separation too. If only she were forgiving enough, or I were brave enough, to end it.

Procrastination has never been a habit of mine. But days of patrol duty with no sightings of my family make it easy to put off visiting home again. I could get used to this lifestyle—not worrying about anyone but myself, at least on a daily basis. I have privacy now, and quiet. If I want to nap during my lunch hour, I don't have to ask Anka's permission to do it. If I want to stay up late reading, no one can prevent it.

But each convenience reminds me that I'm only pretending I don't need my family, and my actions reflect the turmoil. Yesterday, I broke up a fistfight, accidentally stomping on a preteen boy's foot and getting bruised on the knee as retaliation. I don't mean to act like a cat submerged in a tank, but sometimes you can't beat biology.

On August 12, during my thirty-seventh lap around the Atrium as it empties for dinnertime, the Phi twins and Caeli approach me. The boys glare, making me feel sick all over again about abandoning my family—and their willingness to abandon me. But their mother doesn't seem to care.

"It's so nice to see you, Captain Phaet!" Caeli says. "We're on our way back from Education. How are you?"

Before I tell her not to worry, Umbriel points at me. "We need to talk."

Caeli and Ariel give each other a long look.

"All right," Caeli says. "We'll go on home—don't go anywhere *too* private, and Umbriel, be back before 20:00. Okay?"

"Yeah, Mom."

As they walk off, I hold my handscreen in front of my face, staring at the time. Umbriel knows the gesture means *I've got a job to do. Make it quick.*

"Wasn't sure I'd ever see you again. And I heard you haven't talked to your mom or sister or brother since you walked out."

My hands clench into fists, sweating beneath my synthetic gloves. Umbriel always acknowledges the things I can't. Hearing him list my wrongs toward my family is the price I pay for having a perceptive best friend.

"I feel terrible," I say, trying to placate him.

Umbriel's face softens at the string of honest words. "That's a relief."

"Can't describe it . . ."

He didn't want to be angry with me; he immediately gives in. "Oh, Phaet. Even though your mom worries, I know you're still you. The color you're wearing doesn't make a difference. But how long until you come home? How long are you going to keep your rank?"

I shake my head—*I don't know.* "I'll be captain until they tell me I'm a major."

Umbriel doesn't like the idea, but he knows that the Militia has become my future. They won't let me quit for at least five years, and even if they did, I need to keep this job until my family's bank account recovers.

That is, if Mom is found innocent.

His warm hand on mine jerks me away from the hopelessness, and he bends to my ear. "I know things are going to be different for us, but know that no matter what you've done, no matter what else happens, I'll still . . ." He can't go on, and he doesn't need to. Discussing events beyond August 24 is a waste of time.

Speaking of time, I haven't checked on my personnel. My eyes shift from Umbriel's, but he grasps my hands, constructing a cage of living tissue around them. "That's . . . that's what you want, right?"

What a question—useless *and* insensitive. Does he think I can make decisions based on what I *want*?

"Later." I retract my hands and shove them in my pants pockets.

Umbriel's eyebrows descend.

"Hey, Captain!" calls a high voice.

Private Eri Pi stands to my right, grinning. "Stop noodling around with your *boyfriend* and get back to work!"

My eyes narrow. Attached to her arm—and wearing an unfortunate expression—is Sergeant Wes Kappa, which renders her "boyfriend" comment somewhat ironic.

His eyes meet mine. It's a passing glance, but I cling to the memory of it like fire clings to oxygen.

"Eri, let's get some dinner," he says. "You wanted quinoa spaghetti, right?"

"Oh, yeah. Let's go!" With renewed focus, Eri drags him off to Market.

Without another glance at Eri and Wes, I resume walking to distance myself from them. Umbriel tails me, recycling familiar arguments to convince me to leave my job. I stride faster and faster, hardly bothering to bend my stiff knees, until I'm half jogging. Umbriel reaches for my gloved hand, but I jerk away.

"Phaet, can you put that mad face away and listen? I thought you said—oof!"

A set of dirty, stinky robes barrels into him. Without looking back, its owner continues traversing the Atrium floor, weaving between knots of people. From the nearby Financial Department, a paunchy woman cries, "Silver! He's taken silver!"

Umbriel pulls me toward him, but I pull out an Electrostun, elbowing free. At last, something to do.

When the Sputnik was in its early stages decades ago, the Committee backed it with precious metals. Now, Sputniks are digitized fiat money accepted everywhere on the Moon, but Financial keeps gold, silver, and platinum around to prevent spontaneous economic busts.

I've already shot off after the flapping robes. He's tall, slim, and *fast*.

I'm a captain; this is not my job. But many of my underlings are across the Atrium, and I'm already relishing the chase, entire seconds and minutes during which there's nothing but the thief, my goal, and me.

To steer the thief the way I want, I run behind him and to his left, driving him to the right. He checks the Atrium's security mirrors every few seconds to discern my location as I push him toward the entrance of Market. We're in agreement about our destination; hundreds of people swarm at the entrance, a crowd the thief could duck behind.

Too bad. I've already committed his scrawny face to memory—and the boy whose lovely dinner I'm about to interrupt can chase him down, even on an empty stomach.

"Sergeant Wezn and Private Eri," I say into my helmet. "Thief heading into Market. Dirty robes. About one meter, ninety centimeters tall."

A dozen meters away, Wes abandons his still-full bowl of pasta, remembering to push his chair in as he shoots to his feet. When his gleaming eyes locate the flapping robes, he darts through the crowd like a missile, not hitting a single table, chair, or person. Diners scramble out of his way. He gains on the thief; to preserve momentum, he somersaults across a deserted table instead of swerving around it.

Meanwhile, I circle the perimeter of Market, waiting for Wes to lead the thief to me. I can't see the action from the ground, so I mount a pyramid of industrial water dispensers and hunker down on the side opposite the thief's location.

Our target crouches to hide his height, worming under a table—again, a smart move, but performed in the wrong location: right below me. I detect his body odor among the otherwise pleasing aromas of Market.

I set my Electrostun in long-range mode. Why did this man cause so much trouble, when he knew he'd be caught?

With satisfaction suffusing every organ but my heart, I cock my weapon and fire a sticky pellet carrying 50,000 volts onto the skin of his forearm. White veins of electricity wrap around him, knocking him flat. His body performs an involuntary twitching dance, knocking over the table under which he's taken shelter.

Only when his screech hits my eardrums do I realize what I've done.

31

"IT'S OKAY, IT'S *OKAY.*" ERI WAVES HER HANDS at the onlookers, who continue to stare at me and my frozen hand, which still clutches the Electrostun. Theft is rare, and when it does occur, an arrest almost certainly follows.

I wish I could gather all that electricity and shove it back into my weapon. *How badly did I hurt my victim? How could I have had such an urge?*

I allow myself an exhale when the thief, a fifty-something man with a warty face, stirs and produces three silver coins from the pocket of his once-vermilion Tau robes.

"Your dumb Sputniks, all hundred and fifty of 'em. Just let me go home!"

"The rules are the rules, Mr. . . . erm . . . Mr. Leo." Eri clicks magnetic handcuffs around his wrists.

Leo Tau bares his yellow teeth at her and turns to me. "I could ha' kept my four little girls outta Shelter for another few weeks if you hadn't—"

"Come on, now." Eri escorts Leo from Market, her Lazy prodding his spine. Her shiny two-hundred-Sputnik boots scuff the floor. Law will throw Leo in Penitentiary, where Mom spent her miserable six weeks and where he will decay even longer because no one who cares can afford to bail him out. Helplessness and indignation will plague his fledgling daughters, sickening them faster than Shelter's myriad diseases. Four daughters. Soon, four dirt-covered urchins like Belinda.

Wes is watching me in my hiding place. As he turns to go, he shakes his head, wearing an expression resembling pity. I'd rather he were angry.

Someone else demands my attention, yanking me down from the pile of water dispensers and hissing in my ear.

"I can't believe you." It's Umbriel. "I thought you'd never change—and you agreed with me. Where'd that promise go? Into your fat new account in Financial? The least you could have done is let that guy escape, not stun him half unconscious. He took a hundred and fifty—*you* make that much *every day*!"

With a pang, I calculate that I make a hundred and fifty Sputniks about every six hours.

"Have you forgotten where you come from, *Captain* Phaet?" Umbriel demands. "*I* stole you fruit when you were hungry. *I* stole a rose for you because I couldn't afford anything fancier. Are you going to arrest *me* a thousand times, just because you can? I saw your face back there. You looked like you were having *fun*." Umbriel's voice turns to singsong.

"Beater, Beater, make the Bases neater. Stun guns, Lazies, the blood gets sweeter. . . ."

It's a hideous tune that Primary kids chant under their breath. The chasm within me that Mom opened up grows wider, wider, and more darkness sweeps inside.

"Leave."

"Not until you admit what you're turning into."

My hand shoots to my utility belt—an automatic reaction, not an indication that I'd hurt Umbriel. But he doesn't take it that way.

"Arrest me, then! Zap me, put a laser through!" Umbriel towers over me, diminishing my officer powers with the sheer size of his body and personality. "Just don't come running back if you find your old self again!"

He marches off. I take two halfhearted steps toward him before realizing their futility. The floor rises to meet my knees; the impact echoes through my body as if I were hollow inside. And after losing Umbriel, I am.

Although I want to hammer my fists into something—anything—I settle for twisting my fingers together until they grow chilly from lack of blood.

Beater, Beater. My mind repeats Umbriel's chant of its own accord, matching each syllable with my racing pulse. *The blood gets sweeter.*

Yinha finds me sprawled on the floor that night, staring at the seams in the ceiling. Every time I blink, Leo Tau's face appears in my mind's eye, every detail intact from his sunken cheeks to his yellow teeth.

My fury has left me deflated, a floppy sack of skin. Umbriel is right. In the past weeks, I've grown mysterious to myself. That I stormed out of Theta 808 should have been an early indication. If I'd stopped then, I wouldn't have progressed to this point, raging against total strangers.

"Don't mean to be nosy," Yinha says via the Defense inter-handscreen network. My skin tingles. "But how are you?"

I groan and flip onto my stomach.

"Oh, fuzz," Yinha says. "You're flopping around like an overcooked noodle. I'm coming over."

I open the door for her and park myself against the wall. Yinha glides across my kitchen, throwing ice into the blender. She cranks it to the highest speed; the ruckus will hide our conversation from the security pods that we know are buzzing around.

"The first arrest is rough." Yinha sits on my memory foam couch and leans over the armrest to look me in the face. "Nothing prepares you for packing someone off to a Pen cell for who knows how long. Lots of newbie soldiers have issues. Then they get used to putting people away, maybe even start liking it. There's power in it, and that's what makes some stay in this business."

That's what I felt when I fired the Electrostun. I look downward in shame.

"Is that why you're here?"

"I don't know, but I hope not." Yinha avoids my eyes. "This is the only job I have. I do what they tell me to do, not really loving or hating it."

Maybe there's guilt somewhere too, but it isn't obvious. Becoming an officer like her is the best I can hope for. "I should apologize."

"To whom? Leo? It's kind of late for that."

Yes, but to my family as well. Cygnus was right—I should have talked to Mom weeks ago, before my smoldering anger manifested in the form of an Electrostun pellet. Umbriel too.

"I want *your* job," I blurt. No boring, infuriating Atrium duty, no arrests, no Earth recon missions—if I complete a year of regular duty, I can apply to become an instructor. I intend to.

"Think twice, or thrice, or ten times about that. It's cool that I don't have to go on patrol, but it's *not* cool that I send a bunch of you guys out to do it every two months. This latest batch of trainees makes me sad."

Yinha massages her temples. With some dread, I wait for her to elaborate.

"One death already: a boy, fresh out of Primary. His grenade exploded too early. He was only Eri's size. Everyone's too shaken up now to study the manuals for destroyers and pressure suits."

We bow our heads, mourning in miniature. Another Vinasa, and more may follow. Without my Primary study habits—and luck—I could have been just like them.

"Sorry," Yinha says. "Didn't mean to bring up bad memories. Anyway, you'd better smooth things over with your friend—what's his name?"

"Umbriel."

Yinha extends her hand over the armrest to hold mine. "Apologize to Umbriel. And when you can, apologize to Leo. Make it up to him—*legally*, of course. Cool?"

"Mm."

"Do you feel better now? I hate to see you slouch around." Yinha rises from the sofa and turns off the blender. "You're going fizz crazy, stuck in here."

She's right. Despite its size, my apartment is turning into a trap; I've grown too comfortable here.

"Here's an idea. Why don't we fly to the ISS? It's close to the Moon tonight. I haven't visited in years, and I don't want to go alone."

I remember how Yinha couldn't tear her eyes away from the ISS icon during our meeting with Skat and the General. Her preoccupation with it is unusual but understandable. The ISS, a massive satellite containing some of the ancient Earthbounds' most advanced technology, has been in orbit since the twentieth century, long before the Twenty Years' War.

For now, I'll leave memories of Umbriel's taunts and Mom's whispers behind me on the Moon.

ↀↀↀ

With a lurch, my Pygmette latches on magnetically to the floating hunk of metal.

"Beat you!" Yinha's voice roars through my headset. Back in the hangar, she challenged me to a race. I expected to lose, having never piloted a Pygmette off-base, so I didn't mind being left behind in a trail of protons and helium-4. Yinha's ruse has worked; while punching buttons and dodging debris, I had no capacity to think about anything else. I chuckle at her playfulness, smiling for the first time since my falling-out with Mom.

Yinha's celebration ends prematurely, though; she says no more. Unsure whether our connection has failed, I call, "Yinha?"

"I'm here. It's just that . . . well, the last time I visited . . ."

Yinha's Pygmette unlatches from the ISS. I follow her so that I can examine the satellite at a distance, which I failed to do amidst the excitement of our race.

Like an oversized falcon, the ISS has two wings, each with plumes comprised of eight antiquated solar panels. Rising from the steel body of the craft is a short neck, topped with a crest of eight smaller panels.

Seeing the real thing instead of a low-res icon, I realize the panels resemble irregular checkerboards; something has removed solar cells at random, uncovering the bare metal beneath. The wings themselves are crooked; entire plates of steel are gone, revealing the chambers in which ancient Earthbound explorers lived and worked. One attachment on the bottom of the craft hangs on by a hinge. As the ISS follows its orbital path, it turns away from us, seemingly unable to bear the gaze of strangers upon its diminished glory.

"Bai took me here when I turned twenty. Before he got hurt," Yinha says. "This thing used to shine."

Her Pygmette shoots through a hole in the satellite's metal plating and into a room faintly resembling a kitchen. Displaced food carts float around the galley and glance off the walls.

Yinha rounds a corner, bending her Pygmette's segmented midsection with flawless piloting technique, and enters a hallway congested with Earthbound knickknacks: copper wire, metal screws, cracked video screens, and a brown plastic sheet bearing the word SNICKERS as if mocking its surroundings. Clunky rectangular equipment drifts by, metal coverings torn off, thick wires exposed like tangled intestines in an autopsied corpse.

Who wrecked the ISS? Either one of the Earthbound cities with spaceflight capabilities or the Bases themselves. But why? Battery Bay wouldn't travel into space to scrounge metal and plastic when there's so much of both on Earth. And why would the Bases need raw material? We haven't built new structures in four decades, since we completed Base VI—our only settlement on the Far Side.

Yinha's Pygmette halts beside mine. "Let's go home," she says.

Sorrow deadens her voice. Although I don't feel it for the broken ISS, it's within me too. Things in my life are also broken, things I'm glad are invisible.

32

DESPITE MY BEST INTENTIONS, I DON'T TAKE Yinha's advice and apologize to Umbriel—or ask around about Leo Tau, whom I block from my thoughts anew every time the guilt flares up. With route calculations, packing, city tracking, contingency planning, team trial flights, and equipment checks filling my schedule, I don't have the time.

Wes maintains a professional distance from me, a gap he bridges every so often with a questioning, pitying look. Missing someone, even if he's right in front of you, is physically taxing. I'd jog a hundred laps around the Medical quarters if it meant sitting with him afterward, alone.

But there's no time. I go straight from meetings with the team to strategizing sessions with Skat, whom Mom might call less resourceful than an Earthbound desert and less excited than a ground state electron. I imagine her grinning at me, asking if I get the chemistry joke.

I'm terrified I'll never see my family again after August 24. I don't want their memories of me to be forever shaded by my wrath.

On the day before I'm set to leave, foreboding drives me to the place I've avoided, seeking forgiveness—and strength.

"Sweetheart, what are you doing here?" Mom sits up in bed

with a start. Her cheeks have filled out; her skin has more color, even if it's still greenish. Her hair has grown back in patches, grayer than before and just long enough to cover the scars on her scalp. Despite these improvements, I worry that too much movement or feeling could still break her. "Aren't you busy with Militia work?"

She's really asking me: *How could you leave us for so long? And what brings you back now?*

"Done." To avoid sending her fragile heart into palpitations, I don't tell her about the mission.

She laughs, and I see more of the mother I remember: little wrinkles around her nose, teeth bared despite their recent discoloration. "No work today? So why the pinched face?"

"I'm sorry," I blurt, sitting on the bed.

Mom pinches her lips together. "I'm sorry too." She reaches for my hand. I let her take it. "When I saw you outside my cell, you weren't the girl I remembered—you were strong, sharp, almost cruel. Forgive me . . . I thought you'd changed, or that I'd lost you."

I say nothing, willing her to continue.

"I didn't see that love had driven you to join Militia, and that love alone might save you."

But affection for my family didn't keep me from cruelty. "I hurt someone, Mom," I say.

Mom tilts her head sideways, like I do when I'm waiting for someone to keep talking.

"A thief. I stunned him to facilitate arrest. He's in Penitentiary now. I can't count how many times I've imagined apologizing to him, to his family. . . ."

"I was afraid something like that would happen," Mom says. "To have so much power, so young—I should have warned you about how it can change people."

"I loathed Atrium duty. Hours of pointlessness, and wondering what I did to make you send me away."

"I can only imagine how difficult that must have been. And I'm sorry beyond words for asking you to leave." She pauses. "But I hope you're not using the situation you were in as an excuse for your actions."

"It was an explanation." I only hope she won't ask me to go away again, now that she knows about Leo.

"Oh, sweetie." Mom fiddles with my fingers, calloused and corded with muscles, and looks into my face. "Why do you look so scared? Is it about tomorrow—is that why you came back? I'm not afraid. Tomorrow will put everything right, I promise."

Before Mom went to Penitentiary, she feared losing her job, even temporarily. Now, she seems indifferent to losing her freedom—and us—forever. If the worst happens and she's sent back to Penitentiary, I won't be able to get her out, no matter what Militia title I earn.

"I've had months to prepare myself. Years, even."

Years? How many? Why didn't I notice her "preparations"?

"What did you *do*?"

She sighs. "Does that matter? It's already been done."

"Mom!"

"You wouldn't understand. . . . Phaet, I spoke through many voices." Mom looks away from my attentive face and down at the wrinkles in the bedspread.

What could that mean?

"I can't tell you more. Not now . . . Is there anything else on your mind?"

"Nothing."

"*Something.* I know when you want to let words into the universe, but you don't. Is it your job? You can tell me more. I want to help you, to get to know you again."

Shrug.

"I'm your mother—I'm here for you whenever you need me."

How much longer will that be true?

"Look at my big girl." She shakes her head. "Do you still need me at all? You saw the destitution in Shelter and took a job none of us wanted you to have. . . ." She pauses, and then words rush from her mouth. "Goodness, you've seen the real Moon now. What do you think of it?"

I remember Vinasa, how Militia killed her and sent us back to training the next day, forcing us to forget. Belinda, how Shelter's slowly killing her and others like her. My pained expression tells Mom everything.

She bends closer to me. "Society can change, Phaet. What if you could *choose* whether to join Militia? The General and the Committee don't need to know—or command—the minutiae of your life. Imagine returning to the greenhouses!"

"Mom—"

"When you were younger, after your shifts, you'd refuse to wash the soil from your hands because you loved the smell. . . ."

"Mom!"

She stops her monologue, realizing that she's scared me. Few people dare to talk like that—about changing the Bases—even if the Committee's eavesdroppers aren't listening.

"All right." Her eyes close. "I only want you three to grow up happy. When you have children, you'll understand."

I wonder if I'll live that long. "*If* I have children."

Mom misinterprets my words. "You don't want them? But they're so lovely, the people who show you what's important."

I look at our joined hands, a fragile link despite its physicality. Mom tips my chin back up.

"It's hard to be certain of anything at your age, my girl. Especially at a time like this, when the world is full of changes."

"Bad ones," I say.

"Goodness and badness are unquantifiable. I've learned that in the weeks you've been gone. Here at home, looking at the three of you, I've thought about the future . . . and begun accepting the gray areas of the past. Like your decision to join Militia on our behalf—that was neither good nor bad."

That's not the impression she gave me last time.

"My stay in Penitentiary too," she whispers.

"I don't see how that could've been good."

"Free food and solitude," Mom says. "More than Shelter residents can hope for."

I've never thought about it like that. "Even without freedom?"

Mom blinks slowly. "In Penitentiary, I was just as free as I usually am—as anybody is. My mind could go anywhere, which was an improvement from putting other people's thoughts into words and feeding them to an audience that doesn't care. As I watched other inmates suffer, I grew surer that things need to change. No other family should experience what we have."

"I agree," I say, even though it'd be impossible to erase

money problems, illness, and arrests from the population. Is Mom's "crime" discussing solutions to these social problems? That's something the Committee does every day. Perhaps the disruptive print charges aren't as bad as we've feared.

"I'm glad you're speaking honestly. I'd love to see you do that more."

I've gotten that advice from her before, but this is the first time I want to follow it. During these weeks without me, she must have thought hard about how to share her opinion without putting me on the defensive.

"Someday—and I know it might not be soon—when you want to say something, start it with a whisper, grow it louder. Remember that, even as you get older."

Suddenly, I'm scared—she's talking about the rest of my life. "Stop."

She opens her mouth, takes a breath; I prepare to hear her reasons for telling me these things. When she shakes her head and parentheses form around her mouth, I exhale in disappointment.

"I'm sorry, my girl, I don't mean to lecture you. But everything I'll ever tell you, I should tell you now. Just in case I—"

"What's 'everything'?" I don't want to hear the worst.

"Only one more sentence, something I wish I'd said more often." Mom throws her hands up as if surrendering. I reach mine out and hold them, feeling the creases in her calloused skin, lines formed by decades of typing, gesturing, caressing.

"I love you, sweetie."

Isn't it odd how those words can frighten fear itself out of a room? I suppose I came here today, ignorant and confused and not knowing my purpose, to say them back to her.

When Cygnus arrives home from Primary, he pokes his head into Mom's room and gives me a thumbs-up, his mouth spreading into a disproportionately large smile. He tiptoes back into the living room and hunches over the HeRP, whose screen is now so populated with icons that fitting them on there must have been akin to playing handscreen Tetris.

We hear Anka greet Cygnus some fifteen minutes later. She stayed after class to run about with her friends in the gymnasium, just like she always did before Umbriel and I walked her home. *Umbriel.* If Anka's here, then he is too.

I hug Mom with care. After leaving her side, I wave back at her and shuffle into the living room. Two dark eyes fix upon me with fright, and another two with resentment.

"So you're back." Umbriel places Anka's knapsack on the ground and advances toward me.

I thought so hard about what I'd say to him—*I lost control, forgot who I was. Stress was no excuse for how I treated you and everyone else, so I'm sorry. Just ask Mom—she'll tell you I'm remembering how to be good again*. But now nothing comes out.

"Umbriel! Thanks for sending Anka home—oh." Mom has risen and inched in our direction; she's leaning against the wall nearest her room. Recognizing that there's a standoff, she changes her tone. "Maybe you should head to Agriculture, Umbriel. Doesn't your shift start soon?"

"Don't go," I say. I should have taken the initiative, sought him out earlier. But I can be the first to say—

"Sorry," we sputter together, as if we'd planned to synchronize it.

Umbriel has thought hard about his speech beforehand,

judging by its fluidity. "I'm so sorry about getting mad at you. Catching crooks is your job, just like gardening is my job, right? Even if it involves mean looks and too much electricity, you're still Phaet. But you know that. You came home."

"It took a while," Cygnus mutters.

"So?" Anka nudges his shoulder. "Stop bugging Phaet."

"Your sister's right," Mom says. "We don't have much time to be together."

"Right, you four need Theta time. I should get going." Umbriel checks the clock on his handscreen and backs toward the door. "But it's great having you back, Phaet."

The happiness in his eyes numbs the sting of what transpired in the Atrium. Our friendship was grazed, scraped on the surface, but it's grown back thicker.

"Everything okay?" I ask, following him.

"Between us? Things were always okay."

It's not true, but it's soothing to hear. Now that he's forgiven me, I'm closer to forgiving myself.

"Thanks," I sigh.

Umbriel hugs me as if nothing has changed. I'm glad he found me here. At this point in our companionship, we'd be senseless to face tomorrow without each other's goodwill.

As he leaves, Mom stumbles to the sofa. Cygnus holds her arm, lowering her incrementally into a seated position.

"You three, all here again." Mom folds Anka into her free arm, so that my siblings flank her on either side. Her eyes, aglow with affection, invite me to join them.

I cross the room, push our side table closer to the couch, and sit on its rigid surface to face Mom. Her hand finds mine atop my knee.

"Before Phaet and I went away," she begins, "I thought that if only your dad were with us, this home would be complete."

Cygnus, Anka, and I start at the mention of Dad. Mom's actions in years past have made him virtually taboo—we never thought she'd be the first to break the silence.

"The last time he was here, you three were so little. He'd lie on his back and use his shins to float you up like a bird, Phaet. Remember?"

Nod. The memories are vague, tender sensations rather than colorful images.

"And Cygnus, he'd peel bananas for you because you couldn't split the skin. Anka—he constructed a secret language with you, all vowels."

My brother scrunches his eyes, embarrassed. Anka laughs, flushing pink. Watching them, I'm so happy that my mouth muscles grow sore from smiling.

"Do I wish my Atlas could see you three now, grown tall and magnificent? Yes, every day." No frown-parentheses surround Mom's mouth. Admitting her longing for him, at last, has freed her. "It's so hard, now, to gather just the four of us in one place. This is precious. This is enough. Whoever's around you, in the present, is all you need."

More beautiful advice, I think as Mom pulls us into a hug. Advice I'm not sure is true.

Tomorrow, when Mom goes to Law and I descend to Earth, it'll be put to the test.

33

EVERY DAY, IT'S GOTTEN HARDER TO EMERGE from the dreamless cavity where my mind retreats when I sleep. My first thought when I wake has been, *That buzzing in my hand means I need to get up now,* and my second: *Mom's trial is in x number of days.* The shock got severe when *x* equaled three. Then *x* equaled two. Then one.

Today, the countdown ends.

At 16:47, I begin walking toward the hangar; I had meant to leave at 16:30 for our 16:57 launch, but triple-checking my clothes and equipment took longer than expected. I stub my toe twice and make a wrong turn, which eats up another minute while I correct my mistake. When I finally arrive in the hangar, my team and three-person ground crew await me at our assigned destroyer. Wes yawns, squeezing his bloodshot eyes shut. My guess is that he hasn't slept much, preparing for the mission.

Fearful of betraying my state of mind, I open the hatch with my thumbprint and nod at my team to climb into the ship. As Io passes me, I hear the evening news blaring from her handscreen; I doubt she even knows it's playing. She'll have to shut off the program soon, or at least mute it.

After Orion and Nash enter the hatch, I gesture for Wes to go next. As he passes me, he wraps one arm around my shoulders, sending an obvious shudder through them. Months have passed since I've gotten a hug from him, and I wasn't expecting one now, given what he's seen me do under pressure.

"We're going to do a fine job, Phaet. There's no one else I'd rather have as flight leader."

From the look on his face, he'd like to elaborate, but mere minutes remain until takeoff. I wonder what else he's been meaning to say. Maybe after spending so many hours training with me, a girl who once couldn't imagine firing a laser into living flesh, he understands that I'm not the Beater I must have seemed in the Atrium. I nod at him.

After I hoist myself into the ship, the ground crew closes the hatch. As I oversee the final systems check, I can't stop thinking about Mom's trial, which will start three minutes after liftoff.

We strap ourselves into the seats I assigned weeks ago, test the audio system, and check the fit of our flight gloves, which are impervious to temperature, light, and sound. Orion sits in the pilot's seat, flipping switches and reading measurements. Wes takes right wingtip, Nash takes left, and Io sits as copilot. We lift off smoothly, as expected.

To maximize security and efficiency, our flight path will hug the lunar surface until we reach the point closest to Pacifia's current location. For now, we coast past familiar pits and peaks; the acceleration downward due to gravity is still 1.62 meters per second squared. When it drops to zero, and we're on autopilot toward Earth, I might literally get sick.

My teammates concentrate on their respective tasks, except for Io, who's technically backup for Orion. She's muted her handscreen, probably a result of someone's prodding, but her glove's off and she's still tuned in. The news shows an advertisement for a newly developed fruit—the round, khaki-colored, and stringy Celerorange.

As I open my mouth to scold her, the commercial fizzles out. We haven't traveled far enough to lose the signal; there must be a malfunction. Intrigued, I slip off my glove and turn on the evening news on my own handscreen, adjusting the volume to a low setting. In my lifetime, there has never been a glitch on a broadcast.

Yet instead of the usual new discoveries and production statistics, I see a bleak, tiny room stuffed with three people sitting on stools, their backs to one another, their knees all but scraping the walls. A panel above their heads reads LAW CHAMBER 144. Why in the universe would Journalism film the inside of—

Law Chamber 144. I recognize Atlas Phi and another Law worker who must be leading the prosecution. And Mom, skeletal and slumped over on the third stool. Magnetic rings lock her ankles to the front legs. She and Atlas wear transparent lie-detecting glasses; their heart rates, hormone readings, and eye movements appear in real time, wrapping around the room at the bottom of the 360-degree wall screens.

My mother's trial—on the evening news. I'm short of breath, as if I've become asthmatic or the ship has sprung a leak. Such hearings are confidential. Mom wasn't even *arrested* directly; the authorities had her moved to Medical, presumably to keep the situation low-key. Broadcasting her trial now contradicts all the secrecy that has come before. How could the Committee allow this?

Of course—they didn't allow it.

Mom wanted people to see the event. Cygnus must be helping her. He'd do anything for her—especially if it meant taking on a hacking challenge. I squeeze my hands into fists, furious with my mother and with myself. Why didn't I predict this?

Now her humiliation will be visible to everybody on the base. Why, in the months since her abduction, couldn't she think of better retribution against the Committee for her ordeal in Penitentiary? Everyone the authorities think is involved will follow Mom into jail, including Cygnus, if they catch him. And the Phis . . . does Atlas know? What will happen to him, to Umbriel?

I numbly watch my handscreen as we climb the eastern wall of the Copernicus Crater and edge out onto the greater Oceanus Procellarum. Shining trails of ejecta, products of the impact that formed the crater, whizz by as we pick up speed. I see them only in my peripheral vision. We're approaching the breakaway point too soon—only minutes remain before we abandon the lunar surface altogether.

My teeth begin to chatter, and I realize I've been shaking since I first glimpsed the broadcast.

"Phaet, are you . . ." Wes leans over to get a good view of my handscreen.

Now he knows what he brought Mom by carting her off to Medical all those weeks ago. He sucks air in through his teeth, trying to stay calm for both of us.

Above the indicators, the Committee flickers into view, shadowy and faceless. Mom's expression doesn't change, but Atlas jumps back against the wall. *He doesn't know he's being filmed*, I realize, my heart taking off like a frightened baby bird's.

I doubt even Mom expected the Committee to serve as jurors—a random batch of nine Law workers usually does the job. My optimism yesterday was misguided. Mom's alleged crime must have been more disruptive than I imagined if the Committee took time out of their "busy, busy schedule" to pass judgment.

What about the 8,000 Sputniks of bribe money, our last resort? That sum would influence a normal jury, but not the Committee, whose members want for nothing.

The six of them sit motionlessly, forearms balanced on the table. Do *they* know they're being filmed? Nebulus reaches down to adjust his pants leg. I've never seen a Committee member fidget in public. He checks his handscreen as he sits up, earning a sharp look from Andromeda.

"Please disable your handscreen messages, my friends," Andromeda says. Other citizens can't cut off handscreen communications, but it seems the Committee has that privilege. "I don't want *any* disturbances. We must give this case our undivided attention."

The five men oblige her. "It's your base, after all," Hydrus says.

It's a small comfort that they're clueless about Cygnus's cameras. My mind spinning, I consider begging my team to turn the ship around. But my team would never obey an order to abandon a mission; that command might lead my friends to mutiny. Even if I returned to Base IV, what could I do? Cutting the broadcast short wouldn't change the fact that the base has already seen it. An official investigation will be necessary. And the verdict of the trial is in the Committee's hands—no one can change their minds.

Hydrus says, "We the Committee do observe that all three participants in the trial of Mira Theta are present. Atlas Phi, defense. Phobos Xi, prosecution. And the accused."

Andromeda speaks. "Mira Theta is hereby charged with disruptive print. The defense has one minute to make an opening statement before calling upon witnesses for questioning."

That's not right—from years of dinner conversation with the Phis, I know that the Law codes allow three minutes.

"Yoo-hoo," Nash calls. "Everyone's being awfully quiet. Phaet? Wes? What you guys looking at? . . . What in the—"

Seeing Nash's stunned expression, Orion peels his glove back just far enough to tune in to the news on his handscreen. "Fuse!" Appalled, he yanks the glove back into place.

"Never thought I'd see one." Nash could be referring to the trial or a passing landmark. She's picking her words carefully, in case Committee minions are tuning in to *us*. "What, Orion, you scared?"

"I never *wanted* to see one," mutters Orion. "Good-for-nothings"—he points his thumb over his shoulder—"belong in the Pen—"

"Shh!" Wes hisses.

Back in Law, Atlas rises. His voice is steady, as are his vital signs.

"I'm going to argue chronologically. Mira was born to a pair of well-to-do Nuclear Physics workers with pristine records. She showed little aptitude for the natural sciences herself. . . ."

"Upsetting her parents and leading to a minor identity crisis," Nebulus mutters.

". . . but her fifth-year Primary teacher noted that she had 'a talent for finding patriotic words, backed by a precocious understanding of what makes our Bases great.'"

Phobos slaps his hand down on his armrest. "Objection!"

Drumming his spindly fingers, Cassini glances at Hydrus for approval. "Granted."

"Unauthorized procurement of video evidence."

Exasperated, Atlas shakes his head. "It wasn't video. The statement was so important that it shows up on her stats."

Was Phobos so sure he could win that he didn't check Mom's stats beforehand?

"Defense's one minute is up," Cassini croaks. "Please call upon witnesses."

"Sol Eta," Atlas says, looking irritated. "Journalist and Mira's colleague."

On a nearby wall, his handscreen projects the image of a short woman with a close-cropped bob, a pointy nose, and quick-shifting eyes. I remember her; Mom sometimes invited her for dinner. She's another Opinions writer for the *Luna Daily*, a talkative woman with a husky voice that seems to originate in the pit of her belly.

"Present," she says.

Hydrus recites, "Place your right hand on the projection of *On the Origin of Species*."

Sol's hand passes through the projection of an old paper book several times as she awaits further directions. Darwin's work, one of the only Earthbound texts allowed to circulate on the Bases, reminds us that we are as susceptible to nature as any other species, and that we must continually adapt to our harsh environment if we wish to survive.

"Do you, Sol Eta, swear to tell the truth, the whole truth, and nothing but the truth, so help you Reason?"

"I swear."

Nebulus says, "Begin direct examination."

Atlas stands and squares his shoulders. "Sol Eta, what kind of Journalist is Mira?"

"Thorough," Sol says. "Hardworking."

"On the day she was arrested, did she act strangely at work?"

"No—she was well on her way to meet a deadline for an article—'The Miracles of Mathematics.' It called for more Militia alumnae to choose math programs as a Specialization. The Committee asked Mira to write it—Aerospace Engineering needs more analysts, as you know."

"Thank you, Sol. Anything else?"

Sol tosses her head back. Her shiny hair swooshes around her ears. "Mira is one of the most effective Journalists on the base. If she is found guilty, the population will have lost a leading voice in patriotism and positivity."

Wolf bangs on the table before him. "Time's up!"

"What?" says Nash. "Two minutes, not—" According to Law protocol, questioning should last 120 seconds, no less.

"A minute and fifteen seconds," Wes finishes, looking at his handscreen. He's been timing the interrogation.

Nebulus blows his nose into a handkerchief before speaking. "Phobos, would you cross-examine the witness?"

"Unnecessary." Phobos slouches, one foot resting on the other knee. "Can I bring mine in and get this over with?"

Hydrus says, "Yes, by all means."

Sighing, Atlas taps the back of his left hand. The projection of Sol Eta vanishes, replaced by another hologram, this one emanating from Phobos's handscreen.

I let out a gasp that prompts Io to poke Orion in the shoulder and say, "Captain sounds scared."

"Shh!" says Orion.

On my handscreen, Atlas gapes, mouth open like the entrance to a lava tube, but no words flow forth. His heart pounds away; the wall displays show that his stress hormones have spiked. Beside him, Mom's eyes shift rapidly. She's trying to look anywhere but at the witness.

The tear-streaked face of Caeli Phi looks out at her husband and the woman he has tried so hard to protect.

34

AS CAELI SWEARS THE WITNESS OATH, SO help her Reason, I imagine Umbriel, wherever he is, swearing unprintable things of his own. My best friend's family is splitting apart—at least, that's what it looks like. If not, if Caeli's not alone, I can't trust any of them anymore.

Should we turn back? If my siblings and the Phi twins are in shock from Caeli's betrayal, it's my duty to help them. . . . *No, the team will never agree.* And I won't be able to help my family, let alone find them; if Cygnus is using our HeRP, then Anka must be somewhere else, probably with Umbriel.

On my handscreen, Atlas rises, eyebrows bristling, fists clenched. "Caeli. What are *you* doing here?"

To silence him, Wolf says, "Direct examination first."

Atlas tucks himself into his chair, tucks away his powers of intimidation. *Stay sturdy,* I want to tell him.

Caeli's short index finger swipes tears off her cheeks. "They were going to get her, anyway! I did it for us, Atlas, so no matter what that woman—that *traitor*—did, our family wouldn't be guilty by association. Don't you see?"

Atlas opens and closes his mouth, chewing on the words he needs to set loose, words standard trial procedure won't allow.

"I question her first," Phobos says, rising from his chair.

"Caeli Phi, were you in Mira Theta's home on the evening of April 4, 2347?"

"Yes."

"Tell us what you found there."

"I—I was using the HeRP. I forget why. There was a *big* document in Mira's files. Hundreds of kilobytes. Her Opinions articles never go over fifty. I couldn't help myself. I read the first few lines—and it was so unpatriotic, so radical." Caeli shoots a glare at Mom, who doesn't react.

Phobos says, "That will be all."

Atlas leaps from his seat before the Committee has a chance to call on him for cross-examination. "Mira surely protected the document with a thumbprint and a password. How did you get past those?"

"She programmed our thumbprints into the sensors. Her passwords were *easy* to guess. The initials of her children. And their birthdays. It was a matter of time. With the way she was acting, the things she was saying . . . someone was going to catch her!"

"She trusted us, Caeli, as you should have trusted her! Atlas Theta and I . . . After Militia, I owed him my life, and he owed me his, until the day he . . . The twins love Mira—*I* love her, as I loved her husband! Did you ever think of our feelings?"

"Did you think of mine?" Caeli wails, covering her face. "All these years, hiding *her* indecent spirituality, *her* blasphemy, protecting *her* children. . . ."

"Settle down, Caeli," says Atlas. "Breathe."

My mother doesn't seem to hear them. I know the look on her face—from seeing it on my own. She's fled into a quiet space inside her head. Her heart rate is under sixty-five beats per minute.

"Poor lady," mumbles Io.

"Which one?" Nash says.

"Both."

They stop talking when Caeli resumes her rant. "You always *had* to visit them, and you knew I didn't like her. Atlas, you put her before me!" These are words she's held inside for decades, and as they leave her body, she smiles.

Pain shows on my mother's face, in her shining, unblinking eyes. Again, it's echoed on mine. Caeli Phi pretended to love me, my mother, and my family for almost twenty years. She was especially tender toward me and Anka because she "always wanted daughters too."

Atlas's voice loses its stability once more. "That's not fair! You . . . you . . ."

The Committee bangs the conference table, making a terrible racket. "Cross-examination is over."

Atlas just wasted a valuable segment of the trial.

"Phobos, present the evidence," Cassini says.

Atlas towers over Phobos, glaring, as Phobos taps his handscreen. Caeli disappears and a projection of a document takes her place. I gnaw my nails as Phobos reads out loud.

"*Grievances and Propositions for Basic Consideration.*"

Basic. Nice pun. I know before Phobos continues that Mom wrote this.

"The magnificent city of Jinjiang was named for the water upon which it floated: a river filled with silt and chemicals that glowed gold as the sun rose and set. Among towering bronze buildings reaching for the sky remained square temples with tiered roofs that curled upward

at the corners. But Lina hardly saw these things. She and her father, Jon, lived belowdecks, among other poor families. While he worked long hours taking photographs for the Jinjiang Ministry of Broadcasting, she came home after school and stared out their apartment's one window, at the brown water that the Jinjiang government called 'gold.'"

I blink away confusion. Mom began her "treasonous" document with a description of an old Earthbound city?

"On Lina's fourteenth birthday, Jon didn't bring her maqiu*—a sticky sesame and red bean pastry—as he usually did. Instead, he presented her a collection of photos he had taken.*

"'This is what the Ministry doesn't want you to see,' he said. 'Knowledge that it doesn't want you to have.'

"A group of living skeletons covered with thin layers of ashen skin. 'A family of engine room workers. That one, the child missing three fingers, was fired last month because he could no longer lift the shovel.'

"Silver coins, being passed from one well-groomed hand to another, with the tips of rifles making up the background. 'A woman buying her son's promotion in the armed forces.'

"A group of soldiers leading a man to a row of gallows. 'He led a demonstration against our government's pension policy, or lack thereof.'

"Lina began crying. 'This city is horrible, but I never knew.'

"'Truth is ugly here,' Jon replied."

Then the story's meaning hits me like a rib-crushing cannonball. Jinjiang is not the only place Mom is portraying.

In Law Chamber 144, Mom doesn't move. If only I were there; seeing me might jolt her awake, make her remember the three children who need her, and spur her to fight. Yesterday, Mom told us to value every loved one present and not to wish for the departed. I will not let her leave now.

I regain control over my larynx and prepare to give orders. This is *Mom*. Disagreements from subordinates don't matter. "Turn back, Orion."

My request takes long seconds to sink in.

"Huh?" says Io. "Oh. Oh, no no no."

"What the fuse, Stripes!" shouts Nash, abandoning all caution. Then she leans toward me and whispers, "That's career suicide for all of us. Maybe real suicide too!"

"That night, Lina lay awake, clutching the photos to her chest and occasionally leafing through them. While they made her angry and terribly sad, she was glad her father had taken them. At least I know the Jinjiang that's hidden from me, *she thought.* Injustice will continue to exist, whether or not I choose to ignore it.

"The next morning, Lina found a sack of silver coins under her mattress, enough to live on for over a year. Her father kissed her brow before heading to work. 'Everything I do is motivated by affection for this city, and for you,' he said. 'Always remember that. I love you, Lina.'

"Jon never came home."

Mom means to club her readers with the truth, to stop their breath, and it's working.

In the Law chamber, she looks directly at the camera, at me. She's not allowed to talk, but her eyes convey the remains of her resolve.

For years, I've known and responded to that expression. If Mom had a tight deadline for a news story, I'd look at her once and know to program Tinbie with cleaning instructions and begin setting the table for the night's dinner. But now, she needs a different type of help.

"They've got her!" I cry. "They're going to—"

"Be quiet!" Orion says.

But today, I want to be loud. Blast the eavesdroppers—I don't care who's spying on us.

"Please listen to Phaet," Wes tells Orion. "That prisoner"—he points at me, lowering his voice—"her mother. It's quite literally a life or death situation."

"Jon had known that photographing state secrets and showing them to someone else meant death. The government had electronic ears and eyes in every wall, and they easily caught him. Officials took Jon to the gallows. He died knowing that he had shown his daughter the truth of her world.

"Years passed before Lina forgave her father. By then, she had found other people who thought like him—and thought like her. Someday, together, they might make Jinjiang into a place where the government would have nothing to hide. A place where the water ran clear, if not golden."

"Why do you care, Kappa?" Even as Orion argues against us, I feel the ship slowing. He whispers, "Why sacrifice your job—*our* jobs? You can't influence the verdict."

"I don't want to be poor!" Io moans.

"Blast it, Io!" Orion throws up his hands. "Why don't we all say whatever we want now?"

The eavesdroppers must have noticed something funny—if they aren't occupying themselves 100 percent with the trial feed.

"Great!" Nash exclaims. "I'm done hiding!" Then she remembers to lower her voice. "The Committee shouldn't be listening to us in the first place. Don't you see? Those engine workers, Jon, Lina, this Jinjiang city . . . they're stand-ins for the Bases and people living here. That's what Phaet's mom is saying."

Orion turns on her. "So the lunacy has gotten to you, too."

Nash raps her knuckles on the back of Orion's helmet, whispering, "Nah. Just . . . some of this grit matches thoughts I've had. Someone has to try and change things."

"Mm," says Io. "The Committee makes everyone do stupid stuff. Beta has to wear maroon. It's ugly."

Nash beams, relieved that her disobedient thinking isn't occurring in isolation. "So that's four of us who think it's worth going back."

"You going to dump me out the hatch or what?" Orion says. "I'm not coming."

"Orion . . . this is a team effort," Nash says. "We go where Stripes goes."

"She's our superior," adds Wes, careful as always. "We're obligated to follow her orders."

I'm the one who'll get written up for insubordination, not any of them. And there's a chance I'll face charges of disruptive speech, along with Io and Nash. I'm surprised by how little I care.

Exasperated, Orion bangs his forehead on the steering joystick, causing the ship to jerk. "Fine!"

"There's a good Orion!" Nash singsongs, flicking the ponytail that protrudes from underneath Orion's helmet.

He grunts, but doesn't jerk away.

"We no longer print photographs on paper. Our government's eavesdropping ears are not in the walls; they are built into the backs of our hands. Instead of looking up at the Moon, we look down at the Earth. Because of these differences, we think that Jinjiang's history, and the histories of dozens of Earthbound states, are not ours.

"We are wrong."

I'm still trembling; Mom's Journalism skills have served her too well. I fear that she, like Jon, knew this document would mean her demise.

Orion pulls a U-turn.

Io buries her face in her hands. "Are we really . . . Whoa!"

We speed baseward, our engine's reactor eating through hydrogen so rapidly that the pressure gauge enters the red zone. On my handscreen, Phobos continues reading. I catch only snippets of meaning amidst Orion's complaints and Nash's insistence that we're doing "the right thing."

Mom's document segues into a formal tone, using the pronoun "we" and criticizing fundamental tenets of life on the Moon, decrying mandatory Militia service, lack of resources for the underprivileged, and the secret Standing Committee meetings that determine our laws. The petitioners—my mother!—want "favorable foreign relations" with Earthbound cities and regular elections for a larger "legislative body."

Overhauling the system never crossed my mind. But if the system is inherently broken . . .

"Fuzz on a stick," swears Orion. "Patrol ship up ahead!"

"You sissy," Nash sneers. "Scared of a patrol ship. Keep flying, for nukes' sake."

When Phobos stops reading, I glance at my handscreen once more. At the end of the document, Mom has written, in intricate gray script:

"Base minds think alike. Free minds think."

From my handscreen, Phobos's voice says, "Anything to add, Atlas? We've all read Mira's articles. When I ran this . . . thing through the comparison software in Law, it was a ninety-two percent match. Let me put it *simply*, in case you don't understand: Mira Theta oozes from every letter."

ATLAS DROPS TO HIS KNEES. "PLEASE, YOUR Honors, this is illegally acquired evidence."

"It doesn't matter how evidence is procured if it's this incriminating," retorts Janus. "Don't bother arguing. Look at your lie indicators on the graph; they're going wild. You are about to deceive us."

"This document was written in Mira Theta's voice," says Nebulus. "And it was found in her apartment, on her HeRP. Therefore, we conclude that she is . . ."

I clap my hand over the handscreen speaker, knowing what word his mouth will form next, what their verdict will be, what it will mean for the woman I love most in the world.

Guilty.

"Wait! Please!" Atlas raises his hands to the images of the Committee in a supplicating gesture. "Thirteen years ago. The only instance in which a person accused of disruptive print ever walked free. Six thousand Sputniks disappeared from the family's joint account the following day. I'm making a similar offer, but of eight thousand Sputniks."

Cassini sniggers in a brassy falsetto, waggling his fingers at the camera he probably doesn't know is there. People must have tried messaging the Committee that they're being filmed, but they've disabled the function on their handscreens at

Andromeda's request. And no one's told them in person, either, since the trial's location has been kept a secret. Besides, who would dare barge in on a secret Committee function?

"Where does a low-ranking legal counselor like you get that kind of money?" Cassini says.

"I keep excellent track of my finances. And those of my friends."

"A moment."

The Committee members turn inward, whispering among themselves. Cygnus steers a video pod closer to them; the speakers on my handscreen screech and rattle before he adjusts the volume. The destroyer rattles too, as we bump our way into the Base IV hangar.

". . . probably got the money from Theta's daughter," says Nebulus. "The new captain."

"It's a fair sum."

"Not enough to pay for the degree of disruption."

"But we've accepted such payment in the past," says Andromeda's distinctly female voice. "We should let Mira go. We can ensure that she keeps quiet."

Before the craft slows to a stop, I pull open the hatch and leap out.

"Stripes! Want to tell us what you're doing?" Nash shouts after me.

"Or what *we* should do?" hollers Orion.

My feet fall into step, heels barely touching the ground, toes pointed forward. I dash through the hangar and tear down the hallway, dodging stunned soldiers whose eyes are glued to their handscreens. They're transfixed by the first news broadcast in a century that means something.

"This pronoun 'we' in the document . . . Mira obviously has accomplices!" Hydrus rants. "She's also committed unsanctioned assembly. We must detain her."

"But . . ."

"No, Andromeda! Not this time."

"You've been oddly sentimental toward this criminal, Andromeda," says Janus, sounding suspicious. "Mira spent a *month* in Medical while you argued with us. I can't fathom why you thought Caeli might have forged evidence, given Mira's behavior during Peary—or why you thought we'd need a trial to confirm her deviant behavior before execution."

Are these words a hallucination? If not for Andromeda's insistence on a trial, might Mom have been killed as soon as Wes brought her to Medical? I dumbly shake my head within the confines of my helmet. The Committee, the guardians of the Bases, planned to murder my mother and label microorganisms as the culprits. She probably isn't the first they took in this way—or the last.

Andromeda sighs. "Well, you all proved to be right. I'd hoped that her years in Journalism had erased the radical ideas she had in her younger years. Perhaps ingrained ideology can never be replaced. Do with her what needs to be done."

Hydrus turns back to the camera and speaks normally. The image tilts and the resolution blurs as Cygnus steers the video pod backward.

"We decline your offer, Atlas," says Hydrus. "We are not like our underlings. Promises of material goods cannot sway us."

I've found my way to the Atrium. People in brown robes are trickling in, staring at the high-resolution screens on the walls. I dodge them and run along the side of the cavernous space, behind the last row of civilian security mirrors. To facilitate my breathing and increase my speed, I throw my helmet to the floor. My ribs convulse and my lungs hold tightly to every milliliter of air so that I don't sob in fear, which hasn't happened since I was a kid. I'll let my face turn blue before I let strangers see me cry.

". . . guilty as charged!" The Committee's voices project through the massive Atrium speakers and through the dozens of handscreens belonging to the people gathered there.

No—something can still be done. I will free her, and we will run together. . . .

"Throughout this trial," says Cassini, turning to address my mother. "I always wondered why *you* would complain about your lot. You're middle-class, if on the lower end, and educated—not like those useless robepiles in Shelter. That filth leeches off the rest of us. I'd expect grievances from them—but . . ." He scoffs, "Not so well-articulated."

My mother speaks, her voice free of rasps and hitches. "I hope I did them justice."

"A noble endeavor." Janus's voice is a hollow sound that hints at the gap in his chest where his heart should be. "Before you take your punishment, Mira, answer us this: how would *Captain Phaet* and her siblings feel if they knew you chose a failed rebellion over them? That you wasted your life on hopeless heroics when they needed you?"

I stumble, overwhelmed. He knows how to hit us where it will burn. For my family, I gave up my dreams for the future. Mom did the opposite.

Running even harder to gain lost time, I burst through the Law entrance and zigzag to avoid confused-looking soldiers.

I shove past lower-ranked Militia officers wondering aloud where the trial's taking place. Someone elbows me in the back, nearly causing me to plant my face onto the front desk. I grab the edge with my hands to keep from landing atop one of three secretaries.

"Militia order! Where is Chamber 144?"

He looks up at me only long enough to see my captain's insignia. "Take two rights, up the flight of stairs, through the double doors, on your left."

Mechanically, I follow his directions. My fingerprint never fails to grant me access. As I sprint down the bustling first floor hallway, with my hand close to my ear, I hear Mom's voice.

"While you six dangle us from your fingertips, those I love are never safe. Nine years ago, the . . . accident taught me, the hard way."

I bound up the stairs three at a time, sweat dripping into my eyes.

The last hallway is deserted. My thumb slams onto the sensor of Chamber 144, and I tumble inside, my muscles tensed for yet more running.

But there's nowhere else to go; there's nowhere I can hide from the six shadows looming large and still on the walls; if they've so much as blinked at my entrance, the projections don't show it. Atlas gasps; Phobos ignores me. Mom smiles with relief; she must have been wishing I'd find her.

"Well spoken, Mira," says Hydrus. "But our little talk must end he—"

"Wait!"

Hydrus pouts, impatient to deliver the knockout blow, but allows Mom to speak. Her consciousness still occupies that shatterproof space within her. She looks at me, through me, begging me to forgive her for years of secrets.

"My children are innocent—even Phaet! They had no part in this."

What about Cygnus? She put him on the front line. Does she think lying now will help?

Mom clasps her hands and rests her forehead on the knot of fingers. "For the sake of human dignity, spare them! I ask no more."

Silence. Then Wolf says, "Your crimes are punishable by immediate execution."

Mom's hands fall to her sides; the determination drains from her face. There's nothing more she can do. Atlas lunges toward her, but Janus roars, "Stay back!"

Mom's eyes stare into my face until the moment she closes them. I make no move in her direction. I don't forgive her, but I won't begrudge her a few seconds of serenity, not now.

As an automated laser weapon descends from the ceiling, twin metal strips emerge from the defendant's chair and wind around Mom's neck until they meet in the middle, holding her head in place. The steely clasp is the last embrace she'll ever know. When the weapon clicks into place, aimed at her forehead, I wish I were holding her instead.

I clench my eyes shut, but I still see the violet light and feel worlds slip from under me.

36

HER HEAD IS TUCKED INTO HER CHEST, lolling back and forth as if she's asleep. I could almost believe that the laser missed something vital—that I can take her to Medical and they can revive her. She can't be dead, not the only parent I have left.

Broken logic gives way to an unrelated memory: a time in training when I fell off the climbing wall, felt the floor slap against my spine, and lay there trying to remember how to breathe, how to lift my head. I recovered from that blow and within twenty minutes had forgotten the incident, but there is no erasing this. This is worse than anything: I can't recall Mom's last words, the scent of her embrace, what her face looked like before the laser hit. I should have done something more, pushed her out of the chair before the bars slid around her neck, shown my love one last time. . . .

Stop! No more regret. I didn't send that beam her way—these tyrants did. As I remember anger and how to hate, raw energy washes away everything else. Mom never needed to die; Cygnus and Anka never needed to watch.

Before I can move, before I can touch my mother's body or modify the curve of Phobos's haughty nose with my fist, Atlas pins me to his side.

"No—Mom! I hate them! I hate them all!"

Even with a hand covering my mouth, I've never made this much noise.

"I failed," Atlas whispers.

"Let us deal with her." Nebulus gestures for Atlas to step away from me. Reluctantly, he does. I face the six shadows alone.

"You should not be here," begins Janus. "You should be halfway to Earth by now. There is no excuse for your insubordination, *Captain*."

I wasn't here to give one, or to fall like a withered leaf before them. The Committee has done more wrong in five minutes than I have in my life.

"Aside from that," Nebulus says, "You have violated Code 284.75. This is a confidential trial."

"We had high expectations for you, Phaet." Janus tries harder to break me. "Your marks in Primary, your placement in Militia—such potential, all unusable now, like radioactive waste."

Every word slides off my consciousness—acid rain from a waxy leaf, running harmlessly over sealed-shut stomata. Wolf takes over, his cloud of hair seeming to bristle with electricity. "We should have remembered the radical deviants to whom you were born! You're as delusional as your parents, aren't you? They thought they could run a *country*—ha!"

Cassini's hand makes a dismissive sweep, as if brushing me away with his spider fingers. "My fellow Committee members, observe the flat expression, the haughty silence. She's looking at us like some girl-sage who thinks she knows better."

I dumbly latch on to a word, one whose plural form hasn't been used in reference to me in nine years. *Parents*. But Dad died too long ago to be involved in Mom's activities, unless there's more I don't know. . . .

Say something. I can speak to all the residents of Base IV. I want to tell the Committee how wrong they are, how little they understand about our audience. No handscreen-hiders, fruit stealers, or Shelter residents loom above me. The Committee keeps order, but if they comprehended our everyday lives, maybe they wouldn't need to try so hard.

My mouth is dry but my voice is bright. "I don't know better, but I may know more."

Not a movement from anyone on the screen or in the room. I've said enough to petrify them and can now escape.

I stumble to the door, jam my thumb onto the sensor, barge through. The guards gape at their handscreens; they make no attempt to stop me. My feet carry me through the hallway, down the steps, into the lobby. I don't know where they'll take me, only that I need to be alone.

A small crowd has gathered in the Atrium. Although mucus plugs my nasal cavities, I smell sweat and smoke; while tears smear my vision, there's no mistaking the mottled brown robes. Again, the impossible has occurred, and it's another jolt to my state of mind.

The strongest of the Shelter residents have broken out. They form a cluster of about eighty, shouting hoarsely, faces pointing at the ceiling, the bumpy contours of their craning necks exposed. Other citizens, their brighter robes a stark contrast, gather at the mouths of the four hallways that feed into the Atrium, watching the scene with fear and wonder.

As my destination lies on the other side of the base, I run through the center of the Atrium, along the perimeter of the Shelter group. On the ceiling is a photograph of Mom, little and proud in life, surrendering to gravity in death. A shot from

Cygnus's camera plays in a loop on the six surrounding video screens. Again and again I watch myself run into Chamber 144; the camera trains on the back of my head, showing a straight-backed, silver-haired individual whose features have lost their color but not their youthful vigor. As the Committee lectures her, the camera pans to capture her unlined face, pale and adamantly calm. "I don't know better, but I may know more," she says, her wispy voice rendered thunderous through amplification.

As I run onward and duck into a hallway, a hand grabs my shoulder. I put on an extra spurt of speed.

The hand latches on.

"It's Sol Eta, your mom's colleague." Her voice is so full that it's audible even through the din. "I need to talk to you privately."

I kick backward at her shin, but it's a lethargic movement that's disconnected from my brain. With a swift pivot, she evades the attack and grabs my wrist. How amateurish of me.

Sol pulls me to a quieter spot by a wall and stows her left hand in her pocket. Unwilling to incriminate myself by accident, I do the same.

"I'm so sorry, and appalled, frankly, by—by what you've just experienced."

I search Sol's pointy features for any hint that she feels the misery I do, and see only the quivering of her sharp jaw. She defended Mom despite dismal prospects of success, but I still don't want her company. Maybe Sol is quivering—with anger—because Mom led her to believe certain things that weren't true—as she did to me.

"Please forgive me if what I'm about to say sounds callous." Sol clutches my cheeks, her blue eyes flitting across my unanimated face. "You've seen how weak Dovetail is—Mira's trial wasn't in our hands at all. But you . . ." She points at the video clip of me, then sweeps a hand across the vociferous Shelter crowd. "Dovetail needs you. *They* need you."

Working my jaw, unable to comprehend what she's saying or what it means, I back away. Either Sol is deranged or I'm ignorant. It must be the latter—the Committee's comments about Dad, Mom's peculiar words, her manifesto. . . . What else don't I know? In my mind, dozens of questions ram against one another, vying to be the first out of my mouth. "Who's Dovetail?"

"The organization your mom started three years ago. I thought you knew."

Is Sol insinuating—no, *stating*—that between my mother's Journalism job and her duties to our family, she founded a group without Committee approval? If it's true, then the past few months of my life have been useless. No wrenching action I performed—joining Militia, disobeying orders, coming home to her—could have stopped what was already in motion or saved someone who planned to die. All of Mom's advice to me, her acceptance of the horrors she experienced, were because she intended this organization to outlive her.

I could throw something. She favored this cohort, these insane ideas, over people who shared her blood.

Sol advances again, as if she's worried I'll flee at any moment. "Dovetailing—an ancient Earthbound woodworking technique. Two pieces of wood are joined by cutting pieces from each. Your mom named us. Without her, we need you more than ever. Please."

Dovetail. Aside from the meaning Sol's given me, did Mom choose the name because of me, Phaet, her "dove"? I'll never be sure, but the Journalist I knew wouldn't have missed that obvious coincidence of letters and words, and neither would the mother who tried to reform a government to better the lives of her children. New tears ooze from my eyes—the last thing I need is a reminder of how much she loved me.

Sol pushes onward. "We seek to compromise with the Committee, not begin a violent revolution. Infiltration works wonders for us. After what's happened, you can't continue being a Militia captain. But come with me to Shelter, where we're going to hide; tell me everything you know. You'll live under Dovetail's protection. And when we need to rile up the populace, we'll send you out to . . ."

I try again to wrench my arm from her grip. "Why didn't *you* write the 'Grievances'? Why don't you gamble your life?"

Sol's eyebrows shoot up into her hairline. "I've endangered myself as much as anyone else. I only operate through Journalism because I'm better suited to handle public relations. Dovetail has nimbler people like Yinha undercover in Defense. She watches over our members' kids: people like *you*."

Yinha, a captain and a rebel? She watched over me, lived next to me, and never even hinted. Now I'm second-guessing the reasons for her kindness. Was it my skills, my character . . . or my parentage?

"Do you think I wanted this? All Dovetail's preparations, exposed by your hacker brother long before we were ready? And your mother . . ." The muscles in Sol's throat contract as she tries to keep her voice from wobbling. "I never expected to take over Mira's duties as a leader, to beg you to join us. But your family's decisions have forced my hand. Saving this organization, pushing onward, is all I know."

To my astonishment, Sol releases my arms and kneels before me, hands clasped. "See? I'm on my knees. Come with me to Shelter. It's the only safe place for you."

I open my mouth to refuse, but think again before I speak. Sol heads the only organization that can protect my family from the Committee. When they find out that Cygnus hijacked the news, their retribution will be swift. I have to consider Sol's offer, but not here or now, with such a polluted head and the clamor of the Shelter residents' protests ringing in my ears. I block the red tint from the edges of my vision.

"It's not a good time," I say, my voice expressionless. "I'll talk to you later."

"Wait!" Sol shrieks, but I'm already running down the hallway so fast that my legs turn inward again. I don't care, as long as they carry me away from every last thing that breathes.

I rush through halls and doorways of white, float into an empty Greenhouse 22, and inhale the perfumes of plants whose outlines I can barely see. It's dark, lunar night, and everything might as well be made of shadow.

When I reach the rows of apple trees, each hung with ripening fruit, my fingers wrap around the scratchy bark of a trunk and my tired feet give out. This sapling can't replace Mom, but like her, it will stand strong and allow me my silence.

I'm not silent tonight. I press my cheek to the tree's rough bark and cry like I've needed to since Mom went away, months and months ago, muffling my face with leaves so that the security pods won't hear my pain. My eyelids are sheets of fire against the surface of my eyeballs; I no longer smell the peaceful soil and the tangy odor of Umbriel's robes—the scents of my childhood, of things no longer the same.

What a way to learn that you've grown up!

I laugh like the most insane of Shelter residents. The sound surprises me; my voice can be guttural and terrifying if I use it right. "Ha!" I yell, just to hear it again.

I cough out the mucus from my throat and spit it onto the soil. All that grief for a mother I thought I knew. She never needed or wanted anything from me. How can I be upset that, for her, I threw the base into a frenzy, acting like a spoiled child who's smashed a HeRP and doesn't want to pick up the pieces?

Everyone I care for—even people I don't know—could go where Mom has gone, one by one, because of their involvement with me. The guilt will destroy me; the blows will hollow me out until I learn not to feel affection. If I'm lucky, it'll be as simple as arithmetic: I'll become another sort of Beater, surrender a different part of myself.

Total detachment would be better than this awfulness, which I've wanted purged from my life since Dad died. Too bad that when I was six, I didn't work harder at keeping my distance from people I could lose. But I can start now.

When the white handscreen light hits me, I berate myself for wasting precious minutes on grief and madness—and then stop. Nothing the Committee or the Militia does to me will be bad, as long as I don't consider the effects on those I love. I can handle injury, incarceration, or worse. Such scenarios would only bother me because my remaining family would feel more pain than I. If I forget them, I'm free.

What a relaxing state of mind! I should teach myself to stop caring about them.

But someone's come for me. The intruder steps out from behind the trees, dressed in full Militia regalia, weapons at the ready. I squint into the light, thinking: *I may never learn another thing in my life.*

37

"STRIPES!" CALLS A FAMILIAR VOICE.

My brain takes too many seconds to piece together his identity.

Wes. Today I was supposed to lead him on a recon mission, not watch my life disintegrate in a streak of purple light.

"I hate to scare you, but they're after you too." Wes speaks in a whisper. He squats next to me but doesn't touch me—my mania must have scared him off. Mortified, I shrink away from him, rubbing tears and mucus from my face with my sleeve.

He taps his handscreen and flips his left hand over to face the soil. Within seconds, it projects a floor plan of Base IV marked with moving black dots, each of which must represent a person. The dot bearing my name is easy to find, because it's marked with a red target symbol and the words BASEWIDE SECURITY THREAT.

Wes taps his hand again to shut off the projection and stows it in his pocket. "You know the Lunar Positioning System. LPS."

It's old tracking technology, a descendant of the Earthbounds' GPS, installed in ships so that people know where to find each other during lunar-surface missions.

"InfoTech recently downloaded it onto every single handscreen on the Moon. I suppose nonstop eavesdropping wasn't enough anymore for the Committee and the top Defense officers, because most of us have found ways to block the receptors. So the top dogs—colonels and above—wanted to know where everyone is, all the time. They showed me the program because they think I'm most likely to subdue you—but they seemed reluctant to spread the secret. Anyway, the General knows you're here." He pauses. "So does the Committee."

My limbs, curled protectively around my body, begin to tremble.

I gape at my left hand under my Militia glove, wishing my fingers were claws so I could rip out the traitorous piece of metal. I thought I was so *smart*, that by running, hiding, and blocking my handscreen's audio capabilities, I could evade the Committee—but they're always a few steps ahead.

Cygnus. The Committee knows his location too. Do they know he aired the trial?

"I've been sent to kill you by lethal injection. They're going to pass it off as flu." The back of Wes's hand smears the beginnings of tears across his eyes. "I won't do it, though. I'm going to get you out of here."

"Why should I come?"

"Because it's infinitely safer than staying."

I rise and duck behind the tree, trying in vain to put something substantial between us. "Why do they think you'll subdue me? Did they bug you with extra cameras to watch it happen?"

"Phaet . . ."

I inch backward until my foot strikes the base of the next tree and hide behind that too. "How do I know you won't kill me later?"

"Let me answer one question at a time." Wes holds up a

finger in front of me. "They chose me because we seemed close in training. I'm also good with needles." Another finger. "They installed a camera in my helmet before I left, but I knocked it out a few minutes ago. Actually, I knocked out the greenhouse security pods too." Three fingers. "I won't kill you because . . . they're despicable, and you're wonderful."

I shake my head. My hand slides into my boot; my fingers clench around the hilt of a dagger.

"Leave me alone." My voice cracks like an adolescent boy's, betraying the messy wad of emotions within me.

Wes inspects my bloated face. With infinite gentleness, he pulls my hand from my shoe and balances it in his palms like it's something precious and breakable.

I blink.

"I'm so sorry, Phaet. But please remember that there are more important things than how sad you are right now." Wes's left thumb traces the lines running across my palm, perplexing my mind and rebooting my senses; I'm caught between kissing his hand and snatching mine away. "So much depends on you. Cygnus, Anka, *your own life*. If we keep you breathing, things may get better."

He's done it again, seeing inside my soul and choosing words that will sway me. Whatever I was thinking before he arrived, I want to survive and fix what's wrong.

"We need to get you to Base I, where my family can hide you. It's a rough trip, and a long one."

Leaves rustle, stem fibers snap, and he's holding out a glossy red apple. It looks bluish in the murky light of his handscreen.

"You should get your blood sugar up before we start running."

Wes brings the fruit to my lips; the apple trembles before my eye. For once, his hand isn't steady.

The thought of eating turns my stomach. As blood flow to the digestive system decreases in times of stress, I might get indigestion. But his reasoning is impeccable. Blushing beneath the remnants of my tears, I grab the apple from his fingers and attack it with my incisors. Its silky interior, crossed by greenish veins, is pure white and so sour that I nearly spit it out.

Wes plucks another apple for himself, rises to his feet, and takes a huge bite. If it tastes horrible, his face doesn't show it.

"Let's go."

I stand.

We nearly duck again when we hear rustling leaves.

"Phaet?" calls a deep, resonant voice. "Is that you in here?"

We've been seen, but not by anyone dangerous. "Umbriel!"

Umbriel tramples over withering strawberry vines as he rushes toward us, his forehead coated with sweat. He steps between me and Wes, holds me close, and buries his nose in my hair. I drop the half-eaten apple.

"I checked your apartment, my apartment, Law. . . . I was so worried they got you!"

"Umbriel, I understand that you're concerned." Wes swallows before taking another crunching bite. "But Phaet and I need to move. The Committee wants to kill her next."

Umbriel blinks at him. "I'll take care of her."

"I believe you'll do better with Cygnus and Anka. They can't come with us—the escape plan is too risky for untrained kids. Dovetail—"

"Huh?" says Umbriel.

"Phaet's mom's organization. They've got a decent underground following."

"How'd you find out about them?"

"Doesn't matter. They're collecting new members in Shelter. Bring Phaet's brother and sister there."

Umbriel backs away, eyes narrowed. "You think it's okay to hand children over to a bunch of—of insurgents?"

His words strike a nerve. Cygnus, one of those "children," cracked Law and Journalism, exposing the Committee to the whole base.

"Some very respectable people work for them," Wes tells Umbriel. "Phaet's friend Yinha Rho, for example."

"How do you know all this?" Umbriel thunders.

"It's a long story, and your attention is needed elsewhere. Dovetail will provide more than adequate protection for you and Phaet's siblings until we sort out this mess."

Wes's concern for my siblings earns him my faith, but I want to be sure. "I have a few things to say."

The boys fall silent.

"Umbriel, if I don't go with Wes, what's your plan?"

"We—we'll be fine if I keep you close, at least until you can make sensible decisions again."

Wes finishes the apple and tosses the core at the base of a tree. "Not the case, Phaet. I'd say you've always got your wits about you. Though none of your options are very appealing, *you* should choose what you do next."

Should I go with Umbriel, who functions on raw instinct, or Wes, who has presented evidence of a plan? Or I could set out by myself, without anyone to think they know better—but

I learned in Militia never to operate alone.

"I'm going with Wes."

Umbriel sucks in a breath through his teeth. "You can't trust him!"

"I'm not saying I do."

"You don't know a thing about guys, Phaet!"

Wes pats Umbriel's shoulder but keeps his eyes on the ground. "You have nothing to worry about, mate. She's a little sister to me."

"Prove it." Umbriel slips out of Wes's grasp.

"All those weeks Phaet and I spent training together at night . . . if I wanted to try something with her, I'd have tried it."

Umbriel's jaw relaxes, while mine clenches so hard that my masseters cramp.

"If you *had* tried something, you'd be unconscious in Medical now." Appeased, Umbriel steps back from Wes and me. "Fine. Take care of her, you hear?"

"We'll take care of each other," Wes says.

Wherever we go on Base I, I'll miss Umbriel every time I have to speak for myself. But as my best friend sprints out of the greenhouse, flattening more vines, I feel relieved that when he asked me about a life together, I nodded my head instead of promising him anything out loud.

38

UNDERNEATH THE GREENHOUSES, WE careen down a twisting walkway only wide enough for one person at a time. Sprinting flawlessly, Wes glances at his handscreen.

"Don't panic, kid, but my LPS just got disabled. The last thing I saw was a unit moving out of Defense—they're coming to get us because I haven't killed you yet."

Fuse.

Fear for our lives propels my legs faster. *This* is what it's like to lose control, to be moved rather than move.

"We've got to get to the Defense hangar," Wes continues. "I'm sure we can find a ship there."

Defense is a long way off. We'll have to run out of Agriculture, under the Atrium, and cross the distance between. I only hope my resolve can override my cramping muscles, which are ready to quit.

Wes turns decisively every time there's a fork in the path. As our surroundings grow grimy, our shoes lose traction on the slick yellowed floor, and the ceiling droops close to our heads. This is one of the Sanitation lanes, through which workers transport wastes from the other departments. I'm sure they're usually this dirty, but I doubt they're always this loud. I hear the stomping of feet and muffled voices above us—no words, only anger. Above the noise, on giant video screens, the Committee repeats with frightening clarity: "Guilty."

A few seconds later, I hear the first collective shriek of horror, a terrible sound of many tones and timbres.

"What's that?" I cry.

"It's not important," Wes fires back.

The uproar grows louder, laced with the shuffling of Militia boots.

"Please, can we check on the people up there?" I put on an extra spurt of speed and grab the collar of his jacket.

"No time!" Wes hollers as my hand jerks him back.

"Listen!" I screech to a halt, and he stumbles.

Without the hammering of our footsteps on the tunnel floor, the shouts from upstairs take on concrete meaning. "Hurt me, not her!" booms a man's voice, amplified by the speaker system. Cygnus, back at home, has steered the video pods he's commandeered into the Atrium. They haven't caught him yet.

"Not Belinda!" shouts the man.

Wes's hand clutches the canvas of his jacket, over his heart. "Oh . . ." he whispers.

Belinda—could it be the girl I saw in Shelter? So much time has passed since that day. Bright, lively Belinda, tugging my hair with her tiny fingers. If I'm reeling from the man's plea, Wes—who has presumably tended to her on multiple occasions—must be splintering on the inside.

"Please!" begs the voice.

I rub Wes's shoulder with one hand, then lean both my forearms and my forehead against him, breathing him in. I need closeness to a true *human*—not necessarily someone flawless, just someone capable of compassion—so I don't lose all faith.

"Let's go." I try to shake his arm and find it unyielding. "Let's try to help."

Wes takes a few steps back, eyes on the ceiling. "This significantly alters our plan, but I agree. Someone's got to end this."

Nostrils flared, he fumbles in his pockets and pulls out a tan sleeve the size and shape of a finger. I'm unnerved when he slips it onto his thumb. He feels the ceiling with his other hand until his fingers catch on a tiny groove, to which he presses the covered digit. The patch of floor below us shoots upward like an elevator, taking us with it. I'm flabbergasted.

"Sanitation manhole into the center of the Atrium. The workers go in and out to clean up pedestrian residue."

"Your thumb?"

"I worked in Medical, remember? Bloke from Sanitation had a nasty cut on his leg and needed surgery. While he was knocked out, I made a fingertip mold and created a composite in the lab."

Wes shrugs as we rise into the epicenter of a new sort of moonquake.

They ignore us when we step off the lift, whether they're in black Militia gear, clutching Electrostuns and cans of sedative aerosols, or in filthy robes, screaming newly coined slogans.

Three bodies lie between us and the two privates, who flank an emaciated man. His limbs are wrapped around a bundle of dirty cotton and flesh. Everything's the same about Belinda's face, which is just visible beneath her protector's sleeve—except her smile, which is missing. Her eyes are squeezed shut in terror.

On the big screen behind the privates, Belinda, and the

man—who I assume is her father—is a magnification of their faces, or in the Beetles' cases, their soulless helmets.

"I repeat," says one soldier, "you are under arrest for leading an unauthorized exit from Shelter and instigating a disruption to public life—"

"I won't leave Belinda here, not after you waved those—those sticks at her."

"Come quietly, or we will take both of you."

"Why him?" demands a teenage boy behind me. His voice is hoarse from breathing in smoke; looking at him, I remember the young people in Shelter, clinging to their pipes. "You pickin' on him 'cause you can't get all of us at once?"

"Stop!" shouts Wes, extending both arms to restrain him.

Too late—the boy rushes toward the group and into scraggly white fingers of electricity from a private's Electrostun. When two other demonstrators try to break his fall, they too tumble down, writhing.

Sensing that the privates are distracted, Belinda's father dashes toward the nearest hallway, leading her by the hand. Perhaps he imagines that there, they can hide among the citizens watching the spectacle. As Belinda scrambles to keep up, her tiny face wears an expression of pure terror, making her appear childish and weary all at once.

A corporal, standing at the fringe of the Shelter crowd, points a sleek weapon at the runners. The pellet intended for Belinda's father emits sparks as it flies, and strikes his daughter instead.

On the Atrium roof and on their handscreens, the entire base watches her little body hit the floor.

39

AT FIRST, I FEEL NOTHING; I'M BUOYANT AS helium, floating past the big screens, up above the ceiling. In reality, I've fallen to my knees, and within moments Wes is tugging me up by the arm, the strength in his fingers threatening to snap my bones.

The corporal corrects his aim with clinical precision and shoots Belinda's father; the man falls an arm's length from his daughter and drags himself to her side. He puts two fingers to her neck, his face contorted with grief. When he doesn't feel a pulse, he gently closes Belinda's eyes and curls into a fetal position on the floor.

She's gone. No child could survive the 50,000 volts meant for a grown man.

I remember Leo and the pain I caused him. I'll never use an Electrostun on civilians again.

With nothing more to see near the two bodies, the Shelter demonstrators seem to notice our black Militia clothes in their midst. They shout at us and prod my torso until I stand. When they recognize my face, they withdraw, whispering words like *captain* and *tragic*.

Citizens gathered at the mouths of the hallways can't restrain themselves anymore. From all four directions, they shuffle into the Atrium, heads down. The sheer amount of empty floor space emphasizes their pitiful numbers—there aren't even a hundred. Will outrage spread as what they've seen sinks in?

Anka appears among them, fighting her way through with her knobby elbows and knees, calling my name, tugging Umbriel by the hand. *Why are they here?*

"Cygnus has been messing with the broadcasts," Umbriel pants. "At my place. You weren't prepared for that either, no? Why'd he and Ms. Mira keep it secret? I— Hey, look at the screens! He's still going."

Above me are alternating shots of Mom's tranquil face falling to her chest and Belinda tumbling downward, sheathed in electricity. The Shelter crowd piles around Wes, Umbriel, Anka, and me, pushing us into a tight knot. Cygnus knows how to burn people's pain into them, just like Janus—but unlike the mustached Committee member, he's affecting dozens of people without saying a word.

"If they find out Cygnus did this, he's done for," Wes mumbles.

"Everything's gone to grits, anyway," Umbriel says.

I need him to focus. "Where are Ariel and your dad?"

"They're at home. My mom's things are gone—Ariel and Dad were so upset . . . I had to leave."

"Why's Cygnus still in there?"

"He's concentrating on something 'important.' Something else, as if he hasn't already done too much," Umbriel sighs. "Anka didn't want to leave him—and it's close to impossible to get Anka to go *anywhere* she doesn't want to. You know."

Anka brushes her sleeve across her eyes. "Umbriel, you

promised we'd get Mom back. I used to believe anything you said, but now . . ."

Wes stoops down to look her in the face. "*I* asked Umbriel to take you to Shelter. It's a scary place, but your mom's friends are there, and they'll help you."

Anka furrows her brow. "Really?"

"Really." Wes's smile is small and not at all patronizing.

Anka points at me. "What's going to happen to her?"

"Phaet's in trouble. I am too. So we're going somewhere far away for a while, a place where no one can hurt us. But we'll come back for you—as long as we're able to breathe."

Until Umbriel and Anka find Dovetail, they'll need protection. I pull my Lazy from my belt and shove it at Umbriel.

"No! You keep it," Umbriel says. "I can't let you run around unarmed."

"I'm armed," I say, even though all I have left is a set of daggers. "*Take it.*"

He does.

"Don't stay away too long," Anka says.

"Shh." I hug her, burying my face in her soft hair. "Stay strong. Take care of the boys."

Instead of clinging to me, as she would have mere months ago, Anka gently pushes me away and looks me in the eye, chin tilted up.

As we've been talking, the Shelter crowd has backed away in what I thought was a gesture of respect. But when Wes hits me on the arm and points at the dark cluster of five figures pushing closer, I see that it's not us the protestors are avoiding.

It's the Militia's reinforcements.

Anka grabs a handful of Umbriel's robes and pulls him away, even as he fights to reach me. Brown robes obscure their passage. *Good girl.* If something happens to me, I don't want them to watch.

"Phaet Theta," the General's amplified voice drones. Holding his Lazy in one hand and stroking it with the other, he leads the four helmeted soldiers toward Wes and me. "Captain. You disobeyed a direct order, caused a public spectacle, and colluded with an illegal organization, all in under twenty-four hours. We've wasted precious time trying to arrest you for court martial."

"Not court martial," Wes tells him. "Death. You ordered me to kill her."

The General points the Lazy in Wes's direction. "You're up to your ears in grits for the same crimes, Kappa."

His four soldiers move toward us, magnetic handcuffs in hand. Each set of bonds is as soulless as a pair of empty eye sockets.

Someone calls, "You going to kill them too, once we're not around?"

Although people shush the speaker, a young woman from the other side of the Atrium shouts, "A mother, a child. Who'll be next? *Us*? No more dead!"

The four soldiers freeze. In the ensuing silence, I hear the zap of an Electrostun, a falling body, and shrieks of horror.

"No more dead!" a dozen people chant.

"What if someone isn't rich? Won't even have a chance to try and pay her way out!" a man on the far left yells. "No more dead!"

"No more dead!" With every repetition, more people join in, until the Atrium fills with the voices of Shelter, their echoes, and the echoes of those echoes. The brown of their robes pushes into Militia black. Waving their fists, the people nearest us bear down on the General's unit.

The soldiers scattered across the Atrium anticipated this, though, and they spray invisible gas from small bottles. Their helmets protect them, but the protesters sway as it hits their nostrils, euphoric expressions on their faces. The scent is sickly sweet and somehow familiar. Nitrous oxide.

"They must have grabbed the stuff from Medical." Wes puts his visor down and inches away from the invisible poison. If only I were wearing my helmet too. I throw my forearm over my mouth.

While the soldiers are distracted, Wes and I elbow past bodies in various states of consciousness and dash to the side of the Atrium. Sputtering from holding my breath, I lean against the wall and gulp down untainted lungfuls of air.

We've evaded the gas, but we're not free yet. The General strides toward us, accompanied by his subordinates—among them Jupiter and a razor-thin woman whose visor obscures her face. She jogs like clockwork, moving only what's necessary.

"Kappa and Theta, don't move," the General booms. "That's an order."

Our limbs freeze, but my eyes swivel in their sockets, assessing the surroundings. The wall is behind us. Wes is wearing protective gear; he's armed, but passing equipment my way would be perilous. My only other resources are a fallen Lazy to my left and a security mirror to my right.

"Keep your eyes on my dad, little birdy." Jupiter fires

a warning shot near my feet. I crouch down about three centimeters, breathe in and out, and slacken my quadriceps and hamstrings.

"You never fight fair!" Wes aims his Lazy above Jupiter's head, intending to warn him back. As Wes shoots, Jupiter raises a gloved hand. The beam singes his fingers. In self-induced pain, Jupiter hollers obscenity upon obscenity. That deceitful piece of . . .

Wes shouts an unfamiliar swearword.

Jupiter points to Wes, draws his index finger across his throat, and nods to his father.

Before the General's troops can open fire, Wes throws his shield over his upper body. I freeze in place. Fear for him hacks at my heart, even though he's more than capable of defending himself. Unlike Yinha, he has better aim when he's fighting for his life. He shoots holes through the black gloves of two of the General's underlings; they drop their weapons and clutch their hands to their chests. Nausea rises in my throat, but not for long. The General turns his attention—and his Lazy—to my face.

I leap sideways, but I'm not strong enough to dive behind the mirror in one bound. When my left shoulder ignites with pain, I scream. My quadriceps throb as I push off again and sail the last meter to shelter. The General's aim stays true; spots of fire erupt down my arm.

I land hard, roll like a log, and cradle the useless limb to my chest. Raw pain and the odor of burnt flesh make me woozy. I chomp my tongue to stay sharp. Before me, the plastic backing of the security mirror smokes as it begins to liquefy and drip.

It's not over. Using my good arm, I prop myself up and peer around the mirror. Through bleary eyes, I see the General clutching his chest. His armor has been singed away, leaving a pool of blood.

I made the right choice: defense. In his impatience, the General forgot not to shoot concentrated radiation at reflective surfaces. He's a strong man, though, and not unintelligent. He flings his Lazy to the ground and pulls an old-style pistol from his belt.

Copper bullets will render my mirror shield useless. I turn my back to it in case it shatters.

But instead of a shot and breaking glass, I hear a shout of agony. Again, I peek out. A dagger has been driven into the unarmored spot between the General's neck and shoulder by none other than the razor-thin soldier, who disappears into the crowd.

Wes joins me behind the mirror, breathing hard and clutching a battered shield.

"Whoever that was—she's in for it."

"You okay?" I whisper, examining the scene.

He nods. "You, on the other hand . . ."

"Shh." I point to what's happening.

With the General down, the Militia is confused and restive. Two colonels can't decide who will take command, yelling at each other and into their helmet speakers. Then they stop yelling altogether. Some soldiers remove their helmets and tap them suspiciously. Entire clumps drop their Electrostuns and dash out of the Atrium. I look to Wes for an explanation.

He lifts his visor. "Wasn't me. But someone cut the power to the headsets. I can't hear orders, can't see other soldiers' positions."

"Cygnus?" His name sticks in my throat.

"I think he managed to hack the Defense control room. Impressive."

For an instant, I'm unspeakably proud. Then I realize what kinds of trouble he'll be in when they catch him.

The wall screens go fuzzy. Presumably, while Cygnus worked on Defense, InfoTech workers under intense Militia pressure reclaimed the broadcasting system. The Atrium falls silent as six dark figures seated around a conference table appear on the walls and ceiling.

"We'll take over from here," Andromeda says.

40

"PHAET, WE HAVE TO GO." WES TUGS MY uninjured arm. "You're losing consciousness—not to mention blood."

I keep biting my tongue. The pain keeps me awake. I need to hear this, the first unscheduled public address the Committee has given in decades.

"I'm staying."

"I'll pick you up and carry you if I have to."

I glare, knowing that he's brawny enough to keep his word. My eyes remain narrowed until he leaves me alone. I saw off a strip of fabric from my pant leg; Wes takes it and binds my bleeding deltoid.

"Soldiers, drop your weapons," Nebulus says over the din of protestors. "Officers, remember that you are keepers of the peace."

Several soldiers hang their heads. Confused protesters shake their drugged companions, who awaken and sleepily rub their eyes, but they keep shouting.

"We apologize for what you have seen today," says Andromeda, still louder. "You should not have witnessed the accidental death of Belinda Delta or the execution of Mira Theta, a lawbreaker of the first degree. With her manifesto, Mira did not act to keep order but to create chaos. Although her crimes were severe, we believe now that even she did not deserve that fate."

Cassini declares, "From now on there shall be no executions, public or private, anywhere on the Bases, and all efforts will be made to protect children, the heralds of our future."

"What?" Wes and I exclaim together, even as the crowd murmurs excitedly. The Committee and the Militia can continue to execute whomever they like, as long as no one finds out. As for their "efforts" to "protect children"? If authorities damage any youths, including my siblings, the offspring of a dissident, the Committee could easily say they tried to prevent it.

Hydrus stands.

"Mira Theta accused us of illegitimacy, of unjustly holding power. We realize that our emergency rule has extended for over thirty years. We have never been able to schedule new elections, as governing six bases is a massive undertaking, especially in restless times such as these. We apologize sincerely for this oversight. Free and fair elections will take place six months from today, to elect one Committee member per base."

Wes and I glance at each other, wearing the same incredulous expression. This promise—elections—is something that the Committee cannot retract. They're risking their power to temporarily prevent larger uprisings.

Their greatest fear is losing control. I'll make use of that knowledge someday.

Cassini continues. "And to you, Shelter residents, we apologize for the circumstances in which you live and for any neglect you feel. We hope to better integrate you into the base population and acknowledge you as a vibrant, diverse community."

"To this end," the Committee choruses, "we will establish an independent Shelter Assistance Program, or SAP."

Around me, people chorus, "No!" and "Lies!"

The Committee is making an effort, but can they scrape the dirt off the Shelter dome or dredge up the people from its pitted floor?

I smile dimly at Wes, and he smiles back.

"Now that you have witnessed our oaths," says Janus, "we command you to return to Shelter. And quietly."

Grumbling, prodded by Militia, the Shelter residents turn in the direction of their department.

The Committee hates me, no doubt. But no matter what they do to me, they are going to set up elections and a SAP. The population of the base, which has witnessed their promises, will hopefully keep them in line. Perhaps Mom's sacrifice wasn't purposeless. I hope that wherever she is, she knows there's a chance that things will get better.

The Militia stands guard as the Shelter crowd files out of the Atrium in a ragtag line—even the victims of laughing gas and Electrostuns are back on their feet. Soldiers using truncheons thwack the Shelter residents who shout or spit at their feet.

A small black figure sprinting across the floor disturbs what peace of mind I have left. As it approaches, I'm relieved to see that it's Eri, waving her helmet like a warning flag.

"Hey! The rest of my unit's coming after you. I had to run to tell you," she says, her eyes fixed on Wes, "because some juvenile hacker tanked our headsets—fizz! They're here!" Eri darts down a hallway, shouting over her shoulder. "Go, go, go!"

Wes grabs my arm as two Pygmette speeders zip toward us.

"Wezn Kappa and Phaet Theta," drones a mechanical voice. "Stop. You are under arrest."

As if we hadn't figured that out. We increase the frequency of our steps and stretch our legs until our hamstrings threaten to snap, but it's futile. On foot, we can never match the indoor top speed of a Pygmette, which is 120 kilometers per hour—especially with Wes staring downward while sprinting.

"Why haven't they given up yet?!" Eyes still on the floor, he digs inside his jacket pocket and throws a grenade over his shoulder. The explosion leaves my ears ringing.

The voice addresses us from the remaining speeder, closer than before. "I repeat: stop or we will use tranquilizers."

Wes responds by flinging himself to the floor. I follow. The Pygmette passes over our backs, its pilot shouting obscenities. Wes jams his thumb downward into a nearly invisible groove, and the floor beneath plummets us into a smelly abyss.

Back into the Sanitation lanes we go.

I yelp as we land in the dank tunnel. With smarting muscles that can't possibly tolerate any more mitochondrial activity, we pull ourselves up and run. As I shuffle along, swinging only one arm, Wes races ahead. "Sorry, don't mean to leave you behind! I've got to open the next manhole!"

The ceiling is thin, so we can hear the buzzing of the speeders above, pushing us on. My usually reliable legs cooperate less with my brain; my body's resources have been allocated to my wounds, which throb with every pump of my arms.

"Getting close now!" Wes hollers.

As we round a curve, a black-clad figure appears in the distance. We move closer, and another soldier appears behind the first—then two more. Their clothing looks bulky; they've been fitted with body armor. Although Wes and I recognize the danger, we barrel forward. He readies his Lazy and throws his tranquilizing gun to me. The tunnel is narrow, so the soldiers guarding the final manhole into Defense can only approach us one at a time.

Violet light zips from the end of Wes's weapon. It blinds the first private, who throws her arms in front of her visor. Wes collides with her, using a free hand to lift her chin and knock her head into the wall with a *clang*. I lean my head around Wes and fire a tranquilizing dart into the thinly gloved hand of the second private. My victim crumples to the ground as Wes traps the third private's arm between his free hand and Lazy; he twists hard, snapping it.

The fourth soldier, a corporal, has begun running, desperate to evade the fate of her underlings. We pursue her—until she throws herself on the floor over what must be the manhole to the Defense hangar. She rips off one glove and holds her thumb over the invisible groove that'll activate the elevator.

"My other soldiers are stationed right below us." A helmet obscures her face, but there's no mistaking those saccharine tones. "And I'm willing to bring them in."

Callisto Chi stands between us and escape.

I wish I had more than a tranquilizing gun in my hand—my fingers itch to close around the hilt of a dagger and send it through her visor, into her smirking mouth.

"Don't think I'm lying," Callisto says. "My mom had my fingerprint programmed into every access point on the base."

"I believe you." Wes aims his Lazy at her ungloved hand. "But put your thumb on that sensor, and I'll zap your hand off."

Callisto cackles and flips up her visor with her other hand. "You won't, sissy Med. Not while you're looking into my eyes."

But as she stares us down, her eyes grow watery with tears. Wes's jaw muscles tense; he taps the trigger of his Lazy without pulling it, then double-checks his aim. Callisto spoke too soon. He's going to shoot.

"Don't!" Callisto screeches. "Or Andromeda Chi will leave Operation Dovetail!"

What?

Wes and I pitch forward, utterly stunned.

"You have to believe me. Mom told me that she's a member—their best mole. Didn't want me to go along with Militia and kill you today, she said."

"Liar," I mutter. She's trying to trick us so that we'll drop our weapons. Then she'll bring us down. If that's not her plan, she's gone crazy, crazier than me.

"That's what I called her when she said it. She's insane. This whole place is insane. My *mom*, a gritty rebel? *No.* But here's what confuses me: she helped your mom get into Medical; she tried to get the Committee to take your bribe, to save Mir—"

I double over with grief, clutching my stomach.

"Quiet, Callisto. Don't mention any of it," Wes snaps.

"But she did! She asked the other Committee people to disable their handscreen messages before the trial, remember? And it was her idea to poison Mira to make her look sick, give them an excuse to cart her off instead of just . . ."

Hydrus said the same during the trial. I remember Mom's

pink skin and quick breath the day Wes came for her—she must have suffered some kind of food poisoning.

I may be indebted to a Committee member for the last two months of my mother's life.

Callisto rambles on, increasingly hysterical. She must be telling the truth; she begins gesturing with both hands, and her thumb leaves the sensor. I ready my finger on the trigger of my tranquilizing gun.

". . . but Mom's never been . . . that's why I'm confused! So confused . . ."

Callisto's arm motions are cyclic; her ungloved hand rises when her voice crescendos and plummets as she emphasizes certain syllables.

"What does all this make *me*—"

I pull the trigger. The dart burrows into her palm. Within two seconds, her head and hands slump.

"Nice job." Wes squats and rolls Callisto off the manhole cover. "Listen, the soldiers downstairs don't know we're here. When we get into the hangar, we've got to *run*."

"Mm-hmm."

"Please don't do anything loud or stupid."

As if I weren't the antithesis of loud and stupid.

Wes presses Callisto's bare thumb to a tiny groove. The circular patch of floor beneath us drops away, and we land with a recurring echo in the familiar hangar from which my team has conducted trial flights. This time when I leave, I'll wait indefinite days to return.

"Is there another way?" I whisper.

"Are you saying that you want to stay here?"

"We could hide, fix my arm. . . ."

He points at my handscreen. "Not while that's still functioning."

He steps off the elevator and onto the floor of the hangar. The lights switch on, accompanied by a blaring alarm. Black-clad figures stationed along the perimeter rush toward us.

Wes's calm shatters. "God damn!"

He takes my arm—the uninjured one—and runs.

I keep up, my head spinning from the burning in my arm. I picture the soldiers coming after my brother and sister next. "We have to go back!"

"We'll come back for your family later! Remember, the Committee can find you at any moment with the LPS! Do you want to get captured? Do you want to *die*?"

We've almost reached the gates that lead to nothingness. I nearly turn back—because of Cygnus and Anka. There must be a way to keep them safe, to keep the Committee's slithering fingers off them. I repeatedly glance over my shoulder, trying to find a way out of the hangar.

"You've got to run faster!" Wes hollers. "Your family can fend for themselves!"

I remember Cygnus's feats of digital manipulation and Anka pulling Umbriel out of harm's way. "You sure you can get us to Base I?"

"Well, I certainly *could*." He lobs another grenade at a cluster of soldiers that are gaining on us. The familiar odor of burning flesh hits my nose. I could pummel him to make him stop all this, but I continue to interrogate him instead.

"We're going to Base I, right?"

We reach a standard destroyer. Wes pulls himself through

the hatch and reaches his hand back for me. After looking over my shoulder, I clasp his fingers, using the leverage to hoist myself up and tumble into the ship.

"Not exactly."

As the door seals, he elaborates.

"My dear Miss Theta, we're going to Earth."

41

I REACH OVER THE JOYSTICK AND SLAP HIM in the face.

"Ow! What? We're only going home."

Wes Kappa is one of the Earthbound, the reason the Bases even need a Militia. He's also a pathological liar who's taken me from the only family I have left.

Yet he defended my freedom and my life at the risk of his own. *If he were my enemy, I would be imprisoned or dead by now.* After that realization, I'm feeling sane enough to turn on the engine and check systems for liftoff.

Wes rubs his reddened cheek. "Honestly, if you think about it—Earth is safer for you, because there's zero chance the LPS will find you there. I'm not sure why you believed for a second that we were going to Base I, where people could report us. Guess you weren't thinking *off the Moon* quite enough. . . ."

"Shh!"

"Oh, all right."

As my hands cradle the familiar joysticks, preparing for liftoff, Wes taps furiously at his handscreen. The white gate before us opens. I thought only Cygnus was able to do that! How did Wes break into the Defense system?

As our pursuers pile into ships and fire them up, he closes the gate.

Another set of doors opens behind the first. Beyond, there's nothing but deep space and the sliver of blue Earth I have observed for years. I push everything to full throttle, and the ship zips out of the hangar with such force that Wes and I are slammed back in our seats.

By again tapping like a fiend on his handscreen, Wes closes the gates before anyone can follow. "Looks like our superiors are busy elsewhere. No one overrode my command."

He must have illegally transferred flight-leader capabilities to his handscreen. How did he manage to do that undetected, if not through Earthbound sorcery?

As my mind whirls, uncomprehending, Wes launches a missile that crushes the metal of the gates, making it impossible for them to slide open again. Faithless phony though he is, I grudgingly admire his work.

We steer for altitude rather than longitude, moving almost directly upward. As I fall into the familiar motion of the ship, tension drains from my clenched muscles; my wounded arm spasms, and I let out an involuntary hiss. Wes's attuned ears don't miss it.

"Are you . . ."

"Fine."

He sighs, knowing I'm lying, and leans over. Adept fingers sort through bloody cloth, skin, and muscle. "That looks agonizing. Once we get to Saint Oda, Murray can stuff some herbs in it."

Murray, his sister. Saint Oda? That must be his home.

"I'm so sorry I never told you where I came from, but it was necessary, don't you see?"

I feel his hand stroking my forearm and jerk away. "When I met you, my first instinct was to get away."

"Well, you didn't follow it, and look where that got you."

"On a ship, breaking the sound barrier, with a sneaky Earthbound parasite as my copilot."

"Sound doesn't travel in vacuums," Wes reminds me.

I struggle to think of a comeback. "Vacuums—like your amygdalae? Did you hear the rest of what I said?"

This time, *he* can't find the words. He deserves the verbal lashing, but it's shameful to say to the person who's saved my life many times over. Before I can decide whether to apologize, Wes speaks again, all acerbity gone.

"The year I turned nine . . ."

Some of the lilt I've detected before creeps back into his voice.

"There was an attack on my city. Our freshwater was stolen. Our grain stores. Some of our precious metal objects." Wes's accent grows stronger and the speed of his words increases. "And some of our lives."

My heart seizes up, but I continue steering, eyes forward.

"They waited until nightfall to land their spaceships so their black clothes could hide them. All I remember is rushing home and hiding in the cellar . . . the explosions and screams, right over my family's heads. My mum told me it was a thunderstorm, but I knew better. The soldiers burned our gardens, wrecked our buildings, destroyed whatever they didn't take. The First Priest, our leader, didn't want us to be that vulnerable ever again. So my parents told me I would conduct an intelligence mission. I didn't like the idea, not for the first few years of prep, but then I started looking forward to . . . to getting away from them. And, obviously, there's something satisfying about fulfilling a duty.

"Now it's time to head back. I did my job; I found out about Dovetail by poking through some correspondence between jailbroken handscreens—did you know that they were transmitting at a wavelength outside the monitors' detection capabilities? Seeing as Dovetail has started a revolt . . . The best defense is knowledge, my parents said, and I certainly have enough of that now, enough to make me ill."

I, too, feel sick with unwelcome revelations. Militia ransacked his city in a lethal treasure hunt and labeled the ordeal "Earth recon." What else has the Committee commanded people to do? What else are they capable of? My knucklebones might just poke through my skin because I'm squeezing the controls so hard.

"I thought the Bases were sustainable. We don't need to steal."

"That's what they tell you. Also, Sanitation dumps poisonous waste into Earth's oceans. They don't leave it floating in space, because it would ruin their image, so they pass it on to us. You really didn't know, did you?"

He takes my stunned silence as a no.

The ruined carcass of the ISS comes to mind—its metal plates and solar panels ripped away for some unknown purpose. Shaken, I change the subject.

"How did you get up here?"

"I got hold of a handscreen, then reverse-engineered it into my skin—badly, yes, but passably. Left home when I was fifteen. Went to Pacifia, stole a uniform, waited until one of the Base ships landed on some kind of diplomatic mission, boarded, and stowed myself in cargo."

"Diplomatic mission?" The Bases and Pacifia have been enemies for decades.

"A conference about an alliance against Battery Bay; I don't know the details. The Committee does an impressive job faking 'invasions' and such from the Pacifians, telling only their most trusted Militia officers. But I'm not sure how much longer they can hide the collaboration."

"What are they working on?"

"We've got to figure that out later. Anyway, I got off the Pacifian ship on Base IV and entered myself as a transfer from Base I, so no one would question my origins." He glares at his handscreen. "Then, because this *thing* started oozing rainbow pus, I went to InfoTech and got them to rewire it."

Everything I thought I knew about the Bases is being overturned. The Committee—who are predators, not the protectors I believed they were—make me sick. The Earthbound aren't all savages as I'd assumed: while some civilizations, like Pacifia, crave power and blood, others, like Wes's city, merely try to survive. I scrunch my face into an Umbriel-like scowl, suppressing the need to vomit.

"Did they send you by yourself?" I ask.

"There were six of us, each one on a different base. We all faked transfers."

"So few."

"Really, the population of Saint Oda is small enough without us sacrificing more than six young men to spy on the Loonies—I mean, Lunars."

"Your little name for us?"

"Exactly."

I decide that the term fits.

"I used to hate Loonies. All Odans do. But in my opinion, only the Jupiters and generals and Committee members are truly awful. The rest of you are . . . tolerable. And you? Definitely more than tolerable."

I give a surprised hiccup of a laugh, wondering if there's something sentimental in his voice. But I recover quickly.

"Now I see why you wanted first place. A higher rank means more information."

"Quite right."

"Those clunky infrared glasses. Your sister's funny name. The way you talked to hide your accent, like your cheeks were stuffed with cotton . . ."

"I let myself get too close to you." He shakes his head, embarrassed, and twists his upper lip between thumb and forefinger. Both of us stop talking for long, stuffy minutes while I concentrate on steering.

"Why?" I finally ask.

"Why what?"

"Training. Not killing me. *This*."

If he was restless before, he's altogether twitchy now. "I can't give a simple answer. I suppose I found a similar soul, you know?"

Yes, we're very, very alike—dutiful, competitive, solitary. It has brought us closer and driven us apart in equal measure.

"So." He stares intently out the window. "I never want anything to hurt you."

My stomach plunges into a free fall unrelated to the ship's motion. I thought that Wes had ulterior motives related to his Earthbound roots.

"I'm not some pawn you found useful in your assignment?"

"Absolutely not. Well, you *were* the daughter of a woman who despised a regime *I* also despise—but that no longer figures into my opinion of you."

"Oh." After a moment, I mumble, "I don't want anything to hurt you either."

"I was hoping to hear that." He knits his fingers together. "So can we trust each other? I'm asking again because on Earth, you'll be all I have. And vice versa."

"What about your family?"

"I haven't seen them in years. And I have plenty to hide from them, especially my parents."

I don't doubt that, but it seems deplorable to trust someone you just met over your entire family.

"Allying yourself with an accidental Loony rebel might not be safe either."

"I'd have done it the moment you uttered a complete sentence to me."

That was a month after we met.

After I check that the ship is properly cruising, I examine Wes's profile. He's different now that he's not pretending. Even his eyes don't have that once-prominent cold metal quality.

"Your name isn't Wezn."

It's a question disguised as an observation, and he knows it. "And for that I'm grateful. I'm Wesley. People call me Wes at home too."

"Wesley," I repeat. The name tastes grassy and cool. "Are you really eighteen?"

"Of course I am."

Part of me is relieved. He always acted more mature than the other trainees.

"Enough questions. I have one for you too, if you'll answer. After all that I've done, and in spite of who I am, will you please trust me?"

I shouldn't.

"I doubt you have other options."

True.

"I promise you'll be safe. We *will* come back for everyone you care about; we *will* see justice done—"

An explosion jolts us in our seats, and the ship schematic before me flashes a frightening red. Wes shouts foreign swear-words.

What could hit us here, surrounded by the comforting nothing of space?

42

"DEAR GOD, NOT AN ATTACK!" WES PLEADS at the ceiling. He unbuckles himself from the copilot seat, floats away, and straps himself in again at the right wing controls.

Every centimeter of me freezes. Has my autonomic nervous system exhausted itself, given up on me?

Instead of *being* moved, I need to move—or, at a minimum, think.

Because we wrecked the Base IV hangar doors, our pursuers were probably sent from a different base to chase after us. I have to steer our ship out of danger, and quickly, because Wes alone can't possibly take down all of our attackers. There are at least three.

I push hard on the speed lever and try to turn us to the left. The controls shift smoothly under my hands, but the ship doesn't respond.

"We're stuck," I call. "They must have hacked us, programmed the ship to autopilot."

Wes swears under his breath. Another tremor rocks the ship; we've been hit again, in the port side of the belly.

"Blast!" I cry when I see the blinking red light. "I'll fix that."

I turn to the set of buttons and levers that man the repair arms sheathed in the belly of the ship. The arms emerge and grope their way toward the ship's wound, but they're clumsy and slow. Our ship convulses again, and even though I'm wearing a seat belt, my bare head slams into the wall of buttons in front of me. Globules of light, which may or may not be real, explode before my eyes.

Scope out the damage, Yinha tells me in my head. I clear my mind and read the ship schematic before me.

ESCAPE POD FUNCTIONS TERMINATED.

They put a *hole* through the exposed portion of the pod. We're stuck inside the main cabin, wherever autopilot takes us, without a backup craft—and as Jupiter would say, it's damn scary.

"Enemy is retreating," Wes observes tersely.

I check the blinking black radar screen—he's right. The Militia ships are heading back to the Moon; they apparently set out only to wreck our means of steering. But one of them has left us a message through the intra-fleet communication system. It flashes on the screen before me.

PHAET THETA, COME HOME OR ENJOY PACIFIA. THE FOLLOWING FOOTAGE WILL HELP YOU DECIDE.
—STANDING COMMITTEE OF THE LUNAR BASES.

A fresh gust of panic freezes my nervous system as I remember Yinha's warnings about our destination.

Wes busies himself with the ship's repair arms.

The Committee's message is replaced with a pixelated video filmed by Security Pod Phi 273 approximately fifteen minutes ago. I recognize an eye-level view of the hallway leading to

Umbriel's family's apartment and a masked corporal scanning three privates into Phi 343.

The security pod follows the soldiers inside, where my hero of a brother tickles the surface of his jailbroken HeRP without even a glance at the intruders. How long did they know he was the hacker? When he shut down the Militia headsets, or before?

He doesn't look up until the corporal bashes his fingers with a glass truncheon. I cover my ears so I don't hear the scream. Fifteen minutes too late, I cry for his pain.

"Phaet . . ." Wes begins.

"Shh!"

Two privates grab Cygnus by the elbows. He kicks his spidery legs until the Beater swings the truncheon again, putting those out of commission too. Cygnus's lifeless feet sweep the floor as the group exits Umbriel's apartment.

END FOOTAGE, the ship's screen reads.

I wrap my arms around my belly, trying to contain an explosive mixture of shock and guilt. The Committee had taken Cygnus mere minutes after publicly apologizing for Belinda's fate and swearing to protect the children of the Bases. Will his ordeals be as terrible as Mom's, or worse? No one should have to find out. My quivering hand finds the speed lever, begins to pull it back.

"I feel terrible about Cygnus." Wes hangs his head, but only for a heartbeat. "But here's what I think—no, don't slow down. Keep going! They took your brother to lure you back to the Moon."

I won't be able to live with myself if I don't do this. "What would you do if they took Murray?"

"They've likely got an armada of ships waiting outside the

hangar to ambush us. Once they have you, they'll exterminate Cygnus, and you, and your little sister."

He's right—Orion was too. Today, my reasoning ability has hit a new low. Four months ago, dampened cognition would have bothered me. Now it's a petty concern, blotted out by remorse.

Wes leans across me and pushes the speed lever forward. I let him, admitting to myself that the only way to help Cygnus is to find refuge in Wes's city, then sneak back onto the Moon when the time is right. My brother's a clever boy—he'll survive until then. He'll find a way.

As we continue falling, the weight of my heart increases along with the gravitational constant.

I look down at the ship schematic, which is dotted with yellow. Small objects have hit us, and the hull is knitting itself back together. If only my arm and my heart could also self-repair. We're passing through a region of concentrated space debris. It's a small comfort that the Bases have removed the biggest pieces.

"Thanks for understanding, Phaet."

"Mm."

"Now, if you'll permit me a little rant about our present route . . . and the unholy cleverness of your Committee. See, if you'd joined Dovetail, you'd be captured and disposed of. If you'd stayed obedient, you'd have gone to Pacifia on assignment. And though you escaped the Moon, you're still going to Pacifia. We'll probably be smoked on a stick when we get there, and they'll air the footage all over the Bases."

I push his words to the back of my mind as I join him in trying—and failing—to fix our vessel's belly damage. It seems autopilot will govern our flight path until we land, putting us in the vicinity of the hated city. Escape once we get there isn't an option. There's no use trying to lift off from Earth; with the damage, we'll barely have the energy to touch down. We can't turn, accelerate, or decelerate until we're well into the troposphere and the autopilot switches off, but the Pacifian fleet is probably guarding the airspace around the city, leaving us no escape.

As I'm scrolling through and dismissing our options, feeling more and more helpless, Wes fires heavy artillery out of the right wing. Missiles exit the wingtip all in one direction. I'm about to ask what in the universe he thinks he's doing, but then I comprehend the answer. Accelerating objects to a high velocity requires a large force to the right, which will apply a leftward force to our ship. It's not much, considering how massive the destroyer is, but it helps. We must do all we can to veer ourselves off course.

Wes can operate the wingtip weapons, and I was able to use the repair arms. So the autopilot setting hasn't rendered *all* the controls useless. I gingerly try flipping the light switch. It works.

We've entered the ionosphere over Eurasia. The readings on the surrounding composition meter indicate sparse air molecules around us. And it's too bright out. No simulation, accurate or not, could have prepared me for the strength of the sun's rays in the Earth's atmosphere.

Within a few minutes, the mesosphere goes by, and the stratosphere greets us with a gradual strengthening of horizontal airflow and indications of ozone molecules in the surrounding composition readings. All around us is pure azure, a color that's surprisingly gentle on the eyes.

Soon enough, the horizontal wind—we're feeling *wind*—

picks up, buffeting us to the left even more. I pull a scarlet lever with my left hand, causing our ship's massive parachute to open above us. As our fall abruptly slows, it feels as if the ship jerks upward. Wes gives me a smile of approval. I bought more time for the wind to push us away from the directed route.

Now the Earth's crust approaches, partially hidden by clouds. The color of the sky is different here—gray, with an ugly hint of green. I wrinkle my nose at the remnants of pollution from the Earth's so-called "Information Age," when people got rich quick and everyone wanted one of those smelly fossil-fueled automobiles. But I'm more worried about motion sickness than air quality. The gales of wind, huge hands tossing our ship back and forth, recall the manipulative hands of the Committee.

We should come out of autopilot any second. The wind strengthens as drops of water—real rain—pelt the top and sides of our ship. I pull back on the altitude controls. We've been blown around so much that we could land in all sorts of places, from the floating wood city of Taeru to the mountaintop stronghold of Silni. Most likely, though, we'll touch down on Earth's expansive, never-ending ocean.

The water comes up faster and faster. Finally, the ship reacts to my hands—we've escaped the autopilot setting—and flies parallel to the plane of the waves. There are no floating cities in sight.

We have to land, and soon, because the rain is seeping in through the hole in the hull. If it touches the engine, we're done for.

"D'you know how to land this thing in water?" Wes calls over the noise.

"Of course not."

He sighs. "Might as well get ready for a storm."

We reach under our seats and put on the white life jackets. Wes finds the folded-up emergency boat. Clutching it to his chest, he staggers to the back of the ship and retrieves the backpack stocked with disaster supplies. In my panic, I forgot how much we'll need it.

A high-pitched alarm shrieks in the cabin. Water has slithered into the engine through the hole in the side of the ship.

To land, I'll need a smooth patch of sea, but it's impossible to find one. I never imagined water could be so expansive, metric tons of it rolling away in every direction. I never saw more than a few liters at once, and never pictured water as anything but sweet and life giving. This gunk wants nothing but to destroy.

"We should jump." Wes shoulders the backpack and tightens the straps.

"I can't swim."

"You'll be all right. You have a life jacket, and you have me."

I wag my head hysterically. Wes struggles over to me, grabbing appliances to keep from being knocked over by the rocking motion of the ship. He lays his hands on the controls, overlapping my own, and touches the ship to the waves.

The sea throws us up and down. It feels as if we're in another moonquake.

One by one, Wes pries my trembling fingers from the levers and buttons. I grasp desperately at his hands, if only to hold on to *something* in my terror. His eyes probe mine, purer and brighter than the muddy gray of the sea outside.

With a rush of blood to my face, I see how warm, how beautiful they are. The new commotion inside me matches the passionate wind outside—the prickly sensation is returning, intensifying until it feels like pine needles sticking me from the inside.

I stand on shaky legs.

Wes opens the side hatch, revealing the putrid gray outside, and lowers himself into the water. As he holds on to the ship's railing with one hand, his legs drift away. I understand that I must follow.

The water flings itself into my eyes. It smells of salt and filth, stings my laser wounds and pulls at my black clothes. But the taste is familiar, even comforting.

The sea tastes like tears left out in the cold.

I hold on to Wes's hand, and he clutches the ship's railing until it goes under.

Our life jackets keep our heads above the water, but they don't save us from the rain, which feels like bolts of electricity when it strikes my skin. I faintly remember that Earth's rain is acidic, sometimes with a pH as low as four, and hope that this kind isn't so dangerous.

The boat. Wes scrambles through meters of plastic to find the packet of sodium azide, keeping one arm around my middle, and pops it open. The boat inflates with nitrogen gas. I silently thank Engineering for their brilliance and contract my right arm to hoist myself onto the boat. When I collapse on the surface, blood from the three laser burns on my arm leave distinct red pools on the plastic.

The craft rocks as Wes joins me.

"Your arm got wet, didn't it?"

I don't answer.

Sighing, he kneels beside me like he did after Jupiter and Callisto's ambush, on a harrowing night from another era. He fumbles in the backpack and pulls out a packet of disinfectant. After pushing aside my sleeve, he applies the goop liberally to my wounds.

"It could get infected," he chides. "I should have done this earlier."

I hardly register his words. Though I'm on a crude inflatable raft with an Earthbound boy, bobbing atop a stormy ocean that wants to consume me, I feel safer than I have for a long time. I shut my eyes and fall asleep knowing that this will forever remain the day I learned to scream.

UP, AND DOWN, AND UP ONCE MORE. I'M tiny again, and Mom's holding me in her arms, rocking me from shallow sleep into deep, deep slumber.

Some wiser part of me knows that I'm passing through REM cycles, that Mom is dead and I'll never be safe again. Her ghostly hand smoothes the hair on my head.

But the touch can't possibly be hers. It's time to wake up and face what I have done, and what I must do.

I open my eyes to a swath of sky vastly different from the black nothing above the Moon. It isn't the polluted gray mess that I've been lectured about all my life, but pure cerulean, like the surface of Uranus at its brightest. The clouds look as if someone pulled a ball of cotton in different directions and added touches of yellow and purple around the edges. Wes's face hovers above me, and his hand rests on my forehead. I pull myself to a sitting position and wince when I put weight on my left arm.

"Good afternoon." Dark half-moons cradle his droopy eyes. Did he stay awake that whole time, meditating on the ocean and checking me for fever?

"You need sleep." My voice barely escapes my throat.

"*You* need water." He reaches into the backpack, pulling a pouty matronly face to make me laugh, and produces a collapsible canteen. He stretches it to its full size, fills it with ocean water, and shakes it back and forth, providing the mechanical energy that will help the purification mechanism boil the liquid.

When the canteen finishes the condensing process, I push him to drink some before I cough and splutter my way through three greedy mouthfuls.

We gingerly eat some dried fruit. I'm astonished by my hunger; my stomach hasn't experienced pangs like this since I joined Militia, but I limit myself to five pieces of dried apricot, which taste as if they've been sitting in that backpack since prehistory.

Wes clasps his hands to his forehead, staring into the distance.

"God knows when we'll find land."

I don't believe in God. On the Bases, because we aren't allowed to worship, we believe in the hard truths of science instead. But my theorems and laws aren't enough now.

Why did I live, to be reunited with my species' home planet, when so many tried to kill me? Throughout my ordeal, many concrete details—Wes's quick thinking, Andromeda's treason, the soldier who stabbed the General—saved me, moment by moment. But why did those details assemble and bring me to Earth today? Logic can't explain it; perhaps there is something more.

I let out a sound more like a bark than a laugh into the briny air. The girl named Phaet, maybe believing in fate. Mom would love it.

But she's gone, her life snatched away by a violet wave tearing through flesh. Cygnus and Anka—I left them at the mercy of the Committee, which will likely tell the entire Base that I died while attempting a cowardly flight. Receiving the two shocks, one after the other, could destroy my siblings—if that destruction, in Cygnus's case, hasn't already happened.

The probability that Umbriel will do something stupid is approximately 80 percent. He'll throw everything away to find me. Dovetail and Sol Eta will contact him, if they haven't already, and drag him into all this.

To get back at me, the Committee might use Nash, Orion, and my other friends in sadistic ways I can't fathom. For their own good, I hope their allegiance to the Bases is stronger than their attachment to me.

As I sort through the horrible thoughts, as the names echo in my head—Vinasa, Leo, Belinda, Mom, Anka, Cygnus—I realize something that nearly makes me jump over the side of the boat.

People would be better off if they'd never met me.

"Phaet?" Wes peers at me, concern stamped on his every feature.

"Yes?"

He gingerly scratches his nose, right over the freckles. "I wanted to hear you speak. You were being extremely quiet."

I continue being extremely quiet. I wish he'd stop interrogating me and scoop me up like a baby, but he's the wrong person for the job. He's not Umbriel, and he's not Mom.

After a time, Wes tries again. "What's wrong?"

"I'm—I'm lost."

"I don't know where we are either." He chuckles darkly.

Wes turns to the side and contemplates the gentle, glinting waves. The copper wires of his hair have strayed from their strict parallel formation; tickled by the breeze, they liquefy, moving fluidly across his head. Though he doesn't make eye contact again, he slips his pinky finger over mine and squeezes for a moment. It's a singular gesture, but it's what I need.

I lean my head over the side of the boat. The water is opaque, bedrock nowhere in sight. I know Earth's oceans are kilometers deep—the thought makes me fidgety. So I stop trying to find the sea floor and bring my attention back to the rippling surface.

In the water, the reflection blurred by the waves' motion, is someone neither old nor young, her expression neither sanguine nor agitated. If anything, this person looks tired, frayed. Strands of oily hair have fallen out of her droopy, weeping-willow bun.

I haven't examined myself in a mirror for a long time. With painful curiosity I unwind my bun and undo my braid, finger-combing the long, dirty hair. Nets of black come away in my fingers, and I cast them sacrificially into the ocean. Most of what's left is coarse and gray.

A tickle on my ear distracts me from the old-young girl in the water. I reach my hand up and find a feather, soft and light, as pure white as undiluted sun.

Far above me are wings of that same color, riding currents of wind across the earthen sky before blending into a cumulus cloud.

Land must be close. The thought turns the predominantly blue scene around me rosy with hope. When Wes clasps the feather between his fingers, twirling it before my eyes, I let myself laugh in disbelief.

A dove has welcomed us to Earth.

ACKNOWLEDGMENTS

Without the following people, this book wouldn't have left my computer's hard drive. Thanks to:

Kendra Levin, my editor, for her unwavering efforts to shape the manuscript into something we both could be proud of. Ken Wright, who created a cozy niche at Viking for the series. Alex Ulyett, for lending a hand in the whole process and for some really insightful comments.

Simon Lipskar, my agent, for believing in me, and Genevieve Gagne-Hawes, for a rocking year of edits. Every time I start to think writing isn't so hard, the two of you set me straight. Cecilia de la Campa, Phaet's champion abroad. Joe Volpe, for read-throughs, logistics, and picture books.

Christopher Paolini: storyteller, role model, friend.

My teachers, who have inspired me more than they know.

Friends in Baltimore, New York, Princeton, and beyond, for pulling me through these past few years. Here's to shenanigans forever.

Mom, Dad, and Larry, who have shared my life from the beginning.

And thanks to you, reader. I'm glad you came along.

Q&A WITH KAREN BAO

1. How old were you when you started writing *Dove Arising*? Had you always wanted to be a writer?

I was seventeen when I started writing *Dove Arising*, and stayed up long past my "bedtime" night after night to work on it. But I didn't think it would ever be published. Although I'd always loved stories, I didn't dream of being a writer until the first draft of *Dove Arising* was done. It was bigger, better, and more alive than anything else I'd written. I simply had to share it.

2. As a student of science—particularly biology and ecology—what are some of your favorite pieces of tech in the story? Do you think certain inventions are more likely to become a reality than others?

Handscreens are pretty cool, but I hope they never become a reality. Think about a smartphone that never needs charging and is embedded on the back of your hand: it sounds convenient and innovative, but could be addictive and, of course, could give authorities way too much information about you. As "wearable tech" and fitness monitoring devices gain popularity, we'll see technology increasingly merging with the human body. Consumers will eventually need to decide how far that integration can go before it becomes invasive.

3. If you could invent one piece of technology—disregarding the laws of physics and biology—what would it be?

A personal teleportation device. There are so many places to go and people to see, but planes aren't much fun. I'd love to travel across the world without leg cramps and a headache.

4. How much do your studies influence your writing? *Dove Arising* was written while you were in high school—has graduating to a university setting affected the rest of the Dove Chronicles?

I'm an unabashed nerd when it comes to writing. High school physics, which I took while writing *Dove Arising*, influenced fight scenes and space chases, and chemistry class led me to write a lot of corny puns. But it wasn't only science that inspired me; political science courses helped me construct the future Earth's power regime, with its two powerful alliances, in a way that felt believable.

The shift from high school to college exposed me to a world of new things. Living independently helped me write Phaet's transition to young adulthood, when she can't rely on her family anymore. Also, getting to know real scientists—my professors and fellow students—showed me that they come with all sorts of personalities, and I think that helped me humanize the talented scientists and engineers who'll be introduced in Dove Chronicles 2 and 3. Finally, the vastness and newness of college life forced me to open up and become more confident, which is similar to Phaet's experience in the Militia.

5. What kind of research did you do while writing *Dove Arising*? What was the most interesting thing you learned?

Research was almost as important as the writing itself. I had about ten Chrome tabs open whenever I was working on *Dove Arising*. I read about where technology might go in the future—that's how fusion engines and handscreens came to be—and about the Moon itself. As Phaet and her friends know, it's not just a big rock in a vacuum; there are moonquakes, dead volcanoes, mountain ranges, storms of solar radiation.

The most interesting thing I saw while researching was a video of a frog "defying gravity." Some physicists used a super-strong electromagnet to repel the water in the frog's body, making it levitate in midair. That video inspired the Bases' ceiling gravity-magnets, which keep Lunars from bouncing around by creating the illusion of greater gravity. I know the magnets aren't a perfect solution, since they wouldn't work on most non-water materials, would use an incredible amount of power, and might cause health problems in the long run. But I did my best, and paid tribute to a floating frog in the process.

6. Were any of the characters in the book inspired by real people?

I like to add real people's quirks to my characters, but they're all individuals with their own histories, goals, and motivations. Cygnus and Wes are most like people I actually know. And yes, one of them recognized himself and called me out on it.

7. Nicknaming Jupiter the "Giant" was a clever nod to our solar system's largest planet. How did you select the names for your characters, and do they all contain meaning?

Names can say so much about a society, and on Base IV everyone is named after stars, planets, moons, comets, and other astronomical bodies. Lunars are constantly pushing the boundaries of the known universe, and their names reflect that spirit of exploration.

My favorite name is Yinha, which means "Milky Way" in Chinese but translates more directly to "silver river." How cool is that?

8. If you could choose between living on Earth or the Moon, which would you prefer?

Earth all the way. The Moon would make a great geeky vacation spot, but home insurance over there would probably cost a fortune. Plus, Earth is full of wildlife, breathable air, and beautiful land- and seascapes. I hope we keep it like that.

9. How did you develop the social structure of the lunar colony? Did your family's experience with Mao Zedong's "reeducation" camps come into play when writing about the colony's government?

Much of the Bases' social structure is based on typical features of countries in our world under authoritarian rule: restricted speech and press, propaganda and doctored news, repression of minority religions and cultural expression. More specifically, I structured the Bases with elements from stories my parents told me about their childhoods in China. Back then, government officials made up the socioeconomic elite, schools publicly ranked students after big exams, and the highest-scoring kids were pushed to study science, specifically chemistry, in college.

The Cultural Revolution of the 1960s and 1970s—Mao's brainchild—was a campaign that tried to establish Communist ideas as the only ideas in China. Like the Lunar Committee, the Communist Party cracked down on scholarship, religion, and the arts. My maternal grandfather, an urban university professor, was sent to labor with peasants in the countryside to reform his "bourgeois" ways—for ten long years. He returned when my mother was in her late teens, and had changed dramatically. I think my family's experience subliminally led me to write Phaet as a pragmatic science student without a father figure. Maybe it was my way to make sense of what had happened.

10. Which do you think is more important: freedom or safety?

You can't have one without the other. Without freedoms of speech, press, assembly, religion, et cetera, people aren't safe—or at least they won't feel safe, with their governments and even their neighbors restricting them and watching them. And without safety, as when people live in volatile physical environments or in times of conflict, they're restricted by their circumstances and can't choose how to live their lives. Freedom and safety need to come hand in hand; having both in a society is a tall order but a worthy goal.

11. You're selected for a mission to colonize the Moon, and you can bring only three items with you from Earth: What do you choose?

Assuming the mission provides food, water, and a bedroll, I'd bring a good book, a headlamp to light up its pages, and a teakettle. The perfect ingredients for off-world bliss.

MUSIC ON THE MOON: A PLAYLIST FOR *DOVE ARISING*

"Called Out in the Dark"—Snow Patrol

How would it feel to live in a cold, dark, fragile Lunar habitat under the Committee's stranglehold? This song not only put me in the writing mood—it also sounds really, really cool.

"The Listening"—Lights

Feels like Phaet's speaking to us—if speaking were her "thing." She tends toward passivity, and must overcome that tendency in *Dove Arising* to save her family. Whenever I had trouble forgetting my own life as I sat down to write, I'd listen to this song and step into Phaet's voice.

"Papaoutai"—Stromae

Behind the pounding, danceable beat, this song's about the rudderless experience of growing up without a father figure.

"Aerodynamic"—Daft Punk

Militia recruits are careening around in spaceships and exploring craters in pressure suits—what could be more appropriate than a Daft Punk track?

"Dangerous"—Big Data, feat. Joywave

Plenty of things in Militia training are dangerous: Lunar weaponry; sabotage plots; that quiet, martial-artist boy who could be either friend or foe . . .

"Chemical Reaction"—Sucré

Distilled gorgeousness.

"Guiding Light"—Muse

In the first few seconds, a jet whooshes by and time devastatingly stops. Then the desolation only grows from there.

"The Lion the Beast the Beat"
—Grace Potter and the Nocturnals

I put this on repeat while writing the book's climax, when everything happens at once and the dove figuratively bursts out of her cage.

"Lost!"—Coldplay

This song's about meeting setback after setback but never accepting defeat. I can't say much more without spoilers!

PHAET'S MISSION CONTINUES IN

TURN THE PAGE FOR A FIRST LOOK

1

Four months later

THE WINTERTIME SUN MAKES A SPECIAL appearance to welcome Garnet River into the world. She's a squalling pink newborn itching to escape the arms of her mother, a freckled woman who looks weak from childbirth but delirious with joy. Garnet's father, a broad-shouldered fisherman with fluffy blond hair, tickles the baby under her chin. Her resulting sneeze is little more than a squeak. Cocooned in purple blankets, she's adorable—the roundest human being I've ever seen. Her cheeks are two half-moons, her chin a crescent.

There's something hopeful about new life, whether it's a seedling in the Lunar greenhouses or a yowling Earthbound baby. Garnet has every right to fuss—the movements keep her blood circulating, keep her warm. The stratus clouds that usually blanket Saint Oda may have lifted for today, but the cold hasn't.

All of the island community's citizens have gathered in the Overhang, their outdoor auditorium scooped out of the side of a mountain. There's a small platform at the far end, and beyond that lies the ocean. The stone floor slopes upward away from the stage, and a high ceiling shelters the auditorium from the elements. To the side, a disused off-white lighthouse casts its shadow across a thin sliver of the stage.

Eiders circle overhead, cawing. The birds' white wings are tipped with black; the color also appears on their foreheads and around their eyes. Their bills glint silver in the sun. Some birds dip down from the endless sky, fly low, and weave between glass orbs filled with seawater, which hang from the ceiling on hempen ropes around the room's perimeter. Though they're dull by day, the bioluminescent bacteria within them cast haunting blue light after sundown.

On the stage, First Priest Luciana Pinto lays a comforting hand on baby Garnet's forehead, calming her. Saint Oda's leader has a broad nose, wide-set eyes, and medium-brown skin, which seems to glow. Even though Pinto's back is stooped from osteoporosis, the top of her head, covered in curly gray hair, hovers at least a meter and three-quarters off the ground.

"God is closest to our children," she says to the audience. She doesn't have a microphone, but her voice carries fifty meters to where I'm standing, slightly beyond the middle of the auditorium. The Odans constructed their stone auditorium to refract and amplify sound waves, so noises from the stage bend upward and outward. "He weaves a part of his spirit into every living thing before its birth. And so the youngest among us have most recently received his blessing."

"Amen," says the congregation. I move my lips but don't make a sound. Odan services make me uncomfortable, since I'm breaking rules from my old life just by listening. On the Lunar bases, the Committee outlawed religion because it would supposedly counter scientific objectivity. I'd love to believe in the Odans' harmonious vision of the world, with its God who gives a bit of himself to every organism. I'd be happier. But it only takes one counterexample to disprove any theory, and I've come across several.

If God is good, and there's a part of him in all living things, why are the Committee members evil? If God is powerful, why couldn't he stop them from killing my mother? And why won't he drain away my grief? Sometimes, so much sorrow clogs my body that my tears can't flow. I want the Committee—all six faceless murderers—to suffer as I have, as the Lunar people have. To experience hunger so complete that the pangs no longer register; to weather the pain of electric shocks and laser fire. To lose a loved one, if they're still capable of loving anybody. What would *their* screams sound like?

My desires shock me, and they'd appall the Odans, for whom needlessly harming another of God's creations is the greatest sin.

The only person who knows I'm not a believer is Wes, who's standing on the other side of the Overhang with the rest of the men. His face is solemn and his eyes focus on Priest Pinto, but three fingers of his right hand toy with a loose string on his brown wool sweater, coiling it around and around. He saw the same things I did on the Moon—maybe even worse things—and now he seems out of touch with his countrymen's beliefs too.

We keep our doubts to ourselves.

Priest Pinto raises her left hand. Three minuscule red dots—ladybugs—scurry across her palm. She rolls back the baby's right sleeve. "Today, we accept this child as a citizen and a member of our congregation. With these three ladybirds"—the Odans' name for the insects—"I join the divine in me and the city of Saint Oda to the divine in her. Let us welcome Garnet River into our midst."

"Amen!" we chorus.

The three ladybugs scuttle from Priest Pinto's hand to Garnet River's. The baby squeals, delighted or simply tickled.

I smile, remembering the scratching of the insects' feet on the crisp November day when the Odans accepted me as one of their own. It's the happiest event in my recent memory. Wes's grandmother, Nanna Zeffie, spoke on my behalf: "Our garden has become more fruitful than I've ever seen it. The lass does wonders for God's greenest creations—he blesses the work of her hands." Her speech, along with Wes's goodwill, convinced the crowd to vote in my favor. Immigrants like me must receive majority approval from the congregation's adults to become citizens. If they had rejected me, Saint Oda would've sent me away. All the other places I could have gone—floating cities, nomadic pirate ships, the wilderness—would have been hellish compared to this haven.

"Now let us pray," says Priest Pinto.

I bow my head with the women around me.

"Lord, thank you for trusting us with this child. May she grow tall as a fir and sturdy as an oak. May she swim with the dolphin, fly with the eider, and run with the wolf. With your love, may she never find herself alone. Amen."

"Amen," the congregation says.

* * *

The ceremony complete, the Odans mill about, congratulate Garnet's parents, drop off gifts for the baby girl, discuss the good omen of a birth on a sunny day. Men and women from the opposite halves of the hall mingle. By separating the sexes during religious proceedings, the Odans claim, they minimize distraction from God. It's one of many bizarre practices that make me wish I had a digital encyclopedia on Earthbound cultures. Now, whenever I want information, I have to ask someone instead of looking it up on my handscreen, creating much undue social awkwardness.

I trail Wes's older sister, Murray, as she moves through the crowd toward the River family. She and I made our own gift for Garnet; per Odan tradition, we'll present it together.

Dozens of eyes follow Murray, though she's unaware of it. She's tall—if she so chose, she could stand directly behind me without surrendering her line of sight. Sunlight illuminates her tangled hair, the color of parched soil, and the scar, pink against her pale skin, that runs from the left side of her forehead through her drooping right eyelid. I never asked what maimed her. When I first regained consciousness and saw Murray bent over me, I yelped, but I figured that the fear would go away if we didn't talk about it. Besides, asking would've been insensitive. Murray healed my laser burn–riddled arm, stuffing it full of herbs and salves, and stayed by my side for weeks. The least I can do is respect her privacy.

Lewis, her domesticated nightingale, perches on her left shoulder. He's a brown bird the size of a fist, with a white breast and reddish tail feathers. Every few seconds, he ruffles his wings, tickling Murray's cheek; she scratches his belly with one finger, and he chirps in delight. Pets are commonplace at Odan gatherings; today, several attendees carry falcons, frogs, or cats. At the back of the Overhang is an assortment of larger animals: dogs, cows, even horses. I can smell their damp stink from here, but no one else seems to notice or mind.

When we reach the young family, I try my best to smile.

"Fay and I made this for Garnet," Murray says in her high, ringing voice. She holds out the hair clip she's assembled. "Lewis helped too by shedding some feathers he didn't need anymore." The clip has two brown wing feathers on the sides and a longer, reddish tail feather in the center. A chain of pink seashells from clams, scallops, and snails dangles from the feathers' quills.

"As for the shells," Murray continues, "Fay and I picked up whatever caught our eye during our walks on the shore."

"Oh, this is lovely." Willet turns the clip in her hands, admiring it from all angles. "Garnet's going to wear it the moment she sprouts actual hair." She strokes the white-blonde fuzz on her daughter's head. "Aren't you, my little duck?"

Garnet snuggles against Willet's chest and lets out a snore.

"We'll ask her again when she wakes up," Garnet's father, Larimer River, says with a chuckle. He and four of his brothers, all of whom have sunburnt skin and blond curls, supply and run Wes's mother's favorite fish stall in the marketplace. There's a fifth brother too, but he's gone to the Moon as a spy, like Wes did. It's odd, and sad too, that several men from this beautiful city have had to leave it for the bases' barren hallways.

"I remember when *you* stood here," Larimer says to me, "for your own induction. How are the snowdrops?"

Earlier that day, Larimer approached me with his brothers and dropped four bulbs into my hand. "For you," he said. "Snowdrops. They'll flower in the winter when nothing else does. White against the white snow."

I've buried the bulbs like secret treasure, and I'm waiting for the shoots to appear.